The Last Housewife

For Emma Span

The Last Housewife

One

JANE AND I are only about $75,000 away from a really stunning kitchen. We have the space, amid the peeling paint and curling linoleum. The southeast corner of our aging Victorian is sunny and airy. All it needs is cabinets, counters, sinks, appliances, a floor and a new ceiling to replace the one that had been mottled and stained by the leaky toilet upstairs.

Still, the kitchen is one of my favorite parts of the house. I see it as a kind of living history of our family. Emily's thumbprints climb up one wall, a bloodstain from the time Ben sliced into his hand instead of a bagel adorns another. Two of the table legs bear deep and enduring marks from the occasion when Percentage relieved his teething by gnawing on them. There are faintly visible remains of smeared mosquitoes on one wall. We eat there, gossip there, hold family meetings. The kids do school projects at the long, scarred oak table, Jane spreads her case files on it, and I wrestle with my insurance reports.

Mornings, the kitchen is a frantic place. There is never enough time—not for me to make hot breakfasts or for the kids to eat them, not for Jane to get set for her brutal days at the clinic. But the kitchen has its own manic rhythms, and I can tell right away when they are off.

Jane's face was all wrong for somebody scanning the front page of a suburban town's daily newspaper over her first cup of coffee. When she softly gasped, "Oh, my God," and handed me the paper, I froze. Almost nothing that could have occurred overnight in Rochambeau, New Jersey, could account for a reaction like that from my normally unexcitable wife. Something horrible had to have happened.

And the two-inch headline confirmed it: Our son Ben's school principal had been murdered, shot to death sometime over the weekend in her office. The school janitor discovered her body. Thank God she wasn't found by kids pouring into the building sullen and bleary-eyed on a Monday morning.

The murder was shocking enough. But it was the face of the alleged killer staring back at me from beneath the screaming headline that got to me—I recognized it the instant I saw it.

Ben had just left for the bus. Emily hadn't come downstairs yet. I was glad Jane and I had a moment to collect ourselves. I would have liked to tell Ben ourselves rather than have him hear it on the bus, but I wasn't sure what I would have said. I didn't quite know how to tell my son that the principal of his school had been murdered by an outraged parent. Explaining that sort of thing to kids wasn't in any of the stolid but dependable child-rearing guides I had read and reread. If doing your homework could produce good parenting, I'd be up there with the Cleavers.

"But I know her," I sputtered, still staring at the grainy photo.

The numb expression on Jane's face changed. Now she waited for an explanation.

"I met her in the park a few weeks ago when I was walking Percentage. She had this big stupid retriever. We talked a little. I liked her. She was so solid, so cheerful . . ."

Before I could finish the story, the phone jangled. The PTA's Emergency Phone Chain—usually activated for snow closings— was calling, in the person of one Kathleen Coviello. As always, she asked to speak to Emily's mother. As always, I bristled a bit, and suggested she could feel free to speak to me. Did most dads hand the phone over as if it was radioactive? The idea that a father might be the person to talk to about school matters still seems to make many women in Rochambeau uncomfortable. The idea that a father wouldn't be makes me even more so.

Besides, there are pressing practical realities now. Jane works long hours at a challenging job. Mine is more flexible. One person has to know where both kids are all the time, and that person has to be me. I was immensely proud of the fact that my kids had never been left standing outside a school or a birthday party wondering how they were going to get home. It was a record I intended to keep intact.

"Why don't you just tell me what's up?" I asked Kathleen

Coviello, trying to soften the edge creeping into my voice. "I'm Emily's father. Is this about the killing?"

"Well, yes," Coviello said reluctantly. "This is so horrible. We're calling all the parents to ask that children report to school as usual. There will be an emergency response team in the school consisting of parents, psychologists and school administrators. They'll meet with the children in assembly, explain what has happened, and counsel them individually if necessary. The assistant principal is coordinating. We're trying to formulate a media response, to keep the reporters from approaching the children. We're getting a lot of calls from parents who want to know if their children should come to school. We think they should and hope they do."

Jane and I had only a few minutes to prepare our ten-year-old daughter for news of a killing. Sadly, in this country, it wouldn't be the first time or the last. A convenience-store clerk at a nearby mall had been shot and killed during a robbery two months ago, and last year a mailman had been knifed behind the post office by a jealous lover. Not to mention a couple of murders I'd investigated myself. But this was especially threatening and close to home.

I was relieved we could speak to Emily before she got to the bus stop and heard her classmates' version of the weekend's violent events. By their account, there'd be at least a hundred dead, all slaughtered by laser-wielding aliens. I wasn't as concerned about Ben, who took almost any news in stride. Em was more vulnerable. She had few kind words to say about any principal, but the idea of one being murdered could shatter even a preadolescent's contempt for authority.

"Emily, there's some very, very sad news," began Jane matter-of-factly. She—we—try never to speak down to the kids, sometimes even succeeding. The best way to deliver sad or tough news is straight, without embellishment or phony reassurance.

"The principal of Ben's school—her name is Nancy Rainier-Gault—you've probably heard him talk about her. Sweetie, I'm sorry to tell you this, but you'll hear lots of rumors all day in school, some of them untrue. Here's what we know. Mrs. Rainier-Gault was killed over the weekend, shot by somebody with a gun.

We don't know much about it. When we know more we'll tell you.''

"By a killer?'' Em asked incredulously.

I nodded. "By a killer. But no one knows why. I just want you to know that you're safe, that we and the school will take extra special care of you and the other kids today. There isn't anything for you to worry about. We'll talk about it more when you get home tonight. If I were you, I would believe what the teachers told you, not the kids. At least this once.''

Emily nodded solemnly, glanced up at the kitchen clock, and quickly started to collect her things. The real discussions would come later, when everyone got home. I decided to walk her to the corner bus stop for a bit of extra support, and was rewarded by a big—and increasingly rare—hug, which abruptly ended when the bus pulled up.

The bus, often to be heard a block away because of the shrieking kids inside, was unusually subdued. Even the lethargic bus aide—who normally sat munching contentedly from a huge bucket of fried chicken in the shotgun seat while the kids behind her fired water pistols, threw spitballs, tripped and slugged one another—looked uncharacteristically alert and sympathetic. "C'mon, honey,'' she said, one hand resting on Em's slight shoulder. I think these were the first words I'd ever heard her speak.

Percentage and I walked the block and a half back to the house. I sat down with a cup of coffee in the post–school bus lull and read about the killing.

I'd seen Shelly Bloomfield a couple of times, but I'd only talked to her once. In the past few months, the vet had scolded me because Percentage was getting a bit overweight and my internist had scolded me because I was. We'd gone on a diet together—I was glumly eating salads and bran and Percentage had switched to low-fat lite dog food. And several times a week, when the kids are off to school and Jane is headed for work, before I drive to my office, Percentage and I stroll the half mile to Rochambeau Municipal Park, a verdant oasis for cyclists, joggers and dog walkers. We walk briskly around the park for thirty minutes or so. That was about as intense as it was going to get—no running up and down electric steps for me.

That morning—it would have been a month or two ago, in late April or May—our exercise was interrupted by an ebullient and insistent golden retriever who had bounded over and was galumphing in circles around Percentage.

"Hey, Austin," yelled a woman from a couple of trees away, "what are you doing? Come back here or I'll brain you! What are you thinking?"

The idea that Austin or Percentage might be thinking anything at all is pretty astonishing, but people hereabouts often chat with their dogs as if they do. One of the axioms of contemporary life in the suburbs is that the more hours people work and the longer they are away from home, the bigger and more rambunctious dogs they seem to acquire, as if to fulfill their suburban fantasies at all costs. Then they wonder why the dogs, cooped up in empty houses all day, chew through the walls and pogo up and down frantic with joy when their people return home.

Television advertisers know about these fantasies, which explains the many commercials in which shiny, well-groomed retrievers bound in slow motion around new cars or romp with kids who take chewable vitamins. They never seem to be shown pulling their owners across streets, proudly carrying dead squirrels or gnawed-on sneakers, swiping loaves of bread off kitchen counters, or shedding whole carpets in a morning.

We dog owners know that the town is filling with large hunting dogs who break out at dawn and dusk for frenzied bursts of exercise as a chorus of embarrassed owners clucks, "No!" "Bad dog!" and "Beamer, stop that!" The strange thing is that this is exactly the way many people in town talk to their kids—with the same results.

I've learned to run for my life when I hear dog owners cry, "He's usually *very* friendly" or "She's never done that before," although by then it is usually too late. Sometimes it seems that all over town, abashed owners are apologizing for canines that plant their muddy paws on your chinos, slobber all over babies napping in strollers, snatch food out of your hands, munch on your coat as it sits in someone's foyer.

The woman identified in the paper as having been arrested for murdering Ben's school principal was clearly the same one I'd encountered that spring day at the park. Dressed in the combat field gear common among full-time caretakers of small children— thick-soled sneakers, E-Z washable sweatpants and shirt, no jewelry or anything else breakable, valuable, or with sharp edges, chestnut

hair tied back in a ponytail—she looked to be in her late thirties.
She was on the short side, maybe five-three, and didn't have the
drawn face of a jogger or the body of an aerobics survivor, though
the latter was hard to gauge, given the baggy sweats she wore. But
she was attractive in a sort of unkempt, hassled way. I had no
doubt there was a dented minivan parked nearby with melting
Gummi Bears under its seats, dog drool smearing the windows
and a car phone with which to stay in constant communication
with pediatricians, baby-sitters and play-group leaders.

Nobody with a day job—certainly not the women executives,
social workers, editors, shrinks and lawyers who increasingly in-
habit Rochambeau—can go strolling around the park dressed that
way in the morning. Working people, men and women already in
their sober suits, have raced their dogs once around the paths and
are gone by seven-thirty. Only housewives, retirees and private investigators like me could keep this sort of schedule.

The woman immediately affirmed my instincts. "The last housewife," she said, sounding matter-of-fact, offering me one hand
and tossing Percentage a biscuit with the other. When Austin eyed
Percentage covetously, she tossed him a biscuit too. "My name is
Shelly Bloomfield," she added. "I live over on Bryant Street."

"The Last Housewife?" I swallowed a laugh, unsure if she was
joking.

"Not really the last one, but I sometimes think I'm the last one
who's proud of it," she replied. "I am, you might say, a vocal
minority. Though surely not the most fashionable." She smiled. I
smiled back. I warm to almost anybody who doesn't take him- or
herself too seriously. Besides, I knew what she meant.

Few women who take care of their kids full-time sound so assertive about it these days. Housewives are frequently made to feel
uncomfortable even in suburbia, their spiritual home just a few
decades earlier. They feel disdained by the waves of working
women boarding trains to the city every morning, and unappreciated by the men, who either fail to recognize how hard they
work or resent them for not making money.

"I do the most important work there is," Shelly Bloomfield
added. Her smile broadened. "And the toughest, if you do it well.
I believe that when you have kids, you ought to take care of them.
I've got three—thirteen, ten and five. And Austin here." She gestured at the retriever, who grinned fatuously up at her at the

sound of his name. "I know what you do. I recognize you from the paper, right? Kit Deleeuw? You're the guy who solved that case up on the mountain. And the one where some poor guy got killed? That was so sad." She shook her head at the memory. I didn't especially treasure it either. "Don't they call you the Suburban Detective?"

I nodded, as Percentage growled the suddenly amorous Austin away. "I'm him. But your moniker's even better. I guess it isn't always easy being a housewife these days." I knew from a number of friends who were that it wasn't, not only because it's relentless and often thankless work, but because nobody seems to recognize it as work at all. There's a huge difference between someone like me, who juggles child care between stakeouts and trips to my office, and someone like Shelly, who gives her whole life to it.

"No, it isn't easy, but that's not the part that bothers me. It's that nobody's worrying about the children. If I were in the high school teaching everybody else's kids, people would think I was Mother Teresa. But if I read to my own every afternoon at home, it doesn't count for anything. I'm just an anachronism, and a pretty dull one."

"But it makes a big difference to them," I said, not knowing exactly how to respond. She certainly was right, yet I don't think it ever dawned on the women who lived in my house that they *wouldn't* work. When Emily wondered about her future, she puzzled over whether being a veterinarian would be more fun than starring in the Ice Capades. But Shelly Bloomfield was right: what she did was vitally important. "And I bet you help a lot of other parents and kids out, too."

That was the right thing to say. She nodded enthusiastically, her ponytail bouncing. "I'm a walking Emergency Number, the person you call when your daughter has to be picked up at ballet class but you've missed your train, or your son gets sick at school while you're off making deals. I'm acting Mom to a lot of kids during daylight hours, and that's taught me how much kids need one . . ." She flushed. "But listen to me, droning on to a total stranger. I'm sorry. You caught me on a bad morning. One of my neighbors—she's a lawyer in the city—called a little while ago and asked if I could water her herb garden every day this week, while she's in London on a business trip. It really burned me up. If we were sitting next to each other at dinner, the woman'd look right through me like I was an empty fish tank. It's like I have nothing else to do."

"And you said yes, right?"

Bloomfield's answering sigh was so deep that Percentage turned around and looked at her. "I said yes. I mean, really, what can you say?"

I nodded. I'd driven temporary orphans home from lessons myself under those very circumstances.

Shelly called out to Austin who, scorned by Percentage, was now roving the stand of maples that rimmed the park. The dog ambled on.

Percentage was no scholar, but he was Einstein compared to Austin, who in the next few seconds would run headlong into a tree in pursuit of a squirrel and who—despite having been neutered—had an erotic fascination with male dogs, tree stumps and joggers' legs. Bloomfield appeared accustomed to her dog's idiosyncrasies.

"Don't get me wrong. I have nothing against women working, believe me," she was saying. "I just want people to recognize that I'm one of them. But don't get me started. You've got better things to worry about. You must be plenty busy yourself these days."

Shelly Bloomfield probably thought I had tuned out her philosophizing, but she was wrong. She had articulated one of the major conundrums of suburban life in the '90s. Jane and I talk about this only maybe thirty times a week. Either you are a housewife whom everybody deems an insignificant and invisible lump, laboring in boredom as well as obscurity, leaving your vast potential untapped, or you are a harried working woman convinced you must be screwing up your kids. Several of our female friends had left their jobs recently, bowing to guilt and pressure, and decided to stay at home. Shouldn't there be more options? Jane would ask angrily. And, of course, there are. But for many women, the choices are still starkly difficult.

As much as a man can, I identify with both sides. I'm squarely in the middle of this schism, as it happens. My wife works so that I can be a detective; I share child care and housework so that she can work. Every minute spent driving Em to her dance class or Ben to a basketball game is time snatched away from a case and a paying client; the hours spent on cases is time away from helping my children grow up. But at least, as a private investigator, nobody says I'm boring or ignores what I do.

I have, in fact, become a provincial celebrity in our enclave of thirty thousand mostly middle- and upper-middle-class souls. Bloomfield had mentioned my two most celebrated (okay, my *only* celebrated) cases. I'd solved the murder of two teenagers on the Brown estate last winter. And a couple of months ago, I'd figured out who'd killed a hapless husband, a discovery that stunned me at the time, depressed me for weeks afterwards, and haunts me still. These days I have more clients calling than I can accommodate and people recognizing me as I putter around Rochambeau in my dented and venerable Volvo station wagon.

It seems a lot longer than four years since I first rented my office in an upstairs corner of the American Way Mall outside of town and spent long months waiting for the phone to ring. When it did, it was mostly peeper cases—suspicious spouses wanting the goods on their errant mates. But I was an ex-Wall Street commodities trader run out of his job in an insider trading scandal and trying to make a living at the only other skill I'd ever developed (I'd been a criminal investigator in the Army). So as a fledgling private eye I swallowed my scruples and peeped. The best thing about success, aside from being able to clothe my children, is that I no longer take matrimonial work.

Now, here I was, walking through the park with the Last House-wife, thinking she had a reasonably serious point. My wife, Jane Leon, had taken a full-time job as a psychiatric social worker after my Wall Street fall. Jane's convinced that work is the salvation of women—and of their children. Since her health plan and salary had enabled me to get my practice launched, I tend to agree, especially when I see the way some women completely lose themselves in their children's lives, knowing too much, protecting them from too much. These days even the very word *housewife* conjures up something less valuable and important, somehow, than *attorney* or *psychologist*.

But Shelly Bloomfield wasn't wrong. Raising your children lovingly and well doesn't seem to get much appreciation or recognition these days. Nobody makes movies about women who run PTA's, or teach their children how to be compassionate, love books or excel in school.

As Shelly might also have bitterly predicted, I'd forgotten all about our encounter in the park—until that morning's *Rochambeau Times* arrived on our doorstep with its devastating headline about a murder and the arrest of Shelly Bloomfield for committing it.

"I just don't believe it," Jane was sputtering. "A housewife killing a school principal for suspending her son? It's just unbelievable. It's just . . . it's unbelievable."

I scanned the few details available in the front-page article. Nancy Rainier-Gault, principal of the Rochambeau Middle School, had been found dead in her office Saturday, shot once in the chest. She had gone to the school for a meeting with Shelly Bloomfield, who was now being questioned in Rainier-Gault's murder investigation. The grim facts just didn't jibe with the picturesque serenity of upscale, comfortable Rochambeau.

I picked up the phone on the second ring. I was sure someone was calling to see if we'd heard the grisly news. Jane glanced at the clock. She had fifteen minutes to drive to the decaying neighborhood in Paterson where her clinic was located.

"Hello?"

"Mr. Deleeuw? The detective? The Suburban Detective?" The female voice sounded vaguely familiar. There were unmistakably institutional sounds in the background—steel doors slamming, voices echoing in hallways.

"You might remember my nickname too," continued the voice. "I met you in the park a few weeks ago. The Last Housewife? We talked in the park. And I desperately need to be a client of yours. Can you come see me? I'm at the county jail."

I didn't hesitate for more than a second. "Sure. Sure I remember you, Shelly. You're at the county jail? I'll be there in an hour."

I'd handled some sensational, highly publicized cases in my short detecting career, but I'd never walked into the middle of a social civil war before.

Two

I SCRIBBLED "Ben/Dentist/Em/Dance" on a yellow Post-it and stuck it on the sun visor of my Volvo, where I keep track of most of my important appointments. Evelyn de la Cretaz, the sometimes severe but always efficient retired librarian who works for me part-time, has been urging me to invest in a car phone, on which she could call to remind me of such things. It was the only circumstance since Evelyn had joined my budding little operation last winter that she'd suggested I spend money on anything besides file folders. But the idea of high-tech telecommunications seemed too incongruous for my aging station wagon. I was sort of stuck on my Post-it system.

I'd called Chief Leeming as soon as Shelly Bloomfield had hung up and he'd agreed to see me if I stopped by. Before my visit to the jail, I wanted to squeeze out of him what I could.

The chief and I had evolved a sort of routine over the last year or two. Frank Leeming, a beefy, gruff, battle-scarred veteran of the New York City Police Department, had left Brooklyn for what he thought would be a tranquil suburban outpost. Once in Rochambeau, he was horrified to find himself confronted by some spectacular crimes—several murders in a single year, a town up in arms—and by Kit Deleeuw, a greenhorn private detective who kept popping up in the middle of them.

Like most good police professionals, he had little use for private investigators, seeing them variously as hustlers cruising for a fast buck, out of control renegades or bunglers mucking up his investigations. He could hardly believe his bad luck in having someone in his hair who'd been run out of Wall Street by a vengeful U.S. attorney (the FBI had warned Leeming about me).

But the chief had endured too much contact with the FBI to trust the agency totally. He had the street cop's resentment of their fancy clothes, fat budgets and lordly attitudes. Besides, I had busted open a couple of cases that had threatened both his sine-cure and his pension, in the process prying hordes of hysterical parents and taxpayers off his back. If he hadn't exactly come to appreciate me ("You're a Volvo sort of guy, Deleeuw, and I'm more a Chrysler sedan"), he had accepted me as an unpleasant but unavoidable fact of life, like hay fever.

I generally leveled with him, except when I didn't, and even as he cursed me, he always seemed to wind up helping if he could. Leeming had warned me so many times about overstepping my bounds, had threatened me so enthusiastically with license revoca-tion, ruin, disembowelment or worse if I didn't stay out of his way, that I'd be hard put to say if we were colleagues or enemies. More like uneasy allies, I guess, depending on what was going on. At the moment, mostly because I was working on industrial theft and insurance cases out of town, we were getting along fine.

"Underneath all the bullshit, you and I are just two working stiffs," he had pointed out over coffee recently. "We're trying to survive long enough to pay off the mortgage and get the kids off to college before we keel over in the garden like Marlon Brando in *The Godfather.*" I guess that is the bottom line, although I like to think of my life as a little more complex.

Like so many men in the '80s, my comfortable expectations about work had been violently upended, although my troubles were more exotic than many of my laid-off brethren. I hadn't participated in my Wall Street firm's insider trading, but I'd earned the FBI's and U.S. attorney's wrath by refusing to testify against my former colleagues, who were selling one another out more enthusiastically than Wal-Mart sold cheap kitchenware. The feds reluctantly agreed not to harass or prosecute me only if I agreed to leave the Financial District and my career, for good.

At thirty-eight, I was Home Alone, watching the paint peel, the gutters rust and the bills pile up. After six months of my walking the dog and moving dirt from one end of the garden to the other, Jane sat me down one day and announced she was going back to work and suggested I stop feeling sorry for myself and find a new life. And one more thing: she was providing the health plan, so I'd better plan on supplying the child care, since there was nowhere enough money to pay for both. Ah, Jane. Tough, smart and sensible.

It was good advice and I took it. But my stomach still churns when I think of those early transitional months. None of this look-at-me-I'm-a-new-Dad-taking-the-kids-out-for-pizza-once-a-week. I went from 0 to 60 in seconds, suddenly responsible for the care of two kids about whose lives I knew few day-to-day details, in charge of shopping, cooking and running a household about which I knew even less. Meanwhile, every mortgage payment became a white-knuckle event. Not to mention that I had to learn how to become a private investigator, about which there is much mythology but little realistic information.

Somehow to my—and Leeming's—astonishment, I'd become a pretty good private detective, or at least a lucky one. I'd gotten a couple of beatings and a minor bullet wound in the process. Leeming, enraged at my withholding information, had decided to teach me a lesson and had arrested me briefly. But compared to Wall Street in the '80s, those were nicks and scratches. My new work was a lot less scary than the old, or so I reflected as I pulled up behind the Rochambeau police station.

The Public Safety Center, stuffed into a decaying brick building that had once been an elementary school, attested to the fact that the town didn't really want to acknowledge that it had or even needed a police department, and certainly wasn't about to put one in a conspicuous place. The ramshackle headquarters was on a side street; police cruisers and unmarked cars were parked at crazy angles in what had been the playground. The basic idea was that since there shouldn't be any crime, the police shouldn't be seen. Unless some kid's bicycle got stolen—then the cops should flood the streets and get it back. I had come to see how impossible a job like Leeming's could be. He had a tiny budget; his department was a revolving door for rookies who joined the force for a couple of years and then moved on; he was hounded by public opinion every time a burglar purloined a VCR.

The dispatcher, who doubled as majordomo, waved me though to the chief's office, looking harassed. The phones were ringing nonstop. I had no doubt that the Rochambeau PD's switchboard was lit up like Town Hall at Christmas.

Leeming himself was built like an oak desk, heavy, square and with a full head of black hair graying at the sides. His dark brown

eyes were so intense you had to force yourself not to look away.
They were eyes that had seen a lot. He could have slipped on a
uniform and walked the beat and not really looked out of place.

He waved one immense hand in acknowledgment when I entered, and looked at me wearily and warily. "You weaseled your
way into this killing?" he asked. Leeming honestly found it inconceivable that someone would hire me on merit. Whenever I got
work, it was because I had "hustled" or "sweet-talked" someone.
He pointed towards a table with a heavily stained coffeemaker, a
jar of powdered cream and packets of sugar. I had foolishly accepted once. The coffee tasted like dishwashing detergent mixed
with fertilizer and maybe some drain cleaner thrown in. Cops
seemed to love the stuff. Their stomachs are conditioned to handle anything.

"Well, Chief, a better way of putting it is that my legendary
detecting skills have been recognized again."

He rolled his eyes, gulped from his Styrofoam cup, winced and
stared at me. He didn't do how-are-the-kids suburban small talk.
He had two daughters, and his goal in life was to somehow get
them through college and into adulthood, then to flee to Arizona
and live near a golf course. I hoped he made it.

"Sorry, but yes, I'm on the case," I continued. "How bad is it?"

"It's worse than bad," he said morosely. Coping with the killing
of a middle-school principal is not the kind of thing Rochambeau
parents expect to have to explain to their kids over dinner; they
want to talk about soccer practice instead. The New York TV crews
and their vans were undoubtedly cruising the schools right now
and would be outside Leeming's door soon, if they hadn't stopped
by already. The town's real estate brokers would not like to see
their police chief on television saying anything except that the
investigation was concluded and the culprit safely in custody.

"You can't imagine," Leeming growled. "The phones have
gone nuts. In Brooklyn, everybody *expected* bad things to happen.
Here, they come as a complete shock, like they're against the laws
of nature. A school principal getting shot, Jesus. Maybe I should
have my heart attack now. How are you in on this? And you better
fucking behave—" His glare became menacing.

"Easy there, Chief. I'm not anxious to renew my acquaintance
with your holding pen, honest. Shelly Bloomfield has asked to see
me. I presume she doesn't want my chili recipe, so I'm headed for

the county jail to meet with her and her lawyer. She coming out
on bail?''

"Not up to me. But, maybe, I would think. Could go either way.
Not going to run to Costa Rica, is she, not with three kids at
home? Her husband runs a software company in the city, works
with banks there. She's a pretty tough cookie, from what I saw.
Not admitting a thing, not giving us a nickel.''

Leeming looked down at the flashing lights on his telephone.
He had lots of business people, parents and politicians to soothe
and stave off. "What can I do for you, Deleeuw? I have to meet
with the county prosecutor, who wouldn't be too thrilled to know
I kept him outside my office while I filled some suit-turned-detec-
tive in on my most sensitive case. God, the Mayor and the council
are lit up on this one. Every woman in town is squawking. The
women's libbers are not thrilled with the idea that this woman is
dead, I can tell you that. She was apparently pretty active in
women's rights, all that stuff.'' He scowled. "And your client has
some friends and admirers, too. They can't believe we would lock
Betty Crocker up on murder charges. Being in the middle here
ain't my favorite spot.''

Or mine, I thought. I was usually pretty dependably in the feminists' corner, both because I believed "that stuff" and because I'd
be run out of my house if I didn't.

A principal gunned down in her own school had to be the local
equivalent of nuclear meltdown. Rochambeau's schools are the
jewel in the town crown. The high school's Ivy League acceptance
rate is followed much more closely than the football team's won-
lost record. Every parent in town would be horrified over this
violent intrusion into the town's schools, in a large sense Rochambeau's whole rationale for existing. Large numbers of articulate,
educated, politicized women would identify strongly with the dead
principal and all she stood for. And a proudly outspoken homemaker was accused of killing her. The emotional and political
ramifications were daunting, to say the least.

For all the changes men have to adjust to, the work-vs.-home
debate still seems more complex for women. Just two days earlier,
I watched a neighbor run out the door clutching her crammed
briefcase, sprinting grimly for the train while her curly-haired toddler stood on the doorstep yelling, "Bye, Mommy, bye, Mommy,

are you coming back?" Here was a death that brought all of that tragically and brutally into focus.

"Well, I'm sure everyone is upset about it," I murmured, simultaneously stalling and fishing.

"Yeah, but the libbers are louder than anybody else. Except maybe the housewives. And now here comes you, the frosting on the fucking cake."

Maybe he loved me after all. "We all gotta eat, Chief. Just flash me what you can." I love Raymond Chandler talk and rarely get to do it. A bit over six feet, with enough brown hair remaining to have it described as tousled and a slight paunch despite all the dog-walking, I look more like a college professor on the eve of tenure than a private eye. And I had never removed the gun I'd bought from my office safe; the idea of my shooting somebody or of my kids accidentally shooting themselves was too horrifying. But once in a while, it was a great kick to talk tough and crack wise. Leeming never seemed to notice. He talked that way all the time anyway.

"Probably even *you* know that Nancy Rainier-Gault, recently installed principal of the Rochambeau Middle School, was shot through the heart with a shotgun Saturday afternoon," he began. "Her appointment book noted a meeting with Shelly Bloomfield at two p.m. Saturday, the approximate time of her death, according to the medical examiner. Bloomfield's son had been suspended by Rainier-Gault that week. We have all kinds of physical evidence to tie Shelly Bloomfield to the crime scene, not the least of which is the shotgun—it was her husband's—we found stuck in the woodpile next to her garage. It was right near a mama skunk and her babies. That's all I can tell you. 'Cept it's a nice tight case. No holes at all."

Why on earth, I wondered, would anybody in his or her right mind shoot someone with a gun registered to a member of their own family, then hide the rifle a few paces from the back door? Your own property is the first place the police, with their dogs and metal detectors, look. But of course, people in their right minds don't generally kill other people. "How was the body discovered?"

"School janitor found it. The alarm had been turned off, presumably by the principal." Leeming was none-too-subtly easing towards the door. "What else, Deleeuw? I got stuff to do."

I held up a hand. "Who would be so stupid as to leave a murder weapon in their backyard?"

Leeming shrugged. "Easy. A panicked amateur."

I persisted. I didn't have much time.

"What motive could Shelly Bloomfield possibly have? What was her kid in trouble for? You don't kill principals for bad grades." Although, in Rochambeau, that probably couldn't be ruled out.

"Shelly Bloomfield's son Jason, star student and co-captain of the school basketball team, had perfectly good grades. He had just been suspended by Principal Rainier-Gault for sexual harassment. And there was a note on Rainier-Gault's file about Jason that said 'Recommending expulsion. Contact county prosecutor?' Afore-mentioned mother Shelly came roaring into school last Tuesday and threatened real loudly to kill Rainier-Gault if this black mark tarnished son Jason's record. Which it surely would have if he had been charged."

"Sexual harassment. But that's not a felony, right? Is there something more? Are we talking about rape or something like that?"

"We're not talking about any specifics," growled the chief.

"Come on, Chief, what did the kid do?"

"Can't tell you that, Deleeuw. You can ask Mom. She calls her-self the Last Housewife, I'm told. That's great, a town war between NOW and the Rochambeau Moms. Maybe I should just early re-tire now."

"You've already done that once. You don't want to make a ca-reer out of it."

"Welcome to police work." Leeming looked me firmly in the eye. "But if you're sincere about not liking to take people's money when you can't help, I'd recommend you take a pass on this one. We have motive, opportunity, enough physical evidence to make a prosecutor glow in the dark. Any smart lawyer will make a deal on this one. Honest, Deleeuw, I don't see a glimmer of reasonable doubt here. Bloomfield will go down for this one. Go peep into some motel bedrooms."

I used to rise to that bait regularly, but not anymore. "Wouldn't think of it, Chief. Your people seem absolutely helpless without me. About this motive . . . I mean, a rational person doesn't murder a school official for suspending her kid. Was there some

kind of history of animosity between them? Had they come to
blows or something?''

"I don't honestly know what was going through the woman's
mind." Leeming was growing impatient. "My hunch is, she just
got herself into a rage, got all worked up and went there and blew
away the principal. It happens. In this country they shoot priests
for taking three seconds to reach for their wallets." He looked up
at the clock, and his face softened a bit.

"I hate to see anybody killed," he said. "Especially in my town
and even more especially a principal doing her job. But if it's
going to happen, then I like the killer to threaten the victim in
front of several witnesses, have an appointment at the time of
death, then hide the murder weapon—her husband's gun—on
her property. The Last Housewife is going down for this one, Kit.
Murder one. Premeditated, cold-blooded.''

"And does she admit to any of that?''

Was it my imagination, or was the chief just a tad less cocksure
when he answered?

"No, would you? She denies every word of it. Wouldn't even
wait for her lawyer. Told us she couldn't bear to kill mice, let
alone people, and sounded like she meant it. But if you took how
people *seemed* into account, you'd never crack a case. Bye now,
Deleeuw. I have other demands on my time. This principal was a
heroine to a lot of women in Rochambeau. Working hard to help
girls become physicists and to stamp out sexual harassment and
all. We've got a lot of people wanting to see justice done.''

Shelly Bloomfield sat behind a wooden table whose surface was
scarred with the initials of countless lost and troubled souls who'd
come through this depressing cinder-block jailhouse, off a highway three miles south of town, comfortably out of sight and therefore out of mind most of the time. She could hardly have looked
more out of place if she were standing on a Bronx corner ped-
dling crack.

She wore the same sweatsuit I remembered from the park,
though the shoelaces had been removed from her Reeboks. Some
of her brown hair had pulled free from her ponytail and her
makeup looked smeared from crying. But otherwise, she looked
just as Leeming had described her—defiant and proud. Steve

Dougherty, a tax lawyer and town councilman and, it turned out, one of Shelly Bloomfield's neighbors, sat at her elbow.

"No way I can handle a criminal case like this, Deleeuw, as I'm sure you know. Just responding to a neighbor's plea for help," he announced tersely. "Mrs. Bloomfield has read about you, of course, and she remembered meeting you in the park and liking you. We're bringing in some people from Eric Levin's firm and he also likes the idea of hiring you. We need a lot of help . . ." Dougherty shot me one of those man-to-man glances whose meaning was unmistakable: the Last Housewife was in deep trouble. "So—"

Bloomfield, who'd been watching me closely, cut him off. I got the feeling she liked to do her own talking. "I am not guilty, Mr. Deleeuw," she said, looking me squarely in the eye and thrusting her chin still higher. "I am a mother and homemaker. I've devoted myself to bringing life into the world and nurturing it. I could never kill anyone. It's not even conceivable." She bristled, her eyes glinting. Then, as I sat and studied her without speaking, her face crumpled. "Of course, everybody in this situation says that, don't they?"

"They do," I said, recalling Leeming's prophetic comment.

One of the fluorescent bulbs overhead was flickering annoyingly. The smell of disinfectant mingled with cigarette smoke. Shelly leaned back against the metal folding chair, perhaps thinking the same thoughts I would have: what can I possibly say that will convince a near-total stranger whose help I desperately need that I'm not a killer?

I explained to Shelly Bloomfield my own personal creed: I only take criminal cases if I believe the clients absolutely, if I look into their eyes and feel they're telling the truth. Then, I never stop believing. My clients are paying for loyalty as well as expertise, and that's good, because I have lots more of the former than the latter. Sometimes I'm wrong and I get burned. But once I agree to take a case, my client is innocent and it's up to me to prove it.

"Look," Bloomfield said, "I spent the '80s watching almost every woman I know leave home to be whatever it was she wanted to be. And get all kinds of approval for it. Which they all deserve. Diane next door is a lawyer now, Marla's a caterer, Carolyn shows her paintings in SoHo, Ramona down the block is a social worker. Their actions were all praiseworthy and my life—taking care of three children, including one who's hyperactive—sometimes seemed like crap to everybody. At parties nobody wanted to hear about my work. I wasn't on the front line of any revolution.''

Her eyes grew moist. Dougherty handed her his pressed white handkerchief. Behind us, we heard the sounds of cursing and jail doors slamming and, I thought, a few tearful good-byes from visitors. I hate having to go into prisons. I've tried to describe to Jane how suffocated and panicky they make me feel. She understands; her work in stricken Paterson has taken her into several herself.

No civilized culture would put people in cages like this. Certainly it was the last place Shelly Bloomfield had ever expected to be. I thought back to that sparkling morning when I had encountered her and her dumb dog—what was its name?—in the park. Had someone told either of us we would be meeting next in the county jail, while she awaited a bail hearing on murder charges, we'd have roared with laughter.

"You have a hyperactive kid?"

"Jason," she said. "Jason was hyperactive. When he was younger, they wanted to put him on Ritalin. They insisted he needed to be sent to a special needs school. But I wouldn't let them do it. I worked with him for hours every day. Nobody, not even my husband Dan, knows what I went through with that boy. But Jason is now captain of the basketball team, and he's been on the high honor roll two years running. Isn't that important work? Wasn't it worth it? I see kids all over town who are raised by nannies and day-care workers—rent-a-moms—and some of those children are so lonely they want to drink me up. Some of them get into lots worse trouble than Jason. Doesn't my work matter?"

She didn't wait for an answer. "You're goddamned right it does. The most important work in the world. So sure, I went a little nuts when Nancy Rainier-Gault, who's on this big sexual harassment kick, decided to make an example of Jason and ruin all we've worked for. But shoot her? Take a life? My God, no."

Dougherty looked at his watch, then patted her arm. "Shelly, I know this is horrible, but . . ." His colorless voice faltered. There wasn't any "but." It was horrible, period. Dougherty looked uncomfortable. Dressed in a dull gray suit, his hair barber-trimmed, he was the very portrait of the suburban burgher. He belonged at his Kiwanis lunch discussing plans for perking up the downtown and looking for land development deals, not in the county jail with an accused murderer. He was out of his depth.

"Look, Shelly," he said, "you have a bail hearing in about thirty minutes. I think Mr. Deleeuw can best help by getting to work for you."

She nodded, and rubbed her hands over her eyes, further smudging her eye shadow. "I'm sorry, Mr. Deleeuw. It's just that I'm so stunned, so overwrought about all this, what they did to Jason, locking me up like this, hauling me out of my own house in front of my family. I'll never get over it. Never. And I'm terrified that my kids won't either. Think what they're going through! I haven't been shopping, Erin was supposed to perform in her piano recital . . . Oh, God!"

She put her head down on her arms and began to sob. I knew what was racing through her mind. When you take care of small children, their whereabouts, well-being, playdates and lessons never really stop flashing through your head like those electronic schedule signs in airports, no matter what you're doing or where you are. To be pulled away unexpectedly is especially terrifying, because nobody else knows the details of the schedule as well as you do.

She raised her tear-stained face. "I feel terrible about Ms. Rainier-Gault, too, I really do. God, I can't believe she's dead. I can't believe any of this. This can't be happening to me . . ."

Dougherty murmured a few more soothing clichés and reminded her again that she had a bail hearing soon. He sneaked another glance at his watch.

"Mrs. Bloomfield . . ." She looked shocked at my formality, then asked me to call her Shelly. "Shelly," I continued, "the police told me that the principal made some notation about talking to the county prosecutor about Jason. She must have thought whatever your son did was pretty serious. Can you tell me what it was?" I pulled out my calculator-sized tape recorder and pushed the "on" button. Evelyn would transcribe the tape later, if I decided to take the case. I still hadn't made up my mind about that.

She stared at the recorder for a few seconds, opened her mouth to reply, paused as if to make sure she was under control, then spoke quietly, almost softly.

"What Jason admits to doing was wrong, way beyond obnoxious, far past the unacceptable. I would have grounded him for months

if she'd just told me, I would've massacred him. That isn't the way
he was raised. I don't teach my daughters to accept that kind of
behavior, and if somebody did it to them, I'd expect the boys to
catch hell."

I held up a hand. "Wait, Shelly. Slow down a bit. First tell me
what Jason admits to doing."

She massaged her forehead with both hands, as if warding off a
headache. "Jason snapped a girl's bra strap. Some stupid game
these boys play. I guess you reach down the back of her sweater
and snap it. It's wrong, and it's not a game. It must be humiliating
and very disturbing."

"And Jason admitted to that?"

"Yes. He did. He was sorry and ashamed. But you know how fast
things are changing, faster than some kids can understand. That's
probably our fault. Maybe we didn't emphasize it enough. What
he did was wrong, but it was what boys have been doing forever,
usually with a wink from the school authorities. Doesn't mean it
shouldn't be stopped, but c'mon, that shouldn't mark him for life
either." This sounded like a speech she'd delivered before. To the
woman she may have murdered, perhaps?

Dougherty handed her a glass of water from a brown plastic
pitcher embossed with the county seal. An amenity I hadn't encountered before—perhaps the newly elected sheriff was moving
towards a kinder, gentler county jail.

"Nancy Rainier-Gault just came here in September from New
York City. One of the first things she told us parents was that she
was going to react strongly to sexual harassment, make it a big
issue. She told us that she was going to personally visit with the
girls in the school and urge them to come forward, tell them their
complaints about harassment would be taken seriously. She
wanted to make boys conscious of this stuff in middle school, she
said, so when they got to the high school they wouldn't do even
greater harm. I was at that meeting, Kit; I clapped. Dan and I even
talked to Jason about it. Maybe it didn't penetrate, maybe the
other kids dared him, I don't know . . . I take full responsibility.
So does my husband. Jason takes his share too."

She was practically pleading with me now. "He should apologize, he should be punished, he should get counseling if need be.
Do community service. But to make him the symbol of all male

oppression—I can't sit back and let him be sacrificed for that, can I?''

She groaned. ''God, and this will just call so much attention to that stupid game. He'll never live it down. Never. Every story about the murder, about me, will mention it. What crazy, crazy times.''

I could see why Leeming had rather liked her. She seemed honest and level-headed, determined to protect her son without condoning his behavior. It was hard to imagine her toting a rifle to a school building and firing it into a principal's chest. But even my few short years of detective work had introduced me to some stunning liars. I needed to go no further back than my last case.

''But this is what he admitted to, right?'' I asked. ''What the girl accused him of?''

''Bear with me, Kit,'' she said wearily. ''It's hard. I have to tell it in my own way. Otherwise I won't be able to tell it at all.''

Shelly was exhausted now, too drained for defiance, telling the story in sequence, the only way she probably could get through it. ''Jason pulled his stupid stunt, the girl reported him and Ms. Rainier-Gault decided to make an example of him. She could have talked to him, and to Dan and me. We would have punished him, and severely. But instead she called him in and suspended him, then notified us. Then a day or so later, the girl comes back with her parents. Says there was something else. Jason didn't just snap the bra. He squeezed her breasts. She was too embarrassed to talk about it at first. Her parents said it took them a couple of days to pull the story out of her; they could see something was bothering her. Maybe even something worse than that. She'd been out of school for a while. Jason . . . he, well, I have to level with you. He said the boys do this all the time. It's called 'Squeezing the Grapefruit.' Dan was really angry with him. He said, 'Jason, if the boys threw themselves in front of a train, would you do that too?' ''

She paused a second, then spoke quickly, wanting it to be over. ''The first is considered harassment, maybe just mischief to some. The second is on the edge of something else—assault, sexual battery. The girl's parents weren't sure if they were going to push it, to press charges against Jason. They were afraid of going public, of making things worse for their daughter. I wanted to call and tell them how sorry I was, but they wouldn't talk to me. According to the principal, they wanted to think about it, talk to a counselor maybe, talk to their daughter again.

"Anyway, Rainier-Gault called and said that she had been thinking about this, and she was seriously considering notifying the county prosecutor. It was a judgment call, she admitted to me. It wasn't a clear-cut case of sexual abuse, and she wasn't required to report it if the girl or her parents didn't press it. But she thought this decision might be too important to rest with a thirteen-year-old. She said she wasn't going to have sexual assaults in her school, that she had to make an example of my son. She said there was more going on and that she was trying to get this girl to come forward, to tell all of it. She thought she would. Because of confidentiality, she couldn't be more specific, she told me. But she wanted me to know she thought it could get serious."

"And Jason?"

"He denied that he touched her. He admitted the bra strap, but he denied the rest. Swore on his life. He said if he touched her breasts, he didn't know it. He insisted there was nothing else. And I believe him. But the principal wouldn't even talk to him for more than a minute or two. She said it didn't matter what Jason said, he could tell his side of the story to the prosecutor and the authorities. She said it was out of her hands now. She was going to play God. Those are my words, not hers."

"When did you first find out that Jason was in trouble? Tell me all the details about that day."

"She called me Tuesday around lunchtime. My youngest—Sarah—had come home from kindergarten and I was about to make her a grilled cheese sandwich for lunch. I picked up the phone and heard: 'This is Nancy Rainier-Gault at the middle school. I'm sorry to be calling you with this news, Mrs. Bloomfield, but your son Jason is in my office, and I'm planning to suspend him for a week. I'm required to notify you first and I would call anyway, of course. I believe in telling parents about misconduct before anybody else learns of it. Jason reached into a cheerleader's sweater and pulled her bra strap. He says he did it as a "joke," but I'm afraid I have to demonstrate that it isn't a joke at all, that such behavior will not be tolerated. Can you please come in?' "

Bloomfield ran her hands through her increasingly straggly hair. "I dropped Sarah off at a neighbor's and was there at the school in under five minutes. I was pretty upset. I mean, that woman had decided to suspend him without even talking to me first. He's not a mean kid, he just did a dumb thing. I was sure at that point that we could still deal with it among ourselves. I was prepared to take away his Nintendo, to pull him off the basketball team, to ground him. But a suspension goes on your record, marks you for life!

"But she had already decided to make an example of him, that was obvious when I got to her office. Jason was sitting in a chair across from her, and she gestured to me to sit in another. She said, 'Mrs. Bloomfield, I want to explain what the issues are.' "

Shelly's eyes blazed. "Well, people talk to housewives all the time like we never read a newspaper or think about anything besides recipes. I told her I understood perfectly well what the issues were: she wanted to sacrifice my son for a political issue that happens to be valid, and which I happen to agree with, but that didn't require such a severe response. But she didn't want to respond privately or humanely. She insisted that it be dealt with publicly, in the most destructive way. She said that the other boys had to get the message, and if nothing much happened to Jason, the message would be that you could do this sort of thing and get away with it. She absolutely refused to talk to the boy or us to see if there wasn't a better way to handle it, perhaps something less extreme. She absolutely refused to listen to reason.

"Well, we started yelling at each other. She asked Jason to leave the room, which he did. She told me she wasn't going to stand for sexism, not from anybody, and that it was time to take a stand against sexual harassment. I was screaming that five years earlier people like her wanted my boy doped up or sent away and I had gone through hell to bring Jason to the point where he was, and she wasn't going to ruin his life because she had landed here with her PC Manhattan politics. I said boys—and men—had to change, but that it couldn't happen overnight. That Jason couldn't be blamed so harshly for behavior that had gone unpunished forever. She said she understood how I felt, but that we just had completely different perspectives on this issue. She said she expected me to have concern for Jason, but that her concerns were larger, and that, of course, lit me up. I went berserk."

I've heard a lot of stories from clients, some of them more grisly or bizarre, but few more compelling. I was wearing a lot of hats: a

man, the father of a boy and a girl, a town resident, the husband
(and father) of a feminist. I understood the principal's stand; yet I
knew that confronted with the same circumstances I would react
much the way Shelly Bloomfield had. Your instinct is always to
protect your child, to anticipate threats, minimize damage, think
ahead for them. If this had happened to Ben, I would argue as
hard as I could to keep it off his record, to deal with it as privately
as possible. There's no such thing as a politically correct parent
when your kid's in trouble. Examples must be set—but when your
kid is the example, everything seems a lot less clear-cut. But I had
to push away my own reactions as a parent and concentrate on
being a clearheaded private investigator.

"Did you threaten her?"

She looked abashed. "Yes, I said that if she ruined Jason's future for one bad mistake I would kill her. I mean, Kit, for God's
sake, I tell my kids twenty times a week that I'm going to kill them.
I'd never *do* it."

"Go on," I said gently, ignoring the fact that Steve Dougherty's
eyes had been fixed on his watch for the past five minutes.

"We both realized it was getting out of hand. It was her suggestion that we cool down and meet later, maybe over the weekend.
She said she cared about what happened to Jason too, that she
wasn't there only for the girls in the school. It was just that it had
to stop and that process had to begin somewhere." She shuddered. "You know, if she hadn't been talking about my child, I
might even have agreed with her. But I told her, 'There has to be
compassion for both sides, even for boys.' I actually thought I was
getting somewhere. She told me, 'Mrs. Bloomfield, this isn't happening in a vacuum. We have real problems with harassment in
this school, and Jason isn't the only offender or the worst, I know
that. Maybe we should talk on Saturday.'

"I had the feeling that when we got together again, she might
be willing to think about some alternatives. So, why would I walk
in and shoot her without even knowing if she would change her
mind or not?"

The door swung open. An enormous matron with a nightstick
tucked into her belt came in to announce that the van was ready
to transport the prisoner to court for her bail hearing. I only had a
minute or two.

"Then the next thing you heard was a couple of days later, what, Thursday?"

She nodded. "I spent hours talking to Jason, explaining how wrong he'd been, how it wasn't a joke, talking about ways to apologize to the girl, to make it clear to other boys that he was sorry, that these kinds of games were not games at all, but attacks. I swear to you, that boy was miserable and sorry and mortified. No child can fake the pain Jason was in. Then Thursday, Ms. Rainier-Gault calls and tells me about this new thing, about the girl's breast being touched. She said she was leaning even more strongly to reporting all of this to the prosecutor. I begged her to arrange a meeting between our two families to find some other way of dealing with this. I said Jason understood that what he had done was wrong. He was dreadfully sorry and wanted to make amends, to apologize to the girl and her family. Wouldn't that be enough? After all, it was a judgment call on the principal's part, she said so herself. And she did agree—very reluctantly—to meet with me on Saturday."

I wondered about a hundred things, including this: what good would murdering Nancy Rainier-Gault do Shelly Bloomfield? It wasn't as though Shelly could shut the whole mess down by killing the principal. If the girl's parents wanted to pursue matters, they could simply have gone to the prosecutor themselves. Maybe she thought the parents of the girl wouldn't want the public trauma either. Perhaps she just flew into a fury and lost control. But bringing a rifle—that suggested premeditation, that meant a first-degree murder charge.

"Did you bring that rifle with you?"

"No. God, no. I hated that thing. Wouldn't touch it. I was always after Dan to get rid of it. Jason wasn't allowed to go near it, and it was under lock and key. I swear, I have no idea how it got to Nancy Rainier-Gault's office."

She seemed uncomfortable even mentioning the gun. Was she faking that?

"Where was your husband in all this?"

The question seemed to throw her. "Well, Dan runs his own software business. He works long hours, and he's always left raising the kids to me, mostly. He would've come to the conference at the school, but he'd had a grueling week. And to be honest with you, Kit, he just couldn't believe she'd go so far with this, that it would get that serious. He said if every boy he went to school with who put his hand up a girl's dress or down her shirt went to jail, there'd be no men free in America.'' She hesitated, perhaps pondering the wisdom of what she said next: ''And Dan's got a wicked temper. I honestly thought I could handle it better. God, I wish he had come.''

The matron cleared her throat impatiently. I had to wrap it up. ''And when you did go to the school on Saturday?''

''She said these new charges really took things out of her hands. It really was no longer just a matter of a judgment call on her part. And she repeated she had reason to think the problem was deeper. She had to report allegations of abuse, although she agreed that technically this might not clearly constitute that, but that was for professionals to decide. She said that too many women in America had been hurt because they couldn't or wouldn't stand up to protect themselves, and because brutality and harassment and worse had been swept under the rug. She said she didn't mean to be indifferent to Jason, but that this kind of behavior would stop only if women refused to buckle under to it and the men and boys who did it were punished—publicly and firmly. I pleaded, begged, raged—everything . . .'' The matron put her arm on Shelly's.

Shelly rose and nodded. ''She told me there was no more to discuss. She said she hadn't completely made up her mind, pending discussion with the girl's parents, but she wanted to be honest —she expected to proceed. I saw there was no point in arguing. I thought I'd probably have to get a lawyer. When I left, she was going through her files. She turned to wish me good luck and say she was sorry, but she felt that she was doing the right thing. She said she cared for Jason too, and hoped he came out all right. That was some BS, pardon my language.''

Shelly shook her head as she recalled the parting, as if she couldn't yet believe how it had turned out. If she was faking sincerity, she deserved an Oscar as well as a jail term.

''When I left, I swear to you, Kit, she was alive and well. I didn't hurt her. I couldn't. I swear on my children's lives. Will you help me? They say you've worked a couple of miracles.''

The matron, who I thought had been eager to hear Bloom-field's story, told Dougherty they had to board the van right now. The attorney stood up carefully to preserve the crease in his gray suit. "You don't want to tick off a judge at a bail hearing, Shelly. We've got to go."

"Not till he gives me an answer," Shelly said, eyes fixed on my face.

I pocketed the recorder, then stood. "No miracles. I'm not a magician. But you've got yourself a detective." I held out my hand.

Her hands closed around mine; hope flooded her face. "Thank God," she breathed. "I just know you can help me. 'Cause if you can't," she added with a tight smile, "I might really be the Last Housewife."

Three

I BRIEFLY CONSIDERED punching them out, but Chief Leeming and his cops would probably frown at my slugging two earnest yuppie parents in Rochambeau Municipal Park. Besides, I wasn't sure that Percentage and I could make it to the Volvo before the guy, who was lean and muscled, caught up with us and slugged me back.

Still, the temptation was strong. The couple bent over a chubby toddler in a hooded pea-green sweatshirt and matching pants and pointed enthusiastically to the treetops. Both looked fresh off the train from the city—crumpled suits, lots of jewelry for her, his designer tie askew. After a day's work, it was clearly a struggle to appear as enthusiastic and awestruck as Rochambeau parents liked to be around their evolving offspring, but these two were nevertheless focused on little Matthew like laser beams.

"What's that, Matthew?" Mom chirped.

"Buh," said Matthew.

"That's right!" said Dad. "Bird. And what do birds do, Matthew?"

"Fluggg."

"That's *right,*" said Dad with feeling. "They f-f-f-f-f-l-l-l-l-y-y-y. *Fly.* Right?"

"Fluggg."

"And what letter does bird begin with?" Mom picked up the litany.

"Unnnngh."

Young Matthew looked beseechingly towards Percentage and me, but we could do nothing for him. Asking his parents to lighten up would be pointless. People so single-minded always resent your suggesting that they are overdoing it and, of course, it was no business of mine. Who appointed me Superparent anyway?

"With a B!" Dad answered his wife's question. "B for b-b-b-birdie! And where do b-birds live?"

Silence from Matthew.

"In *trees.*"

And what do trees have, I asked myself. L-i-m-b-s. And what would happen if I picked up a l-i-m-b from a tree and brained these whiftos?

"I think he's really getting it," declared the father. "He's doing so well. And he can spell dog now, I'm sure of it. I'll show you. Look, Matthew, what's that?" He was pointing to the dogs in Shelly Bloomfield's canine play group, about a hundred feet away. Matthew had a lot of work to do before he could toddle home and have his cookie, I could see that.

Unfortunately, this wasn't a rare exchange in my town. There are lots of kids in Rochambeau for whom all of nature, every sight and sound, is an opportunity to expand their vocabularies and learn the alphabet. Parents hereabouts don't wait for the educational process to take its course; they try to jump-start it from the minute their darlings first point to something beyond their strollers.

Of course, I was hardly relaxed myself during the few spare hours I'd spent around my own kids at that age. I often wonder just what it is that prompts the child obsession of my generation. My current theory is: fear. Ours is a complicated, dangerous and challenging world, and we have to prepare our children for it. Will they be able to cope? Compete in workplaces where good jobs can no longer be taken for granted? Protect themselves in a country where children may carry weapons to school? These are the questions that haunt parents.

Sometimes all the effort pays off, and these extraordinarily intelligent, attractive and well-prepared young people go sailing off to make their way in the world. Sometimes the deal goes bad, and the kids won't or can't live up to all the expectations. These are the kids I encounter in my work: runaways, kids with drug problems, kids who fly into violent tantrums at school or disappear into dangerous neighborhoods in the city.

Does knowing that B is for bird lead to smooth sailing later on?

I doubt it, but what do I really know? Parents tend to feel passion-
ately about child-rearing, almost needing to doubt other ap-
proaches as a means of reassuring themselves about their own.
The stakes are, after all, high. It isn't like buying a car. If you make
the wrong choices, somebody else will be paying for it the rest of
his life.

Percentage and I were in the park observing Matthew's spelling
lessons because I was hoping to talk with Shelly Bloomfield's
friends and fellow dog walkers in the forty-five minutes before Ben
was expected at the dentist and Emily was due at her dance class,
which would be followed by a hurried dinner and a Board of
Education meeting. Emily and Ben had both come home with
notices announcing that the Board was proceeding with its
planned parents' meeting. On the agenda were crossing guards,
the new language arts curriculum and, ironically, sexual harassment—but parents were encouraged to bring any "concerns"
about the tragedy that had struck that weekend. Knowing Rochambeau parents, they didn't need the encouragement. I wanted
to be anyplace else, but I needed to be there.

I was in search of some insight that could help launch my investigation. I wanted a clearer sense of Bloomfield, some reaffirma-
tion of my own hurried assessment. I liked her. My instinct said
that she was warm, honest, smart, one of those force-of-nature
types, charismatic and memorable. I liked her balance, that even
as she sat in jail facing murder charges, with her son's reputation
and future in peril, she was still able to grasp that the issue involved was complex and serious. Too many people couldn't see
the other side under far better circumstances. And I liked her
loving and courageous battle on behalf of her son.

But I've learned to think skeptically in order to protect myself
and I was struck by her defensiveness about the life she had chosen and the way it seemed to her under siege. The flashes of anger
over her housewifely role, the sense of dislocation, seemed powerful. The question was, how powerful?

Like Rochambeau's other parks, this one was well tended and
shrouded in giant oaks, groves of white pines and leafy maples.
Jogging and bike paths sliced gracefully through its sweeping
green lawns. Over in one corner, a pack of dogs was milling
around.

Bloomfield's dog play group was a chance for people to gather in the park and let their dogs off their leashes for some exercise, which most of the animals sorely needed. Dog owners feel as guilty about leaving their dogs alone all day as they do about leaving their kids in the hands of day-care centers and nannies, and are similarly inclined to overcompensate. They tell themselves that dogs require socialization. I suppose they do, though I don't remember my father ever expressing such concern for the hounds who slept in our basement in the winter or in the backyard in warm weather. (Percentage sleeps on an L.L. Bean cedar-filled bed almost as large as ours.)

Even though the play group was mostly comprised of Labs, retrievers, Dalmatians and your basic large mutts, the little brown poodle seated on the path distinctly commanded some sort of authority.

I regarded the animals ahead of us warily before we approached. While several of the dogs in the morning session were known to us, we didn't often come to the park.

The poodle's bright eyes were fixed on Percentage.

"Polly is the play group leader," advised a stoutish woman wearing a lilac T-shirt and a flowery skirt right out of a Laura Ashley catalogue. She was an upscale version of Shelly Bloomfield, more done up, with a pageboy held in place by a headband that matched the skirt. She eschewed combat sneakers for daintier leather flats. "She belongs to me. I'm Sandra Vlaskamp."

Despite her fashion coordination, Vlaskamp had the same competent demeanor and slightly frazzled air that Bloomfield had. Show me a mother of three with great triceps, Jane likes to say, and I'll show you a nanny back at the house watching the kids. This woman had a stroller within arm's reach, with a toddler dozing in it, and, crawling in the sandbox twenty feet away, a four- or five-year-old boy playing with other kids.

Sandra Vlaskamp displayed another sign of a full-time mom, too —eyes that darted almost continuously from poodle to stroller to sandbox while occasionally flitting over Percentage and me, eyes able to take in ten things at once. These were the proverbial eyes in the back of the head that parents of young boys developed quickly, as soon as their kids could power themselves around. Emily had never needed much close scrutiny, but put Ben anywhere near a strange dog, busy intersection or swimming pool, and he would instinctively go for it.

Percentage seemed to pass muster with the poodle, but I was still getting an unsubtle once-over from Vlaskamp. She didn't seem to buy that I had just strolled by.

"Jessica here is mine too, and Gregory over there in the sandbox. My oldest boy is in school, thank God. Lord," she added, shaking her head, "I'm not going to be one of those who mourns when the kids are gone. There aren't enough pieces of me."

"I know what you mean," I said truthfully. With kids, there are never enough pieces of anybody, employed or not.

Between introductions, she was issuing a continual stream of orders to Polly, Jessica and Gregory. Don't go too far, don't play too rough, look at that flock of ducks in the pond. It wasn't clear who was getting what warning or instruction. All Sandra Vlaskamp really needed, I mused, was a dog to complicate matters.

She read my mind. "We didn't buy Polly. She appeared all bedraggled in the backyard last winter, half-starved and freezing. The kids saw her before I did, and with kids . . . well, you know." I did know. If kids get to homeless puppies and kittens before parents do, it's all over; only the truly strong can hold out.

"So now she's the Enforcer," Vlaskamp went on. "If Polly doesn't like the dog, the dog doesn't get to join our group. But Polly likes this dog—it's Percentage, isn't it?"

I nodded, surprised. We'd only visited the play group once before, after which I recognized that I prefer to dog walk alone. Percentage doesn't have strong social skills, or any skills beyond intense sniffing and walking in circles. His big thing is looking regal. But I remembered that everybody had inquired about the dogs' names, though nobody had asked for any of the humans'.

Around us, other owners—an elderly woman with a hyper Irish setter, a younger man on a bike with a kid strapped into the child seat—shouted ignored commands. Several goldens retrieved sticks, rocks and bits of litter, offering them to everyone in the park. Unless I was mistaken—individual dogs aren't that distinctive to me—one of them was Austin.

I'm not devious by nature. Given who I am, what I look like and where I operate, it seems to me the most direct approach is the best. That was the good advice my friend Benchley Carrollton, proprietor of the Rochambeau Garden Center, bestowed when I set up Deleeuw Investigations. Benchley has this Quaker notion that God resides in every one of us and that good deeds are rewarded, which works reasonably well in his nursery but is a bit more problematic in my line of work.

Still, people in towns like Rochambeau remain a mostly friendly and trusting lot. They have plenty of difficulties and dramas in their lives, but usually they have less to be stressed and suspicious about than city-dwellers do—fewer panhandlers, fewer traffic jams, fewer frayed tempers. Even with burglar alarms more common than they used to be, serious theft and violence are still rare enough hereabouts that people don't flinch when you approach them for directions, don't hesitate before opening the door or hide reasonable information politely sought. So unless I know I'm dealing with liars or psychos, I try to be straight.

"To be honest with you, Sandra, I'm not really here today because of Percentage. While I'm grateful for Polly's approval, I don't really want to join the group either."

Vlaskamp smiled and reached into her skirt pocket for a biscuit. Percentage waggled towards it, until the poodle enforcer yipped him back. "C'mon now, Polly," Sandra scolded. "Percentage is a good boy. Let's let him have a treat too." Polly sulked but backed off.

"You're working for Shelly, aren't you?" Sandra said, her smile unchanging. She reached for another biscuit and tossed this one to Polly. "She told me she met you—and Percentage. We don't get many celebrities in the dog group. In fact, I don't think I've ever met a private investigator before." I let Percentage off the leash and he sauntered towards the other dogs. Percentage was not one for wearing himself out.

"That's her dog Austin, isn't it?"

She nodded. "Shelly called and asked me to take care of Austin. We're friends and neighbors, and I have a key. Dan is a bit overwhelmed, as you can imagine. Three reporters even came up and tried to interview me. I told them to scram. Nobody in our neighborhood will talk. Except to you, probably. But then, none of us really knows anything."

"You and Shelly are close friends, I take it?"

"Best, you could say." Now the staunch smile evaporated, replaced by a look of real pain. "I can't believe this, I just can't. Shelly in jail, for murder. It's crazy, like one of those nutsy unbelievable-but-true stories you see on the tabloid shows. You know: 'The Housewife Next Door Is a Murderer.' Only she's your best buddy and a terrific person, the person you talk to three times a day, walk your dogs with, car-pool with." Her eyes reddened.

I could imagine her spending long days fastening and unfastening car seats, rummaging through the refrigerator a hundred times, dashing out for more milk, scurrying down to the basement to do laundry, walking the dog, cooking meals, keeping schedules and tending to a million never-ending details. Like her friend Shelly, this was a specimen of an embattled and endangered breed.

"Are you one of the last housewives?" I asked.

She laughed. "No, I'm eighty per cent there, but still holding on to what's left of my career." So much for intuition. "I'm a freelance editor. I work at home doing nonfiction manuscripts for a couple of New York publishing houses. I fit it in when I can—at night, during Jessica's naps, early in the morning. I love the business, and I miss it. I want to go back once the kids are a bit older."

I felt a bit rebuked, rightly so. You can't make any assumptions about women in suburbia these days, or where they stand on the spectrum. The woman comforting a yowling, feverish baby in the pediatrician's office could be the head of a megacorporation. "But I am the one who also shops, cleans, cooks, and who has to take her daughter to Tot Swim in twenty minutes and pick up the oldest boy at his pal's, then get dinner started . . . You have kids?"

It proved more effective than a secret password to be able to say that, yes, I had two and I took care of them much of the time. Her nod, and the looming deadline of Tot Swim, encouraged me to push on.

"Forgive an indelicate question, but besides being horrified, what's your take on Shelly's arrest? To start helping her, I need to figure out what really happened. Do you think feelings about being a stay-at-home mom figure into this at all?"

She scanned her kids and Polly, who was eyeing Percentage with growing suspicion. Percentage had pro forma bounded around for a bit, but now that he thought no one was noticing, he'd dropped down next to me on the path and gone to sleep.

"Shelly is the finest parent I know," Vlaskamp said. "Not only to her own children, but to half a dozen others who don't have parents nearby during the day. She's always driving them to the orthodontist when their sitters don't have licenses or their dads meant to get home early but a client called. The Prince of Rides, that's a little joke we have. She has extraordinary patience, enthusiasm and energy. I don't possess those qualities, certainly not to the same degree. I grit my teeth when I have to get down on the floor and play with those dreadful My Little Ponies. For Shelly, it's like she's at *Phantom of the Opera*. She really loves it."

"But?" I prompted. "You have a different view of being a housewife?"

She sighed, then crossed her arms, as if for warmth. "Shelly needs support, and she'll get it. But, as I've told her a number of times, I don't entirely share her point of view about housewifery. We don't fight about it exactly, but we do have heated discussions and, as you know, Shelly isn't halfhearted about anything. I sometimes think her attitude is too defensive. It comes across as self-pitying."

That had bugged me a bit too, now that Vlaskamp mentioned it. When my kids ask for something calmly and reasonably, I'm putty in their grasping little hands. But if the pitch and decibel level climb, I'd rather die than give in. Shelly wasn't exactly whining, but there had been a whiff of poor-me there.

"You know," Sandra went on, "I've decided to stay home for now to be with my kids. We can afford it for a while. I think it's a real gift to kids to have Mom standing there when the school bus stops at the corner. I mean, day care is terrific sometimes, a perfectly acceptable option, but if you're honest, you know it isn't exactly the same as a parent. It's sometimes the best we can do under the circumstances, and we can make it work, but it isn't the same.

"I don't romanticize this stuff. My husband is sweet with the kids but doesn't do much to help with the nitty-gritty. It's easier to shop myself than to make detailed lists for him and then end up throwing out a fifth of what he does buy. Housework is repetitious, dreary, thankless work. Everybody wants something different to eat. Somebody's always unhappy about something. Shelly sees this as a creative challenge. But it wears me out. It's not enough."

She took a deep breath. "But I know women who romanticize work, too. That can be demeaning or frustrating. I think a lot of women will be making Shelly's choice in the next few years."

The dogs had been woofing. As they quieted, I heard the indefatigable yuppie couple urging Matthew to comment on and observe the dogs who b-b-b-arked. Would Matthew be pleasant to take walks with when he grew up?

Sandra Vlaskamp didn't notice. "Then, of course, there are the endless discussions of potty-training techniques, which pediatrician is the most arrogant and unresponsive, which nursery program is the most innovative. No, I wouldn't say my world has expanded. But then, I don't expect lots of recognition for being at home, which is where Shelly and I differ. I think being a shrink or professor—or a book editor—*is* more exciting, frankly, although not necessarily more important. *I'd* rather talk to a lawyer about politics at a party than to compare notes about the nastiest ear infection of the week. That doesn't undervalue full-time motherhood, does it? Just recognizes it's not pioneer work. I'm not breaking new ground here. I'm not even one hundred per cent sure I'm doing the right thing. So why should I insist on validation from everybody else?"

Listening to this articulate, puzzled woman, I felt I could never fully grasp many of the nuances of women's lives. My wife Jane thinks work is crucial, vital to her mental health, her relationship to me and the kids, her self-esteem, her independence. The lack of stimulation and conversation, the repetition, the endless shopping and driving, only ground her down. She nearly suffocated during the years she was at home with our kids, she says, though she also recognizes it was one of the reasons she felt free to plunge into her work and education so determinedly now, taking courses at NYU to become a licensed psychologist.

Jane had leaped at the chance to go back to work when my own career fell apart. She never seriously believed that she was shortchanging Emily and Ben, though she had her pangs. The kids, in turn, thought it as natural for Jane to go to work as it was for me. But Shelly Bloomfield believed people who had children owed it to them to be there—cookies, sympathy and kisses, and a van at the ready—every time they came home from school. And Sandra Vlaskamp thought that was a good but difficult thing to do and obviously ached for her work and a broader world. I didn't know her, and sadly never would, but Nancy Rainier-Gault had been deeply committed to educating women and making schools safer and more hospitable for them. Perhaps she had paid for her convictions with her life. Perhaps nobody was entirely happy with the choices life forced them to make; instead, we were all just slugging it out as best we could.

"So you don't share Shelly's resentment of women who work?"

"Mr. Deleeuw," she said, fixing me with a firm stare, "I *am* a woman who works, okay? And a feminist, too. I guess I just feel more ambivalence about these things than Shelly does. Women who go to an office aren't automatically betraying their children. Women who hang around them all day aren't necessarily cheating themselves or providing lousy role models. It's not that simple. We're all different. We just have to do what works for each of us, depending on a hundred things, from finances to temperament, and try to be tolerant of everybody else. I think women will have arrived when *everyone's* choice is considered valid and important."

"True," I said. But we weren't at that point yet, I knew. There *is* a low-level civil war raging in any given suburban neighborhood or kindergarten class about all this. Some stay-at-home moms are convinced that careerists are harming their children. Some working women, wondering why homemakers don't go mad, resent the time housewives have to spend hounding teachers, running the PTA, picking the perfect piano instructor. Part-time workers feel pulled in both directions, often unable fully to please their families or satisfy their bosses. Men, for the most part, watch in bewilderment, trying to figure it all out and stay out of trouble.

But Tot Swim was drawing closer. I moved on. "What about this new principal, Nancy Rainier-Gault? Did you know her?"

"Only by reputation, and from Shelly. My kids aren't that old. She was single, very political, didn't fit in particularly well here, according to Shelly and playground gossip. She came from a high school in the city. Shelly said she felt this was the kind of place where she was needed. Everybody said she was smart and a terrific principal, but perhaps a little strident." She flipped Polly a biscuit. The poodle ignored it.

"The funny thing was," she continued, "Shelly admired a lot of what Rainier-Gault was doing. Shelly always talked about how much she used to hate the way boys in school felt as if they could make comments about her body. She said a thousand times she'd have Jason's hide if he did that to a girl. We agreed it was time somebody cracked down on this attitude that jocks have—boys and men—that they can do whatever they please."

It has to start somewhere, I thought, and middle school, when everything starts getting sexual, is the perfect place.

"And Jason's a jock?"

"Oh, yes. I don't know him well. But he's a big star on the basketball team, very athletic. He seems quite nice, though," she added quickly. I nodded.

A howl erupted from the sandbox, and Vlaskamp scurried over to settle a dispute about shovels. Turning back to me, she glanced at her sleeping daughter, then over at Polly. All clear.

"But to be honest, Shelly resented Rainier-Gault, too," I reminded her, still fishing. "She obviously didn't feel this woman took housewives seriously. And these days, an accusation of sexual harassment isn't a minor matter. It can really cause damage. Shelly had reason to be angry at this woman for threatening the future of the son she'd worked so hard to protect. That's surely what a jury will be told. The question I have to ask, because the police will be asking it, is how angry was she? How much rage was there?"

"Not *that* much," Vlaskamp snapped. "You know, Shelly's not squishy about disciplining her kids; she has high standards for behavior and enforces them. But she'd gone through so much with Jason. Fought off the supposed experts who wanted to put him on medication or ship him off. Helped him achieve, make friends. Cheered him on. She was a tigress for Jason, but that doesn't mean she was a killer." Though, the prosecutors would point out, people killed for a lot less. Getting a kid on the cheerleading squad had been inspiration enough for that woman in Texas.

Now, Vlaskamp's vigilant eyes searched for and found Austin, who hung back from the circling dogs. He looked a little disconsolate. Even dopey retrievers could sense the kind of trouble this family was in, I thought.

"This case is pretty explosive, Sandra, as I'm sure you know. The media are already portraying Shelly as if she were some deranged Total Woman who hated the principal because she was a militant feminist. Pretty soon the reporters will pick up on Shelly's nickname. I can see the TV movie already."

Sandra shook her head, leaned over and adjusted the stroller visor to keep the sun off her daughter. She looked tired. Taking care of small children and a dog and house will do that. But she seemed emotionally drained, too.

"Why do we view everything so simplemindedly, so divisively in our culture, Mr. Deleeuw? Why are we so intolerant and self-righteous? Shelly makes some noise, but she's about as political as a tennis sneaker, and Nancy Rainier-Gault, well, she and I might not see eye-to-eye on everything, but she was no crazy either. Yet you and I both know how they are going to be portrayed."

Even my brief conversations with Vlaskamp and Bloomfield had made me think a bit harder about my tendency to value professional women above those who stayed home. People do, in fact, talk about them in casually deprecating ways, these women in vans and station wagons frantically driving their kids around all day. When you bump into them at parties or at the grocery store, you never ask them about anything much beyond school gossip and child-rearing because you don't know what else to ask, what else they want to talk about. Maybe you assume they don't have a lot to say. In the very suburban culture they'd so recently dominated, even helped create, these women have become poignant and awkward, almost displaced, near-invisible to everybody but their children and one another.

But Vlaskamp couldn't really answer the many questions I had. She knew nothing of the events on the day of the murder, hadn't seen or heard from Shelly over the weekend, and first learned of the killing the next morning when a hysterical parent of her son's classmate called.

We were quiet for a minute, both glancing at our watches. At that moment our otherwise different lives were driven by precisely the same ethic: we didn't want our kids to spend more than a few minutes waiting to be picked up.

"So there's no way you can imagine Shelly killing that principal? No motive, no set of circumstances?"

"No, not for a second. That gene isn't in her."

"Not even if she were afraid that Jason's future could be in jeopardy?"

Vlaskamp called a two-minute warning to her son, and whistled to Polly. (I'd used the two-, five-, ten-minute warnings too. Kids most resent being ordered around, so you don't say, "Come here right now." You say, "We have to leave in three and a half minutes." If they have a few minutes to get used to the idea, it seems somehow more palatable.) "Mr. Deleeuw, for years much of Shelly's life has been Jason. Taking him to therapists. Reading to him. Tutoring him. She brought him back from the precipice. She saved his life. In that sense, she's a genuine hero. Few people would have done it; even other parents of troubled kids thought she was crazy to try. I never saw such dedication, so much patience, that kind of loving commitment.

"It's true, that principal could have harmed him badly, with her suspension and her threats to prosecute. But how would killing her help Jason? As it is, it will just make the whole family notorious. That wouldn't help Jason. There are other responses Shelly would have tried—protesting, suing, something—and she's smart enough and strong enough to have figured that out. She traveled all over the state trying to find doctors who could help Jason.

"I'm not God, Mr. Deleeuw—I don't know what people are capable of deep down. I just can't believe Shelly could pull the trigger of that gun. If Shelly's the Last Housewife, I'm the Reluctant Housewife. I watch the world move past me while I sit for an hour waiting for a dentist who overbooks to talk about Mr. Brush and Mr. Floss with my preschooler. But whatever else is true about us, Shelly and I are nurturers. We're caretakers. Shelly's proud of that silly title, the Last Housewife. It means she gives and supports life. I'm certain she would never take it."

"Did you talk about the shooting in school?" I asked Emily when she got home. She had troubled to put herself together that morning, a rare occurrence. Mostly, her fashion consciousness seesawed between years when she would wear socks that matched her T-shirts and years when she'd rather die than do so. That was starting to change. Today, her dark hair was pulled back in a ponytail, with one of those gathered ribbon things slipped over the elastic band, and she'd put on denim overalls, a tie-dyed T-shirt and the ubiquitous leather mocs that are the primary footwear of the middle-class suburban girl.

The statement said: *I don't care about clothes or makeup or frills.* But not caring was almost as pricey as obsession. The overalls cost forty-five dollars and the shoes even more. Of course, the laces couldn't simply be tied; they had to be elaborately knotted on each side, for reasons Em refused to explain and which would have been beyond my ken anyway. My daughter was just beginning to edge into the Other Zone, when friends turned cruel and boys stopped talking and the rules and customs slipped out of the sight or comprehension of grown-ups. I would be able to help her less and less.

"Yup," she said. "Mrs. Salinaro talked about it at assembly. It's so sad, Dad. Mrs. Salinaro said the principal of Ben's school was shot with a gun right in the school, in her office. It's so creepy. She said the police arrested somebody, and that we were all safe and that we would be taken care of. That it was all right. Is it?"

I nodded. I could see she sort of knew it was but wouldn't mind hearing it anyway.

"Did Ben like her a lot, Dad?"

"Well, you'll have to ask him. Mrs. Rainier-Gault was new this fall; I don't think Ben knew her that well. But I'm sure it's rough, Em. A principal is somebody who keeps things safe, not somebody who gets hurt, right?"

She nodded, then shrugged. Some things were beyond my understanding, others beyond hers. I never really know how to explain the violence in our culture to either of my children.

"Do you want to talk about it some more?" I prompted.

She shrugged again. "Everybody says that it was a mom who did it and that she was mad because of her son, this kid named Jason, or something." Emily got a lot more interested when I told her this woman had become my client. At first, her friends thought having a private detective daddy bizarre. But when somebody got arrested or killed and I was involved, it was suddenly cool.

We agreed to discuss the murder more later. This was a kid who'd been known to weep over the corpse of a bird. But I felt she'd be okay. The world of a fourth-grade girl is not vast. Its boundaries are friends and classmates, social standing and dance recitals, tonight's homework. Events in upper grades are remote, vague. Still, the death of a principal was a crack in the structure of the universe. I could see it had rocked her, even if she wasn't prepared to open up about it. She went upstairs to change into her leotard. I yelled for Ben to come along so we'd make his dental appointment.

Ben was due for his annual checkup. It had been years since I'd gone in with him. I dropped him off with a check and picked him up when he called. Because he'd been taking fluoride-laced vitamins since infancy, he'd been spared most of the torturous visits that punctuated my own youth. This frankly made me bitter. Ben's teeth were straight, pearly, unscarred by drills or fillings. My mouth could practically set off airport metal detectors. I asked him how he felt about the killing as we all piled into the Volvo for the ride to the dentist's office and then to dance class, wrestling with our seat belts until I heard the familiar clicks.

This was the nerve-wracking driving season in Rochambeau. You had to dodge kids on skateboards, roller blades and bikes, in wagons and on foot, chasing after basketballs, baseballs, Frisbees and soccer balls in various sizes, shapes and colors. Also the dogs, and younger siblings who often tagged along. Once, I was even startled to see a helmeted kid holding on to a wheelclamp whizzing across an overhead wire strung between two houses on opposite sides of Winter Street.

Ben's jaw tightened, as it often did when he was asked anything resembling a personal question. I had to tread more carefully with him. Ben had suffered quite a bit in school when my world fell apart and his friends' parents told their kids I was a crook run out of Wall Street. It wasn't until much later that I'd learned about the shoving matches and cruel teasing that turned him angry and sullen and strained our relationship in a frightening way. Emily and I had always had an uncomplicated dad/daughter love affair, but Ben and I were still working our way back.

"It's pretty upsetting," he said in response to my question, more candidly than I would have expected. Ben was tall, gawky and turning handsome. He had an oh-gosh Jimmy Stewart way of talking that made him even more appealing. "I didn't know her real well, but everybody kind of respected her. She was cool. The girls are really cut up about it. Some of them are really mad."

"Do you know Jason Bloomfield?"

"Just to say hello. I never hung out with him or anything. He hangs out with a bunch of guys I didn't like much."

"Why?"

He shrugged. I decided not to push it. I told him I was representing Jason Bloomfield's mother and asked if it bothered him. He tensed.

"Would it matter?" he asked me dully.

"Sure."

"Well, a lot of the kids won't like it, Dad. They won't like it at all. I mean, this kid is accused of sexual harassment. And his mother is supposed to have murdered the school principal. It's not going to make me popular.'' He didn't say what he was probably thinking: *You're going to make trouble for me again, just when it was getting better.* When I pulled up to the dentist's office, he mumbled thanks-for-the-ride and bounded out of the car. I watched his retreating Lemonheads T-shirt and felt my heart sink. There's little worse than hurting your kid unnecessarily, and I'd done my share. Jane and I had some tough work to do later that night.

This death had brushed too close, I thought as Em and I headed for Gotta Dance. After my last few cases, alas, my kids might be getting used to that. And Jane brought back quite a few horror stories from her clinic, too. My children were no longer kids who doubted that bad things could happen to good people.

I had called Dan Bloomfield from home. He said, in a wary and uncertain voice, to come by. There was a Rochambeau police officer on duty outside, he told me, but he wasn't sure if the idea was to keep them all inside or to protect them from people outside. Strangers were driving by to stare at the house, he knew, and five TV crews from New York and Philadelphia had been parked outside most of the day. Two were still idling there, even though he'd made it clear there would be no interviews. He said he knew Shelly had hired me, but he wanted the ground rules clear: a brief visit, no talks with his kids, not even Jason. At least not yet.

I pulled the Volvo up to the three-story brick-and-frame colonial, parking in front of the police car and getting out slowly so that the officer could get a good look at me. He'd probably run my license plate through his computer. Two battered white vans with no identification but with satellite transmitting dishes on their roofs sat across from the house, a small gaggle of producers and reporters sipping take-out coffee nearby.

Earlier in the day, Chief Leeming had been visibly nervous about the town's response to the shooting. The murder of a heroic school principal was likely to stir the community in explosive ways. I doubted that Rochambeau's feminists would come and torch the Bloomfields' place, but the murder had been all over the New York news and there are plenty of crazies with guns running around this mad country.

The reporters watched me as I locked the Volvo, with 115,000 miles of child-driving, bike-carrying and grocery-hauling on its odometer. The officer motioned for me to come over to the squad car.

"Can I help you?" he asked politely.

"Sure," I said. "I have an appointment with Mr. Bloomfield." I showed him my state license and plastic ID; he waved me ahead.

The front lawn was scattered with toys, balls and a ten-speed hybrid bike, a cross between a racer and a mountain. I suspect none of those items would have been lying around if Shelly had been at home and on the job. One crime skyrocketing in Rochambeau is minor theft, as people from poorer towns drive through and scoop up the middle-class bounty of bicycles, skateboards, bats, gloves and roller blades that dot the town's lawns in all but the coldest weather. Suburban kids don't pitch pennies; they blast one another with nuclear water-weaponry that fires huge streams of water a hundred feet across streets and yards.

Dan Bloomfield was a large, florid-faced man with a big belly, a receding hairline and a stricken look, befitting somebody whose comfortable middle-class existence had just been blown to hell. He was holding a drink with ice cubes clinking in it.

"Uhh, come in . . . I came home after lunch. Went to Shelly's bail hearing. Took off from work. One of the neighbors was here in the morning to be with the kids . . . Can I offer you a drink? I'm having one. Things are kind of . . ."

Catastrophic, I mentally supplied when his voice trailed off.

Last week, Dan Bloomfield had come home every night to kids throwing themselves into his arms, a house that was picked up, dinner waiting, the children's health, homework and recreation all tended to. So it had been for me a few years back, not that long ago in real time, but eons away in experience.

I remembered the feeling. You walked in the door, often with some gift or snack from the city or the train station, and at the sight of you, the kids squealed with joy, all squabbles resolved. You had no idea how many trips it had taken to put that food on the table, to see to it that the children had received their booster shots, gotten art supplies for school projects, been driven to and from playdates and lessons. You couldn't see the effort behind the freshly laundered shirts hanging in the closet or the geraniums flourishing in the window boxes. Nor, wiped out from work and commuting, did you really care. But I could see Dan Bloomfield was just finding out how many trips and how much effort. My heart went out to him, it really did. He would know little peace of mind for a long, long time.

Even though he'd been home for hours, he was still in his work clothes, his tasteful silk tie askew, the tail of his shirt hanging out, the creases on his pants completely erased.

A brown-haired little girl dragging an enormous stuffed bear raced shrieking behind us through the living room and out of sight. That would be Sarah. I only got a glimpse of her, but the trauma around her didn't seem to have sunk in yet, or maybe she hadn't even been told much. There was no sign of Jason, or his ten-year-old sister Erin. Dan Bloomfield erupted.

"Jesus, Sarah, I told you to stay in your room. And I mean it." He turned towards the back of the house, but Sarah had gone flying up the stairs. His words sounded harsh, but there was no anger or menace in his voice, only fatigue and desperation.

The living room was a wreck, even by my highly elastic standards. Mail lay unopened in a heap on an end table. Magazines and flyers overflowed the wicker mail basket next to the door. Toys were scattered everywhere, along with half-empty glasses, a bowl of popcorn and candy-bar wrappings. The house was furnished comfortably but not expensively, the chairs and sofas—dark, with large floral patterns—probably purchased at one of those classic American showrooms in the middle of town. There were frilly curtains at the windows, and little baskets of potpourri and small ceramic dogs scattered around the room. Pictures of Shelly and Dan and the kids sprouted on every surface, in every possible combination.

"You've got to tell them everything a hundred times . . . I tell you," Dan Bloomfield said, pointing me to a leather chair. He didn't have to tell me. "I didn't even have time to change my clothes. Sarah had a doctor's appointment, which I took her to. But we skipped Jason's basketball practice and Erin's music lesson. We're not going to be prisoners in here. We're going to try and live a normal life, for the kids' sake," he grimaced. "Or as normal as you can live while your mother's been accused of murder and there's a police car parked outside. The phone's ringing off the hook, calls from people offering to help and people threatening to kill us. I couldn't possibly get dinner together, I'll just order from Domino's. Thirty minutes, and . . ." He snapped his fingers in wonder at how miraculously the pizza would appear. "Din-

ner. Jesus. I don't know what the hell's happened." He sure
didn't. His bewilderment was clear, and he had lots of reasons. He
was struggling gamely.

"It's going to get rougher, too," he continued quietly. "I know
that. That's why I'm going to get everyone organized, into a routine." He nodded, as if he were giving orders at work. He would
quickly learn that he wasn't.

"Well, I'm here to help," I said. "Everything will work out. Is
Shelly coming home soon?"

"The judge denied bail," Bloomfield said grimly. "The courtroom was picketed by all these protesters—I don't know how
many, it looked like a hundred. There were people chanting,
shouting. The judge said he's taking it under advisement until the
end of the week, but he said this was a heinous crime and he
wasn't going to release Shelly until he was certain she was no
danger to the community. Can you believe it?" He picked up his
drink—looked like Scotch—and took a swig. Then he seemed to
really focus on me for the first time. His corporate voice seemed
to assert itself.

"What exactly do you want, Mr. Deleeuw?" he asked bluntly.
"Why are you here?"

"Well, I'm working for Mrs. Bloomfield and I wanted to meet
you and ask if you can add anything that could help me. And
her."

As it turned out, he couldn't. He'd had important meetings in
the city all week long—he owned a software firm—and since
Shelly handled the school stuff, he'd left this hassle with Jason to
her. "Hell, I thought she could take care of this. She said she
could. I mean, really, even if Jason did what the girl said . . . it's
wrong, and he should be punished. But he's a good boy. Everybody knows that. Shelly's a wonderful wife and mother. That's
what's so crazy about all this, that it's happening to us." That was
usually what seemed so crazy to my clients, I had learned: not that
it was happening, but that it was happening to *them*. As much as we
see on television or in the movies, our imaginations never seem to
stretch far enough to put us in this kind of picture. "These
women are just going overboard now, this obsession with harassment. It's a terrible overreaction."

He seemed to assume that I'd agree that this wasn't a big deal.
Or maybe he didn't care if I agreed or not. Don't be too hard on

him, I cautioned myself. What kind of mood would I be in if Jane was behind bars for murder?

Dan Bloomfield seemed to know only the broadest outlines of what had happened. He was stunned that such a trivial incident at school could take on such frightening dimensions. He hadn't nearly absorbed what had happened yet. He'd been overwhelmed with the accusations against, and the loss of, his wife, the details of taking care of his family. He was adamant that I not speak to the children. "Please, please, they're in shock as it is. Just wait a bit."

I did get a fleeting glimpse of Jason—tall, jet-black mop of tousled hair, intense and good-looking in the baggy denim shorts, oversized sneakers, Chili Peppers T-shirt and turned-back baseball cap that comprised the youthful male uniform of suburbia. A kid with those looks didn't need to grope a reluctant girl. I'm sure he could have found plenty of willing partners. Why grab a kid's breasts?

A second boy—if you call somebody close to six feet tall a boy—followed him. I could only catch a glimpse of blond hair, battered Converse sneakers, jeans and a Rochambeau Middle School Basketball jacket with the letters CAPTAIN across the back. Your basic suburban athlete/hero/prince.

"That's Jason, of course," Bloomfield said, "and the other guy is his best friend, Tobias Tomlinson. Great kid, and a great influence on Jason. He's the co-captain of the basketball team and a really nice young man. Good friend, too. Toby was over here in a minute when this trouble started. Jason hasn't had the easiest time under the best of circumstances, and these aren't those, exactly . . ."

He smiled. "And loaded. Tomlinson as in Tomlinson Manufacturing."

I had heard of the company, although I couldn't recall what it was they manufactured.

Bloomfield's smile melted away. I was surprised to see his eyes begin to moisten. It was as if he'd been fighting to control himself all along and had just lost.

"Look, Mr. Deleeuw, I want to help you. But this isn't real. We're a happily married couple. Fifteen years. We've had this problem with Jason's hyperactivity, but Shelly handled that. Otherwise, we've had happy, healthy, average lives."

He shook his head dumbly. He was like a person in mourning—

not for his wife, but for his life. "I'm sorry. I'm not very collected tonight. I've got to take care of the kids. And I have to take time off from work at a bad, bad time. I'm not complaining, it's just like I've walked right into a tidal wave. And Shelly, poor Shelly. She could never, never hurt somebody like that. Never. I've got all this stuff to attend to. Please . . ."

He was begging me to leave—before I could ask about his shotgun, about his whereabouts on Saturdays, about anything I needed very much to know.

His eyes met mine. I waited a second or two, then said quietly, "I'm going. I hope we can talk in the next day or so. It's imperative we do so. But before I go, I have to ask you this. The gun they found out back—the rifle—where did you keep it?"

He sighed and ran his hands through his hair. "It was locked in the storage closet downstairs. The shells were locked away too. Neither was ever in sight. I never even took the thing out to show to Jason. I wish to God I'd never seen it. I used it once, twice maybe, to go deer hunting in upstate New York with a couple of buddies. As I told the police, I haven't even seen the damn thing in five years. I just can't imagine how it got out of the house or who took it."

"Did Shelly know about it?"

"Sure, she hated having it here. Didn't like a gun in the house. But I think both of us forgot that it was here, frankly. It just hasn't come up." He shook his head.

"Did she know where it was hidden? The gun or the shells?"

Bloomfield shrugged. "I just dunno. I don't think so. I didn't want anybody to know where it was. I can't even remember the last time it was mentioned. When the cops told me they found it in the woodpile, I was shocked."

I took a couple of notes. "Who else knew about the gun?"

"Well, I suppose my buddies did, from the office. But none of them lives around here—they all live in New York, and they certainly don't know where I kept the thing."

You had to be incredibly stupid to drag a rifle back from a murder scene to your own house and hide it right in the backyard. Or incredibly naive. I wasn't sure yet, but Shelly didn't seem that stupid.

"Can you imagine any circumstances of any sort which would compel your wife to take a gun to that school and kill that principal? Is it even remotely possible she has that kind of anger or rage in her?'' I didn't expect him to say yes, but I wanted to see if he hesitated, looked troubled, thought about it too long. Dan Bloomfield didn't strike me as an experienced liar. He seemed a nice guy who had, as he put it, been strolling along the beach and been hit by a tidal wave. Under the circumstances, I don't think I would have held together as well.

There was total silence in the room. Upstairs, I heard boards creaking, sounds of a TV set or video game. Austin came bounding in the back door, let in by Sandra Vlaskamp, who waved through the window. He ran to Bloomfield, then to me, then upstairs for the ritual wiggling, slobbering and pawing that usually accompanied retriever arrivals.

Bloomfield didn't appear to hesitate. ''No. Dear God, I swear it. Never. I couldn't believe it when they came to the house to get her. I don't believe it now. I'll never believe it.'' There was no flinching in his eyes, no balking at some spooky memory or uneasy incident, nothing but absolute conviction. That was important to me. You don't live with somebody for fifteen years and not notice danger signs, even if you are a bit out of it when it comes to your family's daily life.

I said I'd like to come back when he thought it appropriate.

''Of course, of course,'' he murmured. ''I guess you have to talk to Jason, just not yet. It's too soon.'' I agreed, but uneasily. I guess I was expecting something else from him, more of a how-can-I-possibly-help-you attitude. If an investigator had come to help absolve Jane of murder charges, I would have turned my house, kids and life over to him right then and there. I wasn't getting that kind of cooperation. But then, was it fair to judge somebody else in those circumstances? He was trying to keep his family above water.

Poor Dan Bloomfield. He suddenly had to run a household he knew little about—not where the spatulas were kept, whether Sarah's leggings were clean, what setting to put the dryer on, how much dishwashing detergent to use. He had to learn about his children's moods, tastes in food, fears and quirks, needs and flashpoints. He had to try to comfort, support and guide them through a normal life while their mother stood accused of murder, reporters circled their house and intense passions had been stirred all around them. All while he also had a computer software company to run. I knew a lot of men like Dan Bloomfield in Rochambeau. In many ways, I had been one of them.

I climbed into the Volvo, jarred once again by the realization that life in suburbia, however privileged and comfortable, could abruptly turn incredibly fragile. Yesterday's American Dream was today's front-page tragedy as dumbstruck families wondered what the hell had hit them.

Four

SEVERAL YEARS AGO, under some pressure from my beloved, I cut back sharply on my attendance at public meetings having to do with education in Rochambeau. This was partly
due to the frantic pace of our lives. Jane's grueling work at the
mental health clinic, and her NYU courses mean that when she's
home she is either studying, catching up with the kids, advising
me on my cases or plowing through clinic paperwork. Her beloved mysteries—most of them about tough, single women who
live happily with no men under eighty in their lives—pile up on
her bedside table unread.

This all leaves us about as much spare time as spare money. And
we both agree the kids need a parent at home at night. Besides
that, school meetings are hazardous to my health.

Educational meetings are, for a number of my fellow towns-
people, the favored recreational activity. They're cheaper than
movies or the theater. And school officials are a handy target,
required by law to sit and listen to everybody's hectoring. The
suburban taxpayer wants nothing less than a perfect community
in exchange for his or her hefty property tax bill, and nowhere is
this expectation of perfection higher than when it comes to education.

The issues vary, from school bus routes to curriculum battles,
but the tenor of discussions is always the same: no issue is so trivial
that you can't be outraged about it. From September through
June, long lines of parents form weekly at microphone stands to
accuse teachers, administrators and Board of Ed members of inef-
ficiency, incompetence, corruption, insensitivity, homophobia,

Eurocentrism and general conspiracy. It's enough to make me embarrassed to be a liberal.

There is too much academic tracking. Or not enough. Too few innovative and challenging electives or insufficient emphasis on basics. Minority kids are being disproportionately suspended. The Columbus Day holiday is insulting to Native Americans. December pageants are insulting to Jews. There is too much emphasis on getting into college; there is not enough. Condoms should be distributed in the high school. Or not.

To survive, the bureaucrats seem to become stonelike, battered into nonresponsiveness. I can't imagine why any right-minded person would take this kind of abuse to sit on a school board for free.

Though the problems aired at meetings are infinitely varied, they are governed by certain elemental laws: whatever it is, it's never your own fault or your kids', it's always the teacher's or the school's. No matter how unexpected, someone should have foreseen the problem and prevented it. Paying taxes gives you the right to be insulting. The schools you went to were tougher and better. Nobody really cares but you.

In the years I commuted to Wall Street, I rarely set foot in the schools except for the annual parent-teacher conferences or for special concerts or plays in which my children were performing. I was lucky if I could remember Ben's teachers' names. So when I found myself abruptly unemployed, free to exercise all my parental prerogatives, I diligently attended all such meetings.

Problem was, they gave me nasty headaches. I came home fuming and sputtering so many times that Jane finally made the reasonable suggestion that I either shut up about them or stay home. I'd stopped going, at least until tonight.

Actually, Jane, wise woman and aspiring psychologist that she is, has taught me that school officials are so shocked if you approach them with a problem quietly and politely that they'll do almost anything for you or your kids.

Take the time we wanted to move Em away from an angry second-grade teacher who hated kids and once gave Emily detention for getting the date wrong on a spelling test on which she scored 100. I had vowed that I wouldn't leave the building until Em was assigned to a new teacher. That, I assumed, is what devoted fathers did.

Jane silenced me with a coded stare and smiled warmly at the wary principal. "Mr. Thompson, our daughter is so unhappy that we'd like to see her in a different class," she said smoothly. "But we understand the pressures you're under and we'll leave it to you. We know you'll do the best for her."

I could see Jane was going to be a knockout psychologist, maybe even in time to help our mortgage payments. Mr. Thompson nearly fell to the floor in gratitude, pumped our hands, slapped my back, urged us to come back any time and switched Em to another class the next morning.

Another Rochambeau parent, the wife of a cardiovascular surgeon, learned last fall that a popular teacher was scheduled for open-heart surgery, prompting a stampede by parents frantically trying to switch their kids out of his class and away from his unknown and possibly ineffective substitute. Unfortunately (or fortunately, depending on your perspective) the sub turned out to be an even better teacher. There promptly followed another round of frantic calls, visits and letters demanding to get kids switched back in.

This, then, is the particular backdrop against which Principal Nancy Rainier-Gault was murdered, a child-worshiping culture in which the notion of a parent's killing to protect a child's reputation and future is not as entirely inconceivable as it ought to be. If feelings run so high about the grading policies of a seventh-grade language arts teacher, how wrought would people get over this killing? This was a school meeting I absolutely could not miss.

Jane was still at work. But a call to Rochambeau Gourmet Pizza (the busy parent's best friend), whose driver was a high school kid Ben knew from the neighborhood, brought a large pie with extra cheese in fifteen minutes. I left the number of the school and the emergency number for Jane's clinic on our phone pad. Ben and Em both knew the drill: that Ben was in charge and would be paid for baby-sitting; that homework must be done before the TV could be turned on or video games launched or girlfriends talked to in earnest, whispered tones; that sibling fights and sniping had to be postponed until a parent was on the premises. They knew that nobody got in the house that they didn't know. They understood that if anybody smelled smoke, they were to bolt first and think about it later. Jane or I would be back before bedtime.

I fed Percentage, let him run around the backyard for five minutes, then headed for the school. I wasn't enthusiastic about go-

ing. The usual suspects would be out looking for blood. You're
getting grumpy in middle age, Deleeuw, I chastised myself. They
just love their kids, just like you do.

The Board of Education meeting was supposed to have been
held in the high school cafeteria, so that coffee, tea and cookies
could easily be served. But it was clear that tonight's turnout
would be five or six times the usual forty parents, so the meeting
had been moved to the auditorium.

Seated up front near the microphone were several rows of the
outraged. I recognized some from my own school meeting days.
But this night they were supplemented by scores of other parents.
The murder of a school principal touched our deepest nerves,
shattered our most cherished assumptions and struck like a dag-
ger at our suburban hearts, at the very reason there *was* a Rochambeau that people worked so hard to get to and spent so
much money to stay in.

Outside, I'd passed three television vans idling by the curb. Inside, half a dozen men and women with notebooks, presumably
newspaper reporters, were working the arriving crowds. After its
two recent bouts with murder and scandal—both of which I'd
been smack in the middle of—this town had become media-savvy.
TV cameras were no longer permitted inside the schools, which
drastically curbed the volume of coverage.

I was embarrassed when two reporters recognized me and came
scurrying over. "Mr. Deleeuw. You're the Suburban Detective,
right?" the first one said, flourishing his notebook. "Sam Calder-
one, the *Star-Ledger*. There are rumors you're working on this case.
Is that true?" He even pronounced my name correctly, De-*Loo*.

It was even more unsettling when a woman standing nearby
jabbed me on the shoulder and hissed, "You're not working for
her, are you? What's the matter with you? Is money the only thing
you care about? Or maybe housewives are the only women you are
comfortable with?" I didn't recognize this person. She was in her
late thirties, dressed in a brown suit, carrying a battered leather
briefcase. The back of her head, which was what I was now looking
at, was a mass of dark brown curls.

I guess my jaw must have dropped. I take more or less the same
view as defense attorneys, that everybody is entitled both to the
benefit of the doubt and to legal representation and investigative
help. The media sharks and/or the community rumor mill had

worked exceedingly fast. I was beginning to see that this one wasn't going to be pleasant for anybody. *How do you know for sure that she's guilty?* I wanted to shout at the back of the woman's curly head. *And my feminist credentials are in good order, thank you!* But she was already stalking away.

The reporter tried again, but I smiled pleasantly and shook my head and moved on. I never give interviews or comment on my cases.

The evening papers had already dubbed Shelly the Killer Housewife. One tabloid headline bleated: "A Housewife's Murderous Revenge Against a Feminist Principal?" It was a great story, a suburban '90s tale if ever there was one, and the press was running with it as an outbreak of bloody combat between stay-at-home mothers and working women.

I was beginning to wonder myself. Spokeswomen for feminist groups were all over the evening news denouncing the killing, lauding Rainier-Gault for her stand on sexual harassment, demanding justice. "This is an attack on all of us," one bitter Columbia student had declared. "Part of the effort to push us back to being nothing but objects of men's control. We have to not only take back the night, but reclaim the schools." There was a plaintive housewife-on-the-street in that story, too, interviewed at a mall somewhere on Long Island. "I resent people putting this killing on housewives. I'm tired of people talking down to me, saying, 'So where do you work?' and then looking strangely at me when I say, 'I work at home, raising my children.' " She didn't say that therefore she was happy the principal got killed, but she didn't seem all that horrified about it either.

I cringed at the thought of joining in the feeding frenzy. But the reporters were smart enough to know the difference between "no comment" and a denial. It was a tacit admission that I was on the case.

Moving into the auditorium, I noticed Jeannie Stafford and Carol Goldman, the lesbian couple who had moved into the house next door with their daughter Tracy a couple of months ago. Charlie Pinski, the neighborhood lawn obsessive, was still hoping for a man to show up. But even Charlie had to respect Jeannie and Carol's commitment to crabgrass treatment. I gave them each a hug and asked if they were regulars.

"No," said Jeannie quietly. "We actually came in support of Shelly Bloomfield."

I was surprised but wasn't sure why. I was already forgetting my own injunction to make no assumptions about women. "How come?"

"Because she's a woman in trouble." Jeannie flipped her long brown braid back off her shoulder. "We know what it feels like to be surrounded by hostile people. We don't like mobs."

I told them I was working for Shelly, and it was their turn to raise eyebrows.

"Say, you're the Suburban Detective, aren't you?" trilled a familiar voice behind me. It was Jane. "What kind of scum are you, taking this case?" Another joke, I assumed, although she didn't laugh.

"Kids okay?" she asked. I nodded. Ben chafed—the adolescent's permanent rash—at the notion of baby-sitters, and welcomed some money for watching Em, who chafed at the notion of Ben baby-sitting for her. Lots of chafing, but it was nice to be freed of finding, driving and worrying about sitters.

I took Jane's eighty-pound briefcase, which bulged with case files on her clients and which she almost never let out of her sight, then put my arm around her and gave her a grateful squeeze. Murder always made me appreciate Jane and my family even more than usual. After talking to battered, assaulted, addicted and impoverished women all day long, Jane didn't come home looking as daisy-fresh as the women in TV commercials. Her beige linen jacket was rumpled, her makeup a bit smeary, the lines around her eyes radiating fatigue. But she still looked great to me. Her wrinkles and rumples were badges of honor, battle ribbons in her work on the front lines.

Under the circumstances, Jane stayed remarkably even-tempered. I loved her clearheadedness, her sharp sense of irony. Her mind sliced through pretense like a honed knife. She had become an invaluable source of counsel in my work, more than once guiding me in a direction I certainly would never have discovered myself.

"So I was listening to the radio on the way over," she said, grabbing my free arm, nodding at some parents we knew, and guiding me towards a seat. "I hear we're happily turning women against women here. The underappreciated housewives versus the fanatic feminists. With my husband representing the devoted housewife."

"Yeah, I know," I said. "I just got snarled at by some woman about working on this case. She stamped off before I could point out that Shelly Bloomfield is entitled to help *and* to the presumption of innocence."

Jane waved to somebody across the room. "Yeah, but does it have to be help from *you?* Can't you refer this one to somebody else? I gather they practically caught her pulling the trigger."

There was an unmistakable edge in her voice. I stopped in the aisle. The auditorium was filling up fast. Spirited debates buzzed, and a line had already formed at the Wacko Stand, as I called the microphone set up for the public. But I didn't rush for a seat.

Jane is not a distant partner, and I am not casual about her opinion. Her disapproval of my taking this case was serious stuff. "You think I should've turned it down?" I asked, ignoring the people pushing past us for their seats.

"Sorry, Kit, but yes—this one does bug me. To be honest."

"But Jane, why? You didn't flinch a couple of months ago when I worked for Marianne Dow, who was charged with murder. Or a dead kid the police thought had killed his classmate and then himself. Are you saying it's okay to work for accused murderers as long as their politics aren't out of fashion? Why wouldn't I take Shelly Bloomfield as a client? You can't have any clear idea whether she shot the principal or not. I'm surprised at you, joining a lynch mob like this. I mean, even if she did kill Rainier-Gault, it didn't have a thing to do with being a housewife. Whatever she did, she believed she was protecting her son. Besides, she says she's innocent. And I believe her."

Jane brushed a hank of dark hair behind her ear, so she could look at me straight on. "Kit, you believe *everybody* you work for. It's your strength, and maybe your weakness. I'm not joining the mob, I know Bloomfield's entitled to a defense. Let's sit down before we get trampled."

Once we were seated, she continued in a low voice. "It's just all this claptrap that wells up around her. Maybe I'm just being defensive because I work too hard and drive into the city twice a week, but you can work hard at your job and still be a great mother. I really resent this stuff about women's sacred duty to stay home and take care of their kids, who aren't even home themselves after they've turned four. What about fathers staying home? What about two parents each working part-time? What about teaching these Nintendo-whiz eight-year-olds to operate a washing machine? Or letting them solve a few problems for themselves? What about a society recognizing that caring for children is everybody's concern? Why does the welfare of children have to come only out of women's hides?" She stopped and took a deep breath. I consider myself on the higher end of the sensitivity scale, but I could see that in this case I'd been about as aware as a tree stump.

But Jane and I would have to talk about this later. The school superintendent, Helene Springfield, flanked by six uneasy-looking members of the Rochambeau Board of Ed, was gaveling the meeting to order.

Suddenly, seven young women in T-shirts that read *"Fight Back!"* jumped up in the front of the auditorium and started chanting: "They can't kill us all. They can't kill us all. There's no going back. No going back."

In the nonplussed silence that fell upon us, three TV crews rushed in through the side door, their spotlights illuminating the protesters' angry faces. From the other side, an exasperated and outfoxed Chief Leeming pushed in with a dozen uniformed officers and swiftly surrounded the demonstrators, one of whom produced a placard which read: NANCY RAINIER-GAULT, *Martyr in the fight against sexual harassment.* Other signs read: BOYS WILL BE BRUTAL and NO MORE VICTIMS!!!! A chorus of murmurs and boos rose up as Helene Springfield banged her gavel and yelled something at the chief. Leeming and his officers efficiently herded the young women, who kept chanting as they were hustled out, towards the exits. Their seats were quickly grabbed by some of those who'd been standing along the back of the now jammed room.

The superintendent hammered until, finally, the crowd quieted. "Look," Springfield began. "I know feelings are running high tonight, but we have enough excitable people right here in Rochambeau. We don't need people from out of town." Of course, I thought. It's okay if Rochambeau parents act like unstable yoo-hoos, but let's not have any outsiders do it. There were more boos and cheers, though it wasn't clear who was reacting or why.

"I have a prepared statement," she continued. "First, thank you all for coming here tonight. I know we all mourn this week-

end's terrible tragedy that took the life of one of our most dedicated principals. Nancy Rainier-Gault's death was inexplicable.
Last night, in executive session, the Board of Education voted to
establish a scholarship in her honor, to be awarded annually to
the Rochambeau High School female student who most embodies
the ideals Ms. Rainier-Gault fought for.''

There was a burst of applause from the crowded room, but I was
startled to notice that a number of people—maybe one in five—
weren't clapping. Some sat quietly, others pointedly crossed their
arms. And they were almost all women, it seemed to me. Could
the town possibly be so polarized by this killing? No matter what
your politics or employment status, surely it was appropriate to
memorialize this person who'd died violently in her own school?

Chief Leeming and his officers returned and shooed out the TV
crews who, it occurred to me, had been suspiciously quick to respond to the mini-demo. The T-shirted activists had gotten the
publicity they wanted; the stations, their action footage for the
eleven o'clock news. Now, both groups would be headed for the
George Washington Bridge within ten minutes.

The superintendent went on, decrying the violence and explaining the laborious steps the system was taking to explain the
tragedy to students, to reassure parents, to counsel those who
needed it, to get on with the business of educating. "I hope you'll
trust us to keep the psychological and physical well-being of our
students first and foremost," she concluded. Good luck, I
thought. Most of these people don't trust you to buy the right
toilet paper. And then—I almost thought I saw her wince—Springfield invited comments from the floor.

The first speaker mumbled her name unrecognizably, but I was
very familiar with the tone. "I am outraged at the killing of Nancy
Rainier-Gault," she said ringingly. "I demand a full investigation
of how this horrible crime could occur and a full explanation of
why it wasn't stopped. For this to happen at all is a travesty. For
this to occur in a school building is a disgrace—'' Cheers and
applause drowned her statement.

I felt the equally familiar pounding begin in my temples. Of
course, why hadn't *I* thought of that? The school system *should*
have anticipated that somebody would gun down a principal one
weekend afternoon. Should the cops have frisked parents coming

to school conferences? Installed metal detectors like airports have? Would that have satisfied her?

The next three speakers said: (a) that the killing showed us that society was infected by sexism; (b) that the curriculum needed to be radically altered from the first grade on to prevent attacks like this; and (c)—the inevitable—that with property taxes as high as they were, there should be no such thing as crime or violence in Rochambeau. Jane and I waited through nearly a half hour of it, then realized we would both be more productively engaged elsewhere.

We drove home in our separate cars. She went in to check on the kids, and I took Percentage for a short stroll. The day, not to mention the night, had been disquieting, and I felt the need for some peace and some thinking time.

I was musing about Dan Bloomfield, feeling sorry for him and all of the things he suddenly had to deal with. But something nagged at me about my visit. I think I was put off by the fact that while he hadn't been hostile, he had hardly turned himself inside out either. Why wouldn't he try harder to help me? Why didn't he ask what he could do? Why didn't he invite me to come back at the earliest possible opportunity, so that I could ask what I had to ask and get going on the big problem—proving his wife's innocence and returning her to him and their family?

I was rattled, too, by Jane's—and that other woman's—suggestion that I shouldn't be taking this case. Jane had never reacted in any way to the moral character of my clients, some of whom were reasonably scummy. And I was unnerved by the ugly tone of the school meeting. Why would women refuse to applaud the memory of Nancy Rainier-Gault? And how many denunciations of various parties did everybody have to sit through? The rhetoric was undoubtedly still raging back at the school.

When I got in, Jane had changed into her fuzzy blue bathrobe and settled in at the kitchen table with her folders. Em ran down and kissed me, then vanished upstairs to go to sleep. Ben, said Jane, had been on the phone for half an hour, talking with some mysterious female. The idea of Ben actually speaking to anyone for thirty minutes was stunning; we were lucky if we heard him utter fifteen words in a full day. But Jane had made a throat-cutting motion for him to hang up and he had, a bit sullenly of course.

I dialed Sandra Vlaskamp's number. She answered quickly but tentatively, as if she was expecting bad news. I guess she'd been getting some lately.

"Sandra? Kit Deleeuw. Were you at the school tonight?"

"Oh, yes. I was there. I left before it ended; I have a manuscript due this week. But I saw you there."

"Good. Sorry to bother you, but there's something I'm wondering about. I noticed that a lot of people sat on their hands when the scholarship was announced. Do you know why? Were you one of them?" I needed to know.

Vlaskamp was silent for a bit. "Yes, I noticed too. I did applaud, but I understand why they didn't. They thought they were supporting one of their own. None of them condones murder. But they've watched for years now as certain kinds of women take glamorous jobs, write books, do surgery, raise hell, file suit, march, take back the night. Rainier-Gault was that kind of woman. They've had too many conversations where they've been patronized, too many dinner parties where they've been ignored or felt diminished because of what they do. And what do they do? They sit with their sick kids, drive them for years to lessons so they can be the musicians, athletes and scholars their mothers aren't, and in the course of doing that, they put a lot of their dreams and ambitions aside.

"Now, one of them has gotten into terrible trouble and the people they see as having tormented them stand around making righteous pronouncements. If it were the other way around, if Shelly'd been shot, would anyone establish a scholarship in her name, just because she'd worked like an animal to raise her kids well and save her son from a lifetime of discrimination? Not clapping—it isn't about Nancy Rainier-Gault, I don't think. It's their way of saying their hearts go out to one of their own. Does that offend you?" I was sure I wasn't meant to miss the controlled but unmistakable anger that crept into her voice. I might not come out of this case with any new fans.

"No, it doesn't offend me. But it did trouble me some." I thanked her and said good-bye, shivering a bit, though it was a warm evening. The silent minority. These women weren't marchers or shouters; they had chosen the other, less public path. They'd been pushed out of the way by the rest of the culture, or so they felt. And their protest, fittingly, was to sit quietly.

I placed a quick call to Evelyn, to let her know that, for the foreseeable future, work on other investigations, attention to paperwork and general orderliness would all be out the window. I told her I'd be in the office tomorrow, when I had planned to have lunch with my friend and adviser Luis Hebron.

On impulse, I called the Bloomfield house. My instinct, when I was troubled or confused about something, was to keep circling it, confronting it, chewing on it until things became clear. A kid answered on the second ring.

"Yeah?"

"Is Dan Bloomfield there, please?"

"Hesbusy." Like a lot of teenage boys, this one could compress phrases or even entire sentences into single words.

"Is this Jason?"

There was no response.

"This is Kit Deleeuw. I'm the private investigator your mother hired to help her. I know tonight isn't a good time, Jason, but I'd like to talk to you when you get time."

There was no silence now.

"Sorry, but I don't have a good time," he said bluntly, and I was staring at a receiver and hearing a dial tone.

I turned to Jane. "I may be crazy," I said, "but the men in Shelly Bloomfield's house are not lining up to cooperate with me in getting their mother out from under murder charges."

"You are crazy," she said matter-of-factly, "but that doesn't mean you're wrong."

Five

THE NEXT DAY began with the usual mayhem. I have only recently begun to develop the combination of humor, patience, skill and lowered standards required to launch a household that includes a working mother, two groggy kids and a dumb dog, with some measure of efficiency and good cheer. Any number of disasters could threaten a morning's equilibrium: an alarm that wasn't set, forgotten homework, someone's especially foul mood, the discovery of yet another pet rodent dead in its cage.

Today, it was a skirmish that erupted when Em came downstairs in a vast purple T-shirt covered with kittens and a too-small pair of red pants. "I don't like your outfit," blurted Jane, knowing better. "I don't care," Em snapped back. Ben rolled his eyes.

These spats could go from 0 to 60 in seconds, and I didn't like anybody to go off to school or work feeling mad or guilty. This clothes thing was a mother-daughter rite I'd normally stay out of, but we were pressed for time, so I intervened.

Jane and I each have hot buttons about the kids. I can't stand it when kids engage in their primary passion: lying around like zombies reading comics or playing video games for hours on a beautiful spring day while their three-hundred-dollar mountain bikes gather dust in the garage. She loses it when the ratio of fried to green things tilts too far to the crispy side or when Em goes to school looking like she just stepped off a flight from Bucharest. Deleeuw's Law: feminist or reactionary, professional or housewife, women have real trouble when their daughters go out of the house looking like hell.

It was obvious even to me that the shirt and pants were a Fashion Don't and equally clear that Em would care less the more her mother got on her about it, so I rousted Jane, guiding her warmly but firmly out the back door with a kiss on the cheek and her briefcase in hand while murmuring, "I love you, have a great day." Another of Deleeuw's Laws: clothes fights and food fights cannot be won, at least not by parents.

Jane smiled, nodded ruefully, blew a kiss to Em and took off. Battle averted. I grunted good-bye to Ben and got a wave and a "yo" in response, which was effusive for him, especially in the morning. Em gave me a hug (she still shows affection in private) then dashed for her bus.

As each person left, the house seemed to grow significantly more spacious and I felt calmer. I loaded the dishwasher, poured the uneaten cereal and fruit down the disposal, turned on the answering machine and grabbed Percentage's leash and pooper-scooper. We headed out for our morning constitutional, giving a wide berth to the Pinski estate next door.

My lawn-obsessed neighbor Charlie had been driven half-mad trying to ward off the dogshit that most people accepted as an inevitable part of suburban life. A combination of safety concerns and child obsession has resulted in more and bigger dogs all the time, while new chemicals and equipment were providing them with greener, ever more inviting lawns. Charlie was on the front lines of this escalating conflict. He'd tried odiferous sprays, repellent cakes of unknown chemical content and increasingly hostile signs: first "Please Clean Up After Dogs," then "Curb Your Dog," and finally "Don't Even *Think* of Letting Your Dog Eliminate Here!"

Some months earlier, as Percentage and I walked past his house, a young pin oak seemed to growl as we approached. Percentage jumped three feet and tried to flee, but I courageously advanced on the tree, which growled or woofed as I approached. Tugging my cowering dog behind me, I reached the tree's base and pulled a small plastic box out of the mound of cedar mulch. The noise stopped abruptly when I rang Charlie Pinski's doorbell. He came to the door, saw what I was holding and sputtered, "Why, hey, Kit. Whatcha got there?"

"I've got a Radio Shack walkie-talkie that's barking at me, Charlie. Is it yours? I was afraid somebody might steal it. Or, more likely, piss on it."

Not his, Pinski swore, turning purple. I put the contraption back in the mulch. I don't know if it's still there, but the tree has not growled at us since.

These and other efforts on Charlie's part were doomed to failure, of course. Crapping dogs are as endemic to suburbia as the lush green lawns they dump on.

I was nearly on schedule. I wanted to be at the Rochambeau Middle School before nine, after the milling, gossiping, preening and jostling had ebbed a bit but before the first classes began. I took Percentage back inside the house, then walked to our tottering garage. The Volvo sprang to life, as it had every single day for nearly a decade. No vans, four-wheel drives or all-terrain vehicles for this suburbanite. What a faithful station wagon—every nook and cranny, crumb and ding a reflection of our family history. I'd bought it for Jane when she was ferrying Ben around to soccer practices. Now I used it myself.

My first stop at the school was the office of assistant principal Nathan Hauser, whom I'd gotten to know pretty well from parents' meetings. I'd gotten to know him even better when Nathan called and asked me to work pro bono on rumors that a drug dealer was operating in the park across from the school, offering uppers to the eighth-graders. I'd helped flush out the little creep. It took less time than PTA work and I didn't have to attend the dreadful school meetings they would've called if the parents had found out about him.

The dealer was an amateur, a skinny kid in an expensive leather jacket who appeared two days in a row precisely at three twenty-nine, as the first waves of kids started pouring out of the school. He hung back among the trees and bike paths, visible to kids walking by but not to administrators or most motorists. But I'd spotted him meeting some of the students, palming bills, his hand slipping in and out of his pocket, his eyes darting back and forth, everywhere, in fact, but on the aging Volvo idling outside the school in the long line of newer, bigger Volvos and the increasingly common Jeeps and minivans.

I took notes and pictures with my snazzy and rarely used telephoto lens, a souvenir of the desperate early peeping days when I'd investigated errant spouses. It had taken the state narcotics squad all of one afternoon the following week to bust the guy, who was not gifted in big-time crime.

Now, as they say in the detecting trade, Nathan Hauser owed me. Maybe I could collect.

I walked in just as an electronic beep sounded to mark the end of the homeroom period. Bells were a thing of the past, of course, like typewriters and carbon paper. The principal's office, just inside the main entrance, sat darkened and sealed, marked by "Police Crime Scene" tape. The students crowding the hallways seemed to veer instinctively away from it, in the way kids manage not to see things they don't want to see.

Despite the brown paper that had been taped inside the office's glass walls, there was a slit of an opening on the right side between the paper, the beige drapes and the wall. Sunlight streamed in from the outside window. Peering through the narrow slit, I saw a huge wooden desk and an overturned table and lamp. Behind the desk on the brown carpet, I glimpsed a dark bloodstain. That would be where Nancy Rainier-Gault had been shot.

A Rochambeau cop with a big belly, badly scuffed black shoes, a sagging belt hung with equipment, a bulletproof vest outlined against his shirt and a nasty scowl, came up and tapped my shoulder. "Help you, buddy?" His tone was distinctly unhelpful.

"I'm here to see Nathan Hauser."

"Well, this isn't his office," he snapped, steering me to the assistant principal's office next door. I could hear Hauser chewing out somebody for bringing water pistols to school. "Confiscated," he intoned. "Now the property of the school. You got yourself a lunch detention, buster." Considering what had happened next door, it was probably a relief to grab water guns. His secretary took my name and buzzed him.

Hauser came out right away and led me inside, banishing the water-gun offender, who scurried away minus his weapon. Hauser was still holding the water gun, a tiny pocket-sized derringer the kids loved to smuggle into school and surreptitiously squirt at one another while the teachers were looking the other way. Ben had bought and lost dozens.

"Hey, Kit," Hauser said, tossing the derringer into the bottom drawer of a metal file cabinet. It was a water-gun arsenal, with scores of guns in the shapes of Uzis, AK-47's, .9-mm Glocks. "This cabinet is a monument to the drive and resilience of the human spirit. We search the kids, suspend them, confiscate their guns, but they can't be deterred. Every June, I send the contraband over to a church thrift shop, which sells them to poor kids who bring them back in here come September.''

He sighed, then pulled a key out of his pocket and relocked the cabinet. ''If they worked a tenth as hard at their schoolwork, they'd all be headed for Harvard.'' Smiling, he offered his hand. ''Now, how can I help our town's most distinguished private eye? I have to be frank with you, I've talked to a lifetime's worth of police and investigators this week.''

Nathan Hauser was respected, even liked, by most of his middle-school charges, a rare circumstance for a school administrator. He had worked his way up through the school system as an English teacher, then a department head, then assistant principal. He'd been expected to get his own school to administer any day. Under the circumstances, the school he'd be given was probably this one.

He looked the part: tall, handsome, black, his beard flecked with gray. He managed to seem distinguished and casual at the same time, his navy sweater vest in sharp and fashionable contrast to a crisp canvas shirt and bright silk tie. He radiated authority but not pomposity, which was probably why kids liked him.

''I've been hired by Shelly Bloomfield,'' I said, realizing he'd need some time to absorb that one. He did. He frowned, tapped some fingers on the table, leaned back in his swivel chair, crossed his legs, looked me in the eye, then winked.

''Good luck,'' he said. ''But I hope you're not looking for an ally in me, Kit. This is shaping up as the toughest week of my life, and I've had some rough weeks. I worked for Nancy Rainier-Gault and I liked her a lot. Besides, I'm under strict orders from the police and the Board of Ed to keep my mouth absolutely shut. If I do, I might just be principal of this school. These aren't the circumstances I would have chosen, but I want the job and I've earned it. If I screw up, that's twenty years with this school system down the toilet. I'm not going to do that for a woman who killed my boss and friend.''

''Maybe.''

''Almost surely. I'm in your debt, Kit, but I absolutely will not discuss the killing. Not a word.''

''Understood. And I won't insult your intelligence or integrity by asking you to do that. I need other information that you might feel more comfortable supplying. If not, just tell me and I'll just disappear.''

His phone beeped. "Yup. Hauser. Where? Anybody hurt? Jeez, send them both down, okay?" He put the telephone down, then buzzed his secretary. "Anita? Two boys coming down from Cadwalader's class. One locked the other in his locker. Cadwalader just got him out, but he had to pry the door open with a crowbar. Call maintenance. Keep the kids apart. Send the, uh, victim to the school nurse just to be sure." He leaned back in his chair, shaking his head.

I smiled. "Happen often?"

"No. I'd say once a week. We've asked for money to put shelf dividers in the lockers so they can't do it, but there are other priorities, I guess."

He looked at me. It was now or never.

"What can you tell me about Jason Bloomfield? You have my word—as a parent, a friend and professional—that what you say stays with me."

He didn't look convinced.

"C'mon, Nathan. My kid goes to school here; I'm not the enemy. Your assessment of this kid has no bearing on the actual killing. I'm not asking about that."

Hauser fiddled with a huge package of bubble gum, undoubtedly a prize in the day's search-and-seizure campaign.

"For the record, we're discussing Ben's homework habits, okay? So. Jason Bloomfield." Hauser squirmed a bit, looked uncharacteristically hesitant. He was usually blunt and direct. There was some sensitive spot.

"Jason's supposed to be a real made-for-TV-movie kid," I prompted. "Brought back from the abyss by Mom. Beloved co-captain of the basketball team. Solid student."

He shrugged. "I'm not in the business of dumping on my kids. But you know how it is about myths. People love a good story, mom-steps-in-where-insensitive-school-system-fails. And his mother *was* heroic. Nobody could have been more dedicated. But he's still no angel. The teachers know better. Life is almost always more complicated than it seems, especially when you're dealing with kids this age. In fact—this never leaves this room, Kit, or I'll deny it—Jason Bloomfield is a bit of a bad seed."

Shelly's friend in the park would have been jolted to hear Hauser's assessment. I nodded.

Hauser went on. "I know he was diagnosed as hyperactive, but

that was just one of his problems. She hasn't been as effective with
the other problems. Kid gets off on hurting smaller kids and has
this real problem with girls. Hangs around with a couple of kids—
don't even *ask* me their names—who are headed for real trouble.
They stick their hands up girls' dresses, rub their hands against
their butts. Sometimes they play what they call K-9, where they
come up behind a girl who's bending over her locker and grab
her around the waist and rub their crotches against her behind.
Sometimes they just pretend to stumble and grab a girl's breasts
for 'support.' Sometimes it gets worse. There are these rumors,
some pretty ugly, but we can never pin them down. It makes me
sick.''

Shouting erupted in the hallway. Hauser bounded out of his
chair and out of the office, and I heard some bellowing that shook
the walls. When he returned, he continued as if we had never
been interrupted.

"People say sexual harassment talk is exaggerated, and maybe
so, but I'll tell you it happens more than these parents want to
know. Every day. Jason and his buddies fit every profile of boys
who will date-rape or assault girls as soon as they get their hands
on some liquor and an empty house." His tone chilled me. "I bet
Jason has pulled this stuff a dozen times, but this is the first time
the girl has had the support and encouragement to come forward.
I can't tell you how reluctant these girls are to go through the
trauma of reporting harassment. They're often abandoned by
their own friends, shunned by some of the boys, ostracized, stig-
matized. The boys, meanwhile, actually get praised by their buddies, even by some of the girls. It confers some weird kind of
status. It took us a year to find a girl willing to speak out. And, Kit,
don't even try to find this girl. The authorities will be all over
you.''

His look made it clear that he would be right there alongside
them. I wasn't positive I could honor his request, not if I balanced
it against my client spending the rest of her life in jail. "This was
Nancy's special mission," he said. "She was uncovering some ugly
things. And soon after, she was dead. Jason Bloomfield deserved
everything Nancy was going to give him, and more. So it will be
my mission, if I get the chance. One thing people like Nancy have
managed to do is raise the stakes for boys like that. If they do get
caught, there's hell to pay. Not like it was.''

There was a lot of emotion in Hauser's voice. Once again, here was somebody I respected who clearly thought I'd chosen the wrong side. Had I?

"Nancy was no crazy extremist," he went on glumly. "She knew how serious charges like this can be. But she wanted to do something for these girls, to encourage them to come forward, to support them when they did. She wanted to help the boys, too, to teach them that the world is changing, and protect them and prepare them for those changes. She wanted this to be the place where one school system broke the cycle. She wanted it for the boys, too, to stop rewarding them for this behavior, to stop treating it as a prank, to teach them other ways to relate to women. Maybe she came on a bit strong to some of these parents. Direct confrontation isn't really the way we do things around here usually. But handling it quietly, out of sight, didn't change the boys' behavior. If anything, it taught them there were no consequences for it. And if Nancy made a mistake, she sure paid for it."

We sat in silence for a minute or two. Sometimes, in my work, knowing when to shut up is critical.

"So you have no doubt that this harassment incident was a factor in her death? There was no other reason you know of why somebody would want to kill her?"

Hauser drummed his fingers on the desk, then looked me in the eye. "There is no other reason I know of that anybody would want to kill this woman. And, frankly, I'm sorry we're on opposite sides of the desk on this one. You're a good parent, a good investigator. I know that. You belong on my side."

"You're not the first to say so. But Shelly Bloomfield deserves—"

"Spare me the horseshit," he interrupted. "I know all that. What else?"

Hauser was cooperating, but it was clearly costing him. He looked almost ill.

"Was Rainier-Gault married? Family?"

"No, not around here. She was divorced. Her ex lives in London. No kids. I never heard her mention her parents. Most of her friends are still in the city, which is where she spent a lot of time. She liked museums, the theater."

"No boyfriends?"

"None that I knew of. Sorry, I can't lead you to any other suspects."

Neither did anything else; all roads led straight to my client. I was surprised and disappointed by what I had just heard. Shelly (and her friend Sandra) had painted a different picture of Jason and I had read her as clearheaded enough to have a reasonably balanced view of him. I'd been expecting a young boy with problems, not a rapist in the making. And Nathan Hauser was about as credible an observer as you could find. He'd been watching kids for a lot longer than I had. But then, how clearly do any of us really see our kids? Talk about a conflict of interest. We raise them, sweat blood to help them grow. Can we be detached? Can we bear what their problems sometimes suggest about us?

"What about Tobias Tomlinson?"

"Jason's friend? Now, there's a puzzle. That he's Jason's friend, I mean. Toby's not like Jason's other friends. Great kid. Co-captain of the basketball team. High honor roll. Volunteers in a hospital program visiting sick kids. He's in here once in a while for spitballs and stuff, and I've got one of his SuperSoakers in my gun drawer, but nothing serious. Nancy was asking me about him a month or so ago, but I've never heard even the suggestion that Toby would hurt a soul. What you dream of is a learning environment filled with Tobiases. He's quite the heartthrob, too. Half the school has a crush on him, including a couple of teachers. I hoped he would rub off on Jason, but I guess not."

I frowned. "That doesn't exactly square, Nathan. I mean, this sounds like Cain and Abel are best friends. If your perceptions are accurate, and I don't doubt for a second that they are, then what are these two boys doing hanging out together?"

Hauser shrugged. "One of the great mysteries of adolescent life. Kids don't move in straight lines. Opposites often attract in friendships at this age. It's fairly ordinary: kids get fascinated by other kids you wouldn't think they'd have one thing in common with. My own theory is that one kid is drawn to the part of him the other represents. Maybe Jason wants to be admired like Tobias. Maybe Tobias wants to be a bit more dangerous. But if I were you, and I'm not trying to tell you how to do your job, you could do worse than talking to this kid, you really could." He casually typed a few instructions on his computer keyboard as he talked.

"Toby's got phys ed this period. If I make a call, the gym

teacher might just have him outside on the playing field running a few laps. Remember, you *never* talked to me about it. Now get going."

I got up and shook Hauser's hand. "We're even, Kit," he said, looking pained. "I have no inherent love for the police, but this time I think they've got the right person in jail. I think Nancy Rainier-Gault was trying to do something right, and something important, and it cost her her life because a mother who had given up too much of her life to help her son saw it all going down the drain and just went nuts. I don't mean Shelly Bloomfield woke up planning a murder, I think she just lost it. I can't talk about this, Kit, but I think Jason was in trouble, maybe deeper than we know, and Nancy was going to nail him for it and his mother couldn't bear to see it happen."

He got up and walked to his door to be sure no one was on the other side before he went on. "I believe Nancy was onto some of the stuff that Jason and his friends had been doing—I don't include Tobias in it—and was about to land on him a lot harder than anybody realized. Something sensitive was going on. Nancy had talked to some girls in the school and she'd promised them anonymity so that she couldn't even tell me, I think, or the police."

It took a second for what he had said to click. "Wouldn't tell you? But, Nathan, wouldn't you know if she was closing in on something heavy? You're in charge of discipline. How could she not tell you something that important?"

He shook his head. "You don't understand Nancy. She kept me informed as much as she could; I was in on most things. But she had sworn to these girls again and again that if they came to her, their stories would be kept absolutely confidential, that no one else would hear of it without their permission, no one. That was how she built trust, broke down decades of silence. On top of that, the week before the shooting, I was in South Carolina visiting my mom, who's been sick. Nancy wouldn't have bothered me down there unless it was a real emergency.

"But the secretary told me she'd had some confidential meetings with some of the girls, off the school grounds. She didn't know where or what they were about. There are no notes in Nancy's files about it—I looked, believe me—even though Nancy took notes about everything. Nancy must have taken an oath to

keep their names secret, but I can't believe she didn't write something down somewhere. Neither can the cops. They've taken the
place apart, but so far, nothing. And maybe that's what Shelly
Bloomfield really came here for, to get those notes. We ever find
any records . . . Well, that's all I'm going to say, Kit. You better
get over to that playing field. You only have fifteen minutes till the
period ends. And remember, we're even. Don't come back here
and ask me anything else.''

Six

NOBODY KNOWS BETTER than a private investigator that looks are unreliable barometers of character. All those celluloid PI's who size somebody up with one steely gaze are a Hollywood conceit. Most of us have no such X-ray vision. Like cops, we are often and easily fooled. Some kids are unnervingly adroit at stroking adults, and skilled liars can fool anybody.

So I didn't know if he was for real or not, but Tobias Tomlinson looked to be a pretty impressive package, a stunningly well-produced kid even by the standards of a community specializing in well-produced children. No matter how much we come to celebrate our children's individuality, we all know that life is easier for the bright and good-looking. Tobias was singularly blessed.

He already came highly recommended, first by Dan Bloomfield, whose judgment I couldn't really evaluate, then by Nathan Hauser, whom I had learned to trust.

He was running towards me when I came out of the gym entrance, gliding rather than running along the quarter-mile track, a picture of grace. If he was working up even a mild sweat, it didn't show. He was nearly six feet tall, blue-eyed and blond. Watching him as he ran, I'd never felt more middle-aged and encumbered.

He didn't hesitate when I waved at him. He ran over and offered his hand, as if I'd been an appointment on his Newton message pad.

"Tobias Tomlinson," he said. "Nice to meet you, Mr. Deleeuw." He sounded entirely businesslike, as if detectives came up to him two or three times a day to ask about his best friend's possible involvement in a homicide.

"You know who I am?" I asked, feeling vaguely off-balance at the way this seventh-grader seemed more at ease than I was. I cautioned myself not to make the common adult mistake of underestimating a kid. Lots of kids had plenty of poise when speaking to strangers. Just not my own.

"Oh, I'm sorry. I should have explained. You were at the Bloomfields' house last night. You're working for Jason's mom. And you're kind of famous around here, solving those killings and all. You're Ben's dad, aren't you? And, frankly, I can't think of any other reason besides Rainier-Gault's getting offed why you'd be wanting to talk to me. Is there one?" He smiled, looked at me expectantly, then pulled the bottom of his T-shirt up to wipe his forehead, revealing a flat, hard stomach and chest. There was something provocative, almost sensual, in the gesture. I had the impression the teenager was showing his body off or, maybe, like other natural athletes, he just took it for granted.

"Well, you're right," I said lamely. "I did see you at Jason's, and there really isn't any other reason I'm here. Do you mind talking to me? You don't have to. You can call your parents, of course, if you want." I considered this my own version of the Miranda warning. I wasn't required to read kids their rights, yet I always felt obliged to caution them they could talk things over with their parents first, even though I hoped they wouldn't. How many parents wanted their kids talking with some strange investigator?

But Tobias didn't even blink. "I don't mind," he said evenly. "My Dad always says you can't get in trouble if you tell the truth. And I *intend* to tell the truth. Do you think I should call my parents?"

"Only if you would feel more comfortable."

He laughed. "Well, jeez, Mr. Deleeuw, I feel real comfortable talking to you. I mean, you're the Suburban Detective, right? That's pretty cool. Ben's lucky." I thought I caught a slight hint of a smirk, but the look lasted only a second and I could have misread it. Maybe it was just some facial tic or nervous reaction. Perhaps he was more uneasy than was apparent.

"You look like a pretty fast runner. You do track?"

"Yes, sir, plus basketball. And I'm in the theater group."

"That sounds pretty well balanced. And a lot of work."

"You bet, Mr. Deleeuw, but I think, of all of it, I like track the best, just being out here by myself, running and thinking." He smiled, as if in appreciation of my interest. This *was* a well-produced kid.

He had only taken his eyes off mine for the second or two it took him to wipe his forehead. Now he glanced around the field, then back at me, retaining his earnest, businesslike look. "I'm sorry, Mr. Deleeuw. I don't mean to rush you. But the buzzer's going to ring in a few minutes. I've got an exam."

I nodded, proceeding carefully. I was questioning a thirteen-year-old kid without any parental or school approval. If anybody squawked, I could get in real trouble with the state licensing board, not to mention Leeming or the local school district. But Tobias seemed so composed I thought I could throw in a question or two before the next class. It didn't work out that way.

In fact, what happened next seemed so strange and unexpected that I wondered if my synapses hadn't short-circuited. Maybe I'd suffered a small stroke. When you hear or see something that seems unbelievable, you are inclined not to believe it.

Tobias held up his right hand to stop my question, then lowered all the fingers except the middle one. Then he put his hand down. His expression had changed. He was smiling, but not in the same earnest, natural way. This smile was forced, fake; it was as if someone had flicked a switch and a different, less benevolent, face had appeared.

"You're correct to want to talk to me. I'm the right person. I know everything, Mr. Deleeuw. Everything you want to know about what happened. But I'm not going to tell you shit." I felt myself blink. I wasn't sure I had heard him correctly; in fact, I was sure I hadn't.

He went on: "And there isn't anything you can do about it. I don't want to be bothered. And I hate being asked things. Go away and don't come back and bother me again.

"If you make any trouble for me, I'll say you propositioned me, that you touched my private parts and offered me money to pose in the nude or something even better. That you were so turned on by my half-naked body you couldn't contain yourself. I've done it before, accused a man of that. A woman teacher, too. She gave me an A, and I didn't have to take a single test. So, believe me, I mean what I'm saying. Don't come near me again. You got that? I might just tell people that you touched me anyway."

My mouth opened and shut. He didn't move away, and neither

did I. Ten feet away, he would have appeared his earnest, likable self and anybody watching would have sworn we were having a normal conversation. Up close, the leer in his expression was unmistakable.

I was standing in an open field with a school-age kid, but I was genuinely frightened. Nothing like this had ever happened to me. It wasn't in my repertoire of investigative challenges. Kids are natural sources for me—open, trusting and observant. I like them and feel at ease talking to them. If Tobias had slugged me I would have been better prepared. I clenched and unclenched my fists, put my hands in and out of my pockets. Get a grip, Kit. Real private investigators don't freeze.

"That's a pretty nasty threat, Tobias. I can't believe you'd make it, unless you really had something to be afraid of." I wanted to sound strong and dismissive but ended up sounding weak and uncertain.

"And I'll make good on it, too, fucker." He seemed supremely confident, about his willingness to make the charge and the likelihood of it sticking. I wondered how many times he had. Or how often he'd metamorphosed from model kid to monster.

"It sounds like you *have* done this before," I said evenly. I had this weird sensation of being in over my head. I'd been shot, roughed up, even jailed. Why was *he* getting to me this way?

"Let's say I know how to do it. And I haven't done it so often that they won't go for it, either. So don't think that. But I know that people say I'm pretty sexy." There was his leer again. He seemed to be checking to see if *I* found him sexy. People said a lot of nice things about you, Tobias, I thought. You must be a clever little sucker. This was Hauser's poster boy?

"Look, Tobias, when you say you know everything about what happened, exactly what do you mean? About Jason? About the shooting of your principal?"

He looked around slowly, then his leer evaporated and the sweetest, most wholesome grin replaced it. He *was* gorgeous. I bet he got propositioned all the time. And loved it.

"I did it. Okay? That's all I'm going to say. It'll be unbelievably cool, my saying that and knowing you can't do shit about it. Watching you scramble around knowing that. That'll be neat."

And then he turned, waved as if he'd see me later and started jogging back towards the gym. The words almost echoed across the field. *I did it.* Did what? Killed Nancy Rainier-Gault? Assaulted girls at the school? Did something else I didn't even know about?

"Wait—" I started to say, but stopped. He was already halfway back across the field, loping gracefully. In a single gesture that probably took less than a second, he yanked his running shorts halfway down his butt, then pulled them up again, a half moon of disgust. I swiveled quickly, looking for witnesses, but there was no one else on the field. Someone inside would have had to have been staring directly out the window to have seen it, and even then we were several hundred yards away from the building and Tobias might have been casually adjusting his shorts. The whole thing was so brazen it was brilliant. No one would ever imagine they'd seen anything besides a friendly chat. But I can hardly convey the contempt in the gesture or, for that matter, the humiliation.

I couldn't recall anything quite so deliberately malevolent having happened to me before, even at the hands of murderers, thieves, drug dealers and Deadbeat Dads. I'd been chased, cursed, even thrown into jail, but never treated with such pure disdain. I had no idea how to react. Should I follow him into the gym and confront him? Call his parents? The police? But Tobias was crafty enough to know I would hesitate a long time before calling attention to a false but ugly charge like that. I didn't know what to do.

I was feeling, and undoubtedly looking, stupid.

Before Tobias disappeared inside the gym, he turned to smile. Then he vanished. This seventh-grade boy, a prince of the suburbs if there ever was one, had challenged, threatened and offended me, all within the space of a few seconds. And made me feel like a complete incompetent.

I didn't want to just leave, not that way. A puzzled Nathan Hauser ushered me back into his office.

"Nathan, I'll be blunt with you. How well do you know this Tomlinson kid?"

"As well as an administrator gets to know a kid, Kit. He's been at the school two years. Plus, I've seen a lot of kids in my twenty years, and I have a pretty good record of judging them, if I do say so myself. Why?"

I hesitated, not sure of what to say. For that matter, I wasn't quite sure of what had just happened. "Well, he sure acted strangely—"

Hauser held up a hand. "Deleeuw." His voice turned cold. "I don't know where this is going, but it sounds too far to me. I thought I was doing you a favor, sticking my neck out like that. And this is how you respond? This is a good kid. I thought he could help explain Jason to you, but, believe me, he's not involved in this stuff. I don't want him drawn in. That's not what I'm here for." When it comes right down to it, my work boils down to instinct, just like it did when I was a commodities trader. My instincts said to back off. If I even mentioned that Tobias had threatened me with accusations of sexual misconduct, Hauser would undoubtedly have to launch the whole raft of procedures for responding to abuse allegations. He'd probably have to talk to the state, to the boy's parents, and who knows who else? Maybe Chief Leeming too. And Tobias knew I had a son in this school. Ben had already been through enough with me. I could imagine what middle school boys would do to him after charges like that. And it wouldn't do my social worker wife a world of good either.

Maybe, in fact, that's what Tobias was counting on: spooking me into a confrontation that would leave me defending myself on sexual misconduct charges instead of investigating this murder. Could that boy possibly know that my license would be suspended in a second after such a charge? That they'd shut me down first and check things out later? How could I help my client that way? And *what* clients would I have, for that matter? My work—tracking down runaways and errant fathers, looking into drug use—often brought me into contact with kids. That kind of charge hanging over me meant a second career up in flames. Do you get to have three? There wasn't anything Hauser could do anyway. He'd already told me how he felt about the kid. I had to get out of here and think this through.

"I don't know, he just acted odd, I guess. I—"

Hauser was fuming. "You'll have to look elsewhere for suspects. This is a kid with character, and with an unblemished record. A dozen teachers in this school would walk on coals for that boy. Don't you dare come in here and start casting suspicion on him because your client is in a pickle. It's my job to protect this boy. I know some of these kids look like men, but they're only kids." Some, I thought, look like kids, but they are really men. "I'm afraid I'm going to have to ask you to leave the building. Unless you have some concrete evidence that this boy did something wrong. Which I take it you don't?"

I shook my head, deciding on the spot to put the episode aside until later. Maybe until lunch with Luis, who might be able to make the morning seem remotely comprehensible.

Outside I saw right away that the left rear door of the Volvo was ajar. I hadn't opened it, so someone else had. No windows were broken, and nothing appeared forced or damaged. It was an odd target for thieves, clunky, dented ancient wagon that it is. There was nothing in the car but junk, rawhide bones for Percentage, half-eaten candy bars of Em's, maybe a pair of Ben's smelly old sneakers. Besides, the car was in as visible a place as you could find, just outside the school's main entrance.

I couldn't see anything amiss, but I smelled it quickly enough. Piled on the back seat was a small heap of fresh feces. Someone had taken a dump in my car. I think if it had been stolen, I would have felt a bit less rattled. It's become a cliché, but it's a good word—violated. I closed the door, opened all the windows, held my nose and drove to the edge of the park across from the school. My heart was pounding. What the hell was going on?

Fortunately, I had a plastic bag I used for Percentage's lawn leavings when I was in a civic mood. I removed the pile, gagging as I did, and threw it in a town trash basket. Then I drove five blocks to the Rochambeau Car Wash and told the puzzled, grossed-out attendant that one of my kids had had an accident. They scrubbed and Lysoled the back seat, assuring me it wasn't the first such visit. Then I headed for the Mall, hands shaking a bit, forehead damp. Someone was sending me a pretty stiff message and I wasn't proving to be the cool hand I was supposed to be.

There was little traffic on Route 6; within fifteen minutes I was pulling into the Mall parking lot. I had calmed down some. The worst course, I knew, was to jump to hasty conclusions or act impulsively. I needed to sort through the morning's events very carefully.

The American Way was an unassuming, '50s sort of mall, overshadowed by the newer, more deluxe monsters built farther down the highway. Not a Benetton/Laura Ashley sort of mall, but a sneaker-and-furniture-store sort of mall. Before I rented my office there a few years ago, it had never occurred to me there was a life out of sight of the downstairs stores and food concessions. But the

American Way's second floor was home to credit agencies, a tiny graphic design company and a telephone solicitation firm as well as my own dingy little two-room suite. I enjoy my hidden spot above the Mall's bustling shops, parading teenagers, strolling old folks, tacky fountains and cornucopia of fast food.

I especially treasure my window view looking out onto the eternal stream of traffic on the highway. Occasionally, there is a jack-knifed tractor trailer to liven things up. It sounds odd, but it's sweet and peaceful to sit looking out over a traffic jam you're not in.

Walking past Grobstein's Sneaker World, I waved to Murray Grobstein himself. He was crawling around in the window, hanging a huge poster of Shaquille O'Neal behind a display of state-of-the-art Nikes. It's quite extraordinary the way giant basketball stars, who did not occupy mythic positions in popular culture when I grew up, have transformed Murray's life. His store had evolved from a musty old-fashioned place to buy mocs and white tennis shoes to a cutting-edge teenagers' sneaker mart that keeps pace with the rapidly changing fashions and functions in athletic shoes, caps and shirts—no small matter.

The days when kids owned a single pair of battered canvas Keds are ancient history, of course. Murray stocks shoes for walking, running, hiking, basketball, soccer, baseball and for the most grueling of adolescent sports—looking cool, the mythic goal to which most young Americans desperately aspire. He offers air sneakers, gel sneakers, glow-in-the-dark sneakers and $150 things that appear to be nuclear-powered. Murray, riding the sports cult and its profitable offshoot, the sneaker revolution, had recently acquired a Lexus to supplement his Jaguar.

"Yo, Kit, how's the detecting business?" Emerging from the window to show off enormous white shoes with arrows down the side, Murray beamed. "They light up," he explained. "You put little batteries in 'em, and the arrows flash on and off. The batteries last for five years. But the shoes? A year, at the most. I'm pitchin' em as a safety item, too, 'cause you can see 'em a mile away. Course, for 140 bucks a pair, you could hire a limousine. Next, they'll have video games built in." He howled with laughter. And why not? The joke was on parents, not on him. He was a happy man.

"I'm busy but fine," I told him. "I'm working this school-principal killing, you know, where this woman in Rochambeau was arrested for murder?"

"Whoa," he said, pausing in his sales spiel. "That's a hot one. My wife was going on about that last night. Said they ought to hang her. I wouldn't want to be in the middle of that one." Was there *anybody* who thought I should be taking this case? "Who you representing?"

"The woman your wife wants to hang."

Murray shrugged. I didn't think he was into politics.

I had more than social reasons for telling Murray about my case. Thousands of teenagers and their parents came pouring through his store, and he and his sales staff heard lots of things before the police, parents or principals did. Kids who hated shopping for anything else would spend an hour trying on sneakers, and Murray had been helpful in passing along bits of gossip now and then.

"Yeah, well keep your ears open, okay?"

He winked.

Passing Cicchelli's Furniture Store, which had my favorite family of mannequins in the window, I crossed over to the Lightning Burger ("Food in a Flash"). Luis, the manager, was overseeing the post-breakfast cleanup but spotted my approach.

As was our routine, he had two coffees ready in a paper bag before I had even reached the counter. Evelyn and I alternated the pickup, and I would sooner have bungee-jumped off the World Trade Center than ask her to go get coffee when it was my day. I keep a weekly tab at Lightning Burger (the only charge account we can still afford, Jane says), which I settle each Friday.

I always feel the same stab of embarrassment whenever Luis waits on me. Back in Cuba, he had possessed more status and wealth than I would ever know. And he understood far more about crime, the dark side of human behavior and the law than I did. But he had accepted his new life gracefully. I empathized. Like Luis, I had lost much of what I had worked to build and put aside or altered my dreams. I was a lot happier and felt a lot luckier, and maybe he did too. I wouldn't be doing him any service by avoiding him or his restaurant.

Luis looked, as usual, to be the most elegant fast-food franchise manager in the country. His silver head was perfectly combed, every hair in place, tie perfectly knotted, handkerchief peeping over his jacket pocket. He wore his manager's nameplate polished

as if it was the Legion of Honor. Of course, he had to be the only
fast-food manager in North America who went to work in linen
suits—the same suits, I'm sure, that he wore to court when he was
Havana's leading defense lawyer. Luis is instinctively elegant,
something it seems to me Americans have a hard time achieving.
This American never has.

"I'm looking forward to lunch," he said. "Noon?"

I nodded. "I've got a big case. I'd love to go over it with you."

He bowed as if I had paid him a great compliment. I waved
good-bye and headed through the unmarked door nearby and up
the stairs to my office.

Evelyn was at the computer setup in what we rather grandly
called the waiting room, her hair corralled into a severe bun, her
starched white blouse buttoned to her neck. She looked every
inch the stern librarian, always ready to shush giggly children.

Until a few months ago, when Deleeuw Investigations belatedly
entered the Information Age, Evelyn had used computers only to
look up books. I used mine to write reports and I subscribed to
several on-line services which allowed investigators to trade leads
and information and do out-of-town legwork for one another. I
had tracked down more than a score of Deadbeat Dads and a half
dozen runaways that way, gotten legal advice and research tips.
And I'd also obtained some personal and credit information, the
source of which I didn't really want to know about. The computer
had become a daily link with Willie, a loyal hacker planted deep
inside the electronic files of one of the world's leading credit
agencies.

I was thinking more and more about bringing Willie into my
tiny firm as its first junior associate. But first I'd have to meet him.
All I knew about Willie, who had been handed over to me by a
savvy ex-detective, was that he was young and brilliant, and that if
anyone anywhere used a check or credit card to pay for anything,
had ever applied for a driver's license, filled out a lease, applied
for a mortgage, bought a toaster or a car, the all-seeing and all-
knowing Willie could zero in on them.

I requested information by the phone or computer and, at pre-
arranged times, I would get a call with the information I wanted
or, if it was too elaborate, I'd pick up a plain brown envelope
underneath a dumpster behind a building nearby. Willie had
helped me break several cases.

Dashiell Hammett's Pinkertons could have spent most of the day at their desks if they'd had keyboards and screens.

This morning, though, Evelyn was clacking away at suspicious speed when I came in, then clicked around the keyboard for a second. She had looked slightly flustered, even flushed, a lot lately. I didn't let on that I knew she was sending lots of personal messages to somebody via a singles chat on America Online. I just handed over her coffee and uncapped my own. Time to get organized. All I was getting on this case was more uncertain.

"Kit, what's wrong?" she asked immediately. "You look upset." I guess I didn't appear cool or intimidating to anybody today.

"Well, now that you mention it, I have had a pretty trying morning. And now that I'm thinking about it, I realize I ought to get down some notes on what's happened—a bizarre encounter with a model child and a not-so-subtle message left on my back seat. Evelyn, if you don't mind, let's do old-fashioned dictation. I'm not ready to type this into the computer yet. I want to talk about it with another human being."

Evelyn's eyes widened as I relayed my encounter with Tobias Tomlinson and the droppings left so arrogantly on my back seat. "My Lord," she gasped, her basic exclamation over the outrageous, the unusual, the offensive. But I felt better telling her. At least it was down on paper somewhere, and someone other than me knew about it.

I walked into my own office and closed the door. Late morning is the quietest time of day for the American Way. The blue-rinsed crowd have completed their daily walks, mothers are home giving their kids lunch, teenagers are still in school. The shopkeepers and salespeople stand outside their stores yakking or grab coffee and a burrito from the Food Court.

Evelyn had tried to brighten up my office with her needle-pointed throw pillows on my saggy old sofa. But the place remained pretty basic: a desk, a computer, a safe with my never-used gun locked inside, and a phone whose numbers lit up in the dark. I sat in an old oak swivel chair with a cracked brown-leather cushion. The stillness was calming. With Evelyn outside, I didn't even have to answer the phone and she knew I didn't want to be bothered.

The real issue wasn't Tobias Tomlinson, I reminded myself. It was Shelly Bloomfield. She was paying me to help her, and I felt mired before I'd even really got started.

Where to go on this case? There seemed little doubt in anyone's mind that my client had the strongest motive in the world—her son—for killing Nancy Rainier-Gault. The death took place at precisely the time Shelly and the principal were supposed to meet, and the family gun had been used in the killing. She would hardly be the first American who lost her cool, grabbed a gun and used it. Now, however, there was a new element. A seventh-grade boy had sneered in my face, proclaimed himself guilty of something, and threatened me with an allegation I frankly dreaded, to boot.

This kid had rocked me. I wasn't some wise-guy private eye living out of a bottle in a one-room walk-up. I was a parent, husband and Rochambeau resident. I had things in my life worth protecting. And, fear aside, there was something extraordinarily insulting about the gesture, worse than insults or punches.

I'd lucked out in some of my previous cases, followed good advice or lucky hunches. Was I out of my depth here?

I liked to approach cases quietly, unobtrusively and intelligently. I couldn't rely on swarms of cop buddies on the force, and I lacked the skill and gall to worm information out of reticent sources. My greatest investigative assets were common sense, advice from Jane and friends like Luis and Benchley plus information gleaned by Willie. I was living off my wits and my distant memories of a couple of years as an Army investigator on a base in Georgia that I hoped never to see again.

On top of that, I was undertaking a case of which my wife and secretary and half the town disapproved. One insensitive or thoughtless word could alienate one half of Rochambeau or the other.

I mulled about it all for a while and then, with a worried sigh, headed downstairs to the Lightning Burger.

Luis never complained about his transition from prominent criminal lawyer to burger-joint manager. He simply worked as hard as he could, charming the sneakers off the elderly strollers who came in for his discount breakfasts and imploring an endless procession of indifferent teenaged employees to behave courteously.

We claimed our customary corner booth overlooking the Mall parking lot and, beyond it, the busy highway. It seemed an un-

likely location for friendly confidences, yet I was completely comfortable on a red vinyl seat, elbows resting on a cheap laminated
tabletop. There were no difficult food choices to make and the
atmosphere was informal, to say the least. Jane always rolled her
eyes when I told her Lightning Burger was my favorite restaurant,
but it was the truth. My usual—fish sandwich on a roll, Diet Coke
and a small plate of crispy fries—was waiting. Luis had his usual
chicken fajita.

"Good afternoon, my friend." Luis slid in across me, looking
distinctly elegant in his alabaster linen. I think quality tailoring
was one vestige of his former life Luis wasn't about to give up. I
wasted no time filling him in on the details of the murder, my
growing sense of isolation, the seemingly overwhelming evidence
against my client and the shocking hostility I had encountered
that morning. Luis was horrified.

"Human waste on your car seat? Ghastly. Dreadful." He signaled for two coffees, took his jacket off and laid it carefully on
the seat next to him. "First, Kit, you must type up a full report of
your conversation with this very disgusting young man immediately and forward a copy to your lawyer. Do you understand me?
This will protect you in case he makes good on his threat, which
he won't."

"He won't?"

"No. He may cause you considerable anxiety, but he won't actually bring a complaint, I suspect. The accusation would do the
same thing to him as it would to you, cause embarrassment and
perhaps worse. A boy his age claiming some older man propositioned him, touched him—it isn't manly, not for someone who is
so obviously preoccupied with his own machismo and arrogance."

I looked skeptical. Luis was patient. "Someone who prides himself on his virility will not wish to stand before his peers and acknowledge that he can't protect himself against an older man. He
would lose status. A real victim could do that, but not this boy."

I reassured him that I would take his advice and forward a statement to my lawyer. The more I thought about it, the more I
thought Luis had a point about Tobias. Victimization didn't sit
well with him, I suspected. He much preferred being the aggres-
sor.

"I sympathize with the difficulties of this case." Luis nibbled at
his fajita, keeping an ear on an unhappy customer complaining

that his burger was frozen solid as a rock. The teenager looked warily at Luis, then scurried back to the microwave to warm it. "Please give the gentlemen a fresh hamburger with our compliments, Kevin," Luis said, just the slightest hint of a rise in his voice. "Next time, please try to remember to cook it!" That was as sharp as I'd ever heard Luis get.

"Whether he makes good on his threat or not, Luis, what do you make of Tobias? Is he crazy?"

Luis leaned back, took a sip of coffee and sat silently for a minute or two. He had the ability great lawyers have of sensing truth and weakness. "I would take this young man very seriously, Kit. He sounds extremely troubled, a true monomaniac. He has everything: he's intelligent, handsome and adored. He believes he is omnipotent. Perhaps there is no thrill for him in doing something wrong if nobody knows about it. So he tells you—dares you, in effect, to stop him. The threat is to disarm and unnerve you— which he succeeded in doing, no?" Luis raised one silvery eyebrow.

"Well, even the rumor of a charge like that—"

"You could survive even a charge like that if it is totally false," Luis said evenly. "What jury would accept the allegation that you walked up to this boy in the middle of the school day, grabbed his crotch and propositioned him? And every minute that he doesn't report it makes him look all the more suspicious, especially if you *do* report it. He's psych— How do the kids say it?"

"Psyching me."

"Yes, psyching you. But I believe him when he says he is guilty of something. He's telling you the truth. He's also displaying contempt, his belief that no one is smart enough to catch him. And he's leaving exactly what it is he did for you to figure out. This boy is quite dangerous, I think. Yet everyone loves and trusts him, which means he must have great self-control and intelligence. Take him very seriously, Kit. Under no circumstances go near him unless someone else is with you—he is quite clever enough to lay a trap for you." He paused to dab at his chin with a napkin. "Everything you tell me makes me think you are right, Kit. That you have taken on the right client, that she is innocent. It will be very difficult to prove that, but you are up to it."

Before I could express further doubts, however, Evelyn joined us, looking visibly shaken. She normally made it a point to avoid the crowded, noisy mall beneath our office. "Kit, I thought I should let you know right away that the school just called—Ben's school. He's been beaten up, apparently in some sort of fight or attack, Mr. Hauser wasn't sure. He's all right, Mr. Hauser said, but they've taken him to Memorial Hospital."

Seven

I'VE GOTTEN USED to seeing kids with bruises and broken limbs. Every Rochambeau parent has been to the local emergency room at least once. I know a dozen shortcuts to the hospital, routes that shave precious seconds off trips when the bleeding hands of howling six-year-olds on the passenger seat beside you are swathed in dishtowels or T-shirts.

Rochambeau Memorial is a hundred-year-old medical facility on the easternmost edge of town. Everybody calls it "Memorial." People with lots of kids or particularly accident-prone ones are there so often they're known by name. A well-equipped, convenient version of its overwhelmed urban counterparts, it's clean, attractive, safe and offers the kind of courtesy hospitals provide only when most patients have insurance.

And the hospital understands where its bread and butter is. A jazzy, up-to-date video game room, a toy shop and a fast-food and snack stand adjoin the waiting room for siblings and relatives of injured kids. The new $21 million pediatric wing sees lots of sub-urban-style business. Spring and summer weekends are the craziest times, when infants swallow pebbles, toddlers crash into sidewalks, kids chasing baseballs run into cars or walls or one another.

Memorial isn't a place that has had to develop much expertise in fishing bullets out of twelve-year-olds. Its patients tend instead to suffer dog or squirrel bites, to go flying off swings pushed too high, or to pitch off their skateboards onto concrete sidewalks. Dads, a far smaller but still significant part of the emergency room caseload, run lawn mowers over their sneakers or get their fingers caught in hedge clippers or the other home maintenance machinery they love to play with.

"The kids are reckless and the fathers are morons," one laconic nurse told me after treating her umpteenth lawn-cutting injury one July. "Moms are the only people with common sense out here. Just minor kitchen burns, maybe a knife cut if they get sloppy slicing veggies. These days they get hurt falling while they're running for the trains because they tried to finish the breakfast dishes before leaving for work." Her assessment had the ring of truth.

Once in a while the injuries are serious, even fatal, but the great bulk of hospital visits here involve the small, painful, treatable catastrophes of life in the suburbs. Even Rochambeau's ever-vigilant parents can't forestall every mishap. These traumas are woven into family lore, told and retold. We too infrequently stop to think about the other, grimmer kinds of catastrophes that befall other children just a few miles away.

Ben had flipped over his bike a couple of times, gotten thwacked on the forehead by a fastball and sliced himself open with various craft tools, all requiring visits to Memorial for stitches or X-rays. Em had been rushed here when she was three, with a scary fever that topped 104.

But it was something new to spot Ben on a gurney in a curtained cubicle. Seeing my son lying bloodied, bandaged and motionless in a corner of Memorial's emergency room ranked up there with one of the more chilling images of my adult life.

"Dad. Uh, don't worry. I'm okay." He sounded like he was talking with a sock stuffed into his mouth. His jaw was swathed in bandages. There was a gauze patch on his right cheek. The eye above the patch was swollen shut, and his lip, too, was swollen and split. Much of the rest of his face was the color of an eggplant. His right arm was in a sling, and an ice pack sat on his lower abdomen.

"It looks worse than it is, Mr. Deleeuw," said the nurse who came in behind me, cheerful and efficient-looking in her crisp white pantsuit. "Dr. Ozolins will be right in, but we got the X-rays back a few minutes ago and everything looked fine. Couple of cracked ribs, the bruises you see. The school had pre-signed permission forms."

I vaguely remembered filling in forms that gave the school the right to take Ben to a hospital if Jane and I weren't at hand.

"And no damage to the teeth," the nurse added, as though I

ought to be thrilled by the news. "That's where it can get expensive." She popped out of the cubicle just as abruptly as she had popped in.

I took a shaky breath, trying to absorb this. "Ben." I couldn't really think of anything reassuring or appropriate to say. "Ben. You all right?"

"Yeah." My son actually looked happy to see me. "Hurts like hell, though. How're you? How's Em?" Now I knew he was in agony, if he was worrying about his sister.

I handed him a glass of water. I am notoriously slow to anger, but, watching him take small, painful sips through his bloody lip, I found myself fighting off real fury.

"What happened?"

"Dunno . . . Some guys jumped me while I was at my locker. Something hit me in the back of the head. I had my face in my locker, picking up my stuff. I remember going face first into the locker. I didn't see or hear anything else . . ." He winced.

I shook my head, fighting back tears. My handsome kid, tall and gangly, always trying to project an image of invulnerability. I had never seen him so banged up, not even the day he'd ridden his bike downhill into one of the biggest oak trees in town.

I knew it looked worse than it was, and that was a good thing, because it looked bad. I had to prepare Jane, who was hurrying here from work. Ben probably didn't look as ghastly as the battered women and children she saw all day, yet she'd surely be stunned.

"So if they whacked you in the back of the head, how did you get your face all banged up?"

He looked up at the ceiling, saying nothing. He merely offered what Jane and I call the "Ben Shrug," an all-purpose response to the bulk of parental questions. How was school? How are your classes? Are you having any problems? When did you last take a shower? Or clean up your room? What do you think of the Clinton Administration? The mute shrug didn't mean he didn't have an answer or an opinion. It just meant that he wasn't going to share it with us.

"Just tell me a little more, Ben. I need to know what happened."

He closed his eyes, ran his tongue over his swollen lips. "Next thing I know these paramedics are shining lights in my eyes and

Mr. Hauser is screaming at everybody to get out of the way. They put me in an ambulance, which was cool, and brought me here and took these X-rays. It's kinda fuzzy. I don't remember a lot. The doctor said my head was okay, that I had a—"

"Concussion," said the short, briskly moving young man who came into the cubicle, his stethoscope swinging from his neck, the plastic badge on his white jacket identifying him as Louis Ozolins. He pulled out a small flashlight, peered into Ben's eyes, made Ben squeeze his fingers a dozen different ways, asked him his phone number and address and some sports questions, took his pulse, listened to his heart, then turned and took me by the arm, guiding me out into the hall.

All this in a minute or two. He had the MDD, the Male Doctor Demeanor: courteous, brusque, anxious to get somewhere else, willing to explain himself up to a point but not pleased to field many questions, as if there was a limit to what people like me could grasp.

"I'm sure you're deeply upset, Mr. Deleeuw. It's terrible, terrible. You're afraid to turn on the news these days. But look"—he pulled his glasses out of his pocket and looked down at Ben's chart—"the big thing is the boy's okay. Two cracked ribs, a couple badly bruised, but no serious fractures or breaks. No damage to the teeth or gums. Eyes seem fine, so do all the internal organs. He has a nasty concussion but no signs of any brain damage."

Ozolins flipped through the pages on the clipboard. "I'd guess he was hit with a bat, or something that heavy and hard. Then kicked with force around the stomach and kidneys while he was down. Ben has no memory of the event. We'll have Neurology run some tests this afternoon to make sure, but his motor and acuity responses all seem fine. Memory seems fine too—knows his birthdate, address, that sort of thing. Good, strong grip, solid reflexes."

He patted me on the arm reassuringly, then looked at his watch. He was one of those doctors whose competency you trusted even if his manner needed work, as if his very impatience to move on proved that Ben's injuries couldn't possibly be that serious.

"Still, you have to be extremely careful with concussions for a week or so. There can be memory lapses, fainting spells, headaches, fatigue. He's got to stay off his feet. Lots of rest, quiet. No sudden movements. We'll know more tomorrow. I want him to stay here tonight. Okay? You'll sign the forms, get them from Nurse Weinstein? Gotta go. Ben will be fine. It's just a shame. Call me if you have any questions . . ."

I did have questions, but not the sort this doctor could answer. Namely, what on earth had happened? Aside from some shoving matches Ben had gotten involved with defending my honor, I'd never known him to fight. He was easygoing, skilled at avoiding trouble, quick to forgive and tall, which meant bullies tended to stay clear.

Without a shred of evidence, I had no doubt whose handiwork this was. Tobias's. It had to be, didn't it? He had threatened me; he and his friends had undoubtedly left their little calling card in the Volvo; and who else would have any motive to bludgeon Ben, then kick him as he lay on the floor? It was the third and by far the most dramatic and brutal warning from Tobias Tomlinson in a single day, and it had been delivered to my most vulnerable point.

He sure didn't want me on this case. But why so violent and vehement a response? I wasn't onto anything that pointed me in his direction. Why first confess, then warn me away, then strike at me before I'd even had a chance to back off?

Maybe this much-admired young man just got off on vicious, sadistic behavior. But that seemed utterly at odds with his sterling reputation. Could he be that slick? Or sick?

I gave Ben a kiss on the cheek—for the first time in memory, he didn't grimace—and promised to be back soon. I ran into Jane in the hallway.

"He's okay," I reported hastily. "He's beat up pretty good, but no permanent harm done. No damage to brain, teeth, organs. He just doesn't look so hot. I'm heading over to the police."

Her eyes widened, then she nodded. Jane was pretty unflappable in a pinch. Usually, I was the hysterical one when it came to the kids, calling the pediatrician at the first hacking cough. She put one arm around my shoulder, kissed me. "Kit, you okay?"

"Yeah, I'm not the one they beat up. Why?"

"Because I don't like that look in your eye. You're not going to do some stupid guy-thing, are you?"

Despite my mounting concern and anger, her question made me smile. I am not into stupid guy-things, as my spouse so subtly terms them. The last one I remember attempting was bellowing at some behemoth who'd made a stupid crack about my college girl-

friend. He'd probably still be pounding me if my date hadn't
tossed a trash can at him and frightened him off.

"No. I'm just going to the police station, honest. Then I'll come
back here. Who's with Em?"

"I called Nora. She said Em could come over there and stay
with Holly until we got back. She brought her overnight stuff, just
in case. I told her Ben was hurt, but not seriously, and that he
would probably be home soon. She was a little scared, but she was
handling it."

Nora Kroeger lived down the block, and her daughter Holly was
a year younger than Emily. In Rochambeau, we have a sort of
buddy system common to people with small children. Even
though we weren't especially close to the Kroegers, we had this
understanding where our kids could be deposited at one another's houses at short notice. There they would find refuge, food
and playmates—even a guest bed—if we got tied up or caught in
some emergency. These were odd relationships. Although they
were perfectly nice people, we would probably never have known
the Kroegers if not for the kids, and once the kids were old
enough to watch out for themselves or stay alone, I doubted we
would see them at all. Yet we trusted one another with our children.

Jane and I both knew what we had to do. We had a businesslike
history by now, developed over sixteen years of marriage, two kids
and innumerable crises. When it hit the fan, we each went to our
assigned posts, worked out through years of trial and error and
practice. In this case, one of us would stay with Ben through the
night, the other would make sure Em was cared for, the dog
walked, the hamster fed etc. We didn't have to spell it all out. Jane
would take the hospital coverage. She had the cooler head, was
more efficient, better organized, more likely to challenge doctors.
I had a harder time bearing up at the sight of my kid's blood. My
job or, rather, one of my jobs was to keep the home front running.
No matter how dire the emergency, households didn't shut down.
There was another kid to care for and be with, milk that had to be
bought. But first I had to see Leeming.

I pointed the Volvo towards police headquarters. It wasn't until
I looked in the mirror that I realized my eyes had filled with tears.
I'm not particularly tough under any circumstances, but watching
my kid in so much pain was unbearable.

The desk sergeant seemed to be expecting me. He mumbled sympathy about Ben, and quickly buzzed the chief. Leeming didn't keep me waiting long either. And he had obviously been well briefed on what had happened.

"Kit, I'm sorry to hear about your kid. Danny Peterson says that he's okay, that he's banged up pretty good."

I thanked him for his concern. I didn't want to do the bellowing, how-could-this-possibly-happen-to-my-kid routine, especially since the assault almost certainly had happened because of me, not because of lackadaisical police protection. When I started to tell him what had happened in the schoolyard, however, Leeming brusquely interrupted and summoned Danny Peterson, the detective on the case.

Detective Peterson turned out to be a slender black woman in a navy pantsuit. Her eyes registered my surprise as she took the chair across from us. "Danielle Peterson," she said, with a hint of amusement in her husky voice as she offered her hand. I decided I had seen her around town. Late thirties, I guessed. Taller than average, with close-cropped hair, longish silver earrings. She had the I've-seen-every-damned-thing-in-the-world expression a lot of cops get, but her eyes were plenty lively, scanning me head to toe and swiftly taking in every detail.

Leeming cleared his throat, glanced meaningfully at Peterson, then asked me to start at the beginning. When I mentioned Tobias Tomlinson and my suspicion, the look Leeming shot Peterson was impossible to miss. Something was going on I didn't know about.

"I'll be honest with you, Chief, I'm scared to death," I concluded. "I can't watch Ben every minute. He was badly hurt. Whoever did this is capable of doing worse. I don't know what the hell is going on, but it's got to involve this Tomlinson kid somehow."

Leeming shifted uncomfortably in his chair. Whatever he was about to say, he didn't like having to say it.

"Look, Deleeuw, Hauser said you'd had some kind of encounter with the boy." He opened a file folder in front of him, shuffled through some notes, then nodded at Detective Peterson. "You can speak frankly, Danielle. Deleeuw might not know shit about investigating, but I trust him. Tell him what we have. I mean, we have no choice, do we?"

That didn't sound promising. I had come in feeling like a victim, looking for help; now I had a feeling Leeming and Peterson didn't see my role in quite the same light.

"Mr. Deleeuw," she began coolly, "I know you've helped with some cases here, and the chief speaks highly of you . . ." I looked at Leeming, who coughed and looked away. What was going on?

Peterson met my gaze with what looked like at worst a touch of hostility, deep skepticism at best. "But I've got to tell you, your story just doesn't square with what I'm seeing and hearing. This Tomlinson boy, there's not a dot on his record that doesn't say 'Nice Guy' or 'Harvard.' Teachers, administrators, friends, everybody says this kid is well-behaved, friendly, punctual . . . I mean, some of the kids think he butt-kisses a bit but, hey, that's not a crime in this town, is it, Mr. Deleeuw? And the two words that come up most often with this kid are 'good student.' Maybe he doesn't clean up his room or wash his socks sometimes, but if this boy is Rosemary's Baby, he must have pissed *somebody* off besides you, right?"

She paused, flipped through her notes. "And there's an even bigger problem with your story. This kid, he's accounted for every second of his day. When he left you, he went straight back to the gym, then to French, then algebra, then drama. He was in class. I've got a half dozen kids who say they were with him, and they account for almost every minute. Then he went straight to Student Council after school. Fact is, he left the last class early to go to Student Council, which means—"

Leeming finished for her: "—which means he can't be involved in the attack on your boy."

"And," added Peterson, "he was in the gym when you say somebody took a . . . uh . . . dump in your car. *You* pissing anybody else off these days?" She arched an eyebrow.

Confusion, embarrassment and anger were all colliding inside my head. I could see it from her point of view: I had made unsubstantiated accusations against this perfectly nice kid, one with a rock-solid alibi, no less. That meant either a massive conspiracy against me, implausible at the least, or it meant that I was a liar or a nut. Maybe I ought to give a little more thought to the last possibility myself.

"Look, I resent your tone, Detective. Couldn't he have had one of his friends beat up Ben or take a dump in my car? What are you suggesting—that I made up all this?''

Peterson didn't flinch. She was suggesting exactly that.

"I don't know what to suggest, Mr. Deleeuw. You want to tell me? Or are you still saying this boy said improper things to you? Because your story is looking real weird, to be frank."

I leaned back, took a deep breath, suddenly feeling Twenty Thousand Leagues Over My Head. Leeming sighed. "Look, Danny, that's unnecessary. I know this guy. He might be strange, but unless I completely misread him, he's not into playing around with middle school boys. Take it easy, will you?" He jerked his head towards the door. Peterson snapped her notebook shut and left the room. She didn't look to me like she was into taking it easy.

When she was gone, Leeming cleared his throat. "Look, Deleeuw, I've got to warn you to watch what you say from here on. If this boy makes an accusation against you, which it sounds like he might, you'll be the subject of a criminal investigation. In that case, everything and anything you say can and will be used against you. Danny Peterson's my best. She's tough and she's smart. She won't take anything at face value, not what you say or what the kid says. But if this kid, who will have character witnesses lined up all the way to the Bronx, goes after you, you're going to have a nasty situation on your hands. And so will I."

He thumped his desk. "Goddamnit, this is what I mean when I talk about amateurs doing the work of professionals. I don't read you as a guy who would proposition a young boy, I really don't. But you've been bounced out of Wall Street and this kid is a squeaky-clean jock and student council member. That's the way a jury would see it. I mean, shit . . ."

I'd taken all I was going to. "Jesus, Chief, think about it. This isn't some X-rated movie. Would I walk up to some kid and proposition him in full view of hundreds of people, for Chrissakes? I've got a family, I love my wife, I care more deeply about her and my kids than anything. This is—crazy . . ."

Leeming held up his hand. "Work in Brooklyn, then you'll appreciate crazy. Look, Kit, just do me a favor and tread carefully. There's nothing to charge you with. The boy isn't saying you touched him or anything. We don't have grounds to take it further. But if he gets more specific, we have no choice. We have to go to the state. That's the law, and they come in and investigate if there's any whiff of abuse. Just be real careful. I'll be direct with you. Very direct, 'cause your ass is riding on it. You got lucky a couple of times, but I'm telling you again: detective work is over your head. It's going to get you into trouble. Drop the Shelly Bloomfield case. This one is going to bring you down all over again, just like the Wall Street mess. Get out while there's time."

Eight

I KNEW SOMETHING was wrong at home before I'd even turned off the ignition. Percentage usually barks. Dumb as he is, he's attuned to the sound of the Volvo; whenever the car pulls in, I hear his low, hollow woof. I didn't today. I'd never opened the back door when he wasn't there wiggling, panting and dropping some wretched rawhide strip or chewbone at my feet. But today he wasn't there, even after I called him.

I heard the whimpering even before I walked into the kitchen. The rear window facing the backyard was open, as it usually was on warm days. There was a gash in the aluminum screen. Percentage was stretched out on the floor, a chunk of half-chewed raw meat on the linoleum next to him.

No piece of meat had ever lain uneaten near that dog. Something was wrong. Percentage had vomited where he lay; his body spasmed slightly, even as he thumped his tail in greeting and apology for the mess he had made. He had been poisoned.

I scooped him up, struggling with his eighty-five-pound bulk, and jogged as fast as I could to the car, laying him gently in the back seat. Then I steered towards Charlie Pinski's driveway, leaning on the horn. I thought Pinski would be out mowing or trimming on so nice a day, and he was.

"Charlie, call the Rochambeau Animal Hospital, tell them I'm coming in with a poisoned black Lab. Hurry." Charlie dropped his weed mutilator or whatever the hell it was and ran inside. He was, after all, a veteran of the Anzio beach landing, as he pointed out only three or four dozen times a year. He didn't lose his cool.

Percentage seemed barely conscious, not responding to my voice, his tongue hanging from his mouth.

I made it to the office in ten minutes. Thanks to Charlie's urgent call, the vet was waiting with an attendant. They snatched Percentage out of my arms and rushed him into the back. If he was still breathing, I couldn't see any evidence of it.

I can't honestly explain people's intense attachments to animals. I see this dog as a companion who literally stood by my side while life as I'd known it had fallen apart. We were broke, terrified and cut off from almost everyone we had called friends. Jane and I worked like demons to rebuild almost everything about the way we lived, worked and paid for things. But Percentage was never anything but thrilled to see me, never disapproving or irritated. He was simply always there, bearing genial if oblivious witness to the extraordinary upheaval in my life, making up with his unqualified adoration for some of the emptiness and fright I faced.

Nothing annoyed him, not even the time year-old Emily crawled up to his food bowl and stuck her face in his Purina while Jane and I yelped and lunged for her. The sweetest, most generous of creatures, he dozed in the backyard with rabbits, ran from raccoons, wagged at squirrels, looked in wonder at birds, as if he vaguely knew he was supposed to react to winged wildlife but had no real notion how. It tore me up to see him this way.

The vet's assistant came out, shaking her head. An elderly woman clutching a cat carrier clucked sympathetically, and so did a young man holding back an enormous, snarling German shepherd.

"The dog's in shock," the assistant told me. "We're pumping his stomach, or trying to. Trying to get him to vomit. He's not in good shape. His vital signs are very, very weak. Do you have any idea what he might have eaten?"

I shocked myself by producing a plastic Baggie filled with the remains of the meat I'd found on the floor next to him. Somehow I'd had the wits to bring it along. The assistant took the bag and headed towards the back, ordering me to go home, promising to call me as soon as there was any news. The waiting-room crowd, a bunch of veteran pet people, didn't look optimistic, but they all wished me the best as I left.

Outside, I stopped at a phone booth and called the Rochambeau PD. Leeming wasn't in, but Peterson was.

"Yup," she said.

"This is Kit Deleeuw."

Silence.

"I'm at the animal hospital downtown. My dog has been poisoned. Thought you'd want to know. You'll probably want to accuse me of doing it."

"When?"

"This afternoon sometime. Probably at the exact moment you were doing your skeptical number with me."

A little more silence. Then, "Look, Mr. Deleeuw. You're a professional, right? So am I. I shouldn't have to tell you this, but it's not my job to believe everything everybody tells me. It's my job to check out everything, right? I'm sorry about your dog. But some kid made some serious charges against about you, and I'm not taking your word for anything just because you're the grown-up, right? I'm doing my job, just like you're doing yours, okay?"

Like I said, I hate whiners. And now I'd been whining and gotten called on it. We were both doing work it would have been easier not to do. Of course she had to check out Tobias's story. Was I losing it completely?

"Sorry, Detective," I said. "I know you're just doing your job. But that doesn't really make it any easier for me, does it?"

"I don't know, Mr. Deleeuw. If you're telling the truth and I do my job well, it just might." She hung up. I bet she did her job well. God, I hoped so.

I stopped off at Nora Kroeger's to pick up Emily who, pigtailed and overall-clad, looked like an ad for Pepperidge Farm cookies or something equally homespun. She came bounding out of the house, threw herself into my arms, and we traded heartfelt hugs. Emily was usually relentlessly cheerful and easygoing, a couple of years ahead of the worst adolescent mood swings. But I could see she'd been rocked today. She knew Ben had been hurt, and I'd called to tell her Percentage was sick. I wouldn't swear that the tears were for her brother.

"Dad, is Ben okay?" I nodded, told her how yukky he looked but that it wasn't serious, that he'd be home tomorrow, and made a note to be sure to spend some time with Em. With all that was going on, it would be easy to overlook the fact that these were traumatic events in her life, too. I didn't know what I'd eventually have to say to her about Percentage. But I knew that kids are resilient, and it's pointless to hide things from them. They can almost always handle the facts, sensitively presented, and I wanted to keep one record spotlessly clean: I had never lied to my daughter, never once sugar-coated the truth. Sometimes I withheld bits of it, but at this point I was no longer quite sure of anything; I was treading water furiously.

Ben's well-being taken care of, she asked, "Is Percentage going to be okay?"

I'd been thinking so much about my own relationship to the lughead dog that I hadn't considered the rest of my family's. But I had lots of memories of Emily dozing on the floor, using the dog as a big, warm, black pillow. Of her stepping on him, poking him, careening a pull toy over his ears as he slept, yanking his tail. When she was angry or hurt, she would curl up next to him like a doll and be soothed by his genial warmth. The one methodic habit the dumb canine had was to lick her up one side of the face and down the other.

"I don't know, sweetie. I think so, but I just don't know."

I called Jane at the hospital. She told me that Ben was resting and that she would try to do the same. I would stay with Em. Tomorrow, Ben would come home, and we'd try to return to near-normalcy. It might be possible for my family, but I doubted it would be possible for me.

Nine

WITH ALL THE STUFF rocketing around my mind, I had
no trouble getting up at six a.m., tense and unrested.
There was an accused killer to try to clear, a psychotic stalking my
family, some kid right out of Stephen King threatening me with
molestation charges. I had slept accordingly—not at all—conscious through the night of the absence of the faithful hound who
should have been watching, his tail thumping discreetly, whenever
I opened my eyes.

But that was nothing compared to the image of my firstborn,
bandaged and in pain in Memorial. The picture never left me for
a second, nor did the terror, fury and concern it engendered. A
whole range of nightmare scenarios had popped up during the
sleepless and eternal night. Was Em the next target? Jane? Our
house? Would Tobias file some horrible charge that got my license
pulled? Was my second career going down in flames just the way
my first had—with an unfair accusation I was helpless to combat?
And if it did, we were far more vulnerable this time. When I'd
worked on Wall Street, Jane and I always kept a year's cushion in
the bank—mortgage and car payments, health insurance premi-
ums. Now, our cushion was about two weeks' thick. I felt way over
my head, as Chief Leeming, with all good intentions, kept assuring
me I was.

If I could just manage one full day without somebody in my
household being menaced, poisoned or beaten, I might actually
be able to make some progress on the case. I decided I'd call Mrs.
Steinitz, the retired teacher who also doubled as our grumpy but
vigilant and utterly reliable emergency baby-sitter. I didn't want
Emily alone today, and anybody who tangled with Mrs. Steinitz

would regret it. Of course, so would Emily, but that couldn't be helped.

My first call was to the hospital, however. The night duty nurse said that Jane had just left, that Ben was sleeping and that she'd call me when he woke up. "Your boy is just fine," she reported. "He stayed up watching Letterman till pretty late." A relief: that meant he really *was* fine.

Now I checked on the dog. The prognosis for poor old Percentage wasn't nearly as upbeat as Ben's. I didn't equate the kid and the dog, exactly, but I did take a deep breath before calling the vet, looking out the window at the sun climbing over the canopy of stately trees that edged our street.

It was too pretty a sight for all this grief. June is Rochambeau's best month, unless you are plagued by allergies. Lawn sprinklers hiss on in the morning, then again in the evening; the sounds of kids playing provide a sweet, constant backdrop. This early, there was a sense of lush green stillness, of comfortable expectation. The morning light was pale and clear.

Often, when I gaze out the windows, I have that fleeting but satisfying glow we get when we survey what our hard work has bought. I'm happy that my kids can grow up in this spacious, if decaying house and play in a big fenced yard. Today, though, everything I thought of produced cold dread.

"Oh, yes, Mr. Deleeuw," said the voice at the vet's answering service, which picked up even before the first ring died. "I have a note that Dr. Camersen left for you. It's Percentage, isn't it? Dr. Camersen says the dog is doing better. His signs are good, and the doctor feels he's out of danger. There does seem to be some nerve damage. Percentage doesn't seem to have the full use of his right hind leg. But the doctor will explain all this to you. He says he wants you to come by this afternoon."

I felt my tension ease slightly. Ben must be okay—otherwise Jane surely wouldn't be on her way home. Percentage was going to pull through. A gimpy leg would merely provide a good excuse for not catching the rabbits and squirrels he so halfheartedly lunged after. And no one had arrested me yet.

I heard the key turn in the back door, pulled on a robe and— after peeking in on Em, asleep and nearly invisible beneath a tangle of sheets and stuffed animals—headed quickly downstairs.

"Kit?" whispered Jane, who had jumped slightly as I came

bounding down. She looked hollow-eyed and weary. "Did you sleep? The hospital brought in a recliner for me, so I got four or five hours. I can get by on that."

I folded her in my arms, absentmindedly rubbing the back of her neck, which felt like coiled rope. "Ben should be out of the hospital later today, Kit, maybe tomorrow. He seemed shaken at first, but you know kids . . . They seem to bounce back from almost everything. I had to argue to get him to go to sleep. No permanent injuries or scars. Lots of rest when he gets home." She suddenly sobbed, then just as suddenly stopped. I held on tight, pressing a kiss against her cap of dark hair.

I had this notion that I should be storming around, breaking furniture and vowing to tear the limbs off whoever had hurt my boy and poisoned my dog, but I always felt foolish when such feelings rose up. Mostly, I felt a deep sadness that Ben had been hurt and that Jane had to suffer. I felt anger, too, in powerful but short-lived waves. The problem with male fury is that it never accomplishes anything except getting yourself or somebody else hurt. I had to calm down.

Finally, Jane wiped her eyes—and mine—with a paper napkin from the kitchen table. I could count the times Jane had cried in our sixteen years of marriage. Maybe four, leaving aside old Bette Davis movies on TV. Weepy wasn't her style.

I couldn't help thinking that in an earlier time, coerced into housewifely domesticity, Jane might have become a drunk or a shrew, driven mad with boredom, restlessness and anger. It just wasn't the life for her. For Jane, work was more than a means of income; it was her identity. She was a wonderful mother—warm, attentive, strong—but that was no longer enough. At times like these, she had a lot of strength and I drew from it. There were many ways in which she was much tougher than I was. Good thing, too.

In fact, after drying her eyes she announced that she wanted to spend a few hours this morning at her clinic. She headed for the coffeemaker on the counter. I slumped into a chair.

"Kit, what's wrong?" she asked, halfway through measuring the coffee, looking sharply at me. We'd barely had a chance to talk the day before. I briefed her in detail on my encounter with Tobias, and on my unsettling conversation with Leeming and Peterson at the police station.

She nodded. "What else?"

"Shit, honey, my boy's in the hospital, I might be accused of molesting the school hero, my dog was nearly offed and I don't have squat to tell poor Shelly Bloomfield. What else do I need? A DC-10 to fall on the house?"

She shook her head. "I know all that, dummy, don't patronize me." I had learned the hard way that patronizing Jane was a bad idea, like throwing a stone at a grizzly: it only made her mad.

"The look on your face, it's more than tired and concerned," she said, eyeing me carefully. "It's downright terrified. Almost defeated. You look so, so doubtful . . . so insecure. I don't know, you tell me."

In the time-honored tradition of men, I grunted. Then shrugged. She let it go for the moment, squeezing my shoulder gently before heading upstairs to change her clothes.

Mrs. Steinitz, naturally, was awake when I called. Old bats don't sleep, and she probably hung upside down from the rafters at night. "We have some emergencies, Mrs. Steinitz," I told her. "Could you come over today? I'll explain when you get here. Ben's in the hospital—"

"Of course, of course," she snapped. "I'll be right there." Not one for chitchat, she banged the phone down. Poor Em. Maybe she could lure a pal over to play. There wasn't much·TV and Oreos when the Baby-sitter from Beyond the Grave, as Em accurately tagged Mrs. S., was on the scene.

Jane had changed her skirt and blouse when she came back down, but not her steely expression.

"I don't have time for bullshit, Kit. You're a wreck. What's up?"

I puffed out my cheeks and let out a big sigh. "I guess I am a wreck." I swallowed hard. "Chief Leeming says I'm in over my head, and he may be right. The other cases I've been involved with, I don't know, they almost seemed to fall into place and solve themselves. This time, the trouble is piling up faster than I can cope with it. I mean, Jesus, I still feel like an out-of-work commodities trader most days, not some street-smart tough guy who can protect himself . . ."

I stopped, but Jane finished the sentence for me, a wry smile on her face. "And his kin and dog? It's not all on you, Kit. This is the '90s."

"And his kin and dog." I attempted to laugh. "I can't help it, men are raised to think that way, even when they know better. They're supposed to keep their kids from getting beat up. It just seems like I have to handle more things than I know how to. I've made no headway on the Rainier-Gault killing. I can't fathom what this boy is doing to me, or why someone would hurt Ben this way or poison the dog. I'm just scared silly about what's going to happen next. And I'm more scared about what will happen to us if it turns out I'm really no good at this . . ."

I got up and poured myself a cup of coffee, not wanting to whine, but not able to sound half as confident and strong as I wanted to. It seemed better to say nothing at all.

"So you feel like you're drowning, and you're going to lose your second life," Jane finished helpfully, after a moment.

"That's a bit more stark than I would put it, but yes. I guess so. That's what I feel."

Jane came over and sat down, plopping her briefcase down on the floor. This wasn't a good time for a discussion like this. She had to get to the clinic; I had work to do. But we both knew I wasn't going to be much good in this state. She rested her hand on the table and I put mine on top of hers.

"We've been through a lot, Kit," she mused, half to herself. "Sometimes, when I'm driving into the city or sitting up at night, I think of that year you left Wall Street, of the savings draining away, of how hard it hit you to be run out of your firm that way, of all our friends who disappeared, of worrying if we could keep the house . . ." She smiled. "I thought you were bonkers to become a PI. It was the last thing I ever pictured you doing. I thought you wouldn't last a month."

I blinked. "You did? You never said that."

"That wouldn't have been very supportive, would it? You thought it was great when I went to work, when I started at the clinic and when I went back to school. You deserved no less when it was your turn. And then, to my surprise, you took to it right away, solved a couple of blockbuster cases, got your picture in the paper, even made a living, sort of."

She squeezed my hand. "When you got shot during the Brown case, I admit to some doubts. When you got slugged by that crazy weight-lifter I wondered if this was such a good career move." She shook her head. "And then that divorced thug in Jersey City clocked you, too."

We both burst out laughing.

"But now," she continued, "you've got an office in the Mall, a receptionist—"

"Part-time."

"A receptionist," she said firmly. "And people like Shelly Bloomfield are coming to you for help. I don't really like what she symbolizes, to be honest, Kit, but I am *very* proud of you, and very confident. You're good at this job. You're a natural at talking to people—open and honest. Don't forget, you pulled together a lot of puzzle pieces in the Brown case, and you made the police look ridiculous in the Family Stalker case. You've got a terrific record to stand on—considering we might've been living in a trailer in Boonton about now."

She looked me in the eye, and I saw that she was telling the truth, at least what she thought was true. Jane doesn't bullshit; she isn't good at it. This was her honest opinion. It meant a lot, even if she was a little biased.

She gulped down the coffee, kissed me full on the lips, picked up her briefcase and waved her free hand at me. "Here's the poop, Kit. You're a perfectly competent detective. You had some real shocks yesterday, and you had your resulting loss of confidence. It's anxiety-provoking and it's ugly. But get to work. You can't go back, anyway, and you shouldn't. If we lose everything, we'll start again. Your client is waiting for results. Your family needs you. You don't get to have an identity crisis. You get to put your troubles aside for a few hours and then you get to work."

Ten

I NODDED SWEETLY to Mrs. Steinitz and bolted from the house, overwhelmed by guilt at leaving Emily to wake up to her grouchy, temporary caretaker. I would just as soon avoid Em's wrath as well.

I had to get some handle on the Bloomfield case, but I didn't have much of an idea how to do that. There had to be some connection to Tobias Tomlinson's behavior, if I was positive that he was the one who beat up Ben and poisoned the dog—which I wasn't.

That was the obvious conclusion, but it didn't make tons of sense.

Still, frightening as they were, the attacks on my household were the best leads I had. Something remotely resembling a motive or rationale might help. Was Tobias really confessing to a role in the Rainier-Gault killing and daring me to find out? Not many middle-school kids had that kind of gall. But even if he wasn't, his behavior was suspicious. I tried to cast back to the mysterious labyrinths of the adolescent male mind. Sometimes, I knew, friends tried to draw attention away from other friends who were in trouble. That might explain Tobias's bravado and still be in keeping with his reputation as a decent, loyal and popular kid.

I drove by the hospital and was allowed to peek in at Ben, who was still asleep. He looked young and vulnerable. The IV tube had been removed, as well as some of the bandages from his face. He looked as if he'd been in a car crash, his forehead and cheeks all the colors of the northern lights. I was amazed—and relieved—that the beating hadn't left him more seriously injured. But the nurses on duty brushed off any suggestion that he wouldn't be

home that night. "He'll be taking the garbage out by Saturday,"
said one, a hilarious notion if ever I heard one. I'm not sure Ben
knew precisely where our garbage cans were. It could take a half-
hour harangue to get him to move his enormous sneakers out of
the center of the living room.

I stayed only a minute, leaning over and planting a kiss on his
forehead, dropping a pile of sports magazines and some books on
the table next to his bed. Inside several of the books I'd tucked
unrolled Fruit Roll-Ups. I also left a note: *Ben. Here to check on you.
Back later. The doctors say every single thing will heal & you'll be in top
form in a couple of days. Love you, Dad.* I could just picture him
reading the note and thinking: *Oh, gross.* But even through the
ups and downs of adolescence, his kindness and general decency
were never obscured, at least not for long. He was a sweet kid. I
prayed this violence hadn't happened because of me, even as I
knew that it must have. Another strong reason, along with Shelly
Bloomfield's bleak future, to get cracking.

I liked Jane's approach. Here I was, reeling from assaults on me,
my son and my dog, asking the most basic questions about my
ability to be a private investigator and filled with terror at the
implications if I couldn't be one—and she had firmly reminded
me that I simply had too much work ahead to have time for all
that worrying. A short-term solution for severe anxiety, but cheap
and useful.

I left the hospital, walked across to the parking lot and headed
for my office. The day continued as beautifully as it had begun,
breezy, pleasant and clear. I drank in the sweet air gratefully.

If I were anything like a crackerjack detective, I would have
noticed the blue Ford sedan with SG—state government—license
plates idling not twenty feet behind the Volvo. It wasn't exactly a
high-quality tail. In my defense, I did pick it up on the highway
leading to the Mall, but only dimly registered it as an official-
looking sort of car. It didn't cross my mind that it was following
me. To have that kind of intuitive instinct, to sense trouble, I think
you have to start doing this kind of work earlier than I did. I still
have to make an effort to think suspiciously or deceptively.

Instead, I was feeling relieved about Ben, reminding myself that
he could have been hurt far more seriously. Being brained with a
bat—the image made me shudder. The dog could be dead, too.
But my little interlude of relief didn't last long.

The commuters were all headed for the city in the other direction, so I made it to the American Way quickly, the tasteful lawns
and Victorians of Rochambeau giving way to the tacky split-levels
of the adjoining town, then the endless strip development of
Route 6, where Taco Bell, Chili's, Burger King, McDonald's,
Wendy's and Roy Rogers lined up in a row. How many different
fast-food joints did we need, I was wondering idly. Were that many
people that hungry for more or less the same stuff that much of
the time?

I finally got a little jumpy when I saw the blue Ford pull in right
next to my space in the Mall parking lot. I turned the engine off
and unfastened my seat belt. They were beside my car in a flash. A
shield appeared in my window attached to a young woman in a
beige pantsuit. A man, broad-shouldered and looking every inch a
cop, stood planted on the passenger side, as if forestalling any
effort to bolt. He was holding some sort of ID, too.

The woman on my side didn't look cop-like; she looked frazzled. Her pantsuit, which hung off her shoulders as if she'd
bought the wrong size, was wrinkled, and she held a cheap plastic
briefcase in the hand that didn't hold the badge. I saw no bulge
that could be a gun, and she didn't stand in that challenging
don't-screw-with-me way, feet spread-eagled. She seemed oddly
tentative and distracted.

But her partner was a different story: tall and muscular, his
head shaven, he wore a sharply pressed, expensive-looking gray
suit. Most of the police detectives I know are snappy dressers; they
say it goes with getting respect and with long years of wearing a
uniform. I could see the butt end of his gun peeking from the
right side of his belt, poking menacingly out of a black leather
holster. This wasn't a sales call.

"Mr. Deleeuw," the woman said as I stepped out of the car,
"I'm Joan Rheingold. This is my partner Stanley Gans. I'm with
Digh-fuss," she said. My chest contracted sharply. DYFS was the
familiar acronym for the state's Division of Youth and Family Services, the folks you called if you thought your neighbor was beating up his kid, or if your child told you his teacher had touched
him. You didn't have to leave any name or have any proof, just a
suspicion, and they would come and investigate. That was really
the only way the system could possibly work, since kids couldn't be

protected otherwise, something I suspected I was going to have to struggle to keep in mind in the days and weeks ahead.

These were two people I normally thought of as doing the Lord's work, until they turned up looking grimly at me outside my car. As I learned when I was the subject of a federal investigation of Wall Street, nothing alters your perception of justice more than being the object of some.

"Do you have a minute?" Joan Rheingold asked.

"Do I have a choice?" I said lightly, and instantly regretted it. I guess I really didn't know how to behave. After all, somebody has to deal with creeps. I leaned back against the car. Gans walked around so that he came up behind me. He carried a briefcase too, only his was leather and had a badge embossed on it that said: New Jersey State Police.

"You do have a choice, Mr. Deleeuw," Rheingold said. "We're not here to make an arrest. We're here to investigate a report that you made inappropriate sexual advances to a minor. The source of the report is, as I'm sure you know, confidential. But I'd be very interested in hearing about your conversation yesterday with To-bias Tomlinson." She spoke sharply, almost contemptuously.

We weren't wasting time on small talk. Then again, I suspected most of the people these two talked to weren't the sort with whom one especially wanted to exchange small talk.

I looked over at Detective Gans. His fierce demeanor seemed to have softened a bit, as if he had X-rayed my soul and found it in better shape than he'd thought. Or maybe he sensed I wasn't going to give him any trouble. "You don't have to answer these questions," he said. "But obviously, if you don't answer them here, you'll have to answer them somewhere else. I'm sure you know that, being a private investigator and all." The mildly dis-gusted look on his face suggested that mine was not a line of work he held in especially high regard. Like Leeming, most cops see investigators either as potentially embarrassing competitors or as bumbling troublemakers who get in their way.

"Why the State Police?" I asked.

"Several reasons, Mr. Deleeuw. One, the people we deal with sometimes get a little testy with the DYFS investigators, even occa-sionally rough them up. Don't want that, do we?" No sir, we didn't. "And DYFS is a state agency. If things go further, the local

police will be brought in." Besides, he neglected to say, the state
licenses private investigators.

He buttoned his jacket, apparently convinced at least that I
wasn't going to pull out a gun and blaze away. "And I should warn
you that this investigation could lead to an arrest, in which case I
would be obliged to inform you of your rights. I am obliged now
to tell you that you have the right to have an attorney present if
you wish, and that you are not required to answer any of our
questions." Better here than at the police station, I was thinking.
It also occurred to me that if a formal charge had been made, or if
they had any concrete evidence of serious wrongdoing, we would
already be on our way to the police station.

"And," Gans added, "if you should happen to admit to some
crime or wrongdoing, I've got these handcuffs here that I will slap
on you after reading your rights. We do deal with some people
who are not upright citizens." I'm sure he dealt with some of the
most unspeakable sleazoids on the planet, which made it all the
more unsettling that he was speaking to me. "You understand this
stuff? You want to talk here? In your office?"

We walked into the Mall. I suggested we sit at a table in front of
the soon-to-open Food Court. I didn't know if Evelyn was in yet,
but she'd get pretty upset if she knew what was going on. I was
pretty mortified about it myself.

The model family of mannequins in Cicchelli's Furniture
Store's window were already appearing in summer shorts. They
mocked me with their permanent smiles and eternal calm. Not for
the first time, I wished I was Papa Cicchelli, sitting for all time in
his favorite easy chair, his slippers always on his plaster feet, his
pipe always filled, the fake fire always glowing, his wife's adoring
gazed fixed forever on him, his two children always healthy-look-
ing and obedient. I wished I could melt through the window and
join them all. DYFS investigators would never barge into that living room.

Except for a few elderly strollers getting their exercise, it was
quiet in the Mall. The schmaltzy music hadn't kicked in yet, and
the fountains were silent. Murray Grobstein hadn't yet waded into
the window of his sneaker emporium to move around his nuclear-
powered (and -priced) athletic shoes.

I could only think of the FBI agents who'd pursued me so sin-
gle-mindedly during the insider-trading scandal that wracked my

firm. They never doubted for a second that I was guilty and made it clear they would never forgive or forget me for refusing to rat on my buddies. It was a point of pride with them: people who don't cooperate have to be taught a lesson. Nor would they ever believe that I knew nothing that would be of any use to them; that I had never been aware of or party to any insider-trading talk.

My modest bank account should have made the point. But the FBI investigators remained convinced that I had money squirreled away somewhere and kept watching to see how I spent it. They'd have even more evidence of my innocence now—the saggy garage behind my house, the kitchen ceiling adorned with flaking paint and cracking plaster, the tattered furniture. I hoped these folks were more charitable, but I guess that charity wasn't in their job descriptions.

I didn't notice Luis Hebron coming up behind us, but I was never happier to see him. Luis must have seen us come in, sized up something of the situation and discreetly strolled across the Mall from the Lightning Burger to take a look. He would have spotted Gans as a cop in a second, and probably the look on my face encouraged him to intrude, something he virtually never did.

"Kit," he said, with his most gracious smile, "how are you? I don't believe I know your friends. Can I be of any assistance?" Gans shot him a get-lost glare, but Luis's smile never wavered. He had been through lots worse than this.

"Luis"—I sounded more desperate than I'd intended—"would you mind joining us? Mr. Hebron is a friend of mine." I didn't, of course, volunteer Luis's past as one of Cuba's most prominent criminal attorneys, but I did tell Luis who these two were and more or less why they were there. Thank God I'd briefed him earlier about Tobias.

Ms. Rheingold balked at first, pointing out that DYFS investigations were confidential. Even though I had the right to representation, they clearly hadn't expected any. "These are preliminary and private inquiries—"

"That could lead to criminal proceedings, is that correct?" Luis's smile was intact, but his eyes stayed firmly on Gans.

"Well, if evidence were to develop that there was a crime, I suppose that could lead to a criminal proceeding," Gans conceded.

"And something Mr. Deleeuw might say *could* lead to a criminal charge, couldn't it?" persisted Luis even more quietly.

"If he hasn't done anything wrong, then I don't see what the problem would be," said Gans just as coolly.

"The problem"—Luis's voice sharpened slightly—"is that the person in any investigation in which the person interviewed is seen as a possible suspect in a felony—in this case, sexual solicitation of a minor, at least, is that right?"—neither Rheingold nor Gans said anything—"is entitled to be apprised of his or her rights under the U.S. Constitution and under New Jersey criminal statutes. And to have counsel of his choice present during any kind of questioning. Am I wrong?" The smile had faded now. "Especially as you have no serious evidence and no reason to believe any molestation even occurred."

That got both of them sputtering at once. "Mr. Hebron, how would you have any idea whom we have investigated or what we've learned?" Rheingold demanded. "Did you have any reason to know we were coming?"

"Naturally not," said Luis reassuringly. "But am I wrong?"

Gans shrugged. "All I'll say is that you're not wrong about Mr. Deleeuw's right to have representation, Mr. . . . ?" Gans pulled out a notebook and a pen, a cop's trick to rattle people. I almost smiled. This wouldn't work with Luis.

"H-e-b-r-o-n. Luis Hebron."

"And you're an attorney?"

"Yes," I said.

"No," said Luis. "But I am an adviser to Mr. Deleeuw." His look said very forcefully: *I'm not going anywhere, and if you give us a hard time about it, I know how to make trouble.* Cops didn't need more trouble than they already had.

"I am the manager of the Lightning Burger franchise across the way," Luis said, in the same tone as if he'd announced that he was majority leader of the U.S. Senate. He gestured grandly to the restaurant, whose motto "Food in a Flash" shone brightly in neon in the window.

Rheingold and Gans gave each other a look that almost made the whole thing worth it, if the subject matter hadn't been so horrifying. She leafed through her notebook, looking officious. "We have to protect the rights of the people involved, especially the children."

Luis and I both nodded. By all means, protect the rights of the children. "And the rights of the accused too, no?" Luis reminded her politely. God, I wished he really was my lawyer.

"I don't see how we can make him leave, Joan," Gans said, a bit unhappily. "Let's get on with it."

She looked unhappy too. "All right," she said, then warned us that the names of minors absolutely had to be kept confidential. I got the sense that she and Gans didn't have time for a standoff, that they had a lot of stops to make. I was shaken to be one of them.

Luis must have just baffled them with his spotless linen summer suit, his gleaming cuff links, his leather wing tips. He sat down on a white metal chair and crossed his legs, smiling sweetly at Rheingold and Gans and waiting expectantly. Quite a performance.

The fountain suddenly came to life, gushing to five feet, turning turquoise as the lights clicked on. We all jumped a bit.

Rheingold opened her plastic briefcase, took out a tape recorder. I glanced at Luis, but he just shrugged. Rheingold clicked the recorder on.

"Do you know a thirteen-year-old boy named Tobias Tomlinson?" she asked, pen poised. Gans was watching my face closely, as I would have in his shoes.

"Yes, I do. I've seen him twice. Once at the home of one of my clients, though I didn't speak to him there. That would have been a couple of days ago; he came in through a back door. Then yesterday, I talked with him on the school's athletic field for about ten minutes. I wanted some information about a case I'm working on. I approached him on the playing field—"

Gans interrupted. "Did you have the permission of any of the school authorities?"

I hesitated. Hadn't Nate Hauser told me where Tobias was, but made it clear he couldn't officially approve my talking with him?

"Nathan Hauser says you did have permission," Gans added. "Why would you forget that?"

Classy man, Nate, loyal when he didn't have to be.

"Hmmm," hummed Luis. "Isn't that strange, Detective Gans and Ms. Rheingold? Do molesters usually check in with assistant principals before going out in full view of the school population to bother children?"

No response. Rheingold made a note of something.

"I didn't forget," I said evenly. "I just didn't want to get Hauser in any trouble. I wouldn't say he gave me permission, exactly. But I made sure he knew I intended to talk with the boy."

"Were you alone with the boy at any time?" Rheingold was asking the questions now.

"Nobody was within earshot. But I was never out of sight of half the windows in the school. So no, we weren't alone in that sense."

"Did you touch him anywhere?"

"No. Absolutely not. Did he say that I did?"

"What did you say to him?"

"Well, I started to ask him about the case I'm investigating. I'm not free to tell you the specifics, except to say my discussion with him involved nothing of a suggestive or a sexual nature."

"Did you suggest that it might be fun to take his picture in the nude?"

"No. Never. I would never do that."

"Did you offer to drive him home?"

"No. I had barely asked him a question at all when his whole demeanor changed. He suddenly became hostile and threatening. He told me he had made molestation accusations before, and that if I didn't stay away from him, he would do the same to me. Tobias made it clear that unless I dropped my investigation, he might very well make a charge like this. I subsequently reported this threat to the police chief of Rochambeau, Frank Leeming, and I told both my wife and my secretary, Evelyn de la Cretaz, about it."

"And he told me," Luis added, pulling a small notepad of his own from his jacket pocket. "He told me." He jotted something down and then mused aloud, "Unusual case, isn't it? Suspect checks in with school authorities, then notifies potential witnesses of his conversation with the child."

"Or, looking at it another way," Rheingold said crisply, "he makes inappropriate suggestions to the child and then covers his butt by telling everybody he can find that the boy threatened him." Well, she was no pushover either. I felt slightly dizzy.

"Did you contact his parents before you talked to him?" Rheingold looked as if she might vomit if she had to sit near me for much longer.

"No. I asked him if he wanted to call his parents and he said no. Pursuing it further didn't seem necessary—"

"You routinely question thirteen-year-old children without

adults present?'' She was getting more hostile, past the preliminaries. "Or school officials?"

"I never questioned a thirteen-year-old before," I said, my voice rising.

"Why not?" she demanded. "Is it because you know better? Or maybe other children aren't as good-looking?"

Luis put a hand on my arm, but I couldn't sit still for this. "This is complete bullshit," I said. "Why would I talk to him that way in a public place?"

"Because you're not stupid. You could look innocent, you could say, 'Proposition a boy in front of all these people?'—just like you did now. Look, Deleeuw, you went up to a strikingly handsome young boy who had no reason to lodge false charges against you. You covered your butt to the point that you notified the assistant principal you were there, but you also made sure there was nobody close enough to hear what you said. Sounds good to me.''

It didn't sound good to me. And her sneering tone sounded equally bad.

"Does it bother you that the accusation is totally false?"

"What's the motive for this child to lie, Deleeuw? Give me that, okay?" She was increasingly confrontational. Gans looked uncomfortable, as if he had an open mind and was genuinely curious to hear what I had to say. Maybe it was a good-cop, bad-cop routine. If so, she was holding up her end better than he was. But I thought her dislike was genuine. She looked as though she couldn't wait to get home and scrape the slime off.

I didn't have an answer. There was no convincing motive. It seemed ludicrous to suggest to these people that Tobias had confessed to killing the school principal. And even if I did, I had no evidence to support an accusation like that.

I blurted out: "I have never molested anybody, let alone a child. I would hardly make such an attempt in full view of the entire school. This boy is disturbed, I think profoundly so. He mooned me on the field. A few minutes later, I found my car door ajar and a pile of shit on the back seat. My son was badly beaten at the same school just a couple of hours after that, and my dog was poisoned. I think Tobias was involved—"

"Mr. Deleeuw," Gans interrupted quietly, "we understand that you might be completely innocent of any wrongdoing. But these are pretty serious accusations. This boy has a lot of credibility. His

friends and teachers all think quite highly of him. He has a perfect record in school. It's pretty common, I have to tell you, for
people who've been accused to attack the child involved. These
are complex situations. We do the best we can to sort it out."

I watched the fountain lift a bit higher, and turn lime-green,
accompanied by the first swell of piped-in Mall music, designed to
make strolling from one store to another more pleasant. It
seemed to be a string-heavy version of "Baby, I Need Your
Lovin'." More gray-haired walkers passed by, and the first mothers
pushing strollers. Murray Grobstein looked curiously at our little
gathering from his store window and waved tentatively. Some shut-
ters in the Food Court slid up—the souvlaki stand, run by a Do-
minican; the Philly hoagie stand, owned by two Iranians; and the
Senegalese-operated Great American Cheese and Potato Bar.
Lightning Burger was long open, of course. You couldn't get up
earlier than Luis, as these two investigators were learning.

"Put another way, he's got a spotless record and you nearly
went to prison for insider trading," Rheingold piped up. I saw
Luis hold his hand up, which I took to mean "Don't respond to
that."

"I understand that you have to investigate this," I said calmly,
Luis nodding approvingly at my tone. "What I don't understand is
that the boy was clearly threatening me in order to keep me off
the case. So why would he have called and reported me before I
even had a chance to resign the case, before he knew if he'd
succeeded or not?"

Rheingold snapped her notebook shut in disgust. "How about
because you wanted to take the boy to some motel room and give
him money to take his clothes off, so you could take the pictures
up to your office at night and play with yourself?"

Gans leaned forward. "C'mon," he said softly to her. "Take it
easy."

"I don't take it easy," she snapped. "Not with people like this. I
take it real hard and personal." She snatched up her parapherna-
lia and stalked away without a word, out the Mall entrance. Gans,
looking slightly embarrassed, did not move to follow her.

"Are you permitted to tell us anything about who made accusations against Kit?" Luis asked him. I knew the answer. A kid who
brought a complaint that didn't stick would be a sitting duck for
an enraged parent or abuser.

Gans shook his head. "We don't even know for sure, though our supervisors do. We're just told to investigate the report. Some complaints are anonymous, some are calls, some come in the mail. Sometimes the brass doesn't like us to know, because they don't want our judgment affected."

Tobias was becoming almost mythically evil and mysterious in my mind. Nothing about him made sense: his vicious behavior versus his reputation, his efforts to get me off the case followed by an almost-instant follow-up. What purpose would Ben's beating and the dog-poisoning serve? It added up to a lot of intimidation, some of it quite risky, before he even knew if his threats had been effective.

"What happens in these cases if it's one person's word against the other?"

"Well, let's not get ahead of ourselves," Gans told Luis. "I never said the boy made any complaint. It would be a mistake to jump to that conclusion. To be frank, if he had, we'd be sitting in the police station, probably.

"And you wouldn't be here, probably," he added, glowering at Luis. "What are you, anyway?"

"Look upon me as a Mall angel," said Luis, twinkling. I hadn't seen this fearless side of him before, though given the life he'd led, it had to be there. I didn't know much about the details, but I knew he had spent time in Castro's jails before fleeing to America, penniless and alone. What were a couple of bureaucrats with badges to him?

"We just got a report," Gans said, "and we're checking it out. So far, neither the boy nor his family wishes to make a formal complaint." How, I wondered, had Luis known? "If that doesn't change, there'll probably be no further action. If it does . . ."

Maybe Tobias, as Luis had suggested, hadn't actually made the accusation himself. Maybe he'd managed to ratchet everything up one more notch. Maybe he bragged about the threat to somebody who told somebody who told his parents. Another mystery for my list.

Gans stood. "Mr. Deleeuw," he said formally, as if he was about to read me my rights, "this is to officially inform you that you are under investigation in regards to sexual overtures made to a minor. You are not to go near this child again, nor to make any effort to contact him. Do not attempt to send him messages through other people, go near his home or approach him at school or elsewhere. Do you understand that?"

Luis and I stood up too. "Look," I said, "he could be a critical witness in my investigation—"

"If you do approach him," Gans sliced in, "we'll slap you with a restraining order so fast your tail will spin, the state will yank your license and then we *will* be having this conversation at police headquarters. We're not kidding," he said, as if I doubted him. "This can turn serious real quick. Our investigation will continue. I would strongly advise you to stay away from this kid. The next step will be a court order and possible criminal charges."

I looked at Luis. He shook his head, which I took as a sign to say nothing. He then surprised me again by offering Gans coffee and Danish, and Gans amazed me by accepting. His partner was cooling her heels in the car. Maybe he wasn't looking forward to spending quality time with her.

I suppose I shouldn't have been that surprised that Gans could practically accuse me of child molestation in one breath, then have coffee with Luis the next. I am always taken aback when I have to go to the County Courthouse to testify, and watch lawyers who've just ripped one another apart in court stroll practically arm-in-arm across the street for lunch. Business as usual. It isn't personal, unless it's your reputation or freedom or kid they are fighting about. That's why Rheingold's venom seemed unusual.

Gans and Luis headed across the courtyard to the Lightning Burger, leaving me alone in the Food Court. I walked to the glass doors. Rheingold was standing impatiently outside the blue Ford, checking her watch, crossing and uncrossing her arms. When she spotted me, she gave me as cold a stare as you can give somebody without damaging your eyes. I knew I hadn't seen the last of her.

Even the hint of a charge like this could ruin me in one day. Nobody wanted an accused child molester investigating a case. Even if I did find clients, nobody would talk to a man accused of a sex crime or let him near schools or kids. What an effective—and shrewd—way to neutralize me. Because I had to spend time around schools and kids if I was going to hold on to this case. Tobias had to be unnervingly clever to figure out all by himself how to hogtie me like this.

I had no doubt Gans was right: the state would pull my license until the investigation was completed, and that could take a year, even longer. We couldn't survive a month financially if I lost my license; we'd lose the house for sure. I started sweating and shivering, feeling like some wasted, weak-kneed crackhead with a liquid stomach. I don't think I'd ever felt dirtier or more soiled. Or more frightened.

A few minutes later, the now-jovial twosome walked out of Lightning Burger towards the Mall exit. Gans glanced my way and waved. The next time he saw me might be in court. Luis winked, but motioned me behind his back to stay back. He was carrying a sack of coffee and pastries, urging the cop to come back anytime, walking him out to his car. I saw Gans clap him on the shoulder.

I probably looked as bewildered as I felt when Luis returned. I muttered, "Jeez, pal, don't let our friendship cool your new relationship . . ."

He waved me quiet. "Please, Kit, you know better. It was a useful few minutes." He steered me into his restaurant and brought over a fresh cup of coffee, the large size, which I drank greedily. "I believe that they're good, honest investigators," he said, keeping his voice too low for his employees to hear. "Gans was frank. He told me, 'Look, your pal's jacket is clean and he seems like a straight guy, and we see lots of sickos. The kid didn't call, neither did his parents. It was anonymous.' "

Luis paused while some more coffee arrived. "Gans said he had the sense that Tobias was uneasy when they came to his house. All the boy would tell them was that you, Kit, had come to see him at school and asked him some questions that made him 'uncomfortable.' He refused to say any more than that. Then the father asked the investigators to leave, claimed he wanted to speak with his son. Gans said that Tobias seemed uncomfortable, but that he was very poised for someone that age. He surely showed no inclination towards pressing charges. But you've got to treat this extremely carefully, Kit. A single misstep and you could be ruined. You will have to be very, very discreet, not an American trait."

I finished a second cup, and decided against more. I didn't need to get any more wired than I was. "Luis, how did you know they didn't have a strong case?"

He smiled. "It wasn't too difficult, Kit. You don't yet understand the police mind. First, you would have been brought into a more intimidating setting, probably a police station or interrogation room. Second, when police officers have a case against you that is strong, it comes through in their whole demeanor. Their look says 'gotcha.' I know." We both let a little silence pass at that.

"Luis," I said, "maybe I should walk away from this case. Maybe Shelly Bloomfield should get herself a different investigator, one who can't be completely outmaneuvered by a junior high school kid. Maybe what we need here is an exorcist, not a detective. I feel like my whole life is on the line here."

"Please," he said firmly. "Your life *is* on the line, in certain ways, but not in the ways that matter most. You have your family; you and they are well. Of course you're afraid. But you're a fine investigator. What you're failing to see here is that you are getting close to something, or none of this would be happening. If Tobias didn't make the call to the authorities, he knows who did. We need some other sources of information. Do you have any people who *really* know what's going on in Rochambeau?"

The bulb snapped on. My first good idea. "I know where to find some of the best," I told him.

Eleven

I HAD CALLED what was probably the most unusual meeting of my investigative career for seven p.m., pleased to have stopped reeling and started pushing forward. First, however, I made the stop I dreaded most, now that I knew Ben would be safe.

The vet was standing in the waiting room as I walked in, stroking an old man's nervous beagle. Mitch Camersen never turned away a sick pet or worried pet owner. His animal hospital always had a stray dog, cat or rabbit up for adoption. Once, he'd tried talking me into acquiring a pit bull that had been shot by the Jersey City police and abandoned by its owner, a suspected car thief. Gentle as a rabbit, Mitch assured me.

The waiting room wasn't too crowded. At the end of the row of chairs, a boy suddenly turned and kicked his mother in the leg as she pulled frantically on a leash, only marginally restraining an overenthusiastic spaniel as she yelled, "Stop that! Stay still!" It was not entirely clear who she was yelling at; neither the dog nor the kid paid much attention.

"Joshua," she complained loudly, "I'm extremely disappointed in you."

"Come on, Joshua," said the vet. "Let's get you into the X-ray room." Turned out Joshua was the dog. He gave the beagle a good-bye pat, then handed Joshua's leash over to an assistant, a brawny woman named Rita who took no prisoners, canine or human. I had seen Rita wrestle some mighty dogs into submission. "I'll be with you in a moment, Kit. Why don't you wait in Examining Room B?"

I paced back and forth in the empty, alcohol-scented examining room, looking at snapshots of dogs, cats and assorted reptiles and rodents, all patients of the Camersen Animal Hospital. On the other side of the door, various unfortunates yelped, woofed and whimpered.

I'd never quite gotten around to taking a picture of Percentage for Camersen's picture gallery. I promised myself that if the old guy came through this, I would. Meanwhile, I heard a scuffling and yelping next door, but whether it was Joshua or the boy who was being subdued, I couldn't tell. Either way, my money was on Rita.

No matter what I looked at or thought about, the DYFS visit intruded, causing a lump to rise in my throat. What would life be like, I wondered, if a formal charge was made and I had to spend the next year or so waiting to go to trial?

Suddenly the door burst open. In hobbled Percentage, dragging Camersen behind.

"Hey there, dum-dum," I said, dropping to the floor as Percentage whined, waggled and slobbered, his tongue raking my face, his tail batting against the wall. "How ya doin', guy?" (Men are obliged to do guy talk with their domesticated hunting dogs.)

Even if he hadn't cheated death, Percentage would have looked thrilled to see me. Often, when I came out of the bathroom, he was insane with joy, as if I'd been gone for decades. And he was just as delighted to see the UPS man or Jehovah's Witness missionaries who more than demonstrated their faithfulness by resolutely plying our unresponsive streets without, to my knowledge, ever racking up a convert. Maybe a dog's enthusiastic hello was some compensation.

Actually, he looked better than I'd expected. He looked like he'd lost some weight, but none of his enthusiasm; his big brown eyes shone with joy. But the vet hadn't been kidding about the physical damage he'd suffered. He was dragging his rear right leg behind him as if it was made of wood. Percentage gave me a get-me-out-of-here look, or so I inferred.

I felt a flash of fury. How could somebody do this to so open-hearted and harmless a creature?

Camersen felt the same way. "Bastards," he muttered, scooping up the huge dog and putting him on the stainless-steel examining table.

"The good news is that he's going to be okay," Camersen said. "The bad is that he will never regain full use of that leg. There's very little muscle function in it. If it should atrophy, we might have to remove it one day, but we'll cross that bridge when we come to it. It's some kind of nerve damage, brain damage, if you will." Lucky, I thought. His brain was Percentage's least vulnerable point.

"Arsenic poisoning," Camersen went on, patting Percentage. "A close call, but you got him in here in time. By rights, he should have been dead; the amounts in the meat we tested were enormous, lethal." He shook his head sorrowfully. "How could anybody do that to a dog? His hunting days are over."

I had to suppress a laugh. If all we lost this week was Ben's trash-removal service and the dog's hunting skills, maybe things weren't so bad after all. Camersen gave us some muscle relaxants and told me to ease up on long walks for a while until we could gauge Percentage's tolerance. I was to bring him back in a week. The vet bent and stared into Percentage's eyes, warned him sternly to take it easy, then muttered that people who poisoned animals should be executed.

"Mitch," I asked, almost as an afterthought, "have you had any other cases like this?"

He mulled for a bit before replying. "I remember one last year. Can't remember the details, though. I'll have Trudy look it up. Call us in the morning." As he scribbled a note on a pad, I pulled out a Post-it, sticking it to the dog's medicine bottle, reminding me to check back. Post-its littered my car, the walls of my house, the mirror in the bathroom, a sort of yellow monument to countless undone chores. This one shouldn't be left undone. It was unlikely, but there could be a connection.

I stopped at a phone booth to call Shelly Bloomfield. The dog sniffed and decorated several poles and planters as I dialed the county jail. After her arraignment, Shelly would be transferred to Rahway, one of the toughest prisons in the state. I desperately wished I could help her before then. One thing the past day had accomplished was to bolster my conviction that she was innocent. There was evil stuff happening out here, while Shelly was in there.

For the first time in several attempts, the line wasn't busy. Half the time drug dealers were chatting with their clients, or some inmate far tougher than Shelly was impatient to call her boyfriend.

Her voice, when she was called to the phone, sounded tired,

numb. It had to be a nightmare for her, a place as far away from her well-ordered life as a Rochambeau housewife as you can get. "Oh, Kit," she said, "I'm so glad to hear from you. I sure hope you've got some good news for me; I could use it."

I wish I had. As it was, I had no news for her, only questions. All she needed to hear was that one of her last, best hopes for exoneration was being questioned for child abuse.

"Have you seen my kids? Do you think they're okay? God, I miss them. And Austin, is Austin okay?"

I fudged here, assuring her that the children were fine and the dog was happy under the loving and watchful care of Sandra Vlaskamp.

In the background, I heard mutters and cursing. "I can't stay on too long, Kit. Other people want to use the phone." I felt a wave of guilt; I hadn't done a thing for her.

"Shelly, stay on as long as you can. If we don't get to all of the questions today, I'll come and visit tomorrow. Just a couple of things. First off, did you ever use your husband's gun, the one found in the woodpile?"

"No, never. I told you I hate guns. I never went near it. I don't think Dan did either, much. He went hunting a couple of times, but that was years ago. I would never have it near the kids. Dan had it locked away somewhere in the basement."

"Did Jason know where the gun was? Did any of his friends?"

"Not to my knowledge, Kit. Why?"

"Just trying to figure out how it came to be used to kill Nancy Rainier-Gault, that's all." Behind her, the cursing escalated.

"Well, I hope you're not suggesting that Jason . . ."

"Shelly, we don't have time for this. I've got to get some answers. You'll just have to trust me."

Except for the background cursing, there was silence. School officials had probably told her the same thing when they wanted to put her son on Ritalin.

"I didn't know where the gun was, and the last time I remember seeing it was five years ago when Dan and some of his friends went hunting in Sussex County and nearly blew somebody's German shepherd all to hell. What else?"

"Do you know Tobias Tomlinson well?"

"Sure. Toby practically lives in our house. He's over all the time."

"What do you think of him?"

She paused a hair too long. "He seems like a nice boy, and Jason worships him." Jason's not the only one, I thought. "Toby doesn't talk to me all that much, but he's the toast of the town, your classic superkid—a jock, a scholar, a looker. You sort of want to throttle him." I didn't sense the unqualified enthusiasm I heard from everybody about this kid, which gave me hope. And determination.

"Shelly, this is truth time. I need to know about this boy. Were he and Jason alone together mostly, or were there other kids who hung out with them?"

Another pause. I heard her explain politely to somebody that she would just be a minute or two. "Shit, hurry the fuck up" seemed to be the reply.

"Well, there— God, Jason would kill me if he knew I knew about this. Is it important?"

"Shelly, now! And fast, before somebody throws you off the phone."

She plunged on. "Well, one day he and Tobias *were* up in Jason's room for a couple of hours, it seemed and, well, I don't know, I've just never bought the notion of the perfect kid." (Amen to that, sister, I thought.) "Maybe it's because I don't have one and don't know anybody who does. Tobias is just a little too much. You know—a bit too polite for a kid, too smart, maybe too alert? Maybe it was something in his eyes that I didn't like. I just wondered what they were doing up there all the time and, when I asked, all I'd get was a shrug or some BS about talking. *Please.* When junior high boys say they're up in their rooms talking, call a therapist right away. So this day Jason gets a phone call and the two of them go bolting out of the house—"

"This is recently?"

"Yeah, a couple of weeks ago."

"What was the call about?"

"I don't know. I don't remember if I asked and they didn't tell me, or if I got busy and forgot to ask. He wouldn't have told me, anyway, not Jason. You know how boys are." That surprised me a bit. Shelly seemed a little vague about her son's life, for such a vigilant mother. I did know how boys were, but I would have wanted to know more if Ben got a call and went bolting out of the house.

"Were they alarmed? Angry? Frightened?"

"I couldn't say, Kit . . . But they must have been in a huge rush because Jason left the computer on, which he never does because he doesn't want his sisters sniffing around."

"Would you have any way of remembering the exact day?"

"No . . . Well, wait a minute. I had been reading the *Rochambeau Times*. And there was a front-page story about a new medical building supposed to open downtown. I remember because my gynecologist had said he was going to move into it. So, whenever that was, that would have been the day . . . Late afternoon, close to dinnertime. The boys took off and I went upstairs to get something out of my bedroom. I went past Jason's room and the computer was still on.

"See, I spend some time on my own computer. On America Online. I joined this conference of parents with emotionally disturbed or hyperactive kids. Made a lot of good friends there, got a lot of wonderful support and information. I got on computers in the first place to help teach Jason when he was having his worst trouble, teach him games and stuff."

I reminded her to think about who Jason hung out with besides Tobias.

"I'm getting there, Kit. So, I know I shouldn't have, but I logged onto his Mac . . . There was this locked file, but he was in such a rush to leave he hadn't closed it. I found a whole folder called 'Cyberskulls,' with four names in it—Jason, Tobias, Jamey Schwartz and Harry Godwin. And their telephone numbers. And each of the boys had written about some of the girls in the school, I don't remember which. I just skimmed it. Some of the stuff was pretty embarrassing. I mean, you could look at it several ways, as being normal red-blooded boy stuff or as being a bit disturbing because it was so explicit."

I mulled that one, scribbling down as much of what she was saying as I could. "Was there anything menacing or threatening, or clearly over the line? Anything troubling?" Something had troubled the late school principal a lot.

"Not that I saw. And then I heard Sarah yowl downstairs or something, and I left the room. I really didn't think that much more about it. It relieved me, actually, because I didn't have to wonder anymore what he was doing up there. I mean, boys are supposed to drool about girls, right? They probably hit on girls on

America Online. It's the modern-day equivalent of *Playboy*. Do you think it matters— Oops. Kit, I really ought to go." There was muffled yelling in the background.

"And you didn't read any more?" I persisted.

"No, I was just glad they weren't doing anything illegal. I didn't want to snoop too much. I felt creepy as it was." I leafed through my notes. Our time was running out. "Shelly, were there any girls Jason or Tobias spent time with, any that you can think of? Or talked to on the phone? Any names?"

"They'd been talking lately about a girl named Wendy. I think it was Wendy Mosley; she's in their school. They kept saying she was 'hot.' The Mosleys live in the West End. But that's all I—" The voice in the background yelled, "Okay, bitch, give it up."

"Shelly, give me the names of a couple of your friends in the local support group, please."

"But what on earth . . ."

"Shelly, please." I scribbled the names.

I'd saved the toughest question for last, as detectives do, in case the recipient slugs them or storms out the door. Or hangs up the phone.

"Okay, Shelly. I want you to really think about this. You know that the police found Rainier-Gault's notes on Jason. They suggest she wanted to go beyond a one-week suspension; they suggest she was considering expelling him and there was the possibility that she might go to the county prosecutor. I never felt quite comfortable that all this was about the 'Squeezing the Grapefruit' game. I wonder if there wasn't more than that. You've had a couple of days to think, to go over what happened. I need a very honest answer, for your sake and especially for Jason's. Because if I'm right, and there was something else, then whatever it is Nancy was considering going to the authorities about—well, it's still probably something the school administrators might go to the authorities about. Does that make sense?"

I heard a mournful sigh. "Kit, I've thought about this a hundred times . . ." And then the phone went dead.

The Cyberskulls. It didn't sound like much, but compared to anything else I had, it was a trove. Now I knew that Tobias had some sort of group behind him, and that the accused murderer's kid was in it. I made a mental note to pay another visit to Dan

Bloomfield. He too had had some time to reflect on things. Maybe he'd be more forthcoming this time and had recalled something.

I called Evelyn, who was grumpy and alarmed about my erratic comings and goings. "Kit, where on earth are you? Murray Grobstein said you were at the Mall this morning with some strange people, then you disappeared. The phone has been ringing off the hook. Your insurance reports are overdue—"

"Evelyn, this is an emergency," I told her. "We've got to make a lot of phone calls and fast."

I heard the reassuring click of her ballpoint pen. Evelyn was fiercely independent, but in a pinch, she was the person you wanted behind you.

A few hours later, my family was reunited. I'd retrieved Ben, who was arranged on the playroom sofa with his friend Jared, pondering syndicated reruns of *Beavis and Butt-head*. Percentage collapsed on his L.L. Bean cedar bed and went to sleep, as Em sat by stroking his broad head. "I'll take care of you, sweetie, it'll be okay," she crooned, over and over.

My house was back to normal, sort of, if you overlooked the gauze, bruises and gimpy leg. Ben was barely speaking to me, a good sign. Mrs. Steinitz had issued a ban on candy, Nintendo and Em's walking four blocks by herself to the neighborhood convenience store.

"That woman is a monster!" Em howled. "She should be banned from getting anywhere near children. How could you leave me alone with her? I've been *abused!*" Any other time, I would have laughed.

Jane came in a few minutes after I did, her mother hen instincts clearly aroused by her wounded and troubled flock. She fluttered from son to dog to husband to daughter, checking on medications, surveying aches and pains and emotional states.

"You okay, Kit?" she wanted to know. I smiled tiredly. I decided to wait until later to tell her about the DYFS visit. She'd spent an exhausting day listening to far more gruesome tales of abuse, molestation, addiction, violence and misery.

I don't make a habit of withholding things from her—it pisses her off and she doesn't need protecting—but it seemed to me that enough was enough. We'd talk later, after the rather unorthodox meeting I'd convened next door at Jeannie Stafford and Carol Goldman's.

"Jane, I've got to go out again," I hissed, hoping to escape before Em could launch further tirades about the Baby-sitter from Beyond the Grave. "A meeting. I'll explain later. Cover for me."

Jane leaned over and kissed me. "I always cover for you," she promised.

Twelve

THEY'D DECIDED to christen themselves the Rochambeau Harpies—Sandra Vlaskamp's suggestion, which was instantly and unanimously approved—and they were a potent gathering of unrepentant modern moms.

About the only thing the women sitting expectantly in a semicircle around me had in common was that they were all primary caretakers of children. A couple had part-time jobs, but they were around town most of the week. Otherwise, they were true suburban irregulars: one divorcée fresh from Manhattan who'd recently moved onto Shelly's block, six members of the canine play group, two others whose kids had the same condition as Jason Bloomfield, and a single woman—an adjunct NYU sociology professor—who'd given birth through artificial insemination to (in her words) "a brilliant nine-year-old whose father is reportedly a handsome, mean-spirited med student who's a real prick as well as a figurative one. My fingers are crossed." I liked her already.

The newcomer to Shelly's neighborhood was African-American, and two of the dog owners—Hae Sook (springer spaniel) and Nadja (collie)—were foreign-born, probably standard demographics for a lot of suburbs these days. What made the group more unusual were the long hours they spent in the company of toddlers and preschoolers.

"Let's be honest," Vlaskamp had said as the troops trickled in, "we're all a little odd or we wouldn't be here, would we? I mean, who needs to get involved in *this*?" Nods around the semicircle. The sympathies were obvious.

Perhaps I was making private-eye history. In the process, I might manage to save Shelly Bloomfield's hide as well as my own.

I had convened the Harpies in the large, comfortable living room of my neighbors, Jeannie Stafford and Carol Goldman. I wasn't sure how Jeannie and Carol would react to my SOS, to being identified with Shelly, despite their surprising show of support at the school board meeting. But when I called, Jeannie had agreed without hesitation.

"We know what it's like to be stereotyped and to suffer," she pointed out. "The whole town seems ready to lynch her, and I guess we intuitively think we should stand with women under assault. Even though politically we are real different. No housewives here." Jeannie was a fourth-grade teacher in Ridgefield; Carol was in Manhattan three nights a week, stage-managing a theater company.

By and large, the neighborhood had reacted to the street's first lesbian couple with a yawn, I was happy to note. Not only would property values *not* plummet, but Jeannie and Carol were so painstaking about the house (which far surpassed ours in lawn care and general meticulousness) that a whole bunch of people on the block had guiltily started toning up their own properties. My neighbor Charlie Pinski, initially stunned and deflated by the new arrivals (mostly because he wanted somebody with whom to watch football games), had become great buddies with Carol, a rabid Jets fan and an all-around mechanic always happy to help keep Charlie's vast lawn armada—mowers, trimmers, leaf and snow blowers, mulchers, fertilizer-spreaders—in fighting trim. Their adopted daughter Tracy had made friends up and down the block.

Jeannie was affable and even-tempered, Carol more wary and prickly. But her edginess vanished around Tracy, to whom both were supremely attentive. In fact, both women glowed around their adopted kid. Having two attentive moms had its points, I could see, although both women were clearheaded about the need for some men in their daughter's life. I'd been nominated to be one of them.

Tracy must have understood something about suffering, too. The parents she'd been born to had been butchered in an El Salvador village.

Jeannie and Carol had fit easily into the rhythms and tasks of suburban life. Jeannie said she sometimes wept over the stories she'd heard about lesbian couples in preceding decades struggling to do what seemed so ordinary for them. They were becoming fixtures at school and community meetings, had volunteered for half a dozen local charities, and had even recruited their friend the sociology prof for our little gathering. Jeannie moved around the room with a tray, completing the introductions, offering cookies and veggies and soft drinks.

I was the only man in the room, but I felt oddly comfortable, a bit like a fellow homemaker. I too fussed about my kids' social lives, wedged trips to the market in between work and too many other chores, spent countless hours in crowded pediatric offices, and still always felt I wasn't paying enough attention. In this room I belonged.

I was looking at the very heart of modern suburbia, the cogs that make the engine run, that get the kids to class, coach the games, fill the PTA rosters, drive on class trips, bring other people's sick kids home, keep their houses stocked with cookies, milk, frozen pizza and the latest and best video games. It didn't really boil down to whether or not you worked, but to where your emotional connections were. The Harpies associated themselves in various ways with the plight of the Last Housewife, identified with some of what Shelly stood for and wanted to help her.

"So, Kit," said Liz Hoffman, as I was considering how to begin, "tell us why you've called this meeting. You're hiring all of us crafty dog walkers? All you said was that you need our help." Hoffman, like Shelly, wore the classic no-nonsense gear of the mother at home with small kids—sneakers and sweats, hair pinned up not as a fashion statement but to keep it out of the way of sticky fingers.

"I don't know exactly why I'm here, either," put in Lani Faison, who turned out to be finishing a degree at the Fashion Institute of Technology in the city. Sleek and striking, she wore a close-cropped Afro and a long cotton dress and her dangly amber earrings swayed when she moved. "I have a lot of respect for Shelly, even though I've only known her for a few months. They wanted to put my daughter in a special ed class because they'd misdiagnosed her, something they're pretty quick to do with minority children. Shelly helped me out, she'd been there. She got me to the right psychologist, who discovered that Nia had a learning disability and helped me figure out how to deal with it. So I owe Shelly and I'm here. I don't always agree with her, but she puts her money where her mouth is. But Mr. Deleeuw, I'm not a sleuth. I'd like to know what exactly it is that you want."

I moved to the center of the room. "Look, here's what I can tell you. Shelly is going to be arraigned next week on murder charges. She's in real trouble. The police found the murder weapon in her yard. You've probably read that she was the last person known to have visited Nancy Rainier-Gault, and she had a powerful motive —her son had been suspended for sexual harassment, and the principal was looking into other offenses. I don't yet know their exact nature. Even more damning, Shelly was also heard to threaten the principal, though she does bluster, as you know.

"I believe strongly that Shelly isn't a murderer. But what I need from you is some truth, or some guideposts to the truth. If they confirm Shelly's guilt, then so be it. But if what you help me learn can exonerate her, we've saved an innocent person, a whole family, really."

There were some things I'd decided not to bring up—like the DYFS business. I didn't want to mislead them, though I was. It was the rare suburban parent who wouldn't shy away from teaming up with someone under investigation for molestation. And I had been enjoined to protect Tobias. Whatever I felt about him, he was a kid, though a highly disturbed one.

A stocky woman towards the back of the room, both hands chugging away with knitting needles, put down her pile of pink yarn and raised one hand. "Patricia Caldwell," she said. "Three kids: four, six and nine"—as if that were her Rochambeau ID code. "Just tell me what you need and I'll try to get it for you. I put on three hundred miles a week in the minivan, and I *haunt* pediatrician's offices, through which *everybody* comes. I know the faces of people who don't know I exist. Be specific, please."

Around the room a bunch of heads nodded, but I wasn't sure if they were agreeing with her willingness to help or expressing frustration at my vagueness.

"Look," I told them, "I've taken some heat for signing onto this investigation, more than I would have imagined. Even my wife is sort of ticked. But I'm not interested in the politics here; I need to get some facts. You people have deep and broad connections to this community. I want to know more about what happened. Our best lead is that Rainier-Gault was investigating more serious incidents of sexual harassment, so serious she'd considered going to the county prosecutor. Some boys were involved, some girls were involved. I need to know who. I mean, we have to assume the principal was killed to keep her quiet about something she'd learned. If Shelly didn't commit murder on Jason's behalf, then who did? And why? I doubt she was killed over somebody's grades, even in this town.

"So I need you to help me find out what boys might have been harassing and what girls might have been harassed. What middle-school kids have suddenly switched friends, dropped from sight, are behaving in ways that seriously alarm their parents. And I don't mean losing soccer games. My gut says the answer matters a whole lot."

"But how can we possibly know that's the reason for the murder?" asked Susan, of the dog group. It figured that I'd forgotten her last name, but remembered her basset hound.

"We can't know for sure; it's just my best instinct now—"

"Your best instincts have turned out pretty good so far," supplied Vlaskamp, which I appreciated at that moment more than she could know.

"And," said Faison, "what about the girls' privacy? Isn't there a big ethical question there?"

I held up my hands. "There are lots of ethical questions, and everybody has to answer them in their own way. Here's *my* answer: a woman could spend the rest of her life in jail for a crime I believe she didn't commit. Technically, she could even receive a death sentence. To me, that's the overriding ethical dilemma, the priority consideration, as the lawyers would say. We will be as careful as we can about privacy. But if we don't get some new and specific information about what's going on, Shelly's going away for good. Her kids will never have their mother. And a terrible wrong will have been done.

"And then there's this," I went on. "Some of us have daughters who are teenagers or will be soon. If there's someone running around harming girls, that should be exposed. That's what Nancy Rainier-Gault may have given her life for. We have the chance to do right by *both* of these women. I'll follow the case anywhere it goes. It may not go our way. But none of us would be here if we didn't think the wrong person was behind bars."

I was a bit surprised at the passionate sound of my own voice.

But moral issues cut all sorts of ways: one ethical concern bangs into and overrides another.

I ticked off a few of the details and cues I wanted the group to be alert for, relying as I often did on Jane's insights. "If there's a pack of boys, other kids may know who they are," I suggested. "They give off bad vibes. They brag to their friends. Maybe they pick fights. They probably—says my wife, who is a psychiatric social worker—say suggestive things to girls and about them." Or enter intimate details about them in computers maybe, I thought.

"The girls are a different question. They might be depressed, upset, moody. Somebody who knew them well would see that they were having problems. They may be missing school, or have switched schools abruptly, stopped their piano or ballet lessons, withdrawn from their friends, I don't know . . . You're all parents. They'd probably do the things your kids would do if they were upset."

Vlaskamp contributed some fresh news: a group of women who called themselves the Coalition for Justice was meeting Friday at the high school to condemn the killing of Rainier-Gault and demand that her killer be brought to justice. "What do they think?" she demanded hotly, her face flushed. "That the rest of us *don't* want the killer brought to justice?"

Jeannie nodded. "Women should be very careful of prejudging other women."

"Look," said Carol, "it's not like justice can be taken for granted, not for women. I have no trouble with their meeting. I'll be there."

So, I hoped, would I. "Friends," I said, "thanks for coming. Shelly would be very grateful. But I also have to issue a few cautions. Yesterday, I was threatened in several ways. My boy was beaten up"—there were audible gasps from the room. "My dog was poisoned"—this time, cries of horror.

"We need to be careful. I don't want any of you to get involved officially, to question people or approach potential 'suspects,' anything like that. I'd prefer that you never mention me at all. You should only approach people in the normal context of conversation about the killing—which everybody's talking about now—or about kids, which they're always talking about anyway.

"Anybody who feels uncomfortable after listening to me should feel free, entirely free to decline to participate," I went on. "But I

would ask all of you to respect the confidentiality of this group.
Shelly's life may depend on it. I need a lot of information in a
hurry, and I'm not in a position to be able to get it in the usual
ways. When a friend of mine asked me yesterday"—thank you,
Luis!—"if I knew any people who had access to information about
the town, I immediately thought of the dog play group, the support group, all of you. I thought of all the people you see—
coaches, shopkeepers, therapists, house-cleaners, beauticians,
other parents and kids—and realized I could probably assemble
the best intelligence-gathering network imaginable. But I'm not
looking for spies. I know this is a tough situation for you, with lots
of people in town and lots of the media pitting you against women
who want or need to emphasize the professional side of their lives.
If you'd prefer not to be involved I'll ask you to leave at this point,
with thanks for your time and no hard feelings at all."

One woman, perhaps the youngest member of the dog group,
got to her feet. "I'm sorry," she said softly. "I don't feel right
about it. I'm just not sure. I'm sorry." She didn't volunteer her
name, and I didn't ask it.

"It's okay, Elaine," Vlaskamp said soothingly, patting her arm
as the young woman gathered up her things. "We understand.
Call me later if you need to."

After Elaine left, Vlaskamp turned to the group. "She is confused about all this," she said. "But her husband was very upset
about her even coming to this meeting. It would have been very
tough for her." Murmurs of sympathy around the circle.

I expected a couple of others, at least, to walk out. After all,
what was in this for them? But the rest stayed where they were,
chomping on celery sticks or knitting or just waiting for me to go
on. So I did.

I gave them the names of the boys Shelly had found in Jason's
computer: Jason, Tobias Tomlinson, Harry Godwin, Jamey
Schwartz. I asked them to check sources for any information
about them. I told them I was also interested in a girl named
Wendy Mosley, and that her privacy especially had to be guarded.
We waited while Jeannie passed around some yellow legal pads. I
bet my neighbors had been to countless meetings like this.

"This is kind of exciting," whispered one of the dog owners.

I told them I was interested in learning anything unusual or out-
of-the-ordinary about teachers or coaches at the middle school,

too. I urged them to canvass everywhere for information about
any troubled kids—to talk with the clerks at CD and video and
computer stores, learn what neighbors were hearing about them,
and find out what dog walkers saw, which was nearly everything. If
you walk your dog three or four times a day, you pick up the life of
the street—who's home, who works in town, whose fights you can
hear three doors away. You see the tenor of kids' play, how reckless they are on roller blades, whether they fight or not, how gentle they are with their siblings.

"Here's the sort of things I need to know," I told them. "Who
do Tobias and Jason and these kids hang out with? Where do they
go? What do other kids think of them and say about them? What
was the response to Jason's suspension? Which kids were close to
the principal? Which ones did she talk to a lot? Who are the boys
that kids think are scary, sexually aggressive in the school? What
about the girls? Who hangs out with whom at the video store
Friday nights? Which ones have been acting strangely lately?
Who's troubled? And—well—I would like to know what the word
is about who bashed my son Ben. But don't be obvious about
this," I warned. "Don't push people if they don't want to talk.
You're just curious. You all know how to gather information about
kids: who the likely friends for your kids are, who the good music
teachers are, who are the most sensitive coaches. We need that
sort of stuff."

I looked at my watch. I was due at Shelly's house after this
meeting, to meet with Dan Bloomfield and I hoped—at last—with
Jason.

So I gave the group my final pep talk, reminding them about
discretion and confidentiality, and warning them again in the
strongest way not to confront or question anybody they thought
might be troubled or dangerous. "I need you to listen, not to
investigate. If I thought there was real danger I wouldn't have
called this meeting, but at the same time don't forget that we
know there's a killer out there. So err on the side of caution." I
thought I saw a few eyes widen at that but, again, not a single
housewife opted out.

"We'll need to meet back here Friday and compare notes.
Don't talk with one another about this in between. There have got
to be some patterns out there that would help us understand

what's happening, and I can't find them on my own, so I'm hoping you can help. Any questions?"

Faison wondered aloud why they shouldn't exchange information among themselves. "Maybe that would help us," she suggested. I told her I wanted them to sniff around, then let their information lead me. I didn't want to prejudice them one way or the other.

The Rochambeau Harpies seemed excited. So was I. After two days of menace and mayhem, I had help. Jane had been there, as always. Then Luis. Now, the seasoned infantry. I felt as if I was crawling out of the bog.

I had asked repeatedly if anybody was uncomfortable with what I was seeking. I reassured everybody that they should feel free to refuse, that Shelly would never know, that nobody would hold it against them or even remember it in a day. They didn't seem nearly as rattled as I was.

I was surprised when Carol Goldman spoke, as usual without small talk or preamble. It was an unnerving trait, especially in Rochambeau where "how-are-the-kids-and-family" chatter preceded all human interaction.

"I'm here because I want to feel sure that this person is guilty," she said. The room got quiet. "I don't know Shelly Bloomfield, and some of what I do know doesn't endear her to me. She seems smug, at least some of what I hear her quoted as saying. I know she's been put down for being 'just a mother,' but it seems to me some of that is in response to the fact that *she* puts down mothers who have to or want to work. She thinks that if you don't stay home you're not really taking the best care of your kid. I have a problem with that. I don't want to lead a life that narrowly defined, and I refuse to feel guilty about that. I need to work as much as I need to have a family. And with so many of the people in my theater company sick these days—well, I won't walk away from them.

"But I want to help out here, to know the truth. Shelly Bloomfield might be guilty. If she isn't, though, she deserves to be supported and helped, preferably by other women, not just by men."

I wasn't positive, but I thought that line was directed my way.

"I'm going to the meeting Friday night, too," Carol continued, after taking a breath. "I belong there, standing with feminists for justice, in some ways more than I belong here. I feel a piece of me is in both places, maybe. But I want you all to know that I'll do everything I can to gather information for this group. Maybe I'm straddling the fence, but it's the only way I can work my way around to the truth and to where I really belong. For somebody like me, that's a question you end up asking one way or another your whole life.''

Like those old prairie geezers in black-and-white westerns, Carol didn't say much, but when she did talk it was worth hearing. I thanked Jeannie and Carol for hosting. Many of the women stayed behind for coffee and strategizing, but somehow, I didn't feel as if my presence would help. Besides, I had an appointment. I said good night to the members of my unusual new team and headed over to Shelly's house. Had it been only a couple of days since I was last there?

Dan Bloomfield greeted me at the door. He seemed more relaxed than when we had first met, but his eyes were bleak with fatigue and worry. I could barely imagine how he was coping. His son Jason took up a large share of the living room sofa, playing with the Game Boy in his lap. When Dan introduced us, he grunted the brusque greeting of the adolescent boy. I looked to see if he reacted to me in any particular way—a wink, a leer, some hint of hostility—but there was nothing unusual. Just the usual boredom at being in the company of adults. Could he possibly be unaware of what Tobias was up to? He gave no sign that he knew.

I felt a sudden flash of fear—what if Tobias was here? It hadn't even occurred to me. But I was reassured when I looked around. The younger kids must have been in bed; the three of us were alone.

"Come on in, sit down, have a drink," Dan prattled. "What'll you have? Scotch? A Coke? Seltzer? I kept Jason up 'cause you said you had some questions for him. I hope not too many. He's got to get up at six to finish some math homework . . . and he's got a basketball summer camp tryout. He's captain of the team, you know." Bloomfield's mood was hard to pin down. He wasn't exactly cheerful, but he wasn't somber or grim either. Maybe he was putting on the best possible face for his kids, making life appear as normal as possible. I guess that's what I would have done.

A minute later, I was sitting in the lounger across from Jason, who had been asked by his father to turn the Game Boy off and look me in the eye. He did, more or less. He wore the standard suburban-kid uniform: a baseball cap turned backwards, a Georgetown "Hoyas" T-shirt, baggy shorts down to his knees and four-color basketball shoes. His brown hair stuck out from below the cap. Like most boys his age, he looked bored and uncomfortable when adults forced him to talk. He was a nice-looking kid, but with nowhere near the chiseled good looks of his best friend. I couldn't imagine it was easy being Tobias's best friend, especially given Jason's other difficulties.

I didn't waste a lot of time. "Jason, I've got to ask you some questions so that I can help your mother. I'm sure you're truthful, but I need to remind you that your mom needs help, so I need honest answers . . ."

"Tell the truth, Jason," Dan echoed. "Just like we talked about earlier. Just relax and be completely honest. For Mom."

Jason nodded, face impassive. If his mother's fate troubled him, he didn't show it. "I will, Dad."

"Jason, what's 'Squeeze the Grapefruit'? The game that you were suspended for last week?"

He flushed, but seemed resigned, ready to talk about it, as if he knew it would come up.

His father left the room to get his son a soda, which I appreciated. That might make it easier for the boy to talk. Jason had little of his friend's self-possession or polish. He was restless, looking all over the room, everywhere but at me.

"You go up behind a girl, reach down in back into her shirt. You snap the bra. That's all. Lots of guys do it."

"Did you touch a girl's breasts? Ever?"

He looked to see if his father was within earshot.

"Maybe by accident once," he admitted. "But I didn't mean to."

"But, Jason, the name of the game implies that you touch the girl's breasts. Isn't that so?"

Shrug. "I think some guys used to, but I never did."

"Jason, I need to know this for a couple of reasons. But it's just between you and me. Did you ever do anything else to any of the girls at school? Touch anybody in other places? Talk about sex with them? Ask them to do things with you? Anything like that?" I didn't know any other way to ask these questions but straightforwardly. But I didn't want to press him too hard, either. He was awfully young, despite his gangly size.

"No. I swear it. Did somebody say I did?" His eyes widened.

"No one's said anything much. I'm just asking these questions to try to figure out what happened. To make sure you weren't in some other kind of trouble beyond the suspension, maybe a problem your mother didn't know about?"

The sentence ended as a question. Jason looked rattled, but it was impossible to know whether it was because the questions were being asked or because he knew the answers.

"I never did anything else. I didn't." He was emphatic.

Dan Bloomfield came back into the room with the soda for his son, a glass of water for me, and what looked like bourbon for himself.

"How's it going?" he asked.

"Okay. Jason's answering some really tough questions. I'm asking him whether there could possibly be anything else other than the snap-the-bra stuff that might have gone on, either with him or his friends. I told him I'm not here to make judgments, I just need to know."

Bloomfield mulled that for a bit. "And what was the answer?" he asked his son.

"No, Dad. There was nothing else."

I couldn't read Dan Bloomfield's expression. "Nothing else that you did, son, or nothing else that you know about?" he asked softly.

"Nothing else, period. Nothing else anybody did." Jason's voice had begun to quiver.

I nodded reassuringly. "I'm not a teacher, Jason, or a cop. I'm not here to punish you. I just need some answers to help your mom. Jason, do you have a gang of friends?"

He nodded, and volunteered nothing further. This was going to be brick-by-brick.

"Tobias is your best friend?"

He nodded.

"Did he play this game?"

Jason's eyes widened again, and then he shook his head. His answer was so quick and animated in contrast with his previous grunts that I doubted the truth of it. "No," he said brusquely. "Tobias didn't."

"Could he have played it or some other game without your knowing about it?"

He shrugged. I thought it best not to ask much about Tobias. It wouldn't look good if molestation charges were ever officially brought. "Who are your other friends?" He shrugged. Boys responded to every question with shrugs. It's genetic.

"Tobias, Harry, Jamey, mostly. I hang around with Tobias the most, then the others the rest of the time."

"Did they play this game?"

He shrugged. Clearly, he wasn't going to rat on his buddies.

"Do you know if anybody else did?"

Shrug.

"Jason, I need you to think carefully. You were the one who got suspended, but maybe you weren't the only one playing these games. Did you hear of any boys doing more serious things to girls? Touching them?"

He shook his head and his face was stony. It didn't look as though any more information would be forthcoming.

"If you know, Jason, now is the time," said his father. "For Mom."

I thought that with all of the pressure he was under, Jason would surely have indicated in some way if he knew anything. But he wouldn't budge. Either he really knew nothing else or was absolutely determined not to say, at least not at this point.

"Jason, tell me about the Cyberskulls."

Dan frowned and Jason's mouth opened in shock. Then closed. "What . . . How . . ." His face went white. The cool-adolescent mask was gone. I was looking at a terrified kid. "Uh . . . I've never heard of it."

"You sure?"

He nodded.

"What are the—what did you call them?—Cyberskulls?" Dan demanded.

"It's a computer group," I replied. "Some local boys have a sort of computer club they call Cyberskulls. I was wondering if Jason was part of it or knew anything about it."

His father's question seemed to give Jason time to collect himself. "Never heard of it," he said.

"Would you mind if I took a look at your computer?" I asked. "I hate to do it, but it might be useful for your mother's defense."

"No, I don't mind at all."

Dan Bloomfield now looked completely bewildered, but to my relief, he said nothing.

We marched up the stairs to Jason's bedroom, which was filled with the usual adolescent detritus. Clothes, schoolbooks and underwear were strewn around the room, which was decorated with Megadeth and Nirvana posters. The computer sat on a desk, surrounded by stacks of computer magazines and comics, disks and paper. The only light came from a fish tank that bubbled soothingly along the far wall, in which some neon tetras darted nervously back and forth.

"Can you tell me what this is about?" asked Bloomfield, but I shook my head and he fell silent.

Jason clicked on the computer's hard drive graphic—he had a Macintosh, like mine at the office. A list of folders appeared. Besides the system and applications folders, there were three labeled "School," "Personal Stuff" and "Computer Stuff." Probably all you needed to know about the workings of the young American man. I opened the systems folder and found the normal panels and software that operate computers. The "School" folder had only three files in it, each a book report I quickly scrolled. Nothing. I thought the folder marked "Personal" was my best bet, but it held only a few game and bulletin-board files.

Jason had a software program that could "lock" selected files, which meant you couldn't open them without knowing one or more preprogrammed passwords. Locked files usually had some symbol like a padlock and key, or an alarm sounded if you attempted to open them. But I found nothing I couldn't open, nothing that had been locked. I knew Shelly had found more, or thought she had, but where was it? No Cyberskulls folder or file.

I went up to the main menu and clicked on the "Find" icon and typed "Cyberskulls" into the special box. I clicked again and initiated a search of the computer's files. *No folder called Cyberskulls,* came the reply, after the requisite whirring and clicking. That meant no folder with that name was anywhere in the system. Of course, it might have some other label.

The systems folder had hundreds of items, all the programs that ran the computer's memory, word processing and applications. It would take me hours to go through each one and I couldn't imagine why Jason would put the folder there. He appeared to have gotten rid of it. But I had to make sure. I noticed a few boxes of new computer disks on the shelf next to his bed.

"Mind if I copy these?" I asked. "I'll return the disks to you and I'll guard the privacy of what's on them."

Dan Bloomfield started to speak, then stopped. He knew computer software; he had to know what I was doing. But he seemed confused as to whether or not to let me go on.

I wanted to make copies of Jason's folders and I also wanted to see his reaction. Private investigators didn't need warrants. Just gall. But the boy merely shrugged for the twenty-ninth time.

It took me less than ten minutes to copy his files onto the disks. If there had been anything incriminating in the computer when Shelly saw it, I was pretty certain it wasn't there any longer. Jason wore an I'm-glad-this-is-over expression but didn't seem especially anxious. His father looked more perplexed by the minute. I thanked Jason, said we were finished for now and walked downstairs with his father.

"What was that about?" Dan Bloomfield demanded when we were seated again. "Is there something going on here that I ought to know about?"

A shadow moved at the top of the landing. "Just fishing, Dan," I told him. "I'm afraid you'll have to trust me for now. I heard some reports about kids and computers and just wanted to make sure they don't involve Jason. They don't seem to."

The shadow drifted on upstairs.

Bloomfield wasn't buying it, but it didn't really matter.

"How's it going?" I asked him.

"It's hell," he said wearily. "I've hired a baby-sitter all day for cooking and housework, and to keep an eye on the kids. But I'm a wreck. I try to visit Shelly each day and still keep some focus on my company . . ." He shook his head.

"I thought I might have heard from you," I said, probing a bit. "Usually, the spouses drive me nutso."

"I'm already nutso. I guess I've just been too overwhelmed. I still don't really believe any of this is happening. What do they call it—'denial'?" A good, but not a great answer.

"Listen. About the shotgun," I went on. "If Shelly didn't kill the principal, then somebody else did, right? Somebody else who knew where your gun was. You follow me?"

His face registered shock, as if the thought had never crossed his mind. This guy was spinning, all right. "Yeah, I guess I do. Sort of."

"But Shelly tells me not even Jason knew where it was . . ."

"That's right," said Bloomfield, "though I can't swear he didn't come across it."

"Can I see where you kept it?"

The basement was well ordered and clean, the surest sign in any suburban household of a full-time homemaker in residence. There was a workbench over on the left, with racks and bins for drill bits, screws and nails. The washer and dryer were on the far side of the room, and behind us as we came down the stairs was a built-in storage closet.

"The police were all through here," Dan told me, "but everything is pretty much back where it was."

Shelly was right: nobody could accidentally have stumbled across the gun. To get to it, you had to open the door of the storage closet with a key stashed on top of it, pull open a heavy wooden drawer, then open a steel case inside. The shells were kept in a separate drawer. "I curse the day I ever bought the damned thing," Bloomfield muttered.

"And you're telling me there was no sign of break-in? Nothing moved or disturbed?"

"Not that I can recall. No, everything is still in place. And since the gun isn't here, of course, I haven't locked it up again. When the police arrived Saturday, they wouldn't tell me what had happened at first. Shelly was in the kitchen; I was watching a ball game. They knocked on the door, then came rushing in. Some of them had their guns out. They acted as if we were criminals. They showed me a warrant, asked where Shelly was, then asked if I owned a gun. I said yes. I couldn't even imagine what they wanted. I knew Shelly had gone to see the principal. She came back and told me it was unsatisfactory, that the woman was unreasonable, that she was going to make a federal case out of Jason . . . Shelly said she was going to appeal to the Board of Education. But we hadn't talked much more about it. Then all of a sudden there were cops in the house, the kids were all upset and Shelly started screaming at the police about frightening the kids. I brought the detectives down here, opened up the closet and all, and the gun was gone. I haven't a clue what could have happened to it."

Bloomfield was trembling. This was clearly rough on him, remembering the minutes that had left his family in pieces. He kept looking around as if somehow he would come across something that would help it all make sense.

"I kept saying *what is this about? what is this about?* but they just kept asking Shelly and me about the gun. Did she go out? Where? What time? What was Rainier-Gault doing when she left the school? Did Shelly come straight home? Did she see anybody else? Where was the gun? Then after a few minutes this officer knocks on the back window. He's holding my shotgun, with a handkerchief wrapped around his hand."

Bloomfield took me back upstairs and out the back door. Even with the light on, it was hard to see much of the yard. There was a red brick patio, a lawn that looked pretty long and was enclosed by a wooden fence, a flower bed and the garage beyond. Next to the garage was a neatly stacked pile of firewood, the top half dozen logs removed and piled on the ground nearby. That, said Bloomfield, was where the shotgun was found. I shook my head. Whoever had tried to hide it might as well have propped it against the front door.

"When's the last time you'd been in the backyard before the police came?"

"I don't really remember. I don't usually use the back door, except when I go to the car. I must have been in and out—I went to the hardware store that day."

"Would you have noticed if the woodpile had been disturbed?"

"I doubt it," he said. "For one thing, the kids are always climbing on it and the dog was likely to retrieve a log or two. You know how it is with things right under your nose. You can miss them easily enough." I sure could.

"Where *is* the dog?"

"He's staying with one of Shelly's friends, Sandra Vlaskamp. I can't handle him and everything else too, I'm afraid. The kids miss him." I noticed he didn't.

"Dan, I'm curious. These charges against your son, the suspension—how come you didn't go with Shelly to see the principal?" I tried my best to keep the question chatty and neutral and I had deliberately saved it for the end of our conversation. But I knew *I* would have been there. Jane too. If my kid was going to be disciplined on sexual harassment charges, we'd *both* want to hear all about it.

He seemed to tense slightly but answered without any audible edge. "I feel rotten about that, believe me I do. But Jason was always Shelly's turf, pretty much. We fought a lot about him. Early on I'd agreed that he needed a special school. He was wild, uncontrollable. I thought he should be medicated, or at least that we should try it. Shelly fought like a tiger for that kid, and she sort of always handled things involving him. I don't know, I didn't get the seriousness of it. I mean, yeah, it's probably wrong to pull a girl's bra. But throw him out of school? Make it into a big thing like this? I mean, come on, we all know boys are interested in girls. And their breasts, if we're going to be frank about it." We were obviously going to be. "You know?"

"I don't know, Mr. Bloomfield," I said. "I wouldn't want my daughter to have her underwear touched by anybody without her invitation. And if anybody did, I'd want her to scream bloody murder." If she ever had a bra. "So you didn't go because . . ."

"Because I didn't figure it was that serious. You know, just boys goofing around. And Shelly had always handled Jason's problems. I thought it was a routine thing, maybe a few days' suspension at the most. I didn't get it." Sounded like he still didn't.

I walked around the yard, peered into the garage. There were signs of the police having clomped around—trampled flowers, paw prints on the patio from the police dogs, things all askew on the shelves.

Dan Bloomfield was out of gas and I was out of questions. I had seen a lot, figured out little. Time to head home to tend to my own battered flock. I shook hands with Bloomfield. He seemed nice enough, guileless certainly, but I didn't feel easy about my visit. Not about Jason. Not about him. There were the obvious things—Jason had lied about "Cyberskulls," his father seemed astonishingly detached from his family's most serious problems. Plus I still thought that much of what I had been shown didn't make sense—how the gun was taken out of the basement, where it was stashed. But the Bloomfield boys were acting their roles very convincingly.

Thirteen

THURSDAY DAWNED cloudy and sticky. I had slept better than I had in a couple of days, knowing the Rochambeau Harpies were out there helping me beat the bushes. Percentage appeared at my side of the bed as usual, his tail thumping against the wall, the dresser and my nightstand, his bad leg dragging behind him. I thought he looked like a rakish pirate dog now, injured in some nefarious campaign. But he behaved as genially as ever. He no doubt would have slobbered all over whoever had poisoned him.

The only visible remaining signs of Ben's trauma were a web of deep purple splotches. He'd spent much of his first evening back warring with Napoleon on his computer.

Kids and computers. Jason had had plenty of time, of course, to erase whatever had been in his files. And if he hadn't thought to, our mutual buddy Tobias surely would have. But not knowing what his mother knew, Jason had lied outright, even when told that the truth was critical to freeing her. Why? His father wasn't much help. He seemed unconnected to what was happening within his own family—common enough, I well knew, for harried executives with homemaker spouses.

And the gun kept bothering me. How could someone outside the family possibly get hold of it? Who would stick it in so obvious a hiding place in the backyard? I could hear Leeming's explanation: "Well, Shelly Bloomfield would, if she was in a big rush to get it back to the house and its hiding place and was interrupted." Actually, the chief had a point. What if Shelly had taken the gun out, meant to return it and then, for some reason, couldn't? What if her husband had been coming into the yard, en route to the hardware store? She'd stick it in the first available hiding place—the woodpile—and take her chances. But why would she have taken the shotgun out in the first place? At some point I'd have to line up all of the evidence and seriously consider that Shelly could be guilty.

It was easier to focus now that some steps had been taken to keep things running safely and smoothly at home. Mrs. Steinitz, a.k.a. Mrs. No-No (another of Em's fond nicknames), would be here when the school bus brought Emily home (Ben was going to stay at home for another day or two). Jane's semester was ending at NYU so she could be at home evenings, when she wasn't at the clinic.

Besides Shelly's freedom, I now had my own to think about. This morning, for some reason, I was less frightened about Tobias and the threat of his accusations. Maybe it was because I was finally moving forward instead of reeling back. If I was going to do this private investigating successfully—something that had never in my wildest dreams crossed my mind before my Wall Street banishment—this would be a pretty good test. And if the point of Tobias's behavior was to frighten and paralyze, my best response was to stay calm and active. Besides, if he was as evil as I suspected, somebody had to nail the bastard, expose him and get him help. But that was easy enough to say. I knew all too well I was an accusation away from a nightmare.

Leeming had thoughtfully assigned a patrol car to swing by the house every fifteen minutes or so, and the suggestion had clearly been made to Rochambeau's finest to take their coffee breaks in my driveway. I'd always joked that the official insignia of our police department should be two patrol cars pulled opposite each other so the officers could yak, the steam from their Styrofoam cups rising. Now, I was delighted to look out the bedroom window and see two cars idling in exactly that position.

By this point in an investigation, the heat is on. People have put down their money, are counting on you. Jane was right: you can't stop for brooding or anxiety attacks. The real work is in the details, the conversations, the scut work. I was going to do a lot of that today. I called Evelyn at home and told her I might not get to the office at all. She sputtered about overdue reports and an upcoming court date, then dropped it.

"Oh, well, if you think that's best." Since I never dared act like a boss around Evelyn, it was always nice when she remembered that I was hers. "But do take a few minutes and tell me what's happening," she pleaded.

She seemed a bit hurt that I hadn't filled her in. I had to promise a full update later.

Then I contacted Willie. Though our strange relationship was entering its second year, he remained something of a mystery.

I knew he worked for a giant credit company whose highly computerized headquarters was in one of those antiseptic industrial malls a few miles down the highway from the American Way. I didn't know his age, but he seemed young. On the phone, he sounded, in fact, like a teenager. He never wanted to know much about the cases I asked his help on, just went feverishly to work scanning through real estate, credit card and commercial records. Whatever anybody does that involves the movement of money or goods—real estate transactions, restaurant meals, even medical attention—shows up in a computer, Willie had taught me, if you know how to find it. Willie knew how to find it. I wanted to make him an honest man, offer him a job as the first-ever investigative associate hired by Deleeuw Investigations. But first, I had to meet him.

Willie—whoever he was—was a mostly retired hacker. He'd once been able to tap into heavily encrypted computers as easily as most people opened their refrigerators. But he never did it to steal. He believed strongly, he insisted, in the hacker ethic that all information should be free, beyond the control of corporations and governments. To that end, he despised codes, passwords and locked files. I asked him once why he was willing to bust into records for me. "I need a new trackpad," was all he would say. Or, "There's a sweet little RAM-doubler I have my eye on." I was careful never to ask how he got his not-exactly-legally-obtained info. And he never told me. I could honestly swear I didn't know who he was, should some prosecutor haul me in front of a grand jury and demand to know my source.

Our arrangement was originally dependent on pay phones. Now that Deleeuw Investigations was on-line, I also sent him messages through a private New Jersey bulletin board. The Deadbeat Dads I collared would have been shocked to know they'd been nailed by Willie. They'd invariably left their families pleading poverty, but the first time they took the young receptionist down the hall out for dinner at the toniest flocked-wallpaper restaurant in Hoboken, or bought her a diamond-chip locket with their Amex, they were mine. Willie knew not only where they were but could show they'd been liars about being poor. Astonished and unnerved, the Deadbeat Dads often wrote child support checks right on the spot. Sometimes they even kept them coming.

I paid Willie $250 for each case he worked on, slipping the money beneath the door of his studio apartment in a nearby town. A couple of weeks ago, unable to shake my curiosity about him, I'd driven into the apartment complex's vast parking lot, pulled behind a van that left only half of my Volvo visible and waited with the new handy-dandy infrared binoculars I'd mail-ordered from a private investigators magazine.

The binoculars, a new computer and modem, and a pocket tape recorder were my modern-day arsenal. Plus, of course, the creaky but dependable Volvo, a chariot if ever there was one. Since I'd never been able to stomach touching the gun I'd bought five years earlier, I was considering having a metallurgist melt it down. I couldn't countenance selling it or even giving it away, wondering if it might wind up in some hothead's unsteady hands.

I settled in with my binoculars. I'd just spoken to Willie at his office, so I knew that he wasn't home. Sure enough, half an hour after I dropped off the envelope, a little Hyundai pulled up in front of the apartment door. A young man ambled out, unlocked his front door, scooped the envelope from the blue shag carpeting and stuffed it in his pocket.

I guess I'd been expecting somebody a lot nerdier. Willie looked like a surfer in one of those old Southern California beach movies: lanky, huge mop of blond hair hanging over his face and down his neck. He looked sixteen in his denims and T-shirt though he'd sworn to me he was over twenty-one.

The binoculars were quite good. Willie was whistling, his blond head bobbing up and down to the music coming in via the headphones he wore. He was clearly one of those young Americans who was wired from birth. I watched him saunter back into his Hyundai and speed off, probably to spend his mildly ill-gotten compensation. I liked the looks of him. Plop Willie in any mall in the Northeast and he'd look like he grew out of one of the potted plants.

Next time we'd talked, I couldn't resist. "I guess I was expecting some guy with a white shirt, pen holder and horn-rimmed glasses,'' I said.

He'd laughed. "Was that you in the van?'' At least he was observant.

"No, I was parked in the Volvo hidden behind it. I think we need to sit down and talk. I want to offer you a job.''

He'd hesitated. "Cool,'' he said finally. "But let's talk in the fall, okay? I've got all these plans for the summer, you know, the shore . . .''

Changing careers is okay, but not till you've taken care of the beach place you've rented with some buddies for the summer. Still, it didn't sound like the negotiations would be all that complicated. Willie wasn't much of a talker, but he sure was a fearsome information-getter, smart and quick. Let's see . . . Kit Deleeuw, disgraced Wall Street commodities trader; Evelyn de la Cretaz, retired town librarian and needlepointer; and Willie . . . whatever his last name was. Backed up by Jane Leon, soon-to-be psychologist; Luis Hebron, illustrious criminal lawyer turned fast-food franchise manager; and Benchley Carrollton, eighty-one-year-old Quaker gardener and philosopher. And the Rochambeau Harpies. What a team.

In the morning quiet, I e-mailed Willie from Ben's computer, hoping the beeps wouldn't disturb my still-sleeping son. *Hey friend,* I messaged, careful not to write his actual name. *This time I'm dropping off something different for you. Some disks. I don't know if this is possible, but need urgently to know if any files have been erased recently. Would any deletions be recorded somewhere on some application or on the hard drive? Pick up at the dumpster at 8?*

I wanted proof that Jason was lying and, even more, I wanted to know exactly what the boy needed to lie about. Even if the Cyberskulls file was gone for good, irretrievable, just knowing that something had been erased would at least give me some hard information to take back to Jason and his father. There had to be something pretty disturbing in the files for Jason to risk letting his mother languish in jail rather than tell me about it. And if anybody could figure out this stuff, Willie could.

I wolfed down some cereal and a banana, gazing wistfully at my Exercycle in the dining room, which the kids now draped their jackets and backpacks over. I needed to get back on it . . . someday.

Before leaving, I dashed back up to kiss Jane and Em, both still asleep, and Ben, who would have gagged had he been awake. Then I let Percentage into the back of the Volvo. He often accompanied me on my rounds, gazing happily out the back of the station wagon as I went about my business. Aside from the fact that I enjoyed his company, he was a great distraction. People looked at him rather than me, and weren't likely to associate my aging Volvo with any sort of investigating. And whenever I needed a reason to be walking around, Percentage could go decorate tree stumps. He seemed to have an inexhaustible supply of urine.

I drove out through early rush-hour traffic to our alternate drop site at the industrial park where Willie worked. I drove around the far end of the parking lot a few times to make sure nobody was sleeping in a car or making love (exactly what one couple was doing one night when I was picking up a printout; the screaming was so intense I thought somebody was getting murdered until I listened for a bit). I left the disks taped underneath the dumpster, then let Percentage out to sniff and take a whiz or two; it would appear to anybody watching that I had stopped for that reason.

But there was no life of any sort nearby, just the cars that came and went in the livelier quadrants of the mostly unoccupied lot. The only sounds were the hum of the highway and some gulls diving and squawking in the tall marsh grass at the edge of the asphalt. It was a desolate spot, a dead corner of suburbia amid the teeming traffic and business. Five hundred yards away was a long, windowless, concrete building that housed Willie's company, some medical laboratories and tenants with names that sounded like consumer research groups or maybe telephone brokerage firms.

Colorless, featureless, drained of activity and aesthetics, the place gave me the chills. What a great spot to dump a body, I thought; it could rot here for years with nobody but muskrats and seagulls to notice. The place practically shrieked *dead end.* I couldn't imagine working here and was even more determined to help spring Willie, though there was no question I'd miss having access to the world's credit records. Though I suspected Willie with a computer and a modem would always be able to make his way through the world of electronic information.

The telephone book I carried in the back of the Volvo listed three Mosleys in Rochambeau. But Wendy Mosley lived in the

West End, Shelly had said, and there was only one Mosley, Michael J., in that neighborhood. I hustled Percentage back into the wagon and pulled back onto the highway. A mile or so away, I used a gas-station pay phone to leave a message on Willie's voice mail that the package had been delivered.

It took me fifteen minutes to get to the Mosley house on Crescent Terrace. It was a relief to drive back into a world stuffed with signs of life—cars pulling into driveways, bikes darting along the sidewalk, the sound of dogs barking. The Mosley house wasn't spotless or perfect—the gutters looked rusty and the lawn had dead spots, unacceptable in homes with truly manic owners—but the stucco walls and leaded glass windows had grace and the over-hanging trees and shrubs seemed to cradle the house with shade and greenery. The garage was empty. I hoped I hadn't arrived too late.

I parked the Volvo in the shade, rolled the windows down for Percentage and went up the walk. The door opened almost the moment I rang the bell. A very thin woman in a white shirt and striped trousers opened the door. Late thirties, I guessed. The look on her face was severe, but I couldn't tell if that was her usual personality or just an early-morning-before-caffeine expression. Dressed for work, perhaps about to leave, she looked busy and mildly impatient, as if she knew I was a salesman and had already prepared the brush-off.

"Mrs. Mosley?" I asked.

She looked at me, frowned. "You're Deleeuw, the detective."

My turn to be caught off guard. "Do we know each other? If so, I—don't recall."

"I read the papers," she said crisply. "And I used to exercise at Buns of Steel, Roberta Bingham's aerobics program. I was in class the day you came to interview her, but I was in a sweatsuit and God knows what I'd tied up my hair with. Thanks for your work in that case."

I nodded. The memory still hurt. Roberta Bingham had had a rough life, and there weren't too many days that passed without my wondering if I'd been partly responsible for what had happened to her.

The face I was looking at seemed to be hurting a lot too. I sensed wariness bordering on hostility as Mrs. Mosley mentally rifled through the possible reasons for my visit.

"I'd like to talk to you," I said. "About Wendy." The look of
pain that flashed across her face left me no doubt that I had been
right to come to this house. The very mention of her child's name
seemed to bring her anguish.

I'm never one for preambles. People hate to be bullshitted,
equating blather with lying and deception. Often, if their first
impression is of a straight-shooter, they feel safer talking with you.

"Come in," she said finally, swinging the door open. "I'm
Rhoda."

"I'm working for Shelly Bloomfield," I said, when she'd led me
into her living room.

"I know," she shot back. "I was very sorry to hear that. Nancy
Rainier-Gault was a wonderful principal and a terrific woman. She
died for the same reason those abortion clinic doctors died in
Florida, assassinated by fanatics . . ." She shook her head angrily.
Her frown had turned into a fierce scowl.

"I'm sorry, I don't see . . ."

"Well, forgive me, Mr. Deleeuw, but I guess you really can't,
given whom you represent in this mess. I'm a magazine editor. I'll
be out of here running for the bus to the city in twenty minutes
and often I'm not back till seven or eight. My husband's a lawyer;
he has even worse hours than I do. He has a phone and a fax in
his car. Between us, we've had to miss a whole raft of parent-
teacher conferences—we do those on the phone—and two of
Wendy's school plays. Shelly Bloomfield, I'm sure, got to go to all
of her kids' conferences and plays. And there are . . . other
things . . . we miss." She seemed to sag, then picked up.

"She has the gall, your client, to suggest we're neglecting our
kids—the Last Housewife, isn't that what she calls herself?—and
then, when her boy gets into trouble, she takes care of the problem—"

I held up my hands to stop the increasingly angry words. I
wasn't going to debate her. She was deeply upset, and I didn't
really get the feeling her anger was about my client.

"Whoa," I said. "You're going too fast for me. I wouldn't have
taken this case if I thought Shelly Bloomfield murdered Nancy
Rainier-Gault. It's more complicated than that . . . a lot more
complicated."

"Not for me," Rhoda Mosley snapped. And then her eyes filled
with tears.

There were cases where you try one thing and then another, and all of a sudden something clicks. But this was my nastiest case yet. Nothing in it came easily, fell into place or followed any logic. On top of that, I had to maneuver my way through this intra-gender war.

I guess it was the teariness that made me realize that this wasn't just a matter of a working woman ticked off about being made to feel like an inferior parent. This was something intensely personal for Rhoda Mosley. She either had reason to hate Shelly, or something was making her feel particularly raw. "Do you know Shelly Bloomfield?"

"No. When would I have time for a social life?"

"Well, how do you know her views on family life?"

"Everybody knows them, she's quite vocal. She speaks up at PTA meetings, school board functions, along the sidelines at baseball games. But we've never met."

If she didn't know Shelly, there was really only one likely possibility.

"It's your daughter, isn't it?" I asked softly. "Something happened to her. Nancy Rainier-Gault found out about it, didn't she?"

She burst into tears and hid her head in her hands, sobbing. "Please leave. I don't know what to do . . . I'm so confused. I need to talk with my husband. I don't think I should be discussing this with you." Which meant she wasn't sure she shouldn't.

"Of course. I'll come back tonight or tomorrow," I said quietly, getting to my feet. "I'll call you first. I'll let myself out."

There was a phone booth outside the convenience store a few blocks away. I made a note to explore one of those skinny cellular phones I saw in the PI magazine. I loved that magazine. I dialed the middle school, where I could hear the usual youthful hubbub in the background when the secretary answered. "Hi, there. This is Mike Mosley," I said. "I'm calling from the city. I was thinking of coming by to pick up my daughter . . ."

"Mosley?" The secretary sounded confused. "Wendy Mosley? She hasn't been in school at all . . . not for weeks. Who is this?"

I said I'd call home, then hung up. Wendy was at home, as I'd guessed. And for some time. She had to be the girl, or one of the girls, who had been harassed at Rochambeau Middle School. Or perhaps worse. I had to get back in the Mosley house, but I couldn't bring myself to barge in on Rhoda Mosley in her state. I hoped the husband didn't flip out when he heard about my visit. I had to talk to them, and soon.

I had expected that Wendy wouldn't be in school. I didn't expect the next bit of information. It came via Evelyn when I called the office. What she really wanted was to badger me about my long-neglected paperwork—there was a Deadbeat Dad case coming to trial Friday at which I was due to testify—but she put that aside to forward a more urgent message. Eric Levin, who'd be representing Shelly at the arraignment, wanted me to call him at once. I knew Levin from earlier cases. His experience with criminal law was expanding accordingly, though he usually brought in a couple of big guns from Newark firms as co-counsel on murder cases.

"Levin," he said crisply when I got through.

"Yes, Eric, it's Kit Deleeuw. Welcome to the case. Steve Dougherty said your firm would be handling it. Good news for our side. What's up?" I assumed he was calling to get a report on what I was digging up.

"Kit, I'm sorry to tell you this," he said, obviously uncomfortable. "I just saw Shelly at the prison. She asked me—instructed me, really, over my strong objections—to call and tell you that she is terminating your services. She no longer wishes you to work on her behalf. She asks that you bill me for your time and any expenses, which we'll pay."

"Eric, are you serious? You know how much trouble Shelly's in. I'm just beginning—"

"Kit, I'm not happy about this, believe me. But I have no choice. My client's instructions were very explicit. Your contract is terminated, your expenses will be paid in full. She asked me to thank you for your very good work but she no longer wishes to have an investigator working the case. I told her how much confidence I had in you, how much help she needs, but she was adamant. I couldn't budge her."

"Eric, this is madness—"

"Maybe, but I have a responsibility to carry out her wishes. Don't try to call or attempt to contact her, Kit. And don't try to visit; you're off the prison's list, too. I'm sorry. I was anxious to hear what you were learning. I still am, if you're willing to tell me."

I said of course I was. That I had lots of lines out and would call him before the arraignment and tell him what I'd come up with. "Eric, can you tell me anything about why this happened? I have no clue at all."

He hesitated. "Kit, you know this is lawyer-client turf. I can't really reveal it. But I can give you my impression, which will go no further, right? My sense is that you didn't sit right with the husband. You visited the house last night? He called her first thing this morning. She told me to cut you loose right after that. That's all I know. I have no specifics. Got to run. Got to get a drug dealer back on the streets." He hung up. The call was terminated, and so was I.

Fourteen

I DECIDED to pretend Shelly's call hadn't happened, at least for the rest of the day. I had defied state authorities and was investigating a beloved teenage boy who was one phone call away from having me arrested. I had a computer hacker stealing data and checking private consumer records. I had persuaded a dozen rank amateurs to blunder around asking intimate questions about the town's children. I had wandered into the crossfire of an intense gender battle. And suddenly I didn't even have a client. Detective-wise, I was racing downhill with no brakes. Forget about the PI license—it would be a miracle if I stayed out of jail.

What could have happened between my call to Shelly yesterday afternoon and the call from Levin this morning? Was Levin right? Had I really triggered it with my visit to Dan and Jason? I called Jane on her private line at the clinic, something I only did in emergencies. She had a free hour from noon to one p.m. and thought I should come out and spend it with her. "We need to talk things through a bit, don't we, Kit?" Boy, did we. I could hear the concern in her voice. She was going to tell me to pull out. No way.

But I had to cut back on the mounting pressure. Though terror may be useful on the battlefield, it's distracting in an investigation. I was in plenty of hot water, but I had an idea about how to cool it off—a risky one, but I had little to lose. What would one more indictment amount to? My investigative ethic is simple: you take a case, you fight to the bitter end for your client. The only question was this: would my bitter end come before Shelly's? It seemed increasingly likely.

My cage had been rattled for days; it was time to rattle back.

Make lots of noise, Luis loved to say. Flush the birds from the trees.

I dialed the Rochambeau Middle School again, putting on a deep baritone, hoping to sound like James Earl Jones. His is my favorite voice, the kind of voice that says, "This is God calling. Do what I tell you to do immediately."

"Middle School," said the same secretary I'd spoken to earlier.

"Hello, this is Mr. Tomlinson. I have an urgent family matter to discuss with Tobias. Right away. Call him to the phone, please." I didn't sound much like Jones, but I impressed myself nonetheless. I'd mimicked the CEO voices I knew from Wall Street, voices that were busy, that eschewed small talk, that faced pressing decisions and had no time for fiddle-faddle.

Apparently I impressed the secretary too. "Right away, Mr. Tomlinson. But it will take a few minutes to find and bring him here." She understood that this voice should not be kept waiting.

Tobias's father owned a manufacturing company, I remembered. According to local rumor, he was beyond loaded. I felt a sudden chill when I thought of all the lawyers he could hire to pick clean whatever bones DYFS left behind.

What a waste, for that kid to have all that money. Though I had learned in my work that at least one cliché is true: money not only doesn't buy happiness, it can also bring more big problems than I would have imagined. These were often the kids who rattled around empty houses on weekends; kids who had the money to buy expensive cars they could crack up while drunk, whose big homes and excellent sound systems and stocked liquor cabinets drew unsupervised parties.

I knew what Shelly was forever going on about. Kids did need attentive people around. Her mistake was in suggesting that only stay-at-home parents could be attentive enough or attend in the right way. What she was really saying, deliberately or not, was that only moms would do.

But that was one clock that was never going to be turned back— there just had to be ways for people to work *and* for kids to be cared for.

"Hey, Dad?" The voice seemed incredulous. Didn't sound like Tobias was used to hearing from Dad. No shock there: nobody could have been paying much attention to Tobias.

"Hey, Tobias," I said in my normal voice. "It's your buddy,

from the other day. From the playing field, remember? Listen—
and I *would* listen if I were you—I understand that you've got
problems. You couldn't behave the way you do if you didn't—"

"Hey, you can't . . ."

"I'd listen, Tobias. You're too smart not to hear what I have to
say. I assume there's something wrong with you or you wouldn't
be doing what you're doing. I mean this sincerely. You need help.
But in the meantime, I would be very careful about throwing accusations around, given what I'm learning about the Cyberskulls . . ."

There was a lengthy silence at the other end of the line. At least
I had confused him. His old poise seemed to have evaporated.
Now to cross my fingers, lie and hope I could scare the shit out of
him.

"I've got the Cyberskulls stuff, all the files. I'm printing them
out and I'm making copies. If anything happens to me or to anyone near me, to any person or animal or car, for that matter, the
printouts go straight to the school authorities and the police. I can
burn this stuff or I can burn you." Now I was trying a rough
Deleeuw approximation of Clint Eastwood. "And if one more cop
or investigator comes anywhere near me, even drives by my house,
DYFS'll get the files as well. You'll spend a helluva lot of time
telling shrinks your problems, which you ought to do anyway."

"But you don't . . ." He sounded almost pleading at first,
wounded. His voice had dropped to a whisper. He must have been
extremely uncomfortable having this conversation in the middle
school office. "I mean, that's total bull . . . uh, false, Dad. That's
crap . . . I mean, you can't mean that." Poor Tobias. Guess he
wasn't free to be his menacing, slick self with the school secretary
listening in.

"Sure I mean it," I said bluntly. "Did you really trust Jason to
do the job right? It was all in the trash bin on the hard drive. He'd
forgotten to empty it. Can you believe that? God bless the Mac."
Apple computers all have little trash-can icons that you can toss
unwanted files into. If you don't specifically "empty" the trash,
whatever you've tossed remains, giving you—or someone else—a
second chance. It was a good, plausible explanation, one that even
clever Tobias might momentarily buy into. If only it were true.

"Tobias, I found the contents profoundly disturbing, especially
in light of the accusations you seem to be making against me. The

thought of a lawyer going through this with you—perhaps on a witness stand—is appealing." I brought myself up short. Monster, maybe, but still a kid. Don't overdo it. And I couldn't be one hundred per cent certain he had anything to do with the attacks on Ben or Percentage, either.

"Tobias, I have no quarrel with you. I never did. If you're in trouble, I'll help you. But you've got to give me a chance."

More silence. Bingo. At least, the chance of bingo. If I was totally off the mark, he would have hung up.

"Hey, look . . . I . . . we should talk about this . . ."

"My office number is in the phone book, Tobias. Look it up. Give me a call."

I hung up. Let him sweat it. I murmured a silent prayer I could somehow figure out what *it* was.

I called Evelyn back and told her this was her big chance to help sleuth. Hell, if I was exploiting housewives, why not retired librarians? I asked her to drive that afternoon to the Bloomfield residence, to park across the street several doors down, facing the house. I wanted her to watch whether anybody came in or out between two-thirty and five p.m. "I know it's a long time to just sit there, Evelyn, but I need to know. If a patrol car cruises by and asks you what you're doing there, say you're just gawking, like the people at O. J. Simpson's house were. It's not illegal."

I was alert to any trepidation but she sounded positively delighted with the assignment.

"Great, Kit. I've been bored out of my wits this week. Of course I'll go. And I'll take extremely careful notes."

I added the usual cautions: stay away from the house; don't leave the car; don't talk to anybody; don't follow anybody; and for God's sake don't ask why you're doing this. She snapped that she knew quite well how to carry out a surveillance, thank you, and that I should get along with my business. Right.

Next I called the Rochambeau Animal Hospital, as the Post-it affixed to my windshield reminded me in big letters. Camersen came on quickly. I heard the usual yipping in the background.

"Hey, Kit. How's Percentage?" The vet wanted to know every detail: how many walks Percentage had had; his eating habits; his general comportment and disposition; the nature, frequency and consistency of the dog's bowel movements. Only after my full report did he give me his news.

"Kit, we looked up the other arsenic poisoning. Actually there were two, but one was behind an industrial plant out on the highway, not a deliberate poisoning. Some pesticide laced with the stuff. But there was another incident here in town just like yours. A dog found in a comatose state near some meat leavings laced with enough arsenic to kill a dinosaur. This one didn't turn out as happily. The dog was dead by the time they got him here. That poisoning was in the West End, though, so I presume they're totally unrelated. Sadly, dogs get poisoned sometimes, usually by outraged neighbors upset about barking or something." Camersen launched into some clinical details of the dog's symptoms.

"Got a name, Mitch?"

"Jonah—wonderful dog—a golden retriever—"

I interrupted him before he got carried away. "I meant the owner's name."

"Oh—yes. Owner's name was Rhoda Mosley. Came racing in with the dog one afternoon. Their daughter came in with her. I don't think I've ever seen a child so broken up, though I wish I could remember her name . . ."

So the Mosley's dog had been poisoned too. I had no trouble figuring out which number to call next. Rhoda Mosley still hadn't left for work; she answered on the fourth ring. "Look, Ms. Mosley, I know all this is tough for you. My dog was poisoned this week too. I think I know what's going on. I know why Wendy isn't in school and I think I know who's responsible. It's absolutely essential I come over tonight and talk with you and your husband. I think I can help put a lot of minds at ease. And maybe help save an innocent person. I can't swear to it, but I think I am onto at least a part of what caused Nancy Rainier-Gault's death. I'll wait until your husband gets home. I'll be over at eight tonight. Okay?"

"I don't know." She sounded frightened and uncertain. "I don't know."

I said I'd be there and hung up quickly before she could say no, because we both knew that no matter what she said or did, I was going to be on her doorstep at eight. The worst she could do was not open the door. She could also, I suppose, have her husband mash me. It wouldn't be the first time. Before I became a private detective, such possibilities would have been upsetting. Now, they were just part of the job description.

It took me half an hour—including a quick stop at the dry
cleaner's—to drop Percentage off at home and get out to Jane's
clinic. Paterson is a troubled industrial city whose glory days are a
century past; it has neighborhoods as rough as the worst parts of
Harlem or Watts, but wonderful markets and booming immigrant
communities as well. In her cramped office, Jane got to see the
refugees from the old town's worst troubles, the drug victims,
the nineteen-year-olds with three kids, the wanna-be suicides, the
women beaten unrecognizable by boyfriends and husbands, the
molested and assaulted children, the abandoned AIDS victims
shunned by families, friends and employers. Rough stuff. As much
as I heard her talk about it at all, I only really appreciated what she
faced on the occasions when I came to see her at the clinic, located in the basement of Most Precious Blood Hospital.

Visitors had to pass through a metal detector and sign in
through two checkpoints. At least twice in Jane's time here, jilted
lovers had come in shooting. She had once pointed out to me the
bullet holes still in the ceiling from the second attack, in which
one of her clients had been wounded in the hallway just outside
her office. Had the woman still been talking with Jane, there
might have been two people shot that day. I am sometimes afraid
for Jane, working here, but if I suggested a calmer job, she's surely
ignore me. It just wasn't my decision, however much I wished it
was.

I parked near the emergency entrance and told the guard my
wife worked inside. He waved me on. As I was signing the register
at the reception area, I caught sight of Jane coming out with a
patient, a stocky dark-skinned woman with bruises on the left side
of her face.

Jane's office is little more than a Formica-topped brown desk,
two chairs, and a photograph of some nameless Vermont stream.
The idyllic image had as much relevance to its surroundings as the
moons of Jupiter did, but perhaps her clients found it soothing.

In the hallway outside, a dozen people sat stoically in chairs,
some with laps full of children. Another dozen people sat in the
waiting room. There wasn't a face that didn't look grim. Paterson
seemed a lot farther from Rochambeau than fifteen miles; it felt a
couple of continents away. For all our ups and downs, I felt awash
with good fortune.

"Hello, Mrs. Marcos." Jane smiled at one woman sitting expectantly about five chairs down the line. "I promise you, you're the first appointment after lunch." The woman smiled back and nodded, stroking the hair of the bright-eyed little girl in her lap.

In Rochambeau, a waiting room with such long lines would have sparked an uprising. But there were no complaints in this hallway, just resignation and fatigue. Jane tells me she spends most of her time with people whose lives she can't really improve. What keeps her going is the occasional breakthrough: the referral that pays off, the guidance that registers, the man who gets clean, the woman who earns a diploma.

Jane joined me and we moved away from her office. "Business looks good," I said, when we got out of the hallway.

"Business is always good here," Jane said softly. "It's always good when nobody has any money and everybody has lots of troubles. I haven't seen a health plan card in a month. I'm not going to today, either."

The cafeteria was up two flights of stairs—a long, bingo parlor–style room with harsh fluorescent lights and narrow tables sprinkled with crumpled napkins and soda cans. It reminded me of those dining halls in prison movies: at any moment, everybody in it might start pounding on the tables with tin cups. The American Way felt like the Plaza Hotel by comparison. I found myself longing for the spotless booths and snappy service of the Lightning Burger.

There was a long line and a solitary grumpy cook. "We only have half an hour," Jane said by the time we sat down to eat our droopy-looking sandwiches. We found a relatively quiet corner of the room.

"I'm worried about you," she began bluntly, as was her custom, tucking her dark hair behind her ears, exposing the fatigue in her face. Jane is thin, small, only five feet three, but dignity makes her seem taller. No knockout, but highly appealing, even in her exhausted state and in this dingy setting. Her face radiates character. Lesser spouses might not have endured the last few years with so much equanimity and strength. I am always amazed at how comfortable I feel around her—perhaps "safe" is the word. She has lots of common sense and strong intuitive instincts.

If she is short any of the major personality clusters, it might be charm and social grace. Jane has never mastered the art of small talk, has little patience for gossip and none for what she perceives

as stupidity. Many of the child-crazed denizens of Rochambeau
drive her up the wall. She just doesn't believe six-year-olds should
shove slices of hot pizza in their parents' faces and be told pa-
tiently that, sweetie, that isn't really appropriate behavior.

She is capable of extraordinary caring and affection, though
she doesn't go around announcing it. But we have come to depend on it. In our family, nobody doubts her love for us, her
willingness to help or her ability to do so. We all trust her utterly.

"I'm worried about me too," I said, "but I'm striking back." I
filled her in on the morning and told her about my call to Tobias.
Her expression suggested that she thought the move had been as
reckless as it now sounded in the retelling.

"What do you make of Shelly's decision to fire me?" I asked.

"A Mother Hen call," she said. "I'm convinced of it."

"Say again?"

Jane nibbled at her pickle chips. She said she never had much
of an appetite after the stories she heard at the clinic.

"A Mother Hen call," she said. "You talked to her, and everything was fine. You went to her house, questioned her son, went
into his room, you're fired. It doesn't take an FBI agent to figure
that one out. She's afraid for her family. She's protecting them.
Or she thinks she is."

"But I'm not sure she even knew what I talked to them about."

An elderly man in a blue uniform pushed a wide broom past us,
a pile of plastic cups, napkins, bread crusts and paper plates swell-
ing in front of the broom.

"Sure she did. The Last Housewife would call in every day and
demand to hear every detail. Isn't she the one whose religion is
that moms should be on the case?" I ignored the gibe. "She's
afraid of something there. Maybe something she thinks is on that
disk. Maybe something that doesn't even exist, I don't know. But
you can't ignore the juxtaposition, can you?"

No, I thought. I couldn't.

"But, Kit," Jane said, "this is serious now. You don't have a legal
or even a moral leg to stand on any longer. She doesn't want you
probing into her affairs or her family's."

"I can't accept that . . ."

She pushed her plate aside, dropping any pretense of eating.
"This isn't for you to accept or not," she argued. "That's classic
arrogance. First you take on a client who—if you accept even half

of the evidence—probably gunned down a very admirable school principal for threatening her son. Then you investigate the son, and you're off the case. I mean, doesn't that suggest something to you? When you were running around looking for evidence to clear her, that was fine. The minute you set foot in that boy's bedroom and turn on his computer, you're out. You'll find something that will incriminate the boy, that's clear enough. But not if she can help it. And she'll do whatever she has to do to stop you. Maybe we should be grateful she's in prison."

I had to mull that one. "What do you make of Tobias?"

"Sounds like you threw him, but I wouldn't be so quick to interpret his silence as surrender. He might not have been able to talk. He might have thought you were taping him. He might have been genuinely confused. He might withdraw the allegation and do something else. Look, Kit, this boy sounds disturbed, but you're making a dangerous leap by obsessing on him as the murderer. He might be on some power trip here, wanting to inject himself into a case, to feel dangerous, even to gain some attention. But there's no evidence you've told me about that links Tobias to the murder of Rainier-Gault. There *is* a substantial amount linking your client or, rather, your ex-client. You have no business being on this case now, Kit. Don't you see that?"

I nodded. We both knew I wasn't getting off the case.

"The husband makes me a bit twitchy too," she mused.

"What do you mean, 'too'?"

"Well, you don't really like him, do you?"

She glanced at her watch—lunch hour was running out—then headed for the beverage dispensers and returned with two muddy-looking cups of coffee. I tried to remember if I'd ever said I didn't like Dan Bloomfield or that he made me twitchy. I didn't think so.

"Jane, that remark about Dan . . . did I say anything about him?"

"Not directly," she replied. "It was more the way you described him. He put you off. He didn't seem very enthusiastic about your working on the case. Levin suspects you alienated him somehow. At the least, Bloomfield didn't exactly jump up and down to help you, which bugged you on some primal and unconscious level." She winked. Ouch. But she was right: Bloomfield's passivity had troubled me. Was everybody around me smarter than I was?

I fumbled to explain. "He seemed initially overwhelmed, which

I can understand. But there was no 'What can I do to help?' He hadn't seemed to have wondered much about how his gun came to be stuck in that pile of firewood. He was detached, as if this were happening to a second cousin or something. Why didn't Shelly tell him about the Cyberskulls? Why hadn't *he* looked at the computer—he's the software whiz. And if Shelly was so anxious to keep me away from her family, why did she tell me about the Cyberskulls in the first place?''

Jane stirred some sugar into her coffee, which she always drank black when she was working at the clinic. She seemed unusually weary. I felt a pang of guilt. ''Anything wrong, anything out of the ordinary?'' I asked.

Nothing all that unusual, she told me matter-of-factly. ''I had a nine-year-old this morning who'd been gang-raped by her own family, her father, uncle and older brother,'' she told me. ''She's completely traumatized. Hasn't spoken at all. Her little brother called the police. He saw it.''

I squeezed her hand. There wasn't anything I could think of to say that would ameliorate the sadness. There was plenty of suffering in the world, and if you were in Jane's line of work, it poured into your office in a steady stream. All I could do was acknowledge it. She squeezed back, then looked at her watch again and said it was time to return to Mrs. Marcos.

I was glad to have the drive to the American Way; it gave me time to think. Maybe I *should* walk away from the case, but I just didn't think I could. I was no tough guy, but I hated being told what to do. Somebody was trying to scare me off, and I just couldn't give in.

What Jane said made sense. The principal had been closing in on Jason Bloomfield for something beyond bra-snapping, and my very appearance in his room had caused Shelly to try to fire me. Maybe it had never occurred to her that I'd rush over to her house and search his computer for the Cyberskulls file. She seemed smarter than that, but lots of people didn't know the first thing about how investigators really worked. (And I am occasionally one of those people.)

When I pulled into a station for gas, I had another inspiration. I called Evelyn, who hadn't left for her upcoming assignment yet.

''Evelyn, I need to dictate a telegram to send to Shelly Bloomfield at the Essex County Prison. Here goes: 'Shelly. Am remaining on case. Have important leads to pursue. I believe in you. Kit.' ''

She was quiet for a moment. "Kit, do you want to explain this?''

"No, Evelyn, not right now. I think I may get back to the office before you leave. I'll fill you in then."

Another gamble. Maybe I should move to Atlantic City and shoot craps all day. I just wasn't in a quitting sort of mood. Shelly could hire and fire me, as she had demonstrated, but she couldn't control how I chose to spend my day. Let's see what she did now. I had to keep trawling. I had lots of lines out—Willie was looking at the disks, the Harpies were beating the suburban bushes, the meeting was set with the Mosleys, I'd thrown down a gauntlet to the Hell Child and now to my own client. I needed to check out Dan Bloomfield, whose behavior was coming to seem a bit ominous. He'd seemed good-hearted and confused at first, but Jane was right: I was troubled that he didn't seem focused on the fact that his wife was fighting for her life. And something about me had made *him* twitchy too. Something might just emerge from all of this. If nothing did, I'd be working on Luis's payroll at Lightning Burger, possibly on work release.

With little traffic heading south, I made it to the Mall in twenty minutes. The American Way was nearly empty. It often is, post-lunch. The toddlers are at home having their early-afternoon naps. Older strollers always make it a point to clear out well in advance of school closing. I passed by Sneaker World, waving to Murray, and walked through the unobtrusive doors marked "Offices" and up the stairway. The second floor, home to credit agencies and telemarketing firms, lacked the perky colors and foliage of the ground floor. No Muzak either, thank heaven.

At first, I'd had no sign at all on my office door. Mine isn't exactly a walk-in sort of operation. But Evelyn disapproved. She hired a sign company to paint "Deleeuw Investigations" in discreet gold letters on the door. "It's a question of dignity," she told me. She felt the same way about my *Elvis Lives* mug, which she'd forcibly retired.

The name on the door suggested rows of operatives working the phones, squads of investigators lined up waiting for their next cases. In cold reality, the office door opens onto a tiny reception room, now Evelyn's office. A separate door leads to mine, which is furnished with a hotplate and a poster of Winston Churchill that says "Deserve Victory."

With rare exceptions, Evelyn is the only person there when I walk in. But there was quite a crowd today and Evelyn looked as if she were about to jump out of her socks. I had rattled some cages all right, and the lions had gotten out. Who was sitting there to greet me but my good friends—Detectives Peterson from the Rochambeau PD, Gans from the State Police, and Ms. Rheingold from DYFS.

"What a treat," I said warmly. "This must be Law Enforcement Appreciation day! Or you've uncovered a major money-laundering ring. Three investigators just for me?" I understand the appeal of wisecracking more and more these days: it's preferable to crying or wetting your pants.

Peterson stood up to greet me. "Deleeuw. We need to talk." She looked apologetic.

"Kit," interrupted Evelyn, "should I call Eric Levin?" She aimed some withering glances at my visitors.

I shook my head. Was this going to be one of those images I remembered for the rest of my life? Would my kids be reading about me in the morning paper? Despite the fear invading my abdomen, though, it seemed a tad early for a lawyer. Nobody had any handcuffs out.

"If I buzz you," I told Evelyn, "call Levin."

I sat down at my desk, trying to regulate my breathing. Peterson stood with her arms folded; Gans stayed near the door in case muscle was needed. Rheingold pulled a yellow legal pad out of her briefcase. I suddenly got annoyed with myself. Why was I being so passive? These people were hounding me at the direction of some vicious, manipulative kid. Let them put up or shut up. I didn't want to live like this any longer. If there was going to be a nightmare confrontation, we might as well get on with it.

"Look," I said, "we've done this drill before. If you have any formal charges to file against me, file them. Otherwise, why are you here? My position remains unchanged: I never made any improper advances to any child, sexual or otherwise. Nor would I, ever. And you don't have any hard evidence to the contrary, or I'd be arranging bail. I never got to say much more than hello to Tobias Tomlinson before he started leering at me and assuring me he knew how to press sexual molestation charges. Clearly no idle boast.''

Rheingold tried to say something, but I'd decided I wasn't going to make this easy. "I know you're just doing your jobs, but I'm done with this absurd innuendo. Charge me or leave me alone. If you're checking out this case, you know by now it smells. I've never been alone with this kid, I have no history of this kind of crime. By now you've run all sorts of checks and you know I've never bought a porno tape, don't subscribe to smutty magazines, don't call phone sex numbers. To buy that I did anything wrong, you have to accept the notion that, despite having a completely clean record and no history of this kind of behavior, I was suddenly seized by perversion, walked up to a kid I've never met before in full view of my son's whole school and made bizarre sexual proposals. It's crazy.''

"Mr. Deleeuw,'' Rheingold was insisting through my ranting. "Mr. Deleeuw. *Mr. Deleeuw.* Our office in Trenton called a little while ago. We are suspending our investigation. The allegations against you have been withdrawn. We came to tell you that no complaint will be filed, no charges brought. We are sorry for the distress this must have caused you.'' She sounded as sincere as a car salesperson saying it wasn't a good time of year to buy an automobile.

Gans hadn't said a word; he looked embarrassed. Danielle Peterson was watching me closely, perhaps thinking of civil suits and other unpleasantries. Or more likely that was what she did— watched people carefully. Maybe she thought I ought to be more shocked than I was. What she didn't know was that it had to be my call to Tobias that had wrought this. My strategy had worked. There *was* a Cyberskulls file and it had something ugly on it. So Tobias could be frightened.

I was entitled to feel immeasurable relief. Instead I sat blankly, drained and shaken by the way these people could threaten to shatter my life and then blithely show up and say, "Never mind.'' And, to be frank, I was dying to know what was on those files.

"So that's it?'' I asked. "You appear one day and ask me if I'm a child molester and then the next, I'm simply not one? You know this investigation could have destroyed my work, my reputation? Could have cost me my license?'' I was starting to boil a bit, but mostly I felt honor required some righteous indignation. I was, after all, a taxpayer.

Rheingold shrugged. "I spend a lot of time around creeps. I hope you're not one of them." She made it clear that she was far from convinced. "If I find out you are, I'll be back." Gans rolled his eyes. The two of them left, I thought, a bit hurriedly.

Peterson stayed behind.

"Mr. Deleeuw, you told me once that you understood that I was a professional just doing my job. So are these people. Somebody tells us a kid is possibly being mistreated or threatened, you know we can't just say, 'Well, this guy seems straight, so let's forget about it.' We have to check."

"I know all that," I said. I added that I thought that she and Gans were professionals just doing their job. Rheingold, however, I told her, liked to hurt people. Then I took a deep breath.

I couldn't disagree with a word she said, really. If somebody called DYFS and said somebody was threatening my kids in that way, I would expect no less. My anger wasn't really directed at them, anyway. If I was boiling at anybody, it was at this much-adored junior high school kid who had my life—and my case— hanging by a thread while I dangled helplessly.

"Sorry," I told Peterson. "Not your fault. I appreciate your coming here to tell me. *Is* that why you're here, Detective?"

"I'm sorry for all this too. I wanted to make that clear, because I raised this the other day in the chief's office and I could see how much it hurt. I guess I owe you an apology. I never really bought it, but you know this abuse stuff is red-hot right now. We can't write off accusations because you seem like an okay guy."

My knees were trembling. When I'd come in and saw the trio sitting there, I was certain I was going to be led out of the Mall in handcuffs. And I knew most people were like me. They assumed that if the police dragged you off, it was because you'd done something wrong. Even if I'd been freed the next day, half of the people who saw me on television or in the paper would connect me forever with the charge of molesting a child.

"I appreciate your saying that," I said, trying to keep my voice calm, "but this kid is plenty troubled, and not only is he not getting help for himself, but he has the ability to bring a lot of people down with him. He almost got me."

Peterson leaned forward and met my gaze.

"What's going on, Deleeuw?" she demanded. However heart-felt her apology, the desire to apologize had not brought her out to the Mall. Like every good cop I'd met, she had savvy instincts. She sensed that more was happening than she could see.

I tried to guess how much I could trust her. I liked her direct-ness. She was obviously bright and extremely conscientious. Yet she'd been prepared to write me off as a child molester. "Did you think I asked this kid to pose for nude pictures?" I asked quietly.

"No," she said without hesitation. "It never made much sense, just like you said. At your age, there'd probably be some paper, some history. And you'd have to be dumb as a fence post to ap-proach a kid that way in the Rochambeau Middle School, with Nathan Hauser nearby and coaches, teachers, kids all around. No-body says you're dumb, except maybe the chief, and he doesn't really mean it. I don't *think* he means it."

She leaned back on the sofa and crossed her legs. "You still going with the theory that Mrs. Bloomfield is innocent?"

"I'm dead sure of it now, Detective," I said. "The kid's charge . . . it makes me positive. He's desperate to get me off the case. And why would he be? I think that Rainier-Gault found out about something a lot scarier than 'Squeeze the Grapefruit.' And I'm going to find out what it is no matter what kind of threats this Boy Scout Tomlinson makes."

She shook her head. "I don't think it's all that mysterious. I knew Nancy. We were there on some break-ins and one attempted suicide. One beating, too, if I remember right. I think she was simply determined to change this harassment tradition. If she'd found anything more serious, she would have called us in a flash. Her whole mission was to make examples out of the kids who were harassing other kids, to encourage the victims to come forth, in-volve the authorities, get these so-called 'pranks' taken seriously. If she knew about something even worse, why not tell us?"

It was nearly astounding, this sort of collegial brainstorming with a cop who could just as easily been taking my prints and booking me. Yet I was intrigued by the possibility of sharing infor-mation, something easier to do now that I was suddenly no longer a suspected criminal. Talk about justice being blind.

"Detective, don't misunderstand the question, but do you have kids?"

She shook her head. "Hell, I just got married six months ago.

And I made the poor man wait five years before I agreed. I've got a lot of bad guys to put away before I worry about diapers and baby formula."

I laughed. It was a pleasant sensation. I was returning to earth.

"My point is this: kids don't always behave in logical ways. Rainier-Gault might have suspected something and been close to proving it, as I believe. But somebody might have *thought* she suspected something when she didn't. Someone might have panicked. Or the victims involved might have been unwilling to talk or intimidated into not talking."

Her expression said she was taking this in. I plunged on. "I still don't believe Shelly Bloomfield murdered Nancy Rainier-Gault. She had other options. She could have moved her family away—"

Peterson cut in. "No, she couldn't. You're going too fast, Mr. Deleeuw. Okay—*Kit.* Look, this is unofficial, right? You didn't hear this from me. Nancy Rainier-Gault had contacted the county prosecutor's office asking for a meeting about Jason Bloomfield. It was scheduled for Monday but she was killed two days before. I don't know much about what she wanted to discuss, and what I do know I'm not telling you. But if there were criminal proceedings, not just a one-week suspension, then the Bloomfields weren't moving anywhere, you read me?"

I read her.

"Aside from that," she continued, obviously having thought this through, "there was the whole question of his behavioral problems and learning disability. Shelly Bloomfield spent years turning Jason around. In another school district, she might have had to go through the whole thing again. No—I don't think she'd think of moving."

She didn't seem as sure as she sounded.

"Detective, you obviously have your doubts too. Otherwise, you wouldn't be sitting here talking to me about this."

Cautiously she agreed. She chose her next words carefully. This cop wasn't going to say a thing she'd regret having to repeat in court. She didn't know me that well. "I have doubts about every case I'm on, sure. I'm not one thousand per cent on this one. Bloomfield's not what I think of as the type to pull the trigger. But she is a mother hen"—I was hearing that phrase a lot lately—"and her chick was in hot water, *real* hot water. Let's say things got emotional, she and Rainier-Gault exchanged words—"

"Let's say they did, Detective. In fact, I'll stipulate that they did. Here's the big problem with your theory. We agree Shelly's not a killer, that the only way she might have become one was in the heat of the moment. Maybe the principal told her that she was going to ruin Jason, accuse him of something horrible, get him sent away to a juvenile detention center. But you don't bring a loaded shotgun with you for a talk with the principal unless you're thinking about shooting her. That's a premeditated act. It requires calculation. And what Shelly was fighting about was this 'Squeeze the Grapefruit' charge, which is nothing trivial, but not the stuff even a Mother Hen kills over.

"Shelly wanted the principal to cut Jason some slack on the bra-snapping accusation, to rescind the suspension. The boy denied any grapefruit-squeezing. So it would have been messy, yes, but not murder-messy. Why bring a rifle, for God's sake? And then, why bring it right back home? And stick it in a woodpile so close to the back door that the first cop on the scene would practically walk smack into it? The only way to explain premeditated murder was if Shelly knew Rainier-Gault had extremely damaging information about her son and was definitely going to use it. And there's not one bit of evidence to suggest that Shelly knew anything of the kind."

At least that I knew of. Maybe Detective Peterson did. Fat chance she'd tell me if she did. But she might contribute some information involuntarily. I launched one of those sneaky detective gambits.

"And why would she bring the gun practically to her own back door *and* wipe the prints off it? If she was going to be that careful, she'd surely have dumped the shotgun somewhere else. Got rid of it altogether."

Peterson was nodding. So I'd guessed right—no prints on the murder weapon. That helped.

Peterson got to her feet. She had listened carefully but noncommittally. "Holding back information wouldn't be a good idea, Deleeuw. I'll have you for lunch, and the chief will have your remains for a snack."

Like her boss, Leeming, she always seemed to leave with a threat. I sighed and thanked her for personally delivering my reprieve. We shook hands. I vowed to call her if I uncovered any fresh information.

Then, after taking a few deep breaths, I resumed the business of uncovering some. I left a message on Jane's voice mail about the DYFS visit: a break in the clouds, if not the case.

I leafed through my notebook, locating Dan Bloomfield's business card wedged between the pages. "Bloomfield Software," purred the voice that answered the phone.

"Mr. Bloomfield, please. It's a family emergency." That was to make sure he didn't try to duck me. He didn't.

"Yes, Kit," he said, skipping any chitchat. I skipped it too, asking him bluntly if he knew that Shelly had fired me.

"Yes. She told me."

"Do you know why?"

"She told me she didn't feel you were necessary anymore. She didn't like your coming around the house to investigate us. She said that you're supposed to investigate other people, that there are enough people investigating us. In fact, those were her exact words." And, it was clear, his exact sentiments.

"Look, Dan," I said, "Shelly's innocent, and I am developing some strong leads. I can't guarantee anything, but I believe I can help her—"

"No," he interrupted, "you can't. You're off the case. That's the way we both want it. You and I have nothing further to discuss. And I'd appreciate it if you'd drop off those disks you copied from Jason's computer as well. That was a terrible invasion of his privacy. He was very upset. I don't know what you thought you were doing. I agree with Shelly—you're not paid to snoop around our lives. I don't mean to be rude, but your involvement with our family is ended. Is that clear?"

"But," I protested, "I *have* to snoop around, look into everything. Otherwise, I have no idea what's important or what isn't."

"I see what you mean," he said, in the tone of voice people use to get rid of telephone solicitors. "Now, please submit your bills. They'll be paid in full."

"I don't think you see what I mean at all," I said, my voice rising. "Your wife is about to go to jail for the rest of her life and I just told you I might have some leads that could be of great help to her and you haven't even asked me what they are. You don't seem to even give a shit."

"That's beneath contempt, Deleeuw. And wrong. I have people waiting," he said coldly. "Thank you. Good-bye."

He hung up. If Jane were in jail, I like to think I'd postpone a business meeting to hear about any relevant information from anybody. Dan Bloomfield sure didn't resist his wife's self-destructive impulses. Either the guy was completely out-to-lunch or perhaps he had told her something that made her want to terminate me. What would that be?

I dialed Willie's voice mail. "Hi, this is a Spin Doctors fan," I said, then hung up. The name of his favorite band *du jour* was a signal for him to call back from a pay phone somewhere in his building.

I sat, waiting. Evelyn stuck her head in. "Kit, excuse me, but are you going to jail?"

"No, Evelyn."

"Are we going to talk about all this?"

"Soon."

The phone rang. Evelyn gave me a very uncharacteristic thumbs-up and ducked out, signaling that she was off on her mission. Her face was flushed with excitement. I hoped she'd be careful.

I picked up the phone. Willie sounded exultant.

"Partial score! I can read the disk. A file was deleted week before last. It was 620 K."

That wasn't a huge amount of kilobytes. "Is there any chance you can retrieve it?"

"I don't know. I doubt it. Depends on whether it was saved to the hard disk or not, maybe copied to another file or something, and where and how. Could take a long time, too. But I'll check. I'll talk to this Mac guru I know. You wouldn't believe some of the things I've seen this guy do."

"Okay, but be careful. Don't put yourself at any risk—"

"Not to worry. We were hackers together. We could send each other away for a while. But we're buds." I think that was meant to be a reassurance.

"Willie, before you go—one more thing. I need to know everything you can find about the last three weeks of Dan Bloomfield."

"As in husband of murder suspect?"

"As in same."

"Ah . . . the old husband check, eh? That'll be quicker. We've been there before." He cackled and promised to call back tomorrow.

What a bizarre way to make a living. Accounting suddenly seemed an attractive alternative. I longed to head home and have a stiff drink while awaiting reports from my growing squad of operatives, to check on my convalescing son and dog and give Emily some relief from Mrs. Steinitz. Maybe Em would love me again if I made her favorite macaroni and cheese for supper.

Instead, I sat down to the report in the child support case that Evelyn had been nagging me about with increasing urgency. I had to testify about it in court tomorrow, an event sandwiched between tonight's visit to the stricken Mosleys and tomorrow's reconvening of the Rochambeau Harpies.

This case was jumping in seventeen directions at once. I was finally on the offensive, sort of. I wasn't under suspicion of abusing a child anymore, at least for the moment. But I didn't have a client, either.

Fifteen

I HAD SOME TROUBLE focusing on my paperwork. I kept thinking about the Tough Question.

It had been posed by my friend Benchley Carrollton, a gentle, elderly Quaker accustomed to prolonged introspection. Benchley was descended from a family well entrenched in the New World since shortly after the *Mayflower* drifted in. He now runs the Rochambeau Garden Center, a major local institution, the crossroads through which much of the town passes several times a year —in the spring for mulch and annuals, in the fall for bulbs and biodegradable leaf bags, in December for Christmas trees and wreaths.

Benchley and I have spent many long, languorous hours sipping juice or herbal tea amid his little forest of trees and seedlings. He was instrumental in helping me solve my first big case, a murder on the Brown estate on the hill above his Garden Center. I still get faintly queasy whenever I look up that hill. In less frantic times than these, I drop by to see Benchley regularly. In the summer, we sit outside; in the winter, we pull some lounge chairs into one of the steamy greenhouses and drink hot cider. The Garden Center has become one of my favorite spots in the world.

Benchley talked me through my Wall Street humiliation. He was the first to whom I mentioned my cockeyed notion of a new career, and the first to take the idea seriously and encourage me. And it was in the greenhouse one gray November afternoon that Benchley turned to me and asked me what he called one of life's most important questions: "What do you stand for?" I hemmed, hawed, cleared my throat, squirmed in my chair for several minutes before I realized that I had absolutely no idea. I had never thought about it so specifically, nor had I ever been asked so directly. Questioned by anyone else in any other context, I would have been embarrassed by my inability to respond.

This case was actually helping to bring the answer into focus. I think what I stand for, at least what I want to stand for, is Reliability. It sounds dull, but it's elemental. I want to be somebody who can be depended on. I pick my kids up when I'm supposed to pick them up. I'm there when they wake up with nightmares. My friends can count on me. And Jane—I don't want Jane ever to have to pause in the middle of a tough counseling session to wonder if someone's given Em dinner. Or fear that I'm humiliating her with an affair. Or wonder whether I'll stick around when she gets old.

Maybe Faithfulness is a better word. I'm faithful to my family, my friends, my clients. I try to do what I say I'll do, even though I don't always succeed. I finish what I start.

And I was determined to see through what I'd begun for Shelly Bloomfield. There was a woman without much time for introspection. She'd told me once that she measured her life in spoonfuls —of laundry detergent, cough medicine, vanilla extract. I hoped she wouldn't take legal action against me for investigating her case without her permission, but here was my view: I believed she had been wrongly accused of murder. She had come to me for help. No matter what she thought of me at this moment. It was my responsibility to respond and I would.

More and more, I thought I was developing an answer to the Tough Question. In a weird sort of way, I was learning as well what kind of private investigator I was going to be. This case seemed to have a personality of its own, a menacing and challenging nature that had forced me to ask myself if I could really do this work well, if I would stick with it. I intended to.

Evelyn, breathless and excited, was the first of my unorthodox team to call in. "Lots of activity, Kit, I can tell you that," she reported happily. "I took notes. At two forty-three, two boys came riding up to the Bloomfield house on bicycles and ran inside. Both blond. On instinct"—she paused for effect here—"I got out of the car and took a stroll." I had specifically told her not to get out of the car, but why did I think she'd listen? "Nobody pays attention to old ladies strolling, you know."

I supposed it was true. There is this noxious presumption that the elderly have nothing to do and aren't on their way anyplace important. How thickheaded of me not to have used Evelyn before. She was curious, unobtrusive, smart and fearless as a Marine.

"I walked along a driveway and I saw the two boys—joined by a third boy, who must already have been inside—out in the backyard talking. They seemed excited, agitated. Then a fourth boy, quite tall, with one of those silly hoops in one ear, came speeding down the block on a skateboard. I don't mind telling you he was moving much too quickly for the circumstances. He almost ran down a small child. I was prepared to interject myself, but there really wasn't time." I pondered the image of Evelyn "interjecting" herself between a teenager hurtling along on a skateboard and a small child in his path. Maybe she'd swat him with her needlepoint bag.

But I don't think I'd ever heard Evelyn sound so animated. Maybe she could be a second associate, along with Willie.

"So there were four kids behind the house?"

"Yes, four."

They had to be Jason, Tobias, Jamey Schwartz and Harry Godwin, I thought, feeling my heartbeat quicken. "Was one blond, very handsome, almost like a model?"

"Yes, I know the one you mean. The others all circled around him. He was doing all the talking. I think he was very angry."

"How long were they there?"

"About five minutes. I had the impression they had something urgent to discuss. They weren't playing or having fun or just idling about; they had business to attend to. Then the talker went inside with the dark-haired one—he was the one I didn't see arrive, so I presume he lives there. The other two sat down in the backyard, but were out of sight. I had to keep moving back and forth of course—"

I interrupted in alarm. "Evelyn, don't get cocky. These are smart kids, and at least one of them may be extremely cruel. Don't take any more chances like that, promise me."

She humphed indignantly. "Well, I hardly think I was reckless, Kit. But I'll be careful." Evelyn was nothing if not sensible, though she didn't have a clue, I was certain, about real danger, about the kind of evil of which I felt Tobias was capable.

"One other strange thing, Kit," she continued. "They left quite differently than they arrived. Much more . . . *furtively*. The handsome one did see me—that is, he noticed me, but he didn't pay much attention. It was just a glance. They left one by one, in intervals of a minute or so, and went off in different directions. I got back into my car. They seemed to be looking over their shoulders, to see if anybody was following them."

"That is strange," I said. "Why would they behave differently when they left from when they arrived?"

"Well," offered Evelyn, "I suspect the handsome one—the one doing the talking—told them to. He seemed angry, especially at the boy who lived in the house. He jabbed him hard in the shoulder a few times and leaned quite close, almost nose to nose. He had the demeanor of one who was laying down the law, so to speak."

So Tobias was upset. Angry. Called an emergency meeting of the Cyberskulls, maybe dragged Jason upstairs to look at the computer and warned his nasty little group to start behaving cautiously. He'd also obviously spotted Evelyn, but I doubted even Tobias would tag her as a threat. With her severe bun, blouses buttoned to the neck and proper manner, nobody would think she was anything but a mild-mannered retiree out for a walk. Still, the fact he hadn't missed her showed how, well, professional he was. This boy didn't seem to miss many details, at an age when most kids specialized in complete inattention to detail. Looking at Jason's computer, maybe he'd concluded I'd been bluffing. But it was too late to accuse me of molestation again. The next time he came after me, he'd need a new tack.

"Evelyn, listen to me, please. Don't give me a hard time. I want you to be extra careful for the next few days. I think it's unlikely, but it's possible they noted your license plate. Probably nothing to fear but, as you know, strange things have been happening. I want you to be careful about opening your front door to strangers, keep your car locked and the windows up, be alert when you're out and around. In case one of these boys wants to intimidate you or bother you."

She was cool as ice. "Do you think there's a real chance of that? Just let someone try. I have a paperweight in my purse, and I can swing it pretty hard." The more I thought about Evelyn, armed, the more menacing I thought that might be.

She was considering what I'd said, though. "Perhaps I should spend a few days at my daughter's in Green Hills. It's only twenty minutes away and her husband Whitney is big and plenty tough. He lifts weights. And if I stay there I can still get into work just fine." There was an indomitable quality to Evelyn for which I was enormously grateful. I didn't have much of it, and we might both need it.

I told her that a stay at her daughter's would be an immense relief for me. Tobias had no reason to identify her or to hurt her if he did, but he seemed skilled as a snake at striking my most vulnerable spots. And he wasn't averse to threats and violence. I thanked Evelyn profusely and asked her to type her notes up when she came in tomorrow. "Great job, Evelyn." I meant it.

I called home to check on things there. Mrs. Steinitz answered in her usual businesslike, supremely competent and utterly humorless way. "Everything is okay here, Kit. The dog is fine. Ben says his bruises hardly hurt anymore and he threw a baseball around a bit in the yard with a couple of his friends. I didn't let him overdo it." One thing you could count on: with Mrs. Steinitz around, nobody overdid anything. Nobody ate anything that tasted good, nobody watched more than thirty minutes of TV, nobody had much fun. "There were a few messages for Jane. She called a little while ago. It's been pretty quiet otherwise."

"How's Emily?"

"Good. Oh, she did have a nasty little collision outside. Minor thing, scraped up her knee. But nothing bandages and iodine won't take care of. Good thing the officer was right there, too."

"Collision?" I heard the panic in my voice.

"Oh, it wasn't serious or I would have called. I told Jane about it and she didn't seem concerned. Just some scratches on Emily's hands, the scrapes on her knee. She was walking alongside the house with her little friend Liza and they were collecting flowers for some project or other—I don't know why—when this boy came rushing past on a skateboard. I tell you, those things are dangerous. The officer was parked right there, across the street from the house, taking his coffee break when the boy came roaring along." Mrs. Steinitz clucked. "He bumped Emily as he went past and sent her flying onto the sidewalk. The officer jumped out of the police car and stopped the boy and gave him a good talking-to. I think he got a lesson he won't soon forget. Not that kids like that pay much attention to what anybody tells them," she added, dripping disapproval. "He wore an earring, for goodness sake."

I took a deep breath and remembered to stay calm. The whole point of this stuff was to make me crazy, and I couldn't afford to be. Ben, Percentage, and now Em? Was Jane next? "Mrs. Steinitz, where are the kids now?"

"Why, Em and Liza are doing their homework and Ben is upstairs on the computer. Percentage is in the yard—"

"Look, I want everybody inside and I want everybody to *stay* inside. Nobody goes out for any reason, okay?"

Fine, she said, responsive but a little confused. Was anything wrong?

"I don't know. Let's just be supercareful the next couple of days, okay?" With Mrs. Steinitz, that was like issuing a license to kill.

"But surely you don't think this accident was deliberate? Right in front of a parked police car?"

All the smarter, I thought. "I'm sure not, Mrs. Steinitz. I don't mean to overreact. I just want us to err on the side of caution, okay?" I hardly needed to remind her; caution was her standard mode.

I called Jane on her private number. "Jane, let's go on red alert the next few days. I think this was a deliberate attack on Em, just a delicate reminder that they're still out there."

"Who are they?" she interrupted. "Until now it's always been him—Tobias."

"Well, with the Cyberskulls, we might have more than one kid to worry about. It's possible I'm being paranoid, but I have good reason. You're the only one someone hasn't come after, and I'm sure the idea will occur to them sooner or later. Be especially careful when you come into Rochambeau, especially around the house. I don't think they have the resources to wander around outside the town limits. At least the little psychos can't drive."

Jane wondered if I could be sure Em's accident was connected to the case. I had to concede that I couldn't. "But there's more circumstantial evidence than one normally needs. Or maybe they do this to every little kid they come across. It's so damned brazen."

That was what made this campaign so disorienting, given the nature of Rochambeau. Kids had fistfights, but dogs didn't get poisoned, boys didn't get brained with bats, small girls weren't mowed down on their own sidewalks by malicious skateboarders. At least, they weren't supposed to be.

Jane sighed. "Jesus, Kit, these people, whoever they are and whatever they're doing, are frightening. They're so systematic, so unafraid. It's beyond gall . . ."

"Maybe it's privilege. Maybe they've never experienced fear or boundaries or consequences."

Jane reassured me that she'd be watchful and take no chances. "Maybe you do need to stay on this case, Kit. To get these people off our backs. Especially away from our kids. And from other people's kids."

I snorted. "What is this? First I shouldn't take the case. Then I shouldn't see it through. Now I have to stay with it? I hope you don't give this kind of steady, consistent direction to your clients."

She laughed and hung up.

I called the Rochambeau police dispatcher and asked him to contact the officer outside our house to ask if he'd gotten an identification on the boy, or a description. I waited on hold, seething now, while the dispatcher radioed. Jane was right: these kids were so arrogant and open it was almost as if they believed they were beyond the reach of any authority. Maybe they were.

So it seemed Tobias was sending me another message, a different threat. He'd distributed assignments at Jason Bloomfield's house, and one kid's instructions were to skateboard by my house and look for a target of opportunity. Maybe get the dog if he was hobbling around the yard. Maybe scrape up the car, toss a rock through a window. If he saw Emily, give her some bruises, at least a bad scare, and if she lost a couple of teeth or scraped the skin off her face, so much the better.

I could hear Tobias thinking, "Let me just send this asshole a reminder. He still has things to fear from me." It was a shrewd move, too, subtle and menacing, but perfectly innocuous in appearance. Even the cop on the scene wouldn't imagine there was anything more involved than teenage recklessness of the sort he probably saw ten times a day as kids wheelied their bikes through busy intersections and darted on roller blades between moving cars.

I couldn't fathom this little suburban Moriarty. Could a kid that age possibly be so devious and subtle, and hide it so completely from everyone but me?

The dispatcher came back on the line. "The officer says the kid just grazed your daughter, Mr. Deleeuw. He said the boy was going too fast, especially on a sidewalk where kids were playing, but, hey, what the hell else is new? Jim stopped him and chewed him out. The girl only had a scrape and the kid said he was sorry. No reason to get ID or pursue it further. Happens all the time, you know. And Jim says the kid on the skateboard was tall. Jeans, Nikes, a Redskins windbreaker. And a gold hoop in his ear."

I said I knew it sounded harmless enough, but that I thought this wasn't an accident. That I had no proof but reason to think a group of boys was targeting my house, and that this kid was one of them. "Would you keep the officer there as long as possible?" I asked. "And would you ask him and any others on the detail to be careful about anybody approaching my house, especially a kid?"

The dispatcher, who had a kid on Ben's soccer team, told me he would. "The chief says we should take this seriously." I had to give Leeming credit: he might think I was an idiot, but he was doing his job.

I decided not to call back and talk with Emily. If she wasn't making a big deal out of it, then I wouldn't either. The message had been delivered, just in case I was getting cocky or gaining momentum. But I thought my family was safe at the moment.

A half hour later, having finished off the damned report, I looked out at the thick traffic outside the Mall. Rush hour would start petering out soon. I planned to get to the Mosleys' house good and early, before they could come up with too many reasons not to talk to me. Still, I had a couple of hours to kill beforehand and I had a good idea how to spend at least some of it.

I parked the Volvo right in front of the main entrance to Rochambeau Middle School. The last time I'd been here, I'd gotten a gift on my back seat and a threat that Tobias had come perilously close to making good on.

The main doors to the school were unlocked. I thought it was a good bet that Nathan Hauser would still be in his office. Nate volunteered with the Boy Scouts, the Police Athletic League, counseled troubled students and tutored failing ones—just about anything he could think of to help kids. If he had much of a life outside the building, I couldn't imagine where or when he squeezed it in.

His office light was on in the otherwise dim hallway. There's always an eerie kind of quiet in an empty school.

I looked across at the principal's office, still sealed off by yellow police tape, and tried to picture the shooting. An empty building on a weekend, light streaming in through the tall windows that lined the offices and hallways. Did the killer show him- or herself? Did Nancy Rainier-Gault scream? Think of running? Where would the killer have gone afterwards? The principal's body was found lying right behind the desk, which suggested she was shot in her seat or perhaps standing up to greet a visitor. If she was shot in her desk chair, there was yet another reason to link the killing to Shelly, who could have approached without arousing suspicion. But how could Shelly have concealed a rifle?

Hauser must have heard my footsteps. He peered out of his doorway, tie loosened and his shirtsleeves rolled up. He looked happy and relieved to see me. "Kit," he said, coming out to pump my hand, "glad to see you. Detective Peterson, she wanted to make sure I got the word that those charges were withdrawn. I'm so glad. I *told* her and those other clowns no way, no fucking way. I guess I owe you an apology."

He actually didn't. I owed him an apology for putting him in the vulnerable position of having to admit he knew about my visit to Tobias in the first place. But I didn't want to apologize. Not just yet.

"It's been a rough couple of days, Nate. They came to my office . . . it's a horrible thing to be accused of."

He nodded sympathetically. "I know. I can appreciate what you've been going through. We live with that nightmare every day. I could never have dreamed of such a thing happening when you went to talk to Tobias. It's ghastly."

Good, I thought. He's feeling a bit guilty. I hated to be exploitative, but I needed him to be a *bit* guilty. "Nate, what do you make of this kid?"

He ran his hand through his hair, shook his head. "I don't know what to make of him now. I'm trying to reach his father, so far with no luck. I'm insisting he get counseling in order to stay in the school. State law requires that, even when a kid withdraws a charge. First, they want to make sure the child isn't coerced, then they figure if a kid makes a false charge he or she needs help anyway. But I'm terribly sorry, Kit. You tried to tell me Tobias had problems, and I didn't want to hear it. I let two people down, you and him. I should know better than to buy into a kid's own mythology about himself."

"Listen, I have to thank you, Nate. You told the DYFS investigators that I had cleared my talk with Tobias with you, even though you'd told me I was on my own. That was pretty stand-up behavior, more than you had to do." Nate was too conscientious; none of this was in any way his fault.

He still looked miserable. "I just feel so bad. Looks like I owe you again, fella. That kid came within a whisker of ruining you . . ."

We went inside his office. I sat down in the chair across from his desk. Shoving aside a half dozen water guns and a few contraband baseball caps, he opened his small refrigerator and was pulling out two bottles of mineral water.

"Nate, why wait? I don't really think you owe me a thing, but if you have any such notions, why not square the debt now?" I grinned.

He grinned back. "God, you're relentless, Deleeuw. What now?"

"Nate, here's the dilemma. The big news isn't that Tobias lied, the real issue is his motive. He wanted me off the Bloomfield case, which means he must have had a damned good reason. But what? He's the most popular kid in the school, among both teachers and students. Nancy Rainier-Gault was preparing to bring some evidence to the prosecutor, but we don't know what it was or who it involved, though her notes suggested Jason Bloomfield at least. But he says he snapped a bra strap, nothing more. And all she did was suspend him. You were away, and while I'm sure she would have filled you in, she didn't get the chance."

Hauser got up, looked up and down the hallway, closed his office door and sat down. "We've been over all this, Kit. I wasn't holding out on you. I don't know what else she was onto, really. I would have told the police if I did. Believe me, they've asked me more than once. And I wish to God Nancy had told me; she might be alive today."

I nodded. "I believe you, Nate. Your integrity isn't an issue with me."

"Then how can I help you, Kit? I feel bad about the accusations against you, but I can't make up information I don't have."

I stood up and leaned over his desk. "Nate, I'm not interested in your making something up. Tell me who the bad seeds are, or who you think they are. Tell me who you have the most trouble with, who's the most feared. I'm not talking about cutting classes or schoolyard squabbles. I'm talking about sexual harassment, about targeting girls in inappropriate ways. I'm talking about the creepy boys.

"Somebody is going to great lengths to put the blame for this murder on Shelly Bloomfield and keep me away from the troubled kids. I need to know who they are, besides Jason. I mean, Tobias clearly has problems. But if he were bothering girls, harassing them or worse, wouldn't you have heard *something* about it? Wouldn't there be some buzz? Wouldn't he have a reputation? I keep getting stuck on this point: why is Tobias the all-around star he is? Is he a genius at deception? Is someone else involved with him? Give me a name. I know he hangs out with Jason, Jamey Schwartz and Harry Godwin. Give me a name, the first name that comes to mind when you think of real trouble here."

Hauser tapped a pencil against his desk. "This is tough, Kit. I have a responsibility to keep some things confidential. But—I know, I know, you don't have to tell me, we're talking about some important stuff here. Sexual harassment is something I feel deeply about. Not to mention murder." He sighed and dropped the pencil. Then he reached into his drawer and pulled out a paperback. The title on its cover was: *Secrets in Public: Sexual Harassment in Our Schools*.

"This survey was done by Wellesley College," he told me. "Listen to this: eighty-nine per cent of the girls and young women in public schools say they've been subjected to sexual comments, gestures or looks. Nearly forty per cent of public school students say they are harassed on a daily basis. Despite the fact that three quarters of all the girls in the survey told at least one person about being harassed in school." He shook his head in disgust.

"But that's my point, Nate. Harassment's all over the place. Somebody knows. Somebody talks. So here in *this* school: who do they talk about?"

He rubbed a tired hand over his forehead. "You're describing Harry Godwin to a T," he said reluctantly. "The kid is a real predator. He rubs against girls, 'bumps' into their behinds, 'falls' against their breasts. Asked an honor student for a blow job. There were half a dozen serious complaints against him—almost all withdrawn, the others resulted in suspensions. Legally, we're not allowed to expel kids, no matter what they do. Academically, and in terms of his testing, Harry isn't especially bright. Comes in at the low middle. Poor grades, no initiative, little in the way of imagination." He sighed again and fingered the report on sexual harassment. "I can't be spreading gossip, Kit, but if you're looking for somebody Nancy might have wanted to single out, I would say Harry. Jason strikes me as messed up but not strong, not a predator. And Tobias . . . well, I can't reconcile the kid I knew with the kid you know. I've seen him tutor other kids, volunteer for community service, do all sorts of things he doesn't need to. I don't know. I guess I just don't know shit."

I straightened up. I didn't want to impose on Hauser's faith and good nature anymore. One day, it could land him in major trouble, and I didn't want it to be at my behest. "What's Godwin look like, Nate?"

"Tall, maybe the tallest kid in the school. Dark hair. Got his ear pierced last fall."

I grimaced. "Was Rainier-Gault going to the county prosecutor about him? Was he being investigated?"

"We suspended Harry three times this year," said Hauser, rifling through a file in his desk drawer. "Next time, he would have been forced into counseling. Nancy would have dearly loved to get something more concrete on him, but she was right about this harassment stuff. Girls don't believe we'll protect them, or that their friends will stand with them. They're terrified the boys will shun them. And they're probably right. Nancy was brave to take it on.

"But you're not going to find her killer in this middle school, Kit. That is the wrong tree to bark up. Kids like Harry Godwin might be pigs, but that hardly makes them murderers. I sure hope your client didn't kill Nancy because she suspended her son. Nancy didn't deserve that." His grim face suggested that he believed that's exactly what had happened.

"One more question, Nate. Do you know why Wendy Mosley's not in school?"

He whistled softly. "You're pretty good. Well, I can't tell you

much. Something happened to Wendy, something rough. Whatever it was, it didn't appear to have happened on school grounds.
Nancy didn't talk to me in detail, and she didn't call in the cops.
There would have been written reports if formal charges had been
filed, but Nancy was adamant about keeping her word to girls that
she would never violate their confidentiality without permission. I
don't think she ever got that permission from Wendy. Wendy is a
knockout, a cheerleader, but off the field she's a soft-spoken kid,
self-effacing, not very assertive. In other words, a natural target.
She's been out of school a couple of weeks. But when I've called
the house to check on her, her mother tells me she's just not
feeling well. I can tell there's something wrong. I don't know what
happened to her. But I'm sure Nancy did . . ."

We shook hands. He was too good for this world. I did not enjoy
bringing him nasty tidings about someone he'd considered a prize
student.

I stopped at a pay phone and called Willie's voice mail again.
"Put Harry Godwin, age thirteen or so, at the top of your list, pal.
I'll check in with you tomorrow. Or call the house if you have big
news."

What a group. I couldn't fathom Tobias before and I couldn't
fathom him now. So far, the only reason I had to link him to any
wrongdoing was his bizarre behavior towards me. Otherwise, I'd
not come across a single shred of evidence that he was anything
but what he seemed to be—a gifted, privileged, popular junior-
high jock.

Jason was more complex. Nate had the same impression I had
of him: troubled, but not especially menacing. And the Schwartz
kid . . . Maybe the Rochambeau Harpies had learned something
about him. I had been so fixated on Tobias as the font of all
adolescent evil that I hadn't really considered anybody else. Now,
Nate Hauser's words rang in my ears: anything Nancy Rainier-
Gault wanted to take to the county prosecutor, young Harry Godwin, the evil skateboarder, was capable of having done. The problem was, while he sounded mean enough, he didn't seem bright
enough. And whoever was orchestrating the campaign against me
was pretty creative.

I was nearly forty minutes early for my appointment with the Mosleys. I was surprised by my reception: they let me in right away.

Mike Mosley was every inch the up-and-coming Yuppie law partner, late-thirties, fit, expensive haircut, still in his suit, classic white
shirt and silk tie. He greeted me pleasantly. Didn't seem the slugging type, but probably handy with a lawsuit.

Rhoda Mosley, nursing a Scotch and water in the living room,
must have gotten home from work first. She was dressed more
casually, in slacks and a sweater. They seemed friendly, less tense
than I had expected.

"I've heard about you," said Mosley. "I'm at Benchley Carrollton's Garden Center almost every Saturday. Your name came up
in conversation once, during your last big case, I think it was.
Benchley spoke very fondly of you. In fact, as I recall, he was
trying to drum up business for you."

I'd never mentioned it because Benchley would have been uncomfortable, but I was well aware that he'd sent me every paying
client I'd gotten for the first six months I was in business. Everybody in town told Benchley their woes, and he was in a good
position to recommend help.

"When Rhoda called me at the office and told me you'd been
by, I called Benchley and asked if you were trustworthy and discreet," Mike explained. "He gave you quite a warm recommenda-
tion, Mr. Deleeuw—Kit. Very warm. He said if he were having a
problem, you'd be the first person he'd call. He said that throwing
you out of the house wouldn't do much to deter you, either."

That explained my reception at the Mosleys'. God bless Benchley.
His was an endorsement that meant a lot to me.

The Mosleys apparently felt the same way. Mosley sat down next
to his wife, and I took an upholstered chair across from them.
From the looks on both their faces, this was a deeply troubled
house. Maybe they were relieved to find somebody to confide in.

"Does this mean you're willing to talk to me?" I asked.

Rhoda nodded. Mike added the qualifiers. "We have somebody
else to protect," he said. "Somebody who's been through hell.
This just can't get out. It absolutely can't."

"Are you sure it hasn't?" I asked them. "After all, I'm here."

That seemed to rock both of them; they looked at one another
in surprise. "Look," Mike said, "we want to help, but our kid
comes first. The last time we tried to get help . . . well, we wandered into an even bigger nightmare. After talking with Benchley,
we thought maybe we could use you professionally."

I mulled that one for a few seconds, then decided to buy myself some time to consider things. "Ethically, I'm not sure I can offer you a contract," I said. "I'm working for Shelly Bloomfield, and it might be a conflict of interest to represent someone else, however distantly related to the case this person might or might not be. I'll have to think about it."

Mosley nodded. "I understand. But we're getting pretty desperate. We don't know where to turn. We don't know how to protect our daughter and salvage some normal life for her here. We can move to another town, I suppose. But we shouldn't have to do that. It would be awful for her to leave her friends, her life here. Should we uproot her? Hire a guard? File a lawsuit? Nothing seems right. We're just . . ." He put his arm around his wife. These people had been through a lot. They needed help. And I instinctively liked them. For me, that was the magic combination.

"Perhaps I could start, without accepting any money, just by hearing about the problem, sharing information with you," I told them. "If I find that I can help and there's no conflict of interest, we'll negotiate something later, okay? That might benefit both of us. And you both look like you're going to burst if you don't talk to somebody."

Technically, I didn't have any ethical violation, since I was no longer working for Shelly Bloomfield. And if the Mosleys signed on, I could actually claim to be representing clients in this case and to be working on their behalf. But I still saw myself as working for Shelly, and felt she still deserved the bulk of my time. Helping Shelly could very well be helping them, anyway.

"I want to be as honest with you, Mr. Mosley, as I was with your wife. I believe Shelly Bloomfield is innocent. I intend to help free her. But that doesn't mean I can't be helpful to you as well. I appreciate your faith. What can you tell me?"

Rhoda opened her mouth to talk, then closed it again. It fell to her husband to tell the tale, efficiently and poignantly.

"Wendy is thirteen," he said. "She's very attractive, physically mature—she's had modeling offers on occasion. We've always said no." Good for you, I thought. There's a special corner of hell reserved for parents who send little kids to agents. "She's tall and slender and . . . well, this year she developed real breasts." He got up, went over to a wooden cabinet, poured himself a Scotch. I declined.

He turned back to me, drink in hand. "Wendy's been . . . harassed in school for a couple of years now. I had no idea how widespread, how nasty and, frankly, how dangerous this stuff is. Guys whistling, bumping into her, making cracks about her breasts and her behind. Snapping her bra. She'd gone to a guidance counselor, to the principal before Nancy, to her homeroom teacher. Some of them were sympathetic, but no one took any action, or at least none we know of. One or two told her to lighten up, that it was no big deal. She got the message pretty quickly: nobody knew what to do to help her, nobody was going to do anything."

He took a sip of his drink. The mantelpiece clock ticked. Upstairs music played softly.

"She'd become terrified of this one group of boys—there were four of them. She said they followed her down the hallways, asked her if she would kiss them, made clucking noises, constantly jostled her. Several times they followed her home. They scared other boys—nicer ones—away. One of them had a skateboard he kept running past her."

This skateboard was becoming mythic to me.

Mosley continued grimly: "They were always pretty careful to keep just on the edge of the law. They never actually grabbed her, removed her clothes, used force, things that fall clearly within legal definitions of assault, and believe me I know—I've read all the codes. They never did a thing in front of witnesses. The school authorities told us they couldn't do anything unless the boys touched Wendy inappropriately or did something that went beyond obnoxiousness. They just didn't seem to have any sense of what to do about this stuff, no plan. It wasn't talked about. In fact, the kids made fun of girls who complained, called them 'Frosty,' ostracized them. You can see why we came to have so much respect for Nancy Rainier-Gault."

When Mosley stopped—this wasn't easy for him, either—Rhoda Mosley picked up the story: "When Nancy arrived, she launched a real campaign. She called a special meeting for parents; she organized sessions for groups of kids. She said it was important that girls who felt harassed come to her or to Mr. Hauser. That they would see that something could be done . . ." She drew a shaky breath.

"It's complicated," Mike put in. "Wendy didn't want to be followed around by teachers all day; she wasn't comfortable talking about this with men; she didn't want the whole school to know about it. But she didn't want to be frightened all the time, either. This new principal seemed a godsend, the end to a nightmare. At our strong urging, Wendy went to see her, told her about all the incidents, the whistles, the bumping. The one thing she wouldn't do was tell Ms. Rainier-Gault who the culprits were. She refused to name names. She said she still had to go to that school and get along, that she'd be completely isolated if she ratted on these boys, some of whom are quite popular, over something she knew many of her classmates would dismiss as trivial, just boys being boys." Mosley was having trouble keeping the rage from his voice.

"I'll never forgive myself for not just calling in the police," his wife said, "but we didn't think we had enough evidence to press charges. We didn't want Wendy to have to go public. We were afraid of making it all worse." She stood up to pace. "Rainier-Gault was terrific. She was sensitive to Wendy's position. She gave us hope. She called an assembly, then spelled out very carefully what kind of behavior would no longer be tolerated. She described specifically the kinds of things that had been done to Wendy. But everyone in the auditorium knew that these boys were snickering."

Mike told the rest. "Look, this is real painful for us. But earlier this spring, Wendy came home all disheveled, with bruises on her neck. Something dreadful had clearly happened. She sobbed hysterically for hours before she could even talk to us. She had been walking home from school. The boy on the skateboard whizzed by and knocked her down as she passed the bushes in the park—you know, Rochambeau Municipal." I knew it well. It was the site of Shelly's canine play group. "Turns out two others were waiting there. They pulled her jacket open. They pushed her sweater up. They dumped dirt and leaves and dog droppings all over her."

"We didn't know all this at the time." Rhoda had grown extremely pale. "She wouldn't tell us exactly what happened. She eventually told Rainier-Gault, who told us. At the time, all Wendy would say was that some boys knocked her down."

Mike kept shaking his head. "You read about this and it just goes over your head. You always sort of think it's exaggerated, it isn't so bad. Sometimes you even think perhaps the girls do encourage it. Then you learn . . . Boy, do you learn.

"The most the police said they could do—if Wendy would iden-tify her assailants—was file misdemeanor harassment charges against them. The penalty for that is about the same as smoking on a public bus, but at least it would put their parents and the public on notice. Wendy wouldn't budge. She insisted she wouldn't testify, that it wasn't worth it, that she'd be some friend-less freak.

"We met with Rainier-Gault. She begged us to prosecute, said she was aggressively pursuing the problem within the school, that she needed girls like Wendy to come forth. She told us there were other girls who had also been harassed repeatedly, and that she was hoping to talk to their parents too, in the hopes of having them come forward.

"She told us she suspected that this was an organized ring of sick boys who had to be stopped. But she didn't have concrete evidence and she had to get some to move against them. It was very confusing for us. Wendy didn't know what to do and we didn't either. We should have filed a suit. Or hired somebody to accompany Wendy."

I thought of Emily. What would we do if this happened to her? The last thing adolescent girls want is to be conspicuous. We couldn't have her followed all day, even if she would allow it. And what if she talked about the harassment but the charges didn't stick? What if the boys denied it, and they were believed? Then where would she be? And while I understood that the Mosleys might think of moving out of town, to a new school district, that seemed a pretty desperate solution. How would it make the child feel, to have to flee her school and her friends, as if in shame, as if the fault—the sickness—was hers? What peace can you have when your kid is suffering and nobody seems to know what to do about it?

Mike steeled himself for the rest of the story. I could almost see him square his shoulders. "The odd thing is, for a couple of weeks it all seemed to quiet down. We thought it might have passed. Wendy was doing well in school. Nobody was bothering her. She even had a sort of boyfriend to go to dances with. I don't know . . . you move out here so that your kid can have a normal, healthy life and sometimes you cling past all reason to the idea that they are having one, even when by all rights . . ." His voice broke.

Rhoda reached over, touched his shoulder. "Stop it, honey. We did what we thought best. There aren't clear rules here. It wasn't your fault."

But he seemed unconvinced. "So, three weeks ago, we got home from work and Wendy wasn't here. She came in hours later with her clothes torn, dirty and hysterical. It was just like the first time. She won't say a word about what happened. She hasn't been to school since. We took her to the doctor. She wasn't raped, though there were bruises on her upper thighs, no semen, no visible injuries. Other than to go to the doctor, and now to a psychiatrist twice a week, she hasn't been out of the house since."

He drank greedily from his glass. "Ms. Rainier-Gault called Wendy nearly every day, trying to reassure and calm her, promising to end this torture once and for all. I think Wendy was beginning to trust her, or maybe she was just tired of it all. Anyway, Wendy told her who was responsible for one of the minor incidents, the bra-snapping. It was Shelly Bloomfield's son. And the principal was as good as her word. She looked into it, she suspended the kid immediately. It was the first time anyone had taken Wendy's predicament seriously. We were all very hopeful, and it helped Wendy feel a little stronger. The next time Ms. Rainier-Gault visited, Wendy was able to be a bit more forthcoming. We sat right here in this room with Wendy, holding her hand, as she talked to the principal. She told her about some of the uglier stuff—that this Bloomfield kid and others had actually reached into her shirt and squeezed her breasts. It's some ghastly game they play—and, of course, it's over the line legally.

"I think it was a kind of test, actually," Mosley continued. "If Rainier-Gault would take further action, then she could be trusted with the whole sordid story about your client's son and those other sick boys. You wanted to hear this, Mr. Deleeuw."

So I did. Mosley paused and looked me squarely in the eye. I guess I was being tested too.

"Maybe Wendy was preparing herself to tell everything that happened that day. We prayed she would. So did her therapist. The principal, naturally, was infuriated by what Wendy was telling her. She said it confirmed her suspicions, that this sick stuff had gone on long enough, that she was taking her evidence to the county prosecutor. He had been dragging his feet, saying there wasn't anything substantive, that we could never make it stick.

Nancy said she'd go public, resign if she had to. But something would happen, she vowed, or she'd call a press conference to talk about what was happening in Rochambeau. I remember her saying the real estate agents in town would love that. A few days later . . ."

A few days later, she was dead. I let the silence flow undisturbed as we listened to the clock's steady tick. These tormented parents needed some time to calm down.

"What does the psychiatrist say?"

"She says Wendy suffered a trauma," Rhoda answered. "Something quite terrifying. She feels unsafe anywhere but in the house. She obviously can't go back to that school, not under these circumstances. In the fall, we're transferring her to a private school. Or maybe we'll move." She laughed harshly. "Rochambeau has lost its charm for us."

It wasn't holding much charm for me either. My hands were shaking. I kept picturing Emily undergoing that kind of ordeal and how I would feel if I were helpless to protect her. I thought of Wendy Mosley, hidden upstairs, afraid to live her life outside. It broke my heart to see a family stagger this way. I sometimes lost sight of how many did.

I looked down at my notebook and I saw what I had forgotten to ask. "But what about the dog?"

They looked at each other, wordless for a moment. "We've been through so much since then," Rhoda said. "I'm ashamed to say it, but we sometimes forget about poor Jonah. We never really thought there was a connection, but more and more, of course . . ."

She brought me a silver-framed photo from the end table beside the sofa. It was a color portrait of a beautiful, sweet-eyed, long-haired girl hugging a beautiful, sweet-eyed, long-haired golden retriever.

"When those four boys first started bothering Wendy," Rhoda said, "she went and complained to a teacher. I think it was the gym teacher. He called the boys in and really blasted them, just reamed them out. Right around that time—I couldn't swear as to the exact sequence—was when Jonah died. He liked to doze in the sun in the yard. When I called him one Saturday and he didn't come, Wendy went out to get him. She came back in screaming. I wish I'd found him. He was really her dog. We got him when

Wendy was three. He slept in her room, followed her around . . .
Oh God, that child has suffered so much and we have been almost
completely unable to help her.''

Sobbing, she sat down next to her husband. ''We just weren't
prepared for this,'' he said softly, clasping her hand. ''Is anybody?''

I guess it was my job to be, I thought. ''I'll help you, but it's too
late in the case to sign a contract with you,'' I said abruptly. ''If
anybody asks you, just say we're in touch. And thanks for telling
me this. I understand how difficult it was, but it's enormously
helpful. I'll be in touch.''

Outside, the giant oaks rustled in the June breeze. I saw a couple of dog walkers strolling leisurely down the darkened block.
Strange how this tranquility could be doorbell-deep.

Sixteen

EVEN THOUGH it was nearly nine on a school night when I got home, I immediately whisked Ben and Emily out for ice cream and video games at Screen World on Route 6. I thought we needed a dose, however brief, of all-American suburban normalcy.

Screen World has more than a hundred of the latest fifty-cents-per-second video games, a soft pretzel stand and an ice cream counter. It is dark, cavernous and deafening, the decibel level akin to lying beneath a jet engine. My kids love it.

Em played pinball, to which she was enthusiastically addicted, while Ben furiously worked the levers of some bloodcurdling ninja electronic nightmare. "Dad, stop bugging me, I'm okay," he said with extreme exasperation whenever I wondered aloud how he was or even watched him too closely. Our expressions of concern were driving him nuts. At Ben's age, the fewer the questions the better, especially when they were personal. It was his motto, really.

So I left him alone and tried my hand at Ms. Pac Man, a long-in-the-tooth holdover from the simpler, earlier days of video games where you gobbled dots instead of drop-kicking scores of people to death.

I wondered if Ben and I didn't have some business to finish. He'd never told me much about his assault. Maybe there was more. But there is no problem so sensitive or in need of discussion that the adolescent male won't go to any lengths to avoid talking about it. If I pushed him too hard or too soon, he might never open up.

I'll be up-front about this belief: certain chromosomes come with the American male that defy logic, sanity and all attempts at cultural conditioning. One of them is this notion about ratting. If

I told Ben some kid had thrown a brick through a pet store window and killed ten puppies, he would be disgusted and befuddled. He might even go up to the boy who threw the brick and tell him off. But if I told him that the friend who was with the boy had ratted to the offender's parents, he would be outraged and never talk to the friend again.

Maybe such chromosomes aren't restricted to boys, either. I could see why reporting harassment would be so difficult for girls, why they so feared the reactions of their peers. Nancy Rainier-Gault had told a parents' meeting that it wasn't enough to punish an offender. You had to challenge and transform the whole culture of harassment, its traditions, its acceptance, the responses to it. She never really had a chance to get started.

Emily hadn't yet learned to be as guarded as her brother. As I stood behind her in the beeping, poinging, ear-shattering din of Screen World, she asked (never taking her eyes off the game), "Dad, is everything okay? Are you solving your case?"

Yes, I told her, leaning over and kissing her. I love the age when they accept what you tell them. The conversations aren't as interesting, but it's easier to keep them feeling safe.

Next morning, cuddling in bed for a few moments after the alarm beeped, Jane and I ran down our mental checklist. Ben seemed okay. No apparent emotional or physical aftereffects. The bruises were still visible, however, and would be for a week or so. We both wondered about Monday. Would he feel comfortable in school? I told Jane I'd drive him in and talk to Nate Hauser about making sure teachers kept an eye on him. Yet Ben didn't seem particularly anxious about returning. I couldn't figure that out. By rights, he should have been scared witless; he'd taken a savage beating. We were ready to get him to a counselor in a couple of weeks to have him evaluated and make sure he really was handling the aftermath as well as he seemed to be.

As for Em, who'd been visibly upset at Ben's bruises and at Percentage's disabilities, she'd had a few nightmares and seemed a bit clingier than usual—but she was also making playdates with friends, was excited about seeing the new Disney cartoon opening next week, and sounded thrilled at the news that Jane was taking a long weekend and that she wouldn't have to put up with Mrs. Steinitz today. Em didn't even seem to realize that she might have been deliberately attacked. We decided to keep her in sight at all times, but we were both relieved that neither of our kids was having much evident trouble. "Still," Jane cautioned, "there could be a lot of aftershocks, especially with Ben, and they could show up in indirect ways. We have to really keep an eye on him."

Percentage, meanwhile, was playing injured canine hero to the hilt. Emily brought him biscuits every five minutes or so, cuddled and kissed him. Jane made him hamburgers and praised his heroism. He was, I was sure, completely befuddled by but delighted with all the attention. Perhaps I was imagining it, but I thought he had affected a new look: noble yet vulnerable. Maybe there *was* some traffic between the ears besides "Hi there!" and "Feed me!"

We'd gotten nowhere, though, in figuring out the enigmatic Child from Hell. "The best I can do," offered Jane, "is theorize that this is a profoundly needy child who has found a way to get attention and power. It doesn't explain everything, but it's a starting point. Tobias needs to constantly remind you that he's a threat, that you have to pay attention to him, even when he's taking great risks to do so. And he seems oddly desensitized to violence and cruelty."

No word from Willie yet on the mysterious Cyberskulls. He hadn't called to say the file was irretrievable, which was mildly hopeful, but he had warned me to not get my hopes up. Still, some small measure of progress had been made. I knew there was a group of boys in the school—the Cyberskulls, no doubt—who were preying on vulnerable girls. I knew that Nancy Rainier-Gault had been aware of their existence. I even knew who they were, and that there was at least one dangerous kid running around that school besides Tobias: Harry Godwin.

I had victims, too: Wendy Mosley and her tormented parents. And I hoped to learn the names of some more victims tonight. They were really the key to nailing these boys and establishing a clear motive for murder for somebody other than Shelly. It's true what defense lawyers say, I've found: once the police have their suspect, they stop looking for anyone else. It's as natural a reaction as it is frightening, the whole bureaucracy of law enforcement cranking up to reinforce that initial belief. As I've learned with Chief Leeming, you can get the machinery to change course, but only after you ram it with a bulldozer. Appeals to common sense or pleading don't work, only rock-hard evidence.

It's a good system as long as the cops nab the guilty party right off the bat, a nightmare when they don't.

Fortunately, I had some pretty sharp eyes and ears out there now, scanning the suburban frequencies. The Rochambeau Harpies were gathering tonight at Jeannie and Carol's. We'd see if they could help me find some of that damning evidence. I might pick up a few pointers myself beforehand at the Coalition for Justice meeting at the high school auditorium.

This morning, though, I was hustling Emily and her backpack and bag lunch out to the school-bus stop. I would wait with her, to her humiliation, as a precaution against wayward skateboards or other hazards. Then I had to drive to Newark and testify against a Deadbeat Dad.

Arthur Goodell had abandoned his wife and three kids and expensive Rochambeau colonial, vanished for a couple of weeks, then surfaced in New York City claiming to be unemployed and broke. The bank was moving to foreclose on the house, the family had moved to a dingy apartment in Roseland, Bev Goodell was working two jobs, and the kids were eating TV dinners and wearing thrift-shop clothes. Sometimes, I think poverty is particularly jarring to middle-class families. They have no expectations of ever suffering it and no experience in dealing with it. And there are lots of impoverished families in the suburbs, more than people think.

Thanks to Willie's help and several days of telephone calls of my own to large accounting firms—Arthur Goodell was a successful accountant—I'd found him in a week. He was, as I knew from his credit-card trail, neither unemployed nor impoverished nor miserable. By now, I can anticipate the patterns. Deadbeat Dads head for Hoboken, Jersey City, the Upper East Side. They get a one-bedroom apartment and a girlfriend, and hit liquor stores, furniture outlets and stereo shops. They entertain a lot. And sooner or later (usually sooner), they stray into Willie's electronic clutches.

Tailing people in New York City is a snap. There are always throngs of people on the streets. Nobody in New York ever looks behind them, but if someone does, he's unlikely to pick me out of a teeming commuter mob. (Tailing people in the burbs, by contrast, is a nightmare. Usually there are few cars on the streets, and people know which cars belong in what neighborhood. Suspecting me of being a burglar canvassing houses, they are forever calling the police, most of whom know the Volvo on sight by now and just drive by and wave.)

I'd followed Goodell into his apartment building. I'd greeted his buxom young date courteously. He wrote me a check on the spot, like they usually do, and it didn't even bounce. He didn't want me to come back.

My testimony to this effect went well, but the hearing tied up much of my day. Legal wrangling delayed everything; I didn't actually take the stand until after the lunchtime recess. Afterwards, I came back to the Mall, where Evelyn's extremely detailed but excellent investigative field report was waiting for me.

I also met with the security chief of a giant pharmaceutical firm worried about the theft of drugs from one of the company's local divisions. It was our third conversation, and he finally agreed to hire me. I'd worked hard for the contract, actually writing up a detailed proposal for the job, my first proposal ever. I was starting to feel like a corporation. Or at least as if I might measure up to the reassuring lettering on my office door. And the pharmaceutical job would actually provide some steady, long-term income, $60,000 over eighteen months. It might even give me the means to hire Willie.

I tried calling Harry Godwin's house but got an answering machine. I had only slightly better luck at Jamey Schwartz's.

"Yes!" demanded an impatient-sounding woman. I heard a kid screeching in the background.

"Mrs. Schwartz?"

"Yes, that's me. If you're selling, I'm not buying."

"No, I'm not selling. My name is Kit Deleeuw and I'm a private investigator. I want to talk to you about your son Jamey." That line has hardly ever failed. Nobody hangs up having just been told some stranger wants to talk to you about your kid.

Of the four boys, Jamey was the one I knew least about. I suspected he was the proverbial kid-along-for-the-ride-with-the-tough-guys.

"I've heard of you. You've been in the papers."

I get no kick out of being in the headlines or on television, but I am astonished at how Americans revere celebrity, even a tiny slice of it. Since I've been dubbed "the Suburban Detective" by the New York tabloids after helping solve some well-publicized cases, I can't believe how much more willing people are to talk with me. It doesn't seem to matter why, but if they've seen your name in print or your face on the screen, they think you have to somehow be okay.

"What about Jamey?" Mrs. Schwartz asked, still suspicious but now interested. The screeching behind her turned into piercing wails.

"Well, I'd like to come by and talk to you. Maybe to Jamey, too."

She said no. Emphatically and repeatedly. Then she banged the phone down. Can't win 'em all. Maybe the Harpies could fill me in.

I checked in at home, then went down to the Lightning Burger. Luis and I supped at our usual table in the corner. Fridays are a busy time at the Mall, especially towards the evening. It's astonishing how many people think of going to the Mall as a night out, and I guess it makes some sense. They can stroll, chat, sit on benches and watch the passing parade, get the kids a cheap toy or an expensive pair of sneakers, have a quick meal, then buy dessert from one of the half dozen snack stands, ranging from "gourmet" cookies (this reflects the genius of American marketing: what is a non-gourmet cookie?) to fried dough.

The fried dough stand attracts the longest lines in the Mall. Two Latvian immigrants had quickly grasped the way to Americans' hearts. Dough patties cut into the shapes of cats, dogs, bears and T. Rexes were dropped into boiling oil until they were crisp, rolled in powdered sugar, then topped with jelly or sprinkles. I got queasy just looking at some of the results, but I saw sticky, powdered, happy faces all over the Mall.

I filled Luis in on everything that had happened since I'd last seen him. He didn't look happy. Something was bothering him. Given his unyielding notions of manners, he wouldn't volunteer it unless I pressed him, so I did.

"I believe we may have been too willing to accept the idea of young Tobias as demon," he told me. "I advised you not to underestimate him—good advice always—but doesn't it appear to you that we're dealing with something beyond a crafty thirteen-year-old boy? I always told my associates: just because something doesn't seem to make any sense, that doesn't mean that you have to believe it does. Maybe it doesn't seem to make sense because it isn't true."

"Luis, that sounds brilliant, and I'm sure it's true. But I don't have the slightest idea what it means."

He leaned back and roared. "In many ways I love this country," he said when he was finished laughing. "Americans are direct. Perhaps not subtle, but always direct. Let's put it this way, my friend. It doesn't make sense for Tobias to have threatened you that way. It doesn't really make sense for him to have attacked your boy, your dog, perhaps your daughter, and of course your reputation, before you even had an opportunity to respond to his initial threats. So you keep saying it isn't explicable, yet you keep accepting that this is exactly what occurred. Perhaps you need to listen to yourself. If it doesn't make sense, then perhaps it isn't so."

We had our customary hot apple pies for dessert. The young woman who waited on us looked Cuban and said almost nothing. She wasn't wearing a name tag, either. Luis, while always unfailingly courteous with his staff, seemed especially gentle and patient with her. This wasn't the first time I'd noticed that young people without name tags, speaking little or no English, came and went through the Lightning Burger. I wondered if Luis wasn't operating a sort of fast-food underground railway stop for illegals fleeing Castro. One thing I was sure of: I'd never know.

"But I know what I heard, Luis. I know what Tobias told me."

Luis wiped his mouth with a napkin.

"Yes, but you don't know *why* he said it, Kit. You have no idea what this boy might have been told or what he thought you were doing. I have some difficulty accepting the notion that a popular, well-rounded honors student is as disturbed as this young man seems to be and no one notices it. He warns you to leave him alone, then brutally attacks your son, poisons your dog, without first ascertaining if you will leave him alone or not. In fact, if you think about it, Kit, it's almost as if he doesn't *want* you to leave him alone. I know things are different here, but in my country the way to ensure that a man will *not* leave you alone is to attack the ones he loves, the ones he is supposed to protect."

Luis took another bite of the pie, precise, neat, as formal as if it was a torte in some Viennese café instead of a fried concoction in a middle-aged, middle-class mall. "I would venture to say, Kit, that if someone did this to a man's family in Cuba, everyone would expect him to kill the offender instantly."

Jersey isn't quite that macho, I thought, but the point was well taken. How could Tobias, if he was so crafty, believe for a second that I *could* leave him alone after all he'd done?

I knew what Luis was going to say before he said it, so I did: "Keep beating the bushes. Flush the birds out of the trees." He nodded. The two of us cleared the table, and I was off to flush the birds.

I knew the high school quite well, even though I didn't yet have a child there. During the Brown case I was there often, talking with students and teachers. The teenaged couple found dead on the Brown estate were both students here, and I paused at the plaque mounted in their memory in the school lobby. It was depressing to contemplate, even though I'd never met Ken Dale or Carol Lombardi. Premature death never makes sense, but the loss of these two seemed especially unnatural and cruel. They were my first big case, the one in which the New York papers first called me "the Suburban Detective."

People in suburbia are often consciously or unconsciously smug about their lives. Living in a town like Rochambeau is in itself a statement that you've succeeded in providing yourself and your family a safe, comfortable setting, one of the most family-friendly locations ever created. Misery and failure are as common here as in most places, but here they always come as more of a shock, incompatible with our notions of communities like this.

Were the two teenagers' deaths any more or less pointless than Nancy Rainier-Gault's? Here was a principal in her early forties, almost surely on her way to running her own school system, competent and dedicated, brutally murdered in a community where most people leave their doors unlocked and reports of a bicycle theft sweep through town as if it is big news.

The auditorium was mostly empty when I walked in at seven-fifteen. The only issues that draw full houses in Rochambeau have to do with class size or property taxes. And Friday night is a difficult time in any case, when the city commuters struggle in for the last time and families, split up all week by demanding work schedules, reunite. I guessed there were about a hundred people there, all but fifteen or twenty of them women. The auditorium held nearly eight hundred, and with the crowd scattered throughout it looked like a worse turnout than it was.

I noticed Carol Goldman seated up front and went up to her row. "Okay if I sit with you? I understand completely if you'd rather not. You might be safer."

She looked at me for what I thought was a pretty long time. "Sure, sit down," she said. "I don't guess my image is all that unstained anyway. And we *are* neighbors. We're your alternate UPS delivery point, and you're ours. We *need* each other."

"Well," I said, "it doesn't get much more neighborly than going to protest meetings together, does it? Next year, we'll be at the planning board together denouncing a new 7-Eleven or something."

I sidled down the row. I appreciated the company, to be honest. I felt like I ought to have a scarlet letter branded on my forehead.

A long table had been placed up on the stage with four mikes at four seats. One seat was labeled NOW, another the Rutgers Coalition for Justice for Women—these had people sitting in them—and the other two seats were unmarked. Two young women I had not seen before came in and took them.

Another fifteen or twenty people had filtered in when the last speaker to arrive leaned forward and pulled the microphone closer to her face. "I am Dana Kline," she began, then repeated it when the microphone failed to work. The sound system cracked on. "I represent the Rochambeau Coalition for Justice for Nancy Rainier-Gault. We've decided it would be fitting to name ourselves after somebody who sacrificed her life for a safer environment for young women."

There was muted applause in the auditorium. This crowd hadn't come to raise hell or exhibit their outrage for the eleven o'clock news—which was, I noted, represented by a pair of camera crews moving up and down the aisles. The crews would want to see some shouting to bring back to New York. But the women on the stage seemed subdued, regretful that it was necessary to be here, and clearly still saddened by what had happened to Rainier-Gault.

Kline introduced the other women on the stage, then told us a little more about herself. She was a labor lawyer who worked in Manhattan and had helped organize a number of groups working on behalf of women's issues, most recently women at Long Island University demanding equity in tenure. I found myself getting a little impatient. She hadn't exactly explained the purpose of this meeting.

As if in response to my unvoiced question, Kline pulled a written statement from a folder and began reading. "I want to explain to you all our reasons for gathering here," she said. "First, we want to express our grief for the loss of Nancy Rainier-Gault, who was violently murdered last Saturday in her office at the Rochambeau Middle School, possibly because she was determined to curb the long, dehumanizing and historically winked-at harassment of girls in school. We've come to serve notice to local authorities that we're here and we *care.*"

There was more vigorous applause at that, and the TV klieg lights popped on hopefully. "I am happy to report that in this case the police and district attorney have moved very aggressively," Kline continued. "As you know, an arrest was made within hours of the crime and we have every reason to expect the most serious charges appropriate under the circumstances to be brought at the arraignment of the accused murderer. That is scheduled for eleven a.m. Tuesday, and I hope you and as many of your friends as we can recruit will be in the courtroom to demonstrate our continuing concern about justice in this case."

Scanning the crowd, I spotted Lani Faison sitting in the rear of the auditorium. She nodded at me almost imperceptibly.

"I also want you to know that the four organizations represented here will continue to monitor this cause," Kline was announcing. "We have asked the Board of Education to meet with us to ensure that the work Nancy Rainier-Gault began won't stop. We mean to see that it doesn't." More applause, a few scattered cheers.

With that, Kline turned the proceedings over to the head of the local NOW chapter. "I'm Sarah Woodruff from the New Jersey branch of the National Organization for Women," a wiry, grim-faced woman announced. "I'm here to lend our support to what Dana is doing. And I'm proud to announce that our membership has made a $5,000 contribution to launch what we are calling the Nancy Rainier-Gault Award, to be given annually to the person in the state who's done the most to help the fight against sexual harassment in our schools. We are determined that this not be a pointless death; that the work Nancy Rainier-Gault so courageously began will continue." This time there was a standing ovation, loud and heartfelt. This would be the clip the TV stations

aired. It was pretty touching; some of the women were in tears as
they stood and applauded.

I saw Rhoda Mosley come in. A tall, lovely young girl was with
her. Wendy. This was a charged environment for her first excur-
sion outside her home in weeks, but she must have wanted to
come. I couldn't imagine Rhoda forcing her. I thought it was
probably a good idea. Let her know there was support for her
beyond the house. They took seats near the back of the auditorium.

Suddenly, a slender young woman in jeans and a T-shirt wearing
a black armband popped up in the front of the hall with five
others, all wearing armbands and buttons whose slogans were too
distant for me to make out.

"Sisters and brothers," she announced, turning to face the
sparse crowd. She pulled off the cap she'd been wearing over her
spiky straw-colored hair. "We're from the New York City chapter
of SHOUT, a group working to encourage abused women to
speak out. We have been in Rochambeau all week conducting our
own investigation into the killing of Nancy Rainier-Gault and we
have information we think you ought to know." Maybe *they* were
having some luck, I thought, a touch bitterly.

The TV crews rushed forward, and everyone perked up. Drama
loomed.

"We have reason to believe that sexual harassment has been
epidemic for years in the Rochambeau school system and that
nothing has been done to stop it. We have reason to believe that
both the police and county prosecutor had repeatedly been asked
by Nancy Rainier-Gault to take action against boys at the Rochambeau Middle School who were brutalizing young women. And they
dragged their feet. More men yawning in the faces of women who
are being brutalized. Their foot-dragging was responsible for her
death."

Some of the people in the auditorium clapped, some whispered
excitedly, others groaned. "The PC brigade," moaned a woman
in front of us. Beside me, Carol said nothing.

The rhetoric had risen a notch; the TV stations had their sound
bite. But as predictable as SHOUT may have been, the fact was
that what the woman had said was largely true. Nate Hauser and
the Mosleys knew it, Rainier-Gault and many of her teachers knew
it, even Shelly Bloomfield knew it: epidemic or not, a gang of

middle-school boys was harassing and assaulting female classmates. School officials and the police had been told about them,
yet they were still operating.

"We have been here," said the woman from SHOUT. "We have
talked to some of these victims. We know who they are. And you
should all be aware that at least one person, one man working for
the woman accused of killing Nancy Rainier-Gault, is here tonight
spying on this meeting."

No, I thought, it can't be. But of course it was.

"He's down front," she said. "His name is Kit Deleeuw. He calls
himself the Suburban Detective." No, I said to myself, I never
called *myself* that. "He works for a woman who wants to set the
clock back for all of us. A woman who murdered the first person
in this community who ever stood up to Rochambeau's historic
tradition of brutalizing women." I heard murmurs around me,
felt heads turn. Kit Deleeuw, oppressor. Jane would love it.

"I know," Ms. SHOUT continued triumphantly. "I went to
school here—Ann Jankelow, Rochambeau High, Class of 1986. My
breasts were grabbed in the hallway, my ass squeezed from behind. A boy named Dan Mackey stuck his tongue in my ear. A
high school friend pulled his penis out in front of me in a basement hallway and told me to suck it like a lollipop. I reported
some of these incidents. Nobody did anything about any of them.
I didn't speak out publicly then, but I'm speaking out now. I know
what these girls have gone through, and one of the reasons we're
here is to get them to come forth, to speak out, to do what we
didn't have the courage to do then."

Wendy Mosley was in tears, rushing out of the auditorium on
her mother's arm. People all over the auditorium were whispering
and pointing at me. I hoped I didn't look as red-faced as I felt.
The women onstage were staring at me and conferring. I figured I
was a couple of seconds from getting tossed out.

I hadn't noticed Carol pop to her feet, so I was surprised to hear
her voice. "Excuse me, my friend. My name is Carol Goldman and
I recently moved to Rochambeau with my lover and our daughter.
We had been told that this would be a hospitable community to a
lesbian couple, and so far it has been. Kit Deleeuw is my neighbor.
He is also my friend. He is here as a citizen of this community. He
represents a woman whose guilt has not been legally established
and who has been accused of murder by the very authorities—the

very same men mostly—who have refused to act on the long-standing problems that you're talking about. We all know that these problems exist. They have existed and will exist in our schools tomorrow and the next day and the day after that. But Shelly Bloomfield has the right to a fair hearing, nonetheless. Kit Deleeuw is not a spy. He is a good father and a good man who's just doing his job. So please—knock off this self-righteous stuff. Kit's not our enemy. Let's keep the heat on, but let's keep it where it belongs."

Everyone in the room seemed astonished, myself first and foremost. As Carol looked from row to row, people coughed, smiled, nodded, looked away—but nobody seemed to want to take her on. I repressed the impulse to stand up and hug her. After a moment, Jankelow picked up her speech where she left off. She didn't mention me again.

Nobody had asked me to leave, but after a few minutes I decided that I ought to. "Thanks, Carol. That meant a lot to me," I whispered.

"Anytime," she said. "I'm glad I came. This meeting was important and I'm happy about the award. I'll see you at the house in a little while."

Jankelow was winding up as I walked out the door. I doubted the meeting would go on much longer.

Back at my house, things seemed blessedly normal. Jane was plowing through case files and Emily was trying to train her hamster Blair to sit, something I pointed out the dog had never been able to master. Ben was holed up in his room listening to a Counting Crows CD on his earphones. For the moment, my family was safe and secure, and I gave thanks for that.

I took a six-pack of soda and some pretzels from the pantry and headed next door to Jeannie and Carol's house. Time to see what the Rochambeau Harpies were made of.

Seventeen

THERE ARE MORE MEN hanging around the suburbs these days, but we are still the exception, not the rule. I almost never have the sense of its being our place. Even though I now see other men pushing shopping carts, driving on school trips, sitting in pediatricians' waiting rooms, we remain interlopers in these communities, more visible but distinctly peripheral.

Men are changing, sometimes voluntarily and sometimes not, but I often have the feeling that in families the real action is still happening apart from us, around us, while we males struggle to make sense of it.

I will know it's really changed when shopkeepers, grandmas and moms stop remarking on how sweet and heartwarming it is to see me helping at the school bake sale or running around town with Emily.

"You're so patient," says the salesman in a shoe store as I sit while Em fusses over which moccasins to buy. "Usually men have no time for this." Or: "How touching. You and your daughter seem so close!" Men get so much mileage out of so little. Expectations of us are still so low.

These days I had reasons for my musings. Talking to Shelly and her friends, attending the Coalition meeting, listening to the Mosleys describe Wendy's nightmare, sitting down with the Rochambeau Harpies, even being accused of abusing someone, I felt more conspicuously male than I ever had on a case.

I felt it again in Jeannie and Carol's living room, as Tracy came bounding in for a good-night hug and asked me if I would be her "stand-in dad" at the Kinderkickers soccer game the next day. Her moms had enlisted a half dozen male friends to serve as stand-in dads at school and athletic events. "I have two moms and lots of dads!" Tracy told her friends. It seemed to be working so far.

Jeannie and Carol knew it would grow more complicated, as kids got old enough to pay attention to who the moms and dads were. Given what I had seen of adolescence, a lot of kids wouldn't find Tracy's household admirable or even unremarkable. The coming years were tough under the best of circumstances, and Carol and Jeannie dreaded them.

But for now, life was good for Tracy, who had jumped into my arms and was badgering me about her game. "Can't tomorrow, sweetie," I told her. "Got lots of work to do. Important stuff. I'm a Power Ranger of Suburbia. I'll catch you next week, okay?"

"Okay. I like it when you come, Kit!" I'll bet she did. I generally arrived with my pockets stuffed with Gummi Bears and Reese's Pieces. At this age, kids are still eminently bribable. They love surprises and love you for bringing them, and I find that they keep on loving you even after you stop bringing them.

The Harpies were helping themselves to tea and juice from a tray and settling into a rough semicircle, some in folding chairs Jeannie had carried up from the basement, others on the sofa and upholstered chairs. A couple sprawled on the rug. Almost all, I noted, had brought notebooks or legal pads. This was a diligent bunch. Also an eclectic one. I wished I had a group photograph: Lani Faison, the FIT student and newcomer, traded strep-throat war stories with Patricia Caldwell, she of the three kids and minivan. Hae Sook and Nadja were deep in dog talk with Liz Hoffman, like Shelly a defiant stay-at-home mom, and with Sandra Vlaskamp, the part-time book editor. Susan Baker, the professor who had a kid via artificial insemination, came in with two or three Harpies whose names I hadn't caught.

"I'm passing around an address and phone sheet," I announced. "Some of you I didn't get to meet the other night. I should know who you are and how to reach you."

"Want my car phone?" Patricia Caldwell's heavily-driven van was apparently a mobile communications center as well.

"By all means," I told her.

Carol began by reporting on the Coalition for Justice meeting some of us had just left, including my being singled out as a demon secret agent.

"I've got to say honestly that even though I disagreed with their jumping on Kit in public—they don't know him, after all, and I understand their suspicion—I felt I belonged there," she told the Harpies. I understood the suspicion, too, though I thought I'd been subjected to enough scrutiny for one week. I was the one supposed to be doing the scrutinizing.

Carol's loyalties were painfully, and legitimately, divided. The feminists in the auditorium were probably many of the same women who had battled for years to make it possible for her and her partner to live openly, to adopt children, to move to towns like Rochambeau. Women like Shelly Bloomfield, by the very nature of their politics, their advocacy of the traditional, were on the other side.

"I belonged with those women," she went on. "Jeannie and I and women like those have stood together through lots of fights, countless ones, from discrimination and gay-bashing to police harassment and AIDS. If not for the hell-raisers, my relationship would be against the law. I wouldn't have my wonderful daughter. As it is, Jeannie and I still can't legally marry in any state. And Jeannie can't tell her principal or her students that she's a lesbian; lots of parents would want her out of that classroom in a minute. I don't really know what Shelly Bloomfield thinks about me, but I doubt she would approve of me or my kind of parenting."

I wondered myself, walking over to the tray on the end table and pouring myself a Diet Coke. I thought Shelly fiercely believed that the traditional family was the best one, but I didn't think she was a hater who'd deny gays the right to be parents. Still, that was the other side of the coin: when you stood up and proclaimed, "This is the one true way to raise children," you were almost automatically saying that other ways weren't as good or healthy. That was the subliminal message Shelly sent that set other women on edge, that led them to view her as an enemy. It was a great testament to Carol that she saw further than that, that she wanted to make sure Shelly received the same fair treatment she herself had fought for so hard. Tracy was lucky to have such a parent.

Carol continued, "But I have sympathies in both places. So I'm here to be as helpful as I can until we know more of the truth. Then I'll have to make a choice."

Liz Hoffman raised her arm and stood up. She had a cute-looking dog embroidered on her sweatshirt that I didn't recognize. "Cockapoo," she said proudly, noticing my puzzled squint. Were dog people nuts? Or just too loving to confine their affections to a single species?

"I just want to say everybody has their own point of view and they're entitled to it, but I *don't* belong in both places. I belong *here*. Those women at the high school tonight, you know they think Shelly is a murderer and they think those of us who stay home all day are pathetic. But what we do is important. Parents aren't just abstract specters. It matters if they are there or not. If you have kids, then take care of them, don't rent them out to strangers—that's all Shelly was saying. She has no problem with your lifestyle, Carol. I've known Shelly for years and I've never heard her say a homophobic word, which I can't say for a lot of people I know.

"I think that Shelly is being punished because she's always had the guts to say out loud what a lot of us feel inside. We spend half our life driving other people's kids to school and lessons and play-dates. We keep an eye on kids who aren't ours who only have parents from eight to ten p.m. and on weekends. Those kids suffer. They're lonely. They get into trouble. And we're the ones who have to clean up."

Liz had spoken little at our earlier meeting, so I was surprised by the passion behind her words. How had we managed to make these women feel so unappreciated and invisible that they needed to stand up and say, "Parenting is important"?

Liz Hoffman hadn't finished yet. "I don't think Shelly would be in jail if she didn't have those beliefs. I appreciate what Carol said —and I support her right to do things differently. But we're so anxious to be politically and socially acceptable that we lose sight of what's best for our children. I think what's best for our children is for their parents to take care of them, so that they don't come home to empty houses or to strangers."

The room had tensed up. I didn't want this to become a sociological debate and I sure didn't want these women to have to choose between one model of child-rearing or another in order to continue helping Shelly. The more politicized this group became, the more members would feel they had to take sides. But this was a discussion any man with two brain cells would think twice about before jumping into. Liz Hoffman looked deeply upset; Carol's jaw had firmed. I looked pleadingly at Sandra Vlaskamp, who, blessedly, read my mind.

"Ladies," Vlaskamp said, "I don't want to censor anybody, but let's try to clarify why we're here." She sighed deeply, revealing just how upsetting this kind of exchange could be for her. And probably for lots of others too.

"It's not easy being a woman. Or a man," she added graciously, nodding at me, with a shadow of a smile. "It's not easy being a mother, and I'm sure it's even tougher to be a gay one. These days, frankly, I don't think it's easy being *anything*. My friends who have careers have complicated lives and so, obviously, do women like Liz, who work just as hard for no money and less appreciation and status."

I could feel the tension level in the living room drop a bit as Vlaskamp went on. "We all know Shelly. She has strong views on everything, and more than once I've wished she'd keep them to herself. But she is a wonderful mother and a good friend. We have to understand how badly hurt Shelly was. Hurt by being ignored at barbecues. Hurt by people looking through her like she was a pane of glass. Exhausted by her unbelievably tough struggle to save her child from a system that wanted to segregate him and medicate him. This is a woman who, no matter what she says, was always there for other women. I couldn't begin to count the times she listened to someone crying about her husband, picked up kids when some woman couldn't get home from the city in time, brought a pan of lasagna over when someone had the flu and was too sick to make dinner. She's been the surrogate mom for every kid in this neighborhood. That's how she knows how much mothering is needed.

"She's not a saint. She could be strident and even insensitive. But although Liz and I come from different perspectives on how children need to be raised—my kids don't come home to an empty house or a stranger when I'm away from home, they come home to Roberta, who's been taking great care of them since they were infants—we agree on one thing: I too wonder if Shelly would be in jail if not for her outspokenness." Maybe that was easier than contemplating all the evidence the police had against her.

What an amazing comment on our culture, I thought, to take seriously for a second the idea that a woman could be persecuted for being so committed to housewifery. Unbelievable.

I didn't buy it, myself. Shelly was in jail because she was the first credible suspect the police came upon, because there was more than enough reason to arrest her: the gun, the argument, the appointment, the motive. She would be in jail no matter what her domestic views. Yet I understood what Liz and the others were talking about. Shelly was bitterly resented in some quarters in the town, and there were no rallies to free her. Only the Harpies and me, asking questions, tracking the gossip, listening hard.

Vlaskamp's little speech was moving and unifying. And smart. It reminded everybody why they were there. It gave people on both sides a rationale for staying. I wished the whole town could have heard it. Now it was time to proceed.

"So," I said, taking out my notebook, "let's hear what we've got."

I dispensed, again, my usual caveats about discretion. "This stuff should not leave this room. If it were your kids we were talking about, you wouldn't want it to. I don't want our findings to go further than this, not unless it's a life-or-death difference for Shelly. And again, if it works against her, so be it. We're looking for the truth, not our own preconceptions."

"I've got something," Liz Hoffman said. "Two girls have been absent from middle school for long periods. One is Wendy Mosley . . ." She leafed through the notes she'd jotted on a yellow legal pad.

"Liz, I'm aware of her. I don't think we need to discuss her publicly." She nodded, obviously having heard something about Wendy's troubles. There were, truly, no secrets in this town. "Who's the other girl?"

"Lila Tomlinson." She was reading from her notes. "Sixth grade, blond and pretty, lacrosse, chess club, debating society. She's missed almost three weeks. My neighbor's daughter plays lacrosse with her . . . she's a real loss to the team."

I tried to sound casual. "Tomlinson? That name sounds familiar, Liz."

"Well, that's probably because of Tobias," she said. "He's good friends with Shelly's boy Jason, I believe. He's a doll, a sweet, well-mannered boy. Lila's his younger sister. They're an amazing pair, those two kids. The father owns Tomlinson Manufacturing. The mother is a very successful art appraiser, works out of Morristown, flies all over the world. They try to separate the two children so they're not in each other's shadows all the time, being only a year apart . . . She's in private school, at Rochambeau Academy, he's at the Rochambeau Middle School. They're the envy of half of the parents in Rochambeau; they're both well-rounded, high-achievers."

I was shocked, to say the least. And abashed. I realized that I hadn't done any investigative workup on the Tomlinson family, probably the very first thing I should have done after my initial encounter with Tobias. But I'd been stunned at first and then warned off—how would it have looked after the DYFS visit if I started running credit checks on his family or interviewing neighbors? No damn good at all. Real incriminating, in fact. Still, I could have sublet the work to another PI, made a few discreet phone calls, even quietly asked friends around town. I shouldn't have been blind-sided like this. A sister? And why would she have been absent from school as long as Wendy Mosley had? Could Tobias be that evil?

I took some notes as Liz ticked off a few other factoids she'd run across: a couple of kids home sick for extended periods, parents going berserk at baseball games, a member of the middle-school baseball team who had attacked an opposing player with a bat and then been suspended. I underlined the latter.

Patricia Caldwell and Hae Sook Kim added a few divorces, troubled kids and bitterly squabbling siblings to the list. Caldwell had also heard about Wendy Mosley and about a couple of other girls as well who complained of being followed, bumped or intimidated by boys other than Jason in the middle school. I scribbled their names down. This was useful.

I was beginning to think the discovery of Tobias's sister was going to be the big score when Lani Faison piped up.

"Kit, you mentioned this kid named Harry Godwin?" I nodded. "He's like this skateboard assassin. He's run down a bunch of kids in town, seems to get his kicks from it. Somebody ought to stick that skateboard someplace where he won't forget it. A woman in my exercise class, a good friend, almost called the cops on this boy.

"Anyway, the Godwins moved here only two years ago. My exercise friend Cyndi used to live in the same town. She moved here years back, but she still has friends in Newton, where she and the Godwins both lived before coming here. One of those friends actually called and told her to watch out for this family. The parents seemed nice enough, but the boy Harry was in a lot of trouble back there. In fact, he was one of the reasons the family moved. They both work and the kid was unattended—no babysitter, no nanny—and he got into real trouble, not just the spray-paint-on-the-side-of-the-school-bus kind.''

She flipped through her pink spiral notebook. It was dog-eared and stained, probably from having been left around a kitchen or a playroom. ''You're about to ask me what kind of trouble,'' she said, looking towards me. I nodded.

''Harry was accused—this at ten years old, mind you—of luring a little girl in the neighborhood into his garage, locking the door, pulling her clothes off and trying to push various objects up her vagina. When she started crying, he let her go. He threatened her with dreadful stuff if she told anybody, and for a while she didn't, but after he pulled this stunt a couple of times, she started having terrible nightmares. The parents got her to a therapist and it came out.''

The women in the room shook their heads and murmured in surprise and sympathy. I heard bits and snatches: ''My God, ten years old'' and ''That poor child'' and ''That boy needs help.''

''The parents argued that it was no big deal, just boy-girl you-show-me-yours-I'll-show-you-mine stuff. The police were sort of flummoxed. I mean, you can't put a ten-year-old in jail or charge him with sexual assault. The family agreed to get him into treatment. But word got around. Nobody wanted this boy near their kids, and so they moved. They still work long hours; Harry and his younger brother, who's seven, are still mostly unattended. Maid is there to clean and start dinner, but offers little real supervision. So far as we can tell he's not getting any treatment anymore. But he's still trouble.''

Mostly out of professional curiosity—envy would be too strong a term—I asked why ''we'' thought that Harry Godwin wasn't getting any treatment. That kind of information was way beyond even Willie's reach.

''Well,'' Lani said, flipping through a few additional pages, clearing her throat and looking rather satisfied, ''one of the parents in the middle school called up the Godwins and told them Harry was terrorizing their son, who is in the sixth grade. You know, stealing his lunch money and stuff. They got into this tiff, and the boy's mother—she's the receptionist in my pediatrician's office—said Mother Godwin got very huffy and defensive and said they'd been in therapy before and Harry hated it, and they'd all decided it was a total rip-off and wouldn't ever go back. You know, big-time denial . . ."

Lani had good stuff. She took a sip of tea from a cup sitting on the table next to her. "The woman whose son was getting tortured said that if Harry bothered their kid again, he was going either to a shrink or straight into court. To be fair, the Godwins did apologize. They promised they'd talk to Harry and they apparently did, because he stopped bothering this boy, says his mother while I was waiting for my daughter's instant strep culture." Lani smiled. Everybody chuckled. There was a spattering of applause. It would take a private investigator days and many dollars to wrest information like this. Lani got it in under twenty minutes, I'd bet. Maybe *she* would be interested in joining Deleeuw Investigations.

Jeez, what a pair. Tobias and Harry. Could Shelly possibly have failed to notice that her precious Jason was hanging out with the two worst kids in Rochambeau? Though everybody seemed to know that Harry was a profoundly troubled kid, whereas only I— and maybe some of his victims—knew that Tobias was. And he had a model sister, too? Another angel? What was she like?

I thanked Lani profusely for her efforts. I was anxious to sit down and sort through this material. But there was more.

Jeannie Stafford spoke up from the back of the room. "Kit, as you know, I'm a teacher. So I have access to school staffers. I can't really say more than that. I'm also a working woman, so I have access to dry cleaners." Access to dry cleaners? Jeannie saw my look and laughed.

"Well, I don't know about a big-time investigator like you, Kit, but in my limited experience, a few groups seem to know everything about families in a town—plumbers, house cleaners, school people, gardeners and dry cleaners." I might have added a few categories like baby-sitters, pediatricians and supermarket cashiers. One veteran cashier at my market was a veritable Rochambeau CIA.

Jeannie had to be thinking of Bastable's Cleaners. Everybody in town came there at least once a week. George Bastable was immensely proud of his legendary ability to remove the stubborn, sometimes hideously messy stains of daily life from almost anything. He was a canny marketer, too, offering daily specials on tablecloths or ties and boasting of his environmentally sound reusable dry-cleaning bags.

"George Bastable knows everybody in Rochambeau," Jeannie said. "And everybody comes in there to chat, dads home on weekends, housewives during the week, commuters dropping stuff off in the morning, picking it up at night. I learned—as others have—about this group of boys. The Tomlinson boy, Harry Godwin, Schwartz, Shelly's kid. I gather from a teacher in the school that the chief problem was Harry Godwin. Tobias played with these boys, if that's the right term, but his teachers had nothing but praise for him. Jamey Schwartz, well, he's supposed to be relatively benign but malleable, influenced by stronger wills."

"And Jason?" I interrupted.

She frowned. "Jason's had a lot of problems even before this. There was his disorder, but, more than that, there's the dynamic the disorder created."

She paused to look around the semicircle. "I would really urge you all to be careful about all this," she said. "As a teacher, I know how important it is to be discreet. It's critical that teachers not blab information about their students. If someone's life weren't on the line, I'd never be pursuing this. Jason's reputation has suffered enough." There were nods and murmurs of assent. Maybe I was kidding myself, but I thought this group would be cautious. They all had kids and seemed empathetic. Why else would they be here?

Jeannie shook her long braid back off her shoulder and was about to continue when Tracy appeared and asked if someone would come read to her. Carol moved in, grabbed her hand and whisked her off. I heard the two of them laughing on the way up the stairs.

"Jason had a severe case of hyperactivity, a kind of Attention Deficit Disorder, one of the worst the school counselors had seen, according to the records. Most hyperactives are quite treatable. Sometimes they need special training, sometimes some medication, but the vast majority of them do well in school once their conditions are diagnosed. This was a very unusual case."

I was impressed, and envious. Jeannie'd gotten to the records or, more likely, persuaded someone else to get to them.

"He was acting out angrily, damaging books, breaking windows,

hitting other kids. He was a prime case for a special environment
—a school for special-needs kids. The Child Study team came in
to evaluate him. They unanimously felt he should be transferred
to a special school and medicated.

"Jason wasn't learning. Halfway through first grade he couldn't
read or do simple math or other problems. They felt he was very
frustrated, that he was being set up to fail and needed to succeed,
that his was a severe learning disability and that his anger and
frustration over it posed a real danger to himself and other kids.
When he tore up a classroom in the elementary school, he was
designated for transfer."

Jeannie, obviously affected by her story, continued quietly. The
Harpies listened intently, every one of them no doubt wondering:
What if that was my kid? What would I do? "Shelly went into a frenzy
of activity. She took Jason into the city for intense evaluation. She
got a consult at Harvard, where the med school had done a massive study of hyperactive kids. She hired a lawyer and threatened
to sue. She met with school officials. She volunteered to come into
the school every day for two hours to tutor Jason—she has an
elementary ed degree from Stockton State, you know—and then
work with him for two more hours every day at home. The superintendent reluctantly agreed, on the condition that the teachers
and the Child Study team agreed and that Jason caused no further
disruption. It was a radical approach, but there was a lot of research at the time suggesting that it was healthier for these kids to
be mainstreamed, if possible, and that school systems were too
quick to segregate and medicate them. Few parents were willing to
make the commitment Shelly was.

"Well, to make a long story short, Shelly worked miracles with
this boy. She was phenomenally patient, showed up at school every single morning, got Jason reading, doing math, socializing.
There were rough times when he threw tantrums or acted out,
even hit her once. It was an extraordinary ordeal. The people in
the school said they'd never seen anything like it. After more than
four years, Jason was a B student; he had friends; he wasn't on
medication. He moved up to middle school. The district has reas-
sessed its policy of removing or automatically medicating severely
hyperactive or emotionally disturbed kids. Shelly has become a
clearinghouse and resource center for parents with similar difficulties . . ."

"More than that," Lani put in, "she's hands on. She'll come over and help with tutoring. She'll drive kids to counselors in the city."

It was a powerful story, TV-movie stuff. Shelly had told me about her experience with Jason, but I hadn't really grasped the drama of it, the courage involved, the years of brutally difficult work. It was moving, but it was disturbing, too. I could imagine a prosecutor arguing that her great struggle was more than enough of a motive for murder.

"That's the heroic side," said Jeannie grimly. "Here's the downside. Once she started fighting for Jason, Shelly didn't know how to stop. It's not an uncommon problem when kids have physical or emotional problems. I see it all the time in my classes. You get into this mind-set that the world will screw your kid if you're not there every second to protect him. After a while, the child has trouble taking responsibility for himself, figuring out what he's doing wrong and what he's doing right. Because the parent is always right there, dukes up, ready to fight. And here's a case where the parent was dead right—where the system *was* about to screw her kid—so how does she even know when and where to back off? He was condemned once, so it could happen again."

Liz Hoffman spoke up from the sofa. "So that even when the child does mess up, he doesn't get to learn from that because the parent comes zooming in. I make that mistake myself, and my kids don't even have these kinds of problems."

From her seat on the floor, Nadja Piasecka nodded. "My dog had the same difficulty. Maude often fought with other dogs and I was forced to pull her back. Then one day I didn't pull her back and she was badly chewed by a boxer. She learned from this. She drew from the experience. She didn't fight again." That stopped everybody. There were supportive and approving nods from the canine enthusiasts. I looked at Sandra Vlaskamp, who was the least loopy member of the dog play group, and saw the smile start to break out on her face. She turned away. So did I. But the analogy wasn't bad.

Jeannie handled the interruption with the ease of a teacher trained to encourage contributions. "That's an interesting example, Nadja. And I bet Maude is better off for it. But it didn't quite happen here." She shook her head.

"Whenever Jason got into any trouble, Shelly'd rush to his side and fight like a tiger. There were at least half a dozen complaints about Jason before Nancy Rainier-Gault moved to suspend him. Might seem like minor things, depending on your point of view, but way over the line from mine. He pretended to fall once and ended up with his hand on a girl's breast. He squeezed another girl's buttocks and then said, 'Oh, I'm sorry, I thought this was my locker handle.' He admits to snapping the bra. It should have sent up alarm bells, but it sounds as though Shelly couldn't bear to hear that Jason had any other problems. She'd barely survived the earlier ones.''

I was scribbling notes as fast as she was talking.

''But, Jeannie,'' Sandra asked, ''what does this have to do with Bastable's Cleaners?'' Good question.

''That's a different piece of the puzzle. I talked to a pediatrician, a couple of maids I know, and I wasn't getting anywhere. Then I was in Bastable's talking to George—his niece has also adopted a Latin American child it turns out, so we have things to talk about. Anyway, we were gossiping about the murder—George doesn't need much pushing to gossip—and I led the conversation around to these boys. George said he knew some of them well, that he often had to chase them away from his parking lot with their skateboards. They were in danger of rolling right into traffic. He said Harry Godwin in particular loved to sweep past little kids and women pushing baby carriages, slam into them sometimes, and George would rush out and give him hell. He said ninety-nine out of a hundred kids would run off or say they were sorry, but Harry just looked at him and laughed. George said he knew Tobias and thought he was a great kid, other than the fact that he hung around with Harry.''

Jeannie turned to me. ''Kit, he told me something else I thought you might find interesting. He said Jason was there skateboarding with Tobias and Harry and Jamey one afternoon and George had come out to ask them for the forty-seventh time to be careful. A cop drove by. The boys noticed the shotgun in a rack on the patrol car's dashboard. George was on his way inside and the boys didn't realize he was still within earshot. Jamey said his dad had a shotgun too. Jason said so what, so did his dad. That Jason knew where it was kept, had taken it out from time to time and even loaded it once. Harry said he wanted to see it and Jason said sure. He was bragging, obviously happy to impress Harry, said

George. George remembered it well because he was alarmed at the thought of these kids playing with guns.''

"What did he do?'' Liz wondered, alarmed herself.

"Well, he called the Bloomfields' house and talked to Dan Bloomfield. Told him his son was bragging about their having a shotgun and was going to show it to these other boys, some of whom he didn't think should ever get anywhere near a firearm.''

"How did Bloomfield react?'' I asked. "Or didn't George remember.''

"Oh, he remembered,'' Jeannie said. "Dan was furious. Said he'd give Jason hell when he got home. Assured George the gun was locked up and beyond reach and that Jason was just boasting. He thanked George for calling and said he'd double-check to make sure nobody touched that gun. George says now the one he should obviously have worried about was Shelly, not the boy.''

The story had me spinning. It was a lot more meaningful than Jeannie knew. It sure didn't square with Dan Bloomfield's notions of how secure his own gun had been. He'd never mentioned to me that Jason had gotten his hands on it or even knew where it was. I was further embarrassed, because I'd been in Bastable's myself the day before and George gave me a hearty hello and even pumped me about the case. He'd obviously not thought the story about the boys and the guns important enough to tell me, and I hadn't questioned him about anything he might have heard. I could learn a lot from this group.

I heard another half hour's worth of town gossip, anecdotes about messed-up kids and busted marriages, three drug problems, a fifteen-year-old who beat his siblings. Lots of it was interesting, some of it surprising, but none, I thought, relevant.

Sandra Vlaskamp had talked to Nancy Rainier-Gault's neighbor, who said the principal loved Rochambeau and loved the challenge of the town's well-funded but, in some ways, unenlightened school district. Rainier-Gault had become more and more disturbed about what she was finding out at the middle school and more and more determined to do something about it. But she had never, the neighbor insisted, indicated that she thought herself in any sort of danger. Too bad. A bit more paranoia might have saved her life.

The Rochambeau Harpies had done well—very well. They had gained access to almost everything by means of the interconnected network of merchants, therapists and teachers through whom all things suburban must pass.

I thanked them all profusely for their valuable work. Liz Hoffman said she'd been very happy to help and hoped she got another chance to play detective. Others agreed.

There were various announcements: neighbors inviting the Bloomfield kids over for playdates, a group forming to improve day-care options in town, a school tag sale for which donations would be appreciated. The suburban wheels ground on. Even Carol chimed in: "The abortion clinic in Ridgefield needs defenders next week. The fanatics are coming. Any volunteers?" One or two hands went up. Women seem to grow roots around one another, I thought. If this were a men's meeting, we'd all be in our cars and gone by now.

I was hoping that further Harpies conventions wouldn't be necessary on this case, that some break would come before we could schedule another session. Yet I had found the group not only effective but useful. We had become a kind of small community, one of the associations Americans were always forming to build some sense of connection. In the process, we had shared some opinions and aired some differences. This was the way conflicts should be worked out, I thought, with people face to face and in manageable numbers—not making angry statements for TV news but speaking directly to one another.

I looked at my watch. I was anxious to get home and hear from Willie. The women in the group hugged one another, helped clear the cups and straightened out the room. They seemed to drift out with an air of regret, not so much because the meeting had been so exciting but because they appeared to enjoy being together. When asked, I reassured them that we weren't done yet, but I wasn't being totally truthful. I felt the case was close either to being broken or to being lost. It would soon become clear which.

Eighteen

THE AMERICAN DREAM was looking a bit worn to me as I left the Harpies' meeting at ten-thirty and walked the few steps to my door to take Percentage for his last walk of the day. It was hard not to feel discouraged about the town I lived in. Once I'd started working out here, I'd learned pretty quickly that the suburbs are equal parts reality, illusion and myth.

Back when I was on the train to Wall Street I did lots of the mythologizing myself. I pictured the business world ahead of me as tense, cutthroat, draining—and male. The life left behind was teeming with healthy, laughing, well-rounded little suburbanites, an army of busy, good-hearted moms whizzing them via van and wagon from Kinderkickers to Tot Swim to Gyminee Crickets. I thought of teachers, nannies and coaches tenderly caring for their beaming flocks, exhorting them to run faster, learn more, do better. And I saw myself as just another of the intrepid guys who risked high blood pressure to make it all possible. What did I know? I came home to sleep and to try to atone on weekends by racing the kids to malls and movies.

Such idealized notions of suburbia are always dumb stereotypes, I know. But this investigation had made the disparity between the fantasy and the truth seem starker than ever. I had to remind myself that normal families struggling to lead normal lives were all around me as well. They weren't *all* suffering, in pain or in conflict. It only looked that way.

I couldn't wait for my own family to return to the ranks of the normal, to the rhythms of life—treks to the town pool, vacation preparations, disagreements over back-to-school wardrobes.

There's just no way of knowing about kids. Tobias Tomlinson

was raised in a traditional family; he was comfortable—privileged, even—and well educated. Tracy Stafford next door had been plucked from her impoverished, violence-wracked country, transported thousands of miles to be raised by two women of limited means and great hearts, destined to be much loved and to grow up among the sometimes tolerant but often uncomprehending stares and whispers of her peers. She was doing fine so far, seemed confident, resilient and generous. Tobias was distinctly screwed-up: something had gone very wrong.

We know some things: if you abuse your children, neglect them, give them no space to breathe, no opportunity to stumble, entangle yourself hopelessly in their lives, talk at them instead of listen to them, they can easily be damaged. But there is so much we don't know.

Are parents totally responsible for what happens to their kids, for how they turn out? How much do genes, peers, teachers and just pure dumb luck have to do with it? For all of our theories, therapists, and TV talk-show experts, we really don't understand exactly how it all works, do we?

My best thinking time is spent in dawdly, zigzaggy walks with Percentage. Over the years we have strolled just about every street in Rochambeau, peered into windows, listened to quarrels and raging exhortations of kids, watched the progress of renovations I could no longer afford myself. Percentage and I had observed the unmistakable signs of the suburban life cycle: toys scattered on the lawns, then sandboxes yielding to basketball hoops, then no signs of life in kids' bedrooms in the summer, then college stickers on the bumpers of station wagons. There was something simultaneously sad and celebratory about it, loss mixed with life.

It's easy to ponder during these walks. Percentage and I are like comfortable old shoes together. I almost never have to use the leash; I carry it over my shoulder instead. He knows where I will turn; I know where he will sniff. His injury had hardly slowed his pace, which was already leisurely. So many trees, so little time.

We headed over to Rochambeau Municipal Park, where I had first encountered Shelly Bloomfield and the doggie play group.

This had to be a shortish walk. There'd been a message from Willie when I got home: he would drop an envelope off on my porch sometime after eleven; I was to call him at home after I'd looked over its contents. I was anxious to see what he'd found.

Nothing minor would have caused him to breach our security so dramatically.

Percentage and I ambled easily along the park's familiar walkways. A Rochambeau PD car cruising along the concrete path in the middle fixed its spotlight on us. There had been a rape here a few years back and a series of purse-snatchings a year or so ago, but the park still seemed plenty safe for a late-night dog walk.

What was this case really about, I asked myself as Percentage methodically proceeded from bush to tree, sniffing, lifting his good leg, moving on. What was at the heart of this crime? Figuring that out would reveal the truth, or so I believed.

A school principal, Nancy Rainier-Gault, had been murdered. Killed in her office with Dan Bloomfield's rifle. The rifle had been found in the Bloomfields' firewood, the prints rubbed off. Shelly Bloomfield had an appointment with the principal at nearly the precise time of the murder. She had means, motive and opportunity. At stake was the fate of her son Jason, to whose care she had devoted her life. If anything in the world could turn this supermom into a killer, it would be a threat to Jason. But it would have to be a major threat. Was a one-week suspension major enough?

Apparently working alone, believing she would be more effective getting victims to talk than the police would, Rainier-Gault had been closing in on a group of cruel and dangerous young men who had tormented and assaulted at least one girl, perhaps many others. Until her arrival, administrators and too many parents saw this behavior as noxious but inevitable, to be discouraged but not overreacted to.

These boys almost surely were Tobias Tomlinson, Harry Godwin, Jason Bloomfield and Jamey Schwartz. I had wondered if there might be others, but even the Harpies hadn't uncovered any other candidates. In his young life, Harry Godwin had a history of these kinds of attacks and his family hadn't seen fit to get him appropriate treatment. According to Nate Hauser—and Jeannie's findings—Jason wasn't entirely new to the harassment game either. Tobias Tomlinson was fully capable of threats, manipulation, lying and perhaps worse, though this was not well known or widely documented. I had no idea where his younger sister fit in, but she clearly did, and I meant to show up at the Tomlinsons' home the next morning, DYFS be damned.

If you clung to the idea that Shelly Bloomfield was innocent, which I did—she was still my client, as far as I was concerned—then the key to this case had to lie with this group of boys.

In a way, the group they had formed seemed to support some of Shelly Bloomfield's controversial notions about child care. These boys appeared to roam Rochambeau at will, hanging out in parking lots and stalking girls in parks. Nobody seemed responsible for knowing what they were doing, for reining them in when problems developed, even for noticing that problems *were* developing. Was this because their parents weren't at home or—more likely, in my view—because their parents weren't paying enough attention when they were?

Yet wasn't the Last Housewife's own miracle child among this nasty quartet, despite her sacrifices and efforts? That showed the limits of the philosophy she clung to so fiercely: you couldn't guarantee success for your children by renouncing the wider world for yourself.

A man in a luminous spandex jogging suit huffed past me. It was late for running—lawyer stuck in the city late on a case, maybe. In response, Percentage gave a little woof, not very menacing, but probably enough to convince anybody with malicious intent that he was a real dog capable of inflicting some injury.

I was trying not to overreact to Dan Bloomfield's lying to me about his gun. A lot of dads would have fibbed to protect their sons, or rationalized the incident as unimportant, merely something that had happened a while back of no immediate relevance. But didn't Bloomfield realize that he would be helping his wife by telling the police that Jason's pals knew of the gun's existence, perhaps had even seen or handled it? That meant lots of people could have gotten their hands on the gun, a crucial piece of information. Why would Bloomfield remain silent about it? He might be an oblivious man but, unless I completely misread him, he was not a malevolent one. Maybe he Just Didn't Get It. Maybe he couldn't bear the prospect of a wife and son in trouble at the same time.

Denial. It has become a raging cliché, but I see a lot of it in my work. Wives convinced their long-gone husbands or runaway kids are about to walk in the door. Parents who adamantly refuse to believe their kids are on drugs, even when you shake the vials out of their book bags. Absent fathers who insist their abandoned

families are doing just fine when the kids are subsisting on pasta
and potato chips.

And Tobias, the nightmare kid, the menacing little manipulator
who haunted me and almost did me in with a phone call or two.
How much energy and alertness it must take to keep up that perfect mask, how much strength, how much anger.

Nothing about Tobias made sense. A sister absent from school
for weeks didn't exactly fit into the puzzle either. This kid was a
maze; every path led to another path. And the whole time you
were watching him, he was watching you. He was a modern-day
suburban Frankenstein, pieced together of everyone's aspirations
for their kids. Scholar and athlete, beautiful and brilliant—yet no
matter how attractive the shell, somehow the wires inside were all
crossed. Could he be so damaged, so twisted emotionally that he
would harm his own sister, or permit her to be harmed by his
friends?

I needed to sort through the gleanings offered by the Harpies—
Harry Godwin's troubled history and Jeannie Stafford's warning
about Jason Bloomfield among them. This notion of solving all
your kid's problems is epidemic in Rochambeau. Parents try to
anticipate, evade or overcome every conceivable hurt or challenge
before their children can experience or resolve them. When you
throw in a hyperactive, learning-disabled kid who was nearly
packed off to a special school, well . . . anything could happen.

So was Shelly protecting Jason by trying to drive me off the
case? She'd had a full day to react to my telegram by now, and she
hadn't. What did *that* mean? Why fire me and then remain silent
when I refused to go away? Why hadn't Eric Levin called and
warned me of an impending lawsuit if I didn't stop my inquiries?
My client was becoming less comprehensible to me all the time. I
was unofficially working with the Mosleys now as well, and I barely
knew them either.

Was I overlooking something about the murder itself? There
were only forty-five minutes or so between the time the janitor
found the body and the police were swarming over the Bloomfield
house, according to their reports. It struck me that it required an
enraged adult with transportation and a lot of premeditation to
have brought the gun to the school, used it, driven away and
hidden it. These were not traits widely associated with thirteen-
year-olds, but if you read a newspaper or watched TV news, you

saw a lot of young killers in handcuffs. The killer was somebody
with reason to hate Nancy Rainier-Gault or to want desperately to
silence her. Would people kill to prevent their sexual harassing or
that of their children from being exposed? If so, the list of people
with motive had surely broadened: whomever Rainier-Gault had
been investigating, their parents, friends et cetera. But so far only
Shelly fit all the other criteria.

The killer had to know that the principal would be in the school
that Saturday afternoon. In order to frame Shelly, he or she would
have to have known she was coming too. Somebody Shelly had
told about the meeting. Or somebody Rainier-Gault had told. But
so far as I knew, nobody knew about it outside the Bloomfields,
not even Nate Hauser. I suppose it was possible that Jason Bloomfield knew, perhaps had even told his friends. I pulled a Post-it
and pencil nub from the pocket of my windbreaker and wrote
down "kids knew?" Though I had no idea how I was going to find
out, since I was persona non grata at the Bloomfields and I wasn't
on intimate terms with his pals either.

Percentage and I circled the park twice. As we came back onto
my block, I saw a small foreign car speeding towards us, away from
my house. In the moonless night, the headlights were blinding.
The little car slowed as it neared us; I heard a beep and the raw
sounds of Smashing Pumpkins (Ben loved them) wafting from a
souped-up stereo. "Hey, Kit!" called a familiar voice, then the car
sped off. Willie and I had finally met. Sort of.

A police cruiser pulled across the street from my house and
parked. The officer inside raised a Styrofoam cup to me and I
waved back. Percentage woofed, then looked around to see what
he was woofing at. I was glad to see a cop but just as glad he hadn't
encountered Willie dropping something off on my porch. I didn't
want his name in their files. Chief Leeming was helping me, but
able to keep an eye on me too, something he was always all too
eager to do.

The envelope was sitting on the front porch. I went inside, hung
up the leash, turned off the porch light. Percentage nuzzled me to
remind me about his late-night biscuit, which he took in his
mouth and paced around with, wriggling for joy.

I found Jane asleep at the kitchen table over a pile of case
reports two feet high, woke her and gently steered her upstairs.
Percentage hobbled up too, retreated to his cedar bed with his

biscuit, adjusted his gimpy leg, thumped his tail in farewell and promptly conked out. He wouldn't move for hours.

I went in to check on Ben and Emily. Both were sound asleep. Em's hamster Blair skittered around and around noisily on her squeaking wheel. Emily believed the rodent possessed wondrous qualities of depth and genius. I wasn't sure how you identified such characteristics in a hamster, but Em often saw things in small creatures that I didn't. Ben's room had its usual after-the-cyclone look, clothes, sneakers, CD's and schoolwork piled in various corners. Like fights over food and clothes, battles over neatness were rarely won by grown-ups unwilling to take extreme measures.

I wandered through the house, locking windows and making sure the doors were bolted. I felt reasonably secure, with the police obviously keeping a close watch and Percentage to set up a raucous though pointless din if anybody came near the house.

Then I tucked Jane in and kissed her. She opened her eyes and smiled. I'd been dallying with the idea of making love that night, but between Willie's envelope and her fatigue, I could see that it would have to wait. She conscientiously tried to ask me how my various meetings had gone, but I assured her we'd catch up in the morning. "Good night. Love you," she mumbled, and her eyes closed again.

I went down to the living room. The house was still now except for crickets outside and Blair's squeaky exercising. I clicked on a reading lamp. Willie's envelope contained a thin computer printout.

The top of the file read *Cyberskulls*. It looked like a diary kept by four different people, all with disguised or symbolic identities. I didn't really know which of the four contributors was "Morph," "Flash," "Kryptic" or "Burnout." The printout contained scores of entries from each of the four, dating back to a two-month period late last year. I was at least five pages into it before I really grasped what I was reading, and I didn't come close to believing it until I'd read those pages twice more. The entries were damning, though I cursed at the writers' cleverness. No identifiable names were used, victims' or aggressors'. But now I understood why Shelly had tried to fire me.

It was a good thing the phone rang when it did, though it made me jump. I am not a violent man, but if I could have gotten my hands on Tobias at that moment, I swear I would have rammed the printout down his weaselly throat, then happily called Investigator Rheingold myself.

It was Willie on the phone. "Hey, it's me. You get the stuff? I got a little nervous, thought I saw a cop car pull up behind me. Pretty wild, isn't it?" Willie's was always a cheerful voice, no matter what unpleasantness he'd dug up, but not tonight. I'd never heard him so somber.

"Great work. How'd you get it?"

"It had been saved, then renamed. When you save a file, the computer asks you where you want the file saved to. Somebody saved this to the Applications File, then renamed it. It was probably an accident. I suspect it was put under a different file by mistake, so it was there all the time but under a different name. The computer made an extra copy of it, maybe because the kid hit the save command twice. My friend says people often do that if it doesn't go fast enough, and this was an older Mac. The user probably thought he was deleting when he was just saving it under a different name. Happens all the time. There's probably a lot more that was deleted, though. This file . . ."

I wasn't quite grasping the specifics of what Willie was telling me, and didn't really care. I wanted to read the rest of the Cyberskulls file. I wasn't sure Willie had absorbed the meaning of what he had extracted.

"I'm grateful, Willie. This might not be great bedtime reading. In fact, it turns my stomach. But, as I'm sure you know, this is incredibly important. I'll call you in the morning."

"Wait, there's more. The Godwins moved here from Newton, Mass.," he told me. "The kid has a police file. Investigation for misdemeanor assault."

I told him I knew. I was impatient to return to the file.

"But I found something you might not know," Willie said, sounding aggrieved that I was slighting his discoveries. "Dan Bloomfield wrote a check for $10,000 to a Stanley Rodburg last month." I didn't ask him how he knew that. Working in the credit office, Willie had access to bank-account information in one way or another.

"Who the hell is Stanley Rodburg?"

"Divorce lawyer in Morris County. I looked him up in the phone book. And that's not the only thing . . ."

"There's more?" I was beginning to reel.

"Dan Bloomfield started using his Amex a lot in the city a few months ago. Maybe he's got a new job or something, or maybe he just acquired a new appreciation for fine food. Le Cirque, La Grenouille, Bouley, and there's nearly a thousand bucks in florist bills over a few months. Plus four stays at real nice hotels, and two jewelry hits at Tiffany's."

Willie didn't need to say more about his findings. This was familiar turf. We knew the profile: Dan Bloomfield was a Cheatin' Husband. A Cheatin' Husband who, with the help of a lawyer, was planning to become an ex-husband. Lord.

My revulsion over the things I'd been reading was replaced by a stab of sorrow over what kind of spouse Shelly Bloomfield had and at the ghastly family mess he was evidently planning to leave behind. But sympathy would have to wait. I promised to call Willie in the morning and hung up.

I reached into my jacket pocket to retrieve some of the business cards I'd been handed that week, flipping through until I found the one I wanted. I suspected I'd wake her up, but she had warned me to call if I found out anything significant.

On my last big case, Leeming had actually locked me up for five or six hours for withholding information, until he'd appeared in my holding cell to announce that he had decided to drop the whole thing. But the state licensing board took a dim view of PI's who were less than forthcoming in criminal cases. In locking me up, Leeming had obviously meant to frighten me into being a good boy, one who shared. So I was sharing. At least, up to a point.

Nineteen

BENCHLEY CARROLLTON was chipper and wide awake when I called at six a.m. I knew he got up every morning at five for his Quakerly meditations and a walk among the shrubs and seedlings of his peaceable little kingdom.

"Kit, what a pleasant surprise. How about joining me for some cider and muffins? Fresh batch, baked them myself last night."

Tempting, but not this morning. This was going to be a major day in the lives of lots of people in Rochambeau. My own among them.

"I'm running, Benchley. I'll take a rain check. But I do need a favor, though. I need to borrow your cellular phone, if it's convenient."

Benchley's Garden Center was spread over more than ten acres, including a small apple orchard and several rows of evergreens for Christmas. For years, Benchley had used battered old walkie-talkies to communicate with his staff, but often was unable to respond personally to callers frantic about aphids and leaf drop. A few months ago, he finally yielded to new technology and bought himself a cell phone.

Benchley didn't blink or ask questions. Even though I was bothering him during the hour of silence with which he began every day of his life, he gave the response he always gave when asked for something. "Of course, Kit. When do you need it?"

"I hate to take it on a Saturday, Benchley. I know it's a busy day for—"

"Don't be silly. I managed for nearly half a century to run the Garden Center without being in instant communication with the world. I can manage for one day. Remember, just hit the 'phone' button to dial, and any button on the keyboard to answer.''

"So how would you hit 9-1-1?"

There was a pause.

"Kit. Are you okay?" Assured that I was, but still dubious, he answered: "Push 'phone,' then 9-1-1." Benchley and I had faced a bit of danger ourselves on a case, more than I had anticipated and lots more than an eighty-one-year-old Quaker should encounter. He knew the danger signals. But I wasn't dragging him into this one.

"Thanks, Benchley, I—"

"I'll leave the phone by my back door in its case, Kit. It's a small fold-over and has fifteen hours of battery time. It'll fit comfortably in your jacket pocket. When things settle down, will you stop by and fill me in? I miss you." I promised.

The man was a godsend. No wonder Jane swore that if I ever seriously misbehaved, she'd dump me in a flash and head for Benchley.

I got dressed—standard Deleeuw combat issue: chinos, blue ox-ford-cloth shirt, L.L. Bean mocs, well-worn navy blazer—then leaned over the bed to kiss Jane good-bye. No lovemaking this morning either.

A weary groan. "Whass-up?" mumbled My Better Half.

"Got to go break this case. Or die trying."

That woke her up. "For real? Is it dangerous?"

"I don't think so."

"You didn't think so the night you got shot in the side either," she pointed out. Jane believed strongly in our individual independence, but she had no visible faith in my common sense. She's never let me forget that incident, despite my repeated insistence that it was just an oversight. How was I to know the guy had a gun when I came crashing through his bedroom window in the middle of the night? I wasn't one of those people who took nearly getting killed to be an inevitable by-product of my work.

"If there turn out to be complications, I'll be careful and call in the cavalry. Promise. I don't know if I've got the case solved, not completely. I might have to do some monumental bluffing. I might even end up in a bit of trouble." Now there's an understatement. "But I have one of those strong hunches and I'm going to follow it. This ain't so pretty a town as we thought when we staked our claim, podnah.''

I reminded Jane to keep the kids inside. "I hope this will mean we don't have to worry about them anymore," I said. But the truth was, I had no idea if that would be the result or not. Welcome to America, the world's best-equipped shooting gallery, where every sick person had the sacred right to his own assault weapon.

She gave me a long, sweet good-bye kiss. "Don't be John Wayne, okay?" I agreed and I meant it. You, sir, are no John Wayne, I told myself.

I kissed Em good-bye and waved to Blair, who twitched her whiskers at me. I patted Ben on the shoulder; he muttered something I couldn't make out and rolled over.

Benchley's little phone was hanging on a peg by the back door in a leather case, just as promised. So was a paper bag with a warm blueberry muffin inside. He stuck his head out back as I pulled away, waved and called, "Good luck." I waved back.

The North Jersey Copy Center—open twenty-four hours a day, six days a week—was just down the road from the Garden Center. It took only a few minutes to make two copies of the Cyberskulls file. Feeling somewhat melodramatic, I bought a manila envelope and mailed a copy to Benchley.

It was another ten minutes back past the Garden Center and across town to the Rochambeau Middle School. Two unmarked police cars sat in the circular driveway at the main door, which stood open. Chief Leeming, Detective Peterson and a befuddled, groggy-eyed custodian stood in the doorway.

I wolfed down the last crumbling bite of muffin, stepped out of the Volvo, nodded to the custodian, then smiled at the chief. Leeming looked less than thrilled to see me. His weekend slacks and polo shirt barely concealed the butt of the .9-mm pistol protruding from his pants. Peterson appeared more official in pants and a poplin jacket, though a bit less crisp than usual.

"Why, Chief of Police Leeming," I said, feigning shock. "I am pleased and flattered that a civic official of your stature would be here in response to a call from a private detective of my notoriously inadequate investigative skills."

"Well, you have had some spectacular moments," he shot back. "Let's see, there was the time you got yourself nicked by that bullet. And the time I spotted you burglarizing a retirement home—"

"You didn't catch me in the act," I objected. Though he sure came close.

"But I did get to lock you up for withholding evidence a few months ago. And I've got a pair of fresh handcuffs right here, just in case I should be lucky enough to need them again. But mostly, I'm here to keep you from doing any permanent damage to yourself or somebody else. Like Detective Peterson, for instance. She's too valuable to lose."

I clucked. "Chief, Chief. If I don't cooperate, you say I'm a jerk. If I keep you informed, you still say I'm a jerk. I'm here to cooperate. You walk me through the murder scene again and I'll turn over some evidence you will want to see. I'll be a good citizen and a model private investigator. And you'll make some headway on a murder case you say you have solved but suspect in the darkest recesses of your heart that you haven't."

Peterson groaned. She looked sleepy and irritable. I'd awakened her last night, forcing her to rouse herself at dawn on a Saturday morning. "I hate to interrupt all this boy-talk, but it's early, I'm pissed off, I'd love to get on with the business at hand. If there *is* business at hand."

There was. The custodian, whom Peterson had asked the school administrators to dispatch, stayed out front as Leeming, Peterson and I walked inside. The murder scene was still preserved, the yellow tape in place. I didn't think Rochambeau's parents wanted to see their kids walk by police tapes much longer, constantly reminded that their principal had been cold-bloodedly murdered in her office.

"What's in the envelope?" Leeming asked impatiently.

"First things first. I'm feeling cooperative, but you first." Maybe the Bloomfield arrest really had bothered him too. Maybe he had finally decided to trust me. I suspected Peterson might have put in a good word, or perhaps both of them were feeling bad about the ordeal to which Tobias Tomlinson had subjected me. I hoped so.

I had just a couple of questions about the shooting. "Chief, were there powder burns on the victim? Is the idea that Rainier-Gault was shot at close range?"

Leeming and Peterson exchanged lightning-quick glances. As a rule, cops don't talk about evidence before trial; it makes prosecu-

tors berserk. As a practical matter, however, we were sort of working on the case together and clearly the Rochambeau PD wanted
to hear what I had to say. They knew they could count on my
discretion. If I referred to a word they told me, no cop in town—
in the state, for that matter—would ever talk to me again.

"Deleeuw, for future reference, that's one of the first things you
should ask about a shooting, not the last." Peterson sounded
cranky. "That has everything to do with the nature of the killing.
A point-blank firing is an execution. Farther away can be other
things." She didn't volunteer what.

"So?"

"So," said Leeming, "this wasn't point-blank range. Some distance away—ten to fifteen feet, maybe twenty. She wasn't shot
through the window, the glass was all intact, and she wasn't shot in
her seat. Best we can tell, she was standing up at her desk behind
her chair and she was shot in the chest by somebody firing right in
front of her, perhaps through the open door." He glanced across
the hallway into the school library. Hint.

"So, basically, you're saying somebody pulled out the gun, fired
a single shot through the doorway—"

"Didn't say that exactly, Deleeuw," said Leeming. "It *could* have
been just inside the office. But probably not; the state police ballis-
tics guys confirm it wasn't point-blank range."

"Could the shot have been fired from across the hallway?" I
asked.

The school library faced the principal's office directly across the
hallway. On that Saturday, I presumed, it was dark just like it was
now.

"If the library door was propped open, sure," said Leeming.
"And we did find some indentations on the carpet in the library,
despite the fact it had been vacuumed the night before by our
friend Jerry out there. No way to get footprints or shoe types or
anything. But why would Bloomfield hide in the library? She had
an appointment. She probably just pulled out the gun as she was
leaving the office and fired."

"But wouldn't Rainier-Gault have noticed a shotgun?" I looked
down at the ugly stains that still discolored the carpet behind the
desk. Portraits of Barbara Jordan, Hillary Clinton, Sandra Day
O'Connor and Sojourner Truth hung on the wall along with the
traditional renderings of Jefferson, Lincoln and Henry David Tho-

reau. "Wouldn't she have run? Screamed? The library was the best place to take the shotgun. It's dark there, and she wouldn't have seen it."

Danielle Peterson scowled. If the detective was impressed by my reasoning, she wasn't showing it. "We found a duffel bag in Bloomfield's car," she said. "She could have carried the gun in it. For that matter, she could have stormed out of here, gone back to her car, retrieved the shotgun, come back in and fired through the doorway. She could even have hidden the rifle in the library, then gone back inside for it.

"The office door was open," Peterson pointed out. "Odds are Rainier-Gault wasn't sitting there staring at the doorway. She would have been working."

"But somebody could have fired the shot from the library, sure," Leeming concluded.

Wouldn't that have made the most sense, I thought? Rainier-Gault hadn't tried to run away, probably didn't even see her assailant approaching. I walked into the library. There was a bookcase just inside the doorway that would have made a perfect screen and armrest for someone holding a rifle. It was a little high—I had to raise my arm to rest it there—but the angle of fire was perfect. With the library door open, you looked about twenty feet straight into the principal's office.

"What was on the desktop or on the floor?" I asked. "Anything?"

"Yeah," Leeming said grimly. "Jason Bloomfield's student file." That didn't look so hot.

I glanced around, stepped into the hallway, came back in.

"Look," Leeming said, "I'm happy to cooperate with you, Kit, but I'm not happy to play games. I have to drive my daughter into the city. She's trying out for the New York City Ballet junior company."

"Last question," I promised. "The janitor who was working that Saturday—why didn't he see Shelly arrive or leave?"

"That's easy," Peterson said. "The principal directed him to work elsewhere in the building. Unfortunately for her, she wanted these conferences to be strictly private with all this sexual harassment stuff; she made a big thing about confidentiality. She was trying to be respectful of the supposed assailants as well as the victims. Which probably cost her her life. The custodian didn't see anything—until he heard the shot and came running. And then all he saw was her body."

"Okay," I told them, "thanks. Here's my part of the bargain. Chief, I know Shelly is innocent, which I'm sure you suspect by now too, your being smart and all. I have some computer print-outs here for you to read. You'll grasp the significance of them quickly enough and want to talk to the authors. Meanwhile, I'd like to invite Detective Peterson to come with me, since I hope to get some information in the next hour or two that might help break the case. It's a hunch, granted. But you always say you'd like to be included. So I'm inviting you."

Leeming made his pro forma request to let the police handle this, which we both knew I couldn't honor. I had to represent my client's—okay—ex-client's, interests. Besides, there was no way I'd stand back now and let somebody else close my own case.

In the end, Leeming didn't squawk all that much. He told Peterson to go along but drive separately. Two investigations moving on parallel tracks. Then he flicked on a reading lamp in the school library and settled in with the computer printout. He wouldn't like what he read any more than I had and there would be some disrupted households in Rochambeau this quiet morning, whatever the outcome of my case.

"Chief," I called over my shoulder, "before you read the print-outs, call your wife. Somebody else is going to have to drive your daughter into the city this morning."

Leeming raised his middle finger at me. "Just be careful, okay? Whatever the hell you're doing. And Peterson, stay in touch. I don't give a shit about Deleeuw, but good detectives are hard to find."

Ah, men, and the way they show affection. Next thing, he'd be wanting to arm-wrestle.

We drove in separate cars. It was smart to keep the police investigation distinct from mine and Danielle Peterson was far too independent—not to mention fastidious—to ride along in my Volvo. She followed me as our caravan wound its way to the toniest address in town.

There are no really bad neighborhoods in Rochambeau, but there are some modest or marginal ones. Edgewood Terrace is not among them. It runs along the ridge on the northern edge of town, from which residents can gaze out over the town and the marshes and highways beyond, to the twinkling spires of Manhattan.

My street was zoned four houses to an acre, which gave everybody a bit of breathing space. Up here, the ratio was probably reversed: four acres, one house. There were stucco Tudor mansions with circular driveways and Gothic stone castles and sprawling modern wood and concrete aeries. The richest people in town lived on Edgewood, including the Tomlinson family of Tomlinson Manufacturing, makers of industrial machinery. Tomlinson plants were far out of town, north of Paterson and—these days—scattered through Asia and South America.

But the Tomlinsons remained one of Rochambeau's leading families, always popping up in the local paper doing this good work or chairing that civic event. They were strait-laced, well connected and extremely, obscenely rich.

Their house was a massive white colonial surrounded by lush, well-tended gardens. A refurbished carriage house out back undoubtedly housed the help, and a tasteful stone arch over the side drive sheltered a Lexus and two shiny black Mercedes.

Lawns velvety enough for croquet sloped down several hundred yards to the quiet street below. Only landscaping pros—not the high school kids with borrowed mowers that common folk used—could keep grass that green and carpetlike. I parked the car on the drive below the main entrance so anybody inside could see me.

It wasn't yet seven a.m.

Peterson stepped out of the car and chuckled. "Probably not too many black people get in here except to clean, what do you think? When they see me coming, they'll probably call the police. *I* get to tell them I *am* the police, okay?"

I allowed myself a superior smile. "I don't want to make you feel crummy, but the family next door is African-American. Anthony Parker, the stockbroker—" I pointed through a stand of oaks to a similarly massive Georgian several hundred yards away. "And Georgia Jones-Meadows, the singer, lives up here somewhere."

She smirked. "You're just trying to make me feel good about myself, right, Deleeuw? And call me Danielle, okay?" Okay. She was turning out to be surprisingly easy to work with. And sharp. Maybe *she'd* want to be an associate in Deleeuw Investigations. She was probably only making twice what I could pay. But it was nice to have a pal in the Rochambeau PD.

It was a raid, sort of, without the helmets and flak jackets, the kind of visit I doubted the Tomlinsons had ever had. We banged on the brass knocker and hit the bell. "Good alarm system here," Danielle said, eyeing the sensor set into the door frame. "We probably set it off just walking up the drive."

It was a few minutes before a dark-skinned woman in a bathrobe —Pakistani, perhaps—answered the door, looking wide-eyed and nervous. She opened the outer door, but not the inner one in the vestibule behind her.

"Yes?" she queried, peering at Peterson's ID and then, more doubtfully, at mine.

"We'd like to see—" Peterson broke off and looked at me with annoyance. "Who exactly *are* we seeing here, Deleeuw? Are you going to fill me in on anything? You better know what you're doing here, because all this guy has to do is yell for his next-door neighbor and we're both up the creek."

I shrugged my no-big-deal shrug. "Easy, Detective," I said with far more assurance than I felt. "We need to see *everybody*. The whole Tomlinson family. Are they at home?"

The maid nodded yes. Peterson and I each gave her our cards to take up and asked her to wake Gifford Tomlinson and his wife and both children. It was urgent, I added.

She had us wait in a living room about the size of Giants Stadium. Three vast floral-upholstered sofas sat in a horseshoe in one corner of the room and Danielle and I took up positions in a love seat facing them. We had time to spend gawking at the bronze sculptures, the portraits of weighty Tomlinsons, the massive stone fireplace on one wall. A bay window looked down over the town and across the marshes. I picked out the towers of the World Trade Center looming in the distance. Scores of midtown skyscrapers were visible through the morning haze. It was probably a knockout view at night.

Gifford Tomlinson came quickly and forcefully into the room. He'd put on slippers and a plaid cashmere bathrobe, and he didn't look happy. Somewhere in his early fifties, I guessed, tanned and fit, sandy hair graying in a distinguished way about the temples. He probably spent a lot of time on the tennis courts I had spotted out back.

"What on earth is this about?" he demanded. "Is there some emergency? Why didn't anybody call first? Do you know what time it is? And what's this about wanting to see my entire family?" He stopped, maybe aware that he was asking too many questions to yield any worthwhile answers.

"I'm Detective Peterson of the Rochambeau PD," said Danielle, "and this is Kit Deleeuw, a private investigator. We've both been looking into the murder of the middle school principal last weekend. Mr. Deleeuw would like to talk with your son Tobias and daughter Lila in your presence and your wife's. He has some information he thinks you will want to know. I acknowledge that I don't know what it is. You have the absolute right to refuse and to ask us to leave." She said the last a bit hopefully, I thought.

Tomlinson took this in, then turned to me. "Do I need an attorney here for some reason? For my kids?" Without waiting for an answer, he walked over to a wall intercom. "Ruth, get the children up. No need to get dressed. Bring them down to the living room, but when I tell you it's all right, not before." He wasn't blustery, just assuming command, obviously able to think clearly even under confusing circumstances, something I was sort of hoping he wouldn't be. The most logical move here—the one *I* would make—would be to demand to know why we had busted in at this hour, to toss us out and to call the best lawyer in town.

Unless you'd already been worried sick about your kids and you thought these visitors might help.

"I assume you're both here for a valid reason," he continued bluntly. "I also assume you know the kind of trouble I can and most assuredly will make if you're not or if you harm my children in any way. In fact, I'd like to hear a cogent explanation as to why I shouldn't just throw you out on your tails."

Peterson turned to me with a look that said, *You're on your own, smart-ass, talk fast.* Upstairs I could hear muffled voices and footsteps.

"Mr. Tomlinson, can I be candid?"

"That would be wise."

"Your son is in some trouble, I think. You may know or sense that. You probably also know that earlier in the week he tried to accuse me of making inappropriate sexual advances to him. I suspect him of being involved in other attacks on me and my family as well. Beating up my son. Knocking my daughter down. All to-

wards getting me to drop my investigation in this homicide. I'm
not interested in being punitive, in filing charges against him or
suing. I'm interested in getting my client out of jail. But Tobias
might need some help. I believe you ought to hear us out about
that."

Tomlinson's expression gave nothing away. "It is extraordinarily
difficult for me to picture my son doing those things," he said
stiffly.

Then he was silent, which, under the circumstances, was pretty
telling. If he was going to toss us, this was the moment. I hurriedly
filled him in on my visit with Tobias at the school and the subse-
quent appearance by DYFS investigators. "Your son lied about me.
I'm sure you know that."

"The DYFS investigators were here," he replied. "They told us
they received an anonymous report about you and Tobias. Tobias
was very vague as to what had happened. We couldn't get him to
be specific and were very unsure as to how much to push him.
Ruth and I were quite troubled, but Tobias insisted it was just a
misunderstanding, that your visit had frightened him. I would
have raised holy hell about it, but Tobias was very convincing,
insisting that he had overreacted. And assistant principal Hauser
spoke up for you as well, Deleeuw, and he's a great admirer of
Tobias's. It was very confusing, very difficult. We weren't satisfied,
of course. I was planning a visit to you next week; I was away for
much of this one. But why on earth did you approach him at all
without contacting us first?"

It was a good question. The fact was, I had taken a shortcut. I
was in the school and, to be perfectly honest, I thought Tobias
might be more likely to be straight with me in a casual meeting on
the school grounds than at home, with his mother and father
looking over his shoulder.

"Well, I guess I should have. And next time I will," I told Tomlinson. "But I was just asking him about Jason Bloomfield. I
wanted to know what it was the principal was investigating. I didn't
expect to be talking with him for more than five minutes, frankly.
When he turned to me and said, 'I did it,' I was flabbergasted.
Then when he threatened me with exposure as a child molester if
I pursued him any further . . ." I told Tomlinson about finding
feces in the car, about the dog's being poisoned and Ben's beating. I told him about the Cyberskulls file, too, though not what

was in it, and, finally, about my call to Tobias at the school, the one that had resulted in the investigation being shut down.

"I know about that," Tomlinson said. "Tobias called me in Chicago and swore that he was mistaken about your approaching him. He begged me to have the charges withdrawn, said it was the only decent thing to do. I believed him. He's always been truthful. So I called DYFS. They said they would withdraw the investigators, since there was no other evidence to pursue, but that they would pay a follow-up visit to Tobias in a few months." Interesting. I was lucky that Tomlinson had so much political clout. Otherwise, the investigation would probably have taken its sweet time, the suspicious Ms. Rheingold torturing me to the bitter end with every device at her disposal. My hunch was that the person at DYFS whom Tomlinson called was the commissioner. Gifford Tomlinson was a major political contributor.

I nodded, still sounding chagrined, but pushed on. "I've come about Lila, too," I said. "I think your daughter is in some difficulty. I know she hasn't been in school for several weeks. I think I know why. I don't know whether you do."

He shook his head, but said nothing.

"Mr. Tomlinson, I want to take a risk. I want to ask your children some questions, with you and your wife present. I need Detective Peterson here too, not only because of Tobias's charges against me but because if there's any information that might help my client I want the police to hear it directly. I think there will be, so I need to have the authorities here. As I think we mentioned, I've been working on behalf of Shelly Bloomfield, who has been accused of—"

"The Last Housewife," said Tomlinson quietly.

"The same one," I said. "Look, this is unorthodox. I'm asking for your trust. You are free to stop the questioning at any time. I can't tell you I know exactly where this will lead, but if it goes where I think it will go, we can help everybody, including your children. I suspect you and your wife have been frantic, sensing something's wrong but not knowing what. Let's find out together. You have the resources to help your son and daughter, but only if you know the truth. You also have the means to defend them should they need that. But you're flying blind. And if we're being totally honest, you have nothing to lose. Things are going on that will have to be confronted, if not this morning, then very soon

and under much worse circumstances. You don't want this to go
on."

Tomlinson pulled his robe tighter and walked towards the bay
window with its magnificent vista. "Mr. Deleeuw, are you threatening me?" he asked in a tone that suggested it would be a poor
approach.

I thought about it a second. This was a capital-B businessman.
He would appreciate directness.

"Well, yes, Mr. Tomlinson, I suppose I am."

I thought I heard Peterson expel a sigh. "Wait a minute, Kit,"
she interjected. "I can't be party—"

"Only in this sense, Mr. Tomlinson. Speaking as a parent as well
as an investigator, you have to face this. You have nothing to fear
from me except this: I won't ever let go of a case. I'll keep at this
until I get what I'm after; it's my ethic. There are a lot of injured
parties here. My kids have been threatened this week. There are
other kids involved as well, kids who have been hurt very badly,
especially some young women. Your daughter is, I believe, among
them. And there is a woman's death to be accounted for.

"Your son has to look up and see a solid wall forming around
him. You and your wife, me, the police—and he has nowhere to
go. I'm hoping we can get at the truth this way. Let's try it. You
can call it off at any time, although I hope you won't do that."

He considered this, too. He was impressive, cool and steady. I
could see the pain in his expression as well. None of this, outside
of our sunrise appearance, had come as a total shock to him. My
idea had the practical advantage of making some sense: it was a
better way to get at the truth than in a police interrogation room.
I was trying to give him a scenario in which he really had no
reason not to cooperate.

I confess I had been expecting to find a red-faced CEO type,
storming around the house and threatening to call the Governor.
But being rich didn't automatically make you a creep, though that
was an understandable first reaction from anyone who'd worked
on Wall Street. It didn't make you dumb, either. My guess was that
this was a very smart man who was too busy to stay plugged into
his kids' lives, or who didn't know how, and who'd become discon-
nected. It's an easy thing to allow to happen, even for those of us
who are lucky enough to be around.

"If you think Tobias committed a serious crime, I don't think

I'd be very responsible having him blurt it out without an attorney present," he said.

"I don't think I would disagree with that," Peterson continued. Two different tracks, two separate investigations. There were the police, and there was me.

"I don't know what Tobias did," I said, "but he's a juvenile with no previous record. Unless there's something going on I have no inkling of, he's not going to jail in either case—"

"And not with the legal muscle you could hire, to be frank," interrupted Peterson. "And Deleeuw is right about one thing. Sometimes it's better that things come out in a setting like this. And it's to Tobias's advantage if he volunteers the information. Judges love that. Otherwise things come out at the police station with cops, prosecutors and reporters around. I think this is a valid approach for you, Mr. Tomlinson." I saw what she was doing: maintaining some distance, gaining some credibility, yet still supporting me. It was a slippery slope; she had no idea what I suspected or where I was headed. And she hadn't seen the Cyberskulls file, either.

I tried a final plea. "Let's help these kids, Mr. Tomlinson. And my client. And maybe a bunch of other kids who are in trouble or who are hurting. Okay?"

I held my breath. All Tomlinson had to do was say no, barricade his kids behind a wall of lawyers, and we'd probably never get through it. I'd be back to Square One. But a good parent would want the truth. You don't always get the truth from your kids, however powerful you are in the wider world.

Gifford Tomlinson had had money his whole life. He was used to being treated well, to being listened to, to having authority. He wasn't used to this.

"We feel like we've just lost control and we have no idea how," he said, with a calm he probably didn't feel. "A few months ago, we had what seemed like two perfect kids, happy, popular, accomplished. Now you can almost cut the pain and deception in this house with a knife. We have made appointments for both children to see psychologists." I didn't need to ask whether he wanted to be able to tell the therapists what was really going on or not. He would be thinking that himself.

The intercom squawked. They were getting anxious to know what was going on, Ruth Tomlinson said. Was it okay to bring the children down? Tomlinson said yes, as if it had been a foregone conclusion. I didn't realize I'd been holding my breath until I exhaled in a big puff. Danielle Peterson winked at me. She looked pretty curious herself.

So much for the first step. I had maybe two minutes to come up with the second. Improv Investigating: get a toehold, then wing it. Trust the Force, Luke.

While Tomlinson met his family out in the hallway for several minutes before bringing them in, Peterson leaned over and whispered, "Deleeuw, do you have the slightest fucking idea what you're going to do next?"

I smiled wanly. "Of course not. I'm amazed I got this far."

I don't know what Tomlinson told his family, but I wished I'd seen Tobias's face when he told them. They filed in grimly, first the father, then Tobias and his sister, then their mother, looking every bit as dignified in her cashmere robe as her husband did in his.

Finally, Tobias and I were face-to-face. He had nowhere to dodge, no maneuvering room. But I was no longer feeling vengeful. He certainly didn't look the part of a monster; he looked like a terrified kid. The only Tomlinson to actually get dressed, he'd thrown on shorts and a T-shirt and sneakers. Lila, in a floor-length gown that accurately enough said "Sleeping Beauty," actually looked more alarming. The girl had a vacant and distracted air, as if she'd become totally confused and had given up expecting to understand.

Ruth Tomlinson must have been worried too, but she was clearly more concerned about her kids than herself. She positioned herself between the two children on the largest sofa. The fate of a family was in the balance and I didn't know myself how it would turn out. All I knew was that I didn't understand Tobias. Not his behavior, his motives or his shockingly dichotomous character. In front of the police and his own family, I was determined to get some answers out of him.

The maid came in with a large silver tray that held pitchers of milk, orange juice and coffee, plus muffins and croissants. No one spoke to her or acknowledged her. It wasn't that they were rude, they were just used to having people appear to bring them things.

Tobias and Lila passed on any food or drinks. So did I. Peterson, ever the cop, poured herself some black coffee. I was grateful for her presence. I doubted Tomlinson would have gone for this if she hadn't been there. Everybody looked at me. I gave Tobias a long gaze back. There was a lot of tension in the room.

I said a little prayer to the God of Private Investigators that I didn't blow it, and called the meeting to order. There was no other way to do it but to look both of these kids in the eye and go straight over the cliff. "Tobias, I know why you did what you did. I know why you lied about me. You've had a nightmare. You've suffered a lot. We are going to help you."

He looked at me in total amazement as everyone else in the room turned to him. I was sure he'd been expecting me to rip into him, to chastise him, to tell him how angry I was and how hurtfully and recklessly he'd behaved. What I'd said was obviously the last thing in the world he'd been expecting to hear.

"You've been trapped in the worst kind of situation anybody can get caught in. Your sister was attacked. Your best friend, or friends, almost surely did it. You had to protect Lila. And you had to protect your friend. On top of that you were being threatened, perhaps with disclosure of something you didn't do. I don't know how you stood up to all of it. You're a pretty brave kid. But you're still a kid."

I paused. He was gaping at me, still in complete shock. His mother was watching him closely, her mouth closed in a thin line. Gifford Tomlinson gripped the arm of the sofa. Lila stared at the floor. Peterson stared at me; now she was really out to sea.

"Tobias, I can promise you, I've got everything. I've got it all. I've got the Cyberskulls file. The thing now is to tell the truth and let us help you.

"Lila," I said, turning to the girl, "you've been through an awful ordeal, but it's over now. We're going to take care of you. Your brother thought he was protecting you. He did the best he could. We'll take it from here. Your parents love you and want to help you. Detective Peterson represents the police. Nobody's going to hurt you anymore."

Ruth Tomlinson finally spoke. "Mr. Deleeuw, please tell us . . ." But I held up a hand and she stopped.

"Tobias, there's been enough damage done. The principal. Wendy Mosley. Lila. Jason's mom. Let's stop it, okay?" I pulled the Cyberskulls file out of the manila envelope.

"Otherwise I'll just read this to your parents and to your sister.

The police have it already; they're talking to Harry and Jamey and Jason right now. Here's the choice: you talk to me or I'll read it aloud. Do it, Tobias. Everybody in this room wants to help you. Give us the chance. Stop carrying it by yourself."

Tobias said nothing. Maybe he couldn't. Maybe he wouldn't. I chose a page at random. " 'Three p.m. May eighteenth. Morph and I sandwiched the Ice Queen. He dropped his books in front of her. She stopped. I had my hand out. Put it right on her butt. We said we were sorry. Flash.' "

Tobias flushed, but remained mute.

"But that's pretty mild, Tobias. Here's a paragraph from Kryptic. It isn't dated. 'Stood behind W at her locker, real close. The best bod in school. Slipped my hand under her skirt and all the way home. She yelled but nobody was around. I said, "Watch where you're going." ' "

Tobias looked at the carpet. "There are pages and pages of this stuff, Tobias." I said. "It's hard to read it."

Peterson flipped open her notebook. "Best tell us the truth, son."

"Come on, Toby," said Tomlinson, walking across the room to stand behind his son, hands on his shoulders.

The boy sat frozen, his head bent, his body stiff. For an eternity, I was certain I had failed. Then, abruptly, his will seemed to collapse. A tear slid down one cheek. He buried his head on his mother's shoulder.

"God, I'm sorry," Tobias sobbed. "I'm sorry, Lil. Mom and Dad. God, I screwed up . . . I thought I was doing the right thing. I got in so deep, and I couldn't get out . . . I messed it up so bad."

Twenty

THIS WAS THE PROVERBIAL FAMILY that had everything. From the moment we'd gathered, however, it was all too clear to everyone in the room that life in this sprawling colonial mansion would never be the same.

I was torn between the instinctive resentment the middle class has for the very wealthy, and my reflexive empathy with any and all parents.

Ruth Tomlinson didn't question the proceedings or seem surprised by them. She barely looked at me or Peterson, seemed content to let others handle the questions and answers, as if she had decided her only useful role at this moment was to mother her kids. She whispered softly into one ear, then another, hugging Tobias, squeezing Lila's arm, reassuring them, loving them, letting them know she was there, that everything would be fine. It was the way you comfort a toddler after a scary fall. "It's okay, Toby," she murmured again and again. "Lila, it's all over now, love. We'll help you now."

My own belief was that Ruth Tomlinson had seen much of what was happening all along and probably had sensed a great deal more. Families can have the toughest time talking to one another, yet feel instantly when something is wrong. Which is why, in Rochambeau, therapy is bigger business than fast food.

Gifford was the composed, calm and focused CEO, trying to take charge of something that had spiraled past his authority a long time ago. From now on, it would be damage control. Counselors, doctors, private detectives, even the police would be asking questions, suggesting responses, constantly taking his family's temperature, and they would stay around for a long time.

As for Tobias, I could hardly credit that he was sitting across from me, sobs wracking his body. He was just a kid. *He's just a kid.* How could I have thought otherwise? By the end of this week, he had become a demonic myth, bigger than life, as evil as Satan. How could I have looked so hard and seen so little?

Crying in his mother's arms wasn't some evildoer but a young boy miles in over his head. He should have been a happy teenager at the peak of his youthful good fortune—good looks, brains, charm, money, athleticism. He should have been happy with his friends, sullen and uncommunicative with his family, the rightful order of things. Instead, stricken with grief and guilt, he looked scared to death.

Lila seemed profoundly damaged to me. Like her brother, Lila was beautiful, gorgeous blue eyes set off by streaky blond hair and a creamy complexion. And she was completely expressionless, utterly detached, as if quite apart from what was happening before her.

Peterson, always head-to-toe cop, remained watchful as a hawk. She wasn't sure yet where this was going and was thus prepared for anything. Cops hate to be in this position—to not know whether there is a murderer, a juvenile delinquent or something even less menacing in the room. If things went awry, she didn't want them going awry in front of Gifford Tomlinson, who not only could summon the Mayor to the phone in minutes but could afford platoons of first-rate lawyers.

What she wasn't expecting was that her beeper would start trilling. She jumped a few inches when it did.

That, I thought, would be Leeming. I handed her Benchley's phone, which she accepted thankfully, moving out into the hallway. Meanwhile, we sat quietly, this family and me, the father clearing his throat, the mother ceaselessly reassuring and comforting her kids. Tobias glanced at me from time to time; Lila never took her eyes from the floor. There seemed no need for small talk.

Peterson came back in a few minutes, shooting me a surreptitious glare. I probably should have told her more about the file.

She leaned over to whisper: "Thanks for telling me about that computer printout, asshole. The chief has people running all over town looking for members of a group called Cyberskulls. Wants to know if I'm really needed here."

"More than you know," I said. "Sorry I didn't fill you in, but I thought he'd want to see it for himself first. Believe me, you'll be where the action is today. In fact, we're about to hear from one of the Cyberskulls. You can call the chief soon with all the other names."

I motioned her to sit down so we could get along. I couldn't risk the genies getting stuffed back into their bottles.

Gifford Tomlinson cleared his throat. "I want you kids to know I love you both and will stand by you no matter what has happened. I know that goes for your mother too." Ruth Tomlinson's look said that it didn't need saying on her end. Those were the words I'd want to hear from my parents if I were in trouble. Though they did ring a tad hollow. I wouldn't be happy if a private detective, a total stranger at that, was leading this discussion at my house with a cop seated alongside.

"However," Tomlinson went on, "I can't help you—your mother and I can't—if we don't know what's wrong. So how about bringing all of us up to date? Then we can decide what to do. Okay? Deleeuw, my children are obviously having a rough time. Can you tell my wife and me what you know? Then the children can add to what you say, if they wish."

I would have preferred Tobias to have started the explanation, but he seemed too broken up. He must have been enormously relieved finally to have the truth come out, and at least his tears belied the notion that he was heartless. Maybe I could start the proceedings; that might make it easier for him to fill in the blanks. He seemed to be struggling to get himself under control now, wiping his bloodshot eyes with the back of his hand.

"I'll agree to start," I said, "but only on a couple of conditions. Tobias, you have to be comfortable with us talking about this. *All* of it. The Cyberskulls. The attacks on Wendy and your sister. The truth about Harry Godwin and Jason Bloomfield. You have to agree that I can tell what I know and that you'll tell the truth. Otherwise, I'm outta here." Idle threat. The only way I was leaving this house was if somebody dragged me out by the throat. But I was willing to bet that this was a kid who desperately needed to unburden himself, to shed a lot of guilt.

I turned to his sister. "Lila, I have a daughter nearly your age. I can only imagine how tough this has been on you. You have to be okay with our discussing what happened to you. I understand if you're not, if you want to leave the room or talk in front of a counselor. Maybe you'd prefer to confide in your mother, or father, or doctor. I only want you to stay here with us if you are comfortable."

I had no way of knowing if this was getting through to her. I had no platitudes to offer, just options and a sense that she had some control.

Lila met my eyes for the first time. She squeezed her mother's hand. "It's okay," she said, so softly I almost didn't hear her. "I'm okay."

"You want to do this?" I repeated.

She nodded, then broke off eye contact.

Danielle Peterson stood up. "So now it's my turn to interject something," she said. "Just like you see in the movies. I don't know what Mr. Deleeuw is going to ask and I don't know what this young man or his sister might have to say. But I want you all to understand that I am a police officer. I am sworn to uphold the law. If I hear about illegal or criminal behavior I might have to act on it.

"Nobody has to talk. You can decide to be silent. You can talk to a lawyer before deciding. You can have a lawyer present during the questioning. If you talk about any crimes, whatever you say can be used against you. I have to tell you that if you can't afford an attorney"—there was a hint of a smile as she glanced around the room—"one will be appointed for you." She added that she would be using a tape recorder, which she fished from her purse and turned on, repeating the Miranda warning she had just delivered.

Gifford Tomlinson frowned, then once again rested a hand on Tobias's shoulder. The boy was no longer shaking; though his eyes were red and his face very pale, he had regained most of his composure.

"Toby," said the father, "I want to make sure we're not making a mistake. If you've done something seriously wrong, perhaps illegal, we should call a lawyer. Maybe you and I need to go into the other room and discuss that."

Tobias shook his head. "Dad, we need to talk about it. Let's just do it. I've screwed up, and I don't want to screw up again. I've done things that are wrong, but I haven't killed anybody or anything like that."

Tomlinson searched his son's face, then nodded at me. We were halfway there.

"Tobias, first of all, I have to clarify this," I said. "Did I ever make any indecent proposals to you?"

"No, sir. And I'm sorry."

"Did I ever ask you to pose for nude photographs?"

"No, sir." He looked straight ahead, like a military cadet being disciplined.

"So I never made any sexual overtures to you, of any kind? And you don't need to call me 'sir.' 'Mr. Deleeuw' or 'Kit' will do fine."

He shook his head, then mumbled, "No, you didn't."

"You're sure?" pressed Peterson.

He dipped his head.

"The boy nodded yes," Peterson said into the tape recorder.

"Why did you lie?" I asked. "Why did you say I did?" I wanted this on the record.

"Harry and Jason told me you were working for Jason's mother. I wanted you to stop investigating. We all did. We weren't afraid of the police, but I remembered hearing about that other case, the kids killed up on the Brown estate. And I was scared you'd find out. About me. About Lila. And because you were working for Mrs. Bloomfield, we were scared you'd learn about the Cyber-skulls. Because Jason was one of them. And because of the things we had written in his computer."

Both of his parents seemed to be holding their breath. Peterson didn't take her eyes off the boy.

"And you called your father and begged him to call the state and stop the abuse investigation because you believed that I had found those Cyberskulls files."

He nodded.

"What were you afraid I'd found out about you, Tobias?"

"That I did those things to those girls. That we attacked Wendy Mosley in the park and we . . ." He looked beseechingly at his mother. I thought Gifford would interrupt and demand a lawyer, but he didn't. He seemed to want the truth more.

I spoke up: "Tobias, I've talked to Wendy's parents. I know what happened to her—the incidents in school, the attack in Rocham-beau Municipal Park. Were you a part of that attack a few weeks ago?"

The room was absolutely still. I knew Wendy hadn't been raped, but Tobias's parents didn't.

"I was and I wasn't," Tobias answered. "Harry said she'd agreed to meet us in the park. He said he met her there all the time. He and Jason and Jamey Schwartz grabbed her and knocked her down. At first I thought they were playing, but then I realized they weren't, that Wendy hadn't agreed to meet us at all. They were all over her. They took some of her clothes off."

He put his head in his hands for a moment. A shudder ran through his body. Then he raised his face. "We stuck stuff up her . . . her place. Her vagina. I didn't do it. But I was there. I watched. I didn't stop it in time." He began to sob. His mother cradled him in her arms. "Toby, Toby," she murmured.

He pulled away from her, determined to tell us everything. "Before that, we had done other . . . things . . . to other girls. We grabbed them, bumped into them, followed them home. I knew it wasn't right, I felt creepy about it, but Harry said he'd always done it. He swore it was okay, it was just what boys and girls did. That the girls liked it. A couple of girls *did* seem to like it, that's what it looked like. They even came up to me later and kind of flirted with me. At first I was really frightened, like we were going to get into trouble. But we never did, until Jason got suspended."

"And Wendy Mosley?" I interrupted.

Tobias struggled before answering. "The other guys pulled her down on the ground and yanked her dress up, pulled her underpants down. At first I thought she was laughing, but then I saw she wasn't, she was crying, making these terrible sounds. I got really frightened, more scared than I've ever been in my life. I shouted at them. Dad, Mom, I swear it, I pushed Harry and Jason away. But they had stuck a broom handle up there and—"

His mother gasped. His father was ashen. "Tobias," he said brusquely, "I don't think you should say any more about—"

"No, Giff," Ruth Tomlinson interrupted. She spoke with calm and authority. "He needs to. There's only so much you can hide. And for so long."

"It's okay, Dad." Tobias snuffled, rubbing his nose against his sleeve. Jesus, I thought, how did a kid like this get into such a morass? Could he really have believed this was normal boy-girl stuff?

Tobias didn't seem to need my prompting now. "Afterwards,

Harry said I was a jerk. He said he'd beat me silly if I ever inter-
fered again. We had nothing to worry about, he said. Harry
bragged that he'd killed Wendy's old dog months ago to scare her
into not talking. He'd told her if she talked, her mom and dad
would be next. She's never been back to school since the park."

"Oh, my God," Gifford Tomlinson said, almost to himself.

Tobias looked at his father, hesitated, then went on. "I really
started getting frightened all the time then, but . . . I didn't
know how to get out of it. I stopped bothering girls at all. I said I
was too busy to write new stuff in the Cyberskulls file. But I didn't
tell anyone what happened. I didn't want to look like a rat or a
chicken. I know that's no excuse, I mean, there is no excuse. But it
is the truth, the way I felt."

The maid stuck her head in to retrieve the tray, but Gifford
waved her out and she swiftly withdrew.

"Was that the most serious case, the worst attack?" Peterson
asked.

Tobias nodded.

"What was the other stuff?"

"Just bumping girls in the hallway. Slipping your hand down
their butts. 'Squeezing the Grapefruit.' The stuff Ms. Rainier-
Gault nailed Jason for. I heard that the other guys jumped Wendy
once before, but I had a track meet that day so I wasn't around. I
sort of thought they were making it up. Bragging, you know?" He
stopped for breath. He seemed determined to answer every question truthfully. "Nothing as bad as what we did to Wendy. Or what
he did . . ." He couldn't look at his sister. I saw that tears were
inching down her cheeks as well.

"Toby," said his father firmly. "We need to know what happened to Lila."

Tobias took his sister's hand. "I'm sorry, Lil. I'll never forgive
myself. It was all my fault. I hope you can understand one
day . . ." He turned to me, took a deep breath and then plunged
on.

"We'd formed this group, the Cyberskulls. We had this pact that
each of us had a code name. I was 'Flash.' We each had to keep a
computer diary of what we had done, of the girls we had touched
and things we said and did to them. I didn't do much, in fact the
guys were always on me. I bumped into a couple of girls, but I
always made it look like an accident. See, we agreed that if we all

wrote the stuff down, we couldn't ever give the others up. It was a way of making sure nobody ratted. But it was dumb, because you felt you had to do something. You couldn't just write nothing. It started out as fun, like a dare. And it seemed . . .'' He flushed deeply now. "Well, it was a turn-on, you know. It just sounded like dumb stuff, horsing around. I never thought it would go this far.''

"And Lila?'' I prodded.

"Jason thought his mother was getting suspicious. A few weeks ago, he was in a big panic because we'd run out of the house when Harry called about something, and then later Jason remembered he'd left his computer on. He was always complaining about his mom, about how snoopy she was, how she never left him alone. He called us later that night and said when he checked his computer some of his files had been opened. He could tell from the log next to each file. His mom used the computer sometimes, but she didn't know all that much about how it worked, so she didn't realize she was leaving a record. We decided to copy the files out of his computer and move 'em here. Harry and Jason especially really got off on reading them aloud, laughing. They thought it wasn't safe at Jason's. But nobody's ever home here,'' he added, "and Benazir doesn't understand much English. She doesn't even know how to turn a computer on. Lila would hang around with us sometimes if she was around.''

Ruth Tomlinson closed her eyes.

Peterson leaned forward. "I'm going to have to take that computer with me, folks. I can get a warrant if you want.''

Gifford Tomlinson nodded. A warrant wouldn't be necessary.

Tobias said, "We came over here a couple of times. Harry kept saying how cute Lila was, what a babe and all. One afternoon, the guys were here for a while, typing into the computer files. Then it got near dinnertime and they all left—Jason and Jamey and Harry. I was shutting the computer down so I told them they could let themselves out. You know, Benazir was downstairs. I thought they had all left. But then I heard this noise and then this cry from Lila's room and I ran in there and . . .''

Tobias looked up at the ceiling as if seeking more help than could possibly exist. It was unbearable to hear him recount the story, but to his credit he never wavered.

"Lila was on the floor. Harry was on top of her. I couldn't see . . . I don't know. His pants were down around his ankles. He was moving up and down . . . Oh, God," he cried, and hunched over. "I'm going to be sick!" He darted from the room. His father followed.

Lila still stared at the floor, as if the account she'd just heard had happened to somebody else. She registered no visible emotion of any kind. Ruth's hand stroked and stroked her daughter's hair.

Peterson used the cell phone to call the dispatcher. She asked for Harry Godwin to be picked up and brought into headquarters with his parents. At least assault, she told the dispatcher. Maybe worse. She reported that Jamey Schwartz, Jason Bloomfield, Godwin and Tobias Tomlinson were the Cyberskulls group the chief was looking for. She said that Tobias would come in shortly, that the boy had a statement to make and would be cooperative.

Ironic, I thought. Tobias would end up a rat after all.

"Did you know any of this?" Peterson asked Ruth Tomlinson, clicking off the phone. "Hear or suspect anything?"

She took a long time answering, stroking Lila's blond head on her shoulder. "I knew something was wrong," she said softly. "I knew she didn't feel well, I saw she was very depressed. But she said she was sick, wouldn't say a word more. We'd made an appointment with a psychologist for next week. Giff and I have been so busy, we've both been traveling, and we just didn't focus on it. Oh, Lila, Lila . . . I'm so very, very sorry."

Tobias returned with his father in a couple of minutes. His face was drained of color, and a speck of what he had thrown up had landed on one sneaker. This kid had gotten way out of his league. He was going to need lots of help.

"I pulled Harry off Lila," he resumed. "I yelled that my father was coming home. He ran out of the house. He swore he didn't actually do anything. He said he just humped her. I asked Lila if that was true and she said yes."

We were all startled by the sound of Lila's voice. "He didn't do more than that," she said in a frail, still voice. "Toby got there in time. I think he would've, but Toby got him off of me. But he did . . . other things . . . He made me . . ."

Peterson came over and took Lila's other hand. "Not now, dear. We need to get you to a doctor. We have to get you taken care of. You can tell us about it later, more privately, okay, honey?"

"Son, for God's sake, why didn't you tell us? Or call the police?" For the first time I heard a current of anger in Gifford
Tomlinson's voice. Tobias looked so bleak I feared he might have
finally run out of strength. I jumped in.

"Harry blackmailed you, didn't he? He had copies of the Cyberskulls files, right? Plus he probably threatened your sister with
worse. And you knew he made good on his threats, didn't you?"

"Harry said he'd killed Wendy's dog and he could do something like that to Lila. He said he knew how to hurt people. He
said he had these computer files where I admitted to attacking
girls and that I'd go to the youth detention center for sure. He
told me what guys did there to kids who looked like me. He said
he never raped Lila anyway, just climbed on top of her because
she asked him to. And if I told anyone anything, the Wendy Mosley thing would come out and the other three would all testify that
it was my idea.

"I believed him, Mr. Deleeuw. Jason and Jamey were, like,
scared to death of Harry. They'd do anything he told them to.
And while I was in jail, Harry said, he'd really take care of Lila.
Like he'd taken care of the principal. That really scared the shit
out of me. Jesus, I'm sorry. I didn't know what to do, I didn't
know who to talk to. I'd gotten myself into this horrible mess,
and—"

Tobias wiped his face with the hem of his T-shirt. Had I heard
what I thought I'd heard? I saw Peterson had picked it up too.

"It's up to you, Mr. and Mrs. Tomlinson, but if I were you, I'd
get a lawyer on over here now," she said. "I don't see your son as
being in danger of going to jail or a detention center, not if he
cooperates and is telling the truth. But there's a lot of heavy stuff
flying around, and things may be heating up pretty fast." Gifford
got up to make the call, leaving us all in suspended animation
once more until he returned.

"Tobias," said Peterson, speaking slowly, "I want you to think
hard about the answer to this question. What did you mean just
now when you said Harry told you that he 'took care of the principal'?"

Tobias shuddered, then said, "Jason had told us about the gun
his father kept in the basement. He knew where the key was hidden. He'd shown it to Harry. Harry had taken it out a few times.
Anyway, last week Harry was called to Ms. Rainier-Gault's office.

Afterwards, he was all freaked out. He was really pissed, said she
told him she knew he was running a gang of kids who were humiliating girls. She said she was going to nail him worse than she'd
nailed Jason—no one-week detentions this time, she was going to
the police—and this was his last chance to admit it and get help.
One boy's parents had already been called and this kid's mother
was coming in to see her Saturday, and Harry's parents would be
getting the next call, so this was a good time to start talking, she'd
said. Harry said he told her to piss off, but the talk made him real
nervous, more nervous than I'd ever seen him.''

I bet I knew why, too. I leaned over and wrote *kid has previous
history of assault* on Peterson's open notebook. If Harry got in
trouble again, he probably did face time in a juvenile detention
center. *I know,* she jotted below my entry.

"Harry said he couldn't hack that, that if he went down, we
were all going to go down with him. He said he wasn't going to let
the bitch get away with it." He groaned. "I couldn't believe how
this stupid thing about bumping into girls had gotten so big . . .''

"Did you attack Mr. Deleeuw's son?" Peterson asked sharply.

"No, I swear it. That was Harry."

"What about poisoning my dog?" Ben's and Percentage's troubles didn't loom as large after listening to Tobias, but I had to
know.

"Harry too. We were having these meetings. Harry said since I
was the 'pretty boy' I should be the one to scare you off. He said
the regular police were too busy with other stuff to stick with this
kind of thing for too long. He said there weren't enough cops to
deal with it, that it would go away. He'd dealt with cops and stuff
back where he'd come from. He said if a kid complained to the
state that he was being molested, the cops would come and tell the
person not to go near the kid until it was sorted out. He said you
wouldn't be able to investigate anything. I didn't know about Ben
or about the dog until later. I'm sorry about Ben. He's an okay
kid. I'm sorry about everything."

"But I'm still confused by what you meant when you told me, 'I
did it,' " I asked. "Did what?"

"I," said Tobias slowly, "covered up for the guy who attacked
my sister. Helped attack Wendy. I did plenty. I thought—we
thought—if you saw me as responsible for the attacks on the girls
but you couldn't approach me because of DYFS, then your investi-

gation was dead. Harry said he'd keep the pressure on your family. He said you'd be 'neutralized,' that was the word he used. And since the cops had already arrested Jason's mom, the whole thing would blow over. Especially with Ms. Rainier-Gault dead. Harry told me to say that stuff to you. I guess I thought if I threatened you, the trouble would stop. You'd never be able to investigate us."

My stomach turned. Over my clunky misperceptions. Over the story this privileged boy was telling, over his malleability, his willingness to be swayed by the pack, his ability to rationalize harassment and brutality. What hope was there for everybody else? My stomach was sinking, too, over the other reality beginning to dawn on me.

"Did Harry Godwin shoot Nancy Rainier-Gault?" asked Peterson. "Is that what you're telling us?"

He looked at his parents, who sat stunned and exhausted. His father nodded. "Tell them if you know, son."

"I don't know. He didn't tell me he did. He just said he took care of her. I don't know what that meant."

"Tobias," said Peterson, "this is no time to clam up. You've learned how dumb that is. This is a murder case. I don't mean to scare you, but if you know a single thing I'd better hear it *right now* or you're going to learn what real trouble is." The authority in her voice was startling.

"Really, Detective . . ." Gifford Tomlinson began, but stopped when he caught her look.

Tobias closed his eyes. He'd never forget this visit.

"Almost over, pal," I said. "You can't stop now."

He said, "Jason told me that Harry came to his house Saturday afternoon and said he needed to borrow something. Jason asked him what and Harry said it was better if Jason didn't know. He went into the basement with a big gym bag and came out with something in it. Jason figured he might be taking the gun to shoot at cans up on the Brown estate. He and Harry had done that once before. Harry didn't say anything. He just pushed off on his skateboard with the gym bag. Jason said he didn't see him again. Then the police came and found the gun in the yard, so Jason got confused. Maybe Harry hadn't taken it after all. Harry warned him never to tell that he'd been there at all, or this Cyberskulls stuff would come out and think what that would do to Jason's mother."

"Did Jason tell you he thought Harry killed the principal?" I asked.

"No," said Tobias wearily. He'd been talking for a long time. "He thought his mother might have done it, at least at first, I think. He said his mother was so mad at the principal she even said she was going to kill her. He said his mother went nuts if anybody messed with him. But if Jason thought Harry did it, he didn't say. Next time I talked to him, he said his dad told him not to talk about the case with anybody, even his friends."

"Do you know if he told his dad about Harry's visit?" I asked.

"I don't know. To tell the truth, I didn't want to talk about it anymore."

The Tomlinson family attorney arrived, and that ended the questioning. Tobias was trembling and spent anyway. His father agreed to accompany him to the police station in an hour. At Peterson's urging, Lila went with her mother to Rochambeau Memorial for a full medical workup. Peterson thought the girl might still be suffering from shock.

Lila wasn't the only one.

Peterson called Leeming, who said that Jamey Schwartz was being questioned now but that officers had been unable to locate Harry Godwin. She had asked them, at my request, to hold off interviewing Jason.

I got on the phone. "Chief, remember when I got shot? You ought to, you remind me often enough."

"Sure, why?"

"I don't want it to happen again. I'd like you and a squad car or two to meet Peterson and me at Shelly Bloomfield's house."

"Why, Deleeuw? What are you expecting there?"

"I'm not sure I know," I said. "Maybe just some answers. Let's just say I'm not looking to be a hero twice."

Twenty-one

CHIEF LEEMING had taken me at my word: his black Chrysler and two police cars lined the quiet street in front of the Bloomfield residence. Peterson pulled up behind me.

Lila and her mother were en route to the hospital in a patrol car. Tobias, his father and their attorney would soon leave for the police station. The last thing I saw as I left the big white house was the maid Benazir, who stared at the departing procession in complete bewilderment. No one had explained any of it to her, but I'm sure she knew trouble when she saw it. She too must have sensed that this family was unraveling before her eyes.

I was spinning from what I'd seen and heard, feeling guilty and foolish. Instead of demonizing Tobias, I should have gone straight to his parents. I had been intimidated by an adolescent boy who was far weaker than I'd understood. I should have known better; I would next time.

The shocking thing was that everyone's contradictory perceptions of Tobias were all true: the boy was capable of conscience, and equally capable of turning conscience off. He had surely proven less of a leader than his teachers said, but at his age, leadership was a pretty fluid notion. The really frightening part was that this was clearly a kid with a lot of decency, raised with a strong value system. Look how little it took to undermine and pervert it.

The patrol cars had attracted a gaggle of neighbors who were, at police insistence, keeping their distance. Several dogs had started a persistent yammering, perhaps sensing the alien presence on the block. This street probably had seen more police cars in the past week than in the previous century.

The day had turned brilliant and breezy, the first roses glowing in people's yards. Too nice a day by far for this awful stuff.

I noticed a police van parked five doors up from the Bloomfield house. That would be the local SWAT team, used more frequently than one might think: when somebody drinks too much and fires off a shot, when domestic quarrels turn savage, when a trapped burglar tries to bluff his way out with a hostage. I saw a State Police truck pull up even farther down the block, probably with heavier artillery. Not knowing what to expect, the chief was ready for anything.

He came up to me, still in civilian clothes but with a walkie-talkie in hand, eyes scanning the house, the block, me.

"That Cyberskulls stuff made me sick," he said, while waiting for Peterson to join us. "I can't believe these boys. I saw a lot of horrible stuff in Brooklyn, but I never saw anybody keep a diary about it."

I agreed. "It's pretty stunning. I wish we'd been able to save the rest of it—"

"Who's we?" Leeming interjected alertly. But I'd never give Willie away. I ignored him.

"If a tenth of what I read was true, those boys are going to be answering a lot of questions," Leeming went on, when I didn't answer. "I have the whole detective bureau on overtime and I've asked for State Police help. I won't let this rest. This is what Nancy Rainier-Gault was yelling about for months." He clenched a powerful fist. "But we didn't have any proof. I wish to God we'd had this. How did you get it?"

"Can't tell you, Chief. All I can say is that it came out of Jason's computer. Tobias can confirm its authenticity."

Leeming scowled and I had a premonition this wouldn't be the last time he'd try to find out who cracked the Cyberskulls file for me.

"How much trouble will we have from old man Tomlinson? Several pols have their noses permanently up his butt," the chief groused.

"Not much," said Peterson, joining us. "He's in shock and will probably liven up later, but he just wants to get his family through this. Though he wasn't too shaken to take a high-priced attorney down to the station with his firstborn."

She scanned the Bloomfields' house. All the curtains were

drawn. She was probably wondering the same thing I was. Shelly's van and Dan's Acura were in the driveway; the younger kids must be stirring by now. Why hadn't somebody come out to learn why half the cops in town were encamped out front?

"Who were you calling on the cell phone from your car, Deleeuw?" Peterson didn't miss a trick. "You almost killed both of us weaving back and forth while you fumbled with the buttons. Lucky some patrol car didn't pull you over for DWI. Except I guess they're all here."

I beamed at her. "I called the weather number. Fair and lovely all week."

In fact, I had used Benchley's phone to call the county jail. The line had been clear, for a change. Maybe the other inmates were catching up on their beauty sleep. I'd gotten through to Shelly on the third try.

She'd sounded tentative, but not all that surprised. I swear she'd seemed almost happy to hear from me. "I knew you wouldn't drop the case," she'd said. Her voice was flatter, less animated than I had heard before. Maybe a week in jail could do that to you.

"Then why did you order me to get off it?"

If you could hear shrugs, hers would have come through the phone. No answer was really necessary; we both knew why. Anyway, it didn't matter. We didn't have long to talk, so I'd told her what I suspected. I didn't want her to be surprised. I said I was sorry for my role in what was about to happen, but I owed her the call. The Last Housewife was still my client.

"Thanks for warning me," Shelly'd said. "Is there anything I can say or do to get you to stop, to back off? I was thinking of confessing, of pleading guilty."

"No. It's too late for that, Shelly, and you couldn't get away with it anyway. I won't let you go to prison for a murder you didn't commit."

A kind of panic seemed to wash over her. "I was afraid this would happen, Kit. That's why I wanted you off the case. Can't you let it go? Can't you let me make my own choices? Do you have to play God with my family? Can't you just let me decide?"

Earlier, I had actually thought about doing that. For perhaps two minutes. But I couldn't, even if I'd wanted to. It sort of went back to what you stood for, back to the Question. If I was going to do this work, I had to be faithful to it. I couldn't look away, then move ahead with my life, knowing I could have saved hers. Nor could I have allowed myself to live in a town with a murderer who was walking around free, going to the movies on Fridays, ordering pizza, living a life. I'd told her so.

"Kit, was I wrong? My ideas about families, about being a parent? Was I so far off, all along? I was so frightened for that boy."

"Not possible for me to judge, Shelly. You did the best you could. We all do the best we can." I thought of her and of the Tomlinsons, the Godwins, the Mosleys. All decent people doing their best. Sometimes, though, your best isn't good enough. There is too much out there we can't contol. "It's a crapshoot, Shelly. It's just a crapshoot. You did your best. Do you want me to phone you back, after it's over?"

"No, Kit. I don't think I want to talk to you again." She sounded as if she was past caring. I could hardly blame her if she was.

"I understand." Those would almost surely be the last words I spoke to her. Thinking about the Last Housewife, I barely heard the chief demanding to know what was going on.

"Okay, Deleeuw, I'll say 'Uncle,' " Leeming announced. "You mentioned not being a hero. So I'm here with all this backup. Why? Is this connected to that Cyberskulls stuff? Does somebody have a weapon in there? I don't want my guys going in blind."

I said I didn't really know what we faced, that I wanted to talk to Dan Bloomfield, that the conversation wouldn't be pleasant and that it could shed considerable light on the murder of Nancy Rainier-Gault. I told him I still believed in Shelly Bloomfield's innocence, which meant the real murderer was still on the loose. On the other hand, I added, ever truthful with the authorities, I was acting on some hard information and some soft hunches.

"And I suspect your fourth Cyberskull—Harry Godwin—is in there with his friend Jason," I said, pointing out the killer skateboard propped up against the house next to the front door.

"Damn your amateur ass," Leeming growled, unsatisfied. "The head of the State Police Emergency Services Unit is fifteen feet away and the first words he's going to say are 'Good morning, Chief, what have we got here?' and just what the fuck am I supposed to tell him, that you're about to have an unpleasant conversation and, by the way, don't overlook the skateboard?"

Before I could answer, the front door opened. Dan Bloomfield emerged in jeans and a striped shirt that he hadn't finished tucking into his waistband.

He walked up to us, looking surprised to see me, then unhappy about it. Neighbors were sprouting all over the block.

"What's he doing here?" he snapped at the chief. "He was fired."

Leeming blinked. He didn't know what *he* was doing there, let alone what I was. And it was news to him and Peterson that I'd been dumped.

"I've continued to work to clear Shelly," I said evenly. "Just got off the phone with her, in fact." Before Bloomfield could bluster further, I dropped the bomb. Several of them, in fact.

"And now I'm here to find out why you lied to me and to the police, why you withheld evidence that could have helped clear your wife of murder, and whether those lies are connected to the affair you've been having with Janet Braverman, the twenty-six-year-old software designer who works with you and with whom you've been dining out regularly at some of Manhattan's finest establishments." Dan's mouth opened a few inches wider than I would have thought anatomically possible. "I hope she's enjoying the jewelry," I added, more viciously than was really necessary. God, I hate sneaky cheats.

Leeming looked in surprise at me, then at Bloomfield. Peterson's gaze was fixed on him too. I noticed both of their hands drifting towards their weapons, Peterson's in her purse, Leeming's tucked into his belt in the rear. Their movements caused several other cops to quietly move towards Bloomfield.

I have often been slow to anticipate violence, which has cost me some aches and bruises, but this time I actually was ready. I stepped back even as Bloomfield began his swing.

Leeming kneed him sharply in the groin and he doubled over. Two officers had him on the ground in a flash. This working-with-the-police stuff has its benefits, though you wouldn't want to overdo it.

"None of that," snarled the chief. The neighbors were shouting and pointing, the dogs barking even louder. "I'll cuff you if you give us trouble."

"Fuck him, that son of a bitch," Bloomfield spat, still curled up at our feet. "I don't have to listen to this in front of my own house."

"No, you don't," I agreed. "The police station would be better." The officers pulled him to his feet.

And then the shot rang out.

I froze. I think my mouth was open. "Get down, Kit, DOWN!" screamed Peterson, who emphasized the point by knocking me flat.

All the cops had their guns drawn and were lying flat or in crouches, aiming at the house. "Get away, get them away!" Leeming screamed in the direction of the cluster of neighbors across the street. People grabbed their kids and ran, or ducked behind cars.

The State Police truck had emptied out even before the echo of the crack stopped reverberating. A dozen men and women in blue jumpsuits scrambled to circle the house.

"Shit," hissed Leeming, motioning his officers into position behind cars and bushes and trees. "We should've gone into the house first. Bloomfield, damnit, who's in the fucking house!" It wasn't a question.

"Let me go in," Dan pleaded. His belligerent manner had evaporated. "My kids are in there. My two girls, Erin and Sarah. And Jason with his pal, Harry."

"Stay put and be quiet," Leeming barked. He picked up the bullhorn a cop had scuttled over with and his voice boomed out over the neighborhood. "Is anybody hit? Just answer if you are hit or injured or in need of assistance. Or trapped in an exposed place."

Silence. All of us were trapped in an exposed place.

The neighbors had vanished, leaving toys, bikes, even a few minicams behind.

"Is there *another* gun in there that you know of?" Leeming asked Bloomfield brusquely.

"No. Jesus, what if the kids are hurt . . ."

There was no more noise, no signs of movement from inside the house. Bloomfield said the girls were watching cartoons on the TV in the living room, that the boys were fixing themselves breakfast. The chief got on his radio, ordered the dispatcher to call in all off-duty officers, to seal off the street and neighborhood, to keep any media far away. "Get some ambulances standing by," he rasped. Almost instantly sirens wailed in the distance. The emergency medical crews undoubtedly monitored the police radio frequency.

Leeming picked up the bullhorn again.

"Yo in there. In the Bloomfield house. This is Frank Leeming of the Rochambeau Police. We need to know if everybody's okay. If you can, come out with your hands up. If you can't, or want to talk, you can telephone us at 555-8000. Or you can signal us from a window. Jason, Harry, we want to help you. If you've got guns and aren't coming out, that's a big mistake. Don't be foolish. Jason, your father is here. He's fine. If you want to talk to him, call 555-8000. But you must come out."

Leeming repeated the message half a dozen times, like a tape loop. The State Police captain, sliding a bulletproof stand alongside him, ran up beside Leeming. They conferred in terse murmurs. At a gesture from the chief, Peterson sidled up to join them.

I could imagine what they were saying. Four young kids in a house with some sort of firearm, two boys feeling cornered, the possibility that someone might already be lying on the floor in a pool of blood. They couldn't wait. They had to go in.

Leeming nodded to the State Police captain, who slithered away, whispering into his radio.

"What's happening?" Bloomfield yelled, still prone on the asphalt of his own driveway. "Is my boy okay?"

A little late for that question, I thought, glancing over at him. Bloomfield's return gaze came as close to pure hatred as I'd seen in some time.

In minutes, we heard a series of deafening bangs—sound grenades, we were told later—and black-clad figures rushed the house from almost every direction, crashing through windows, rappeling down from the chimney, breaking in the front door. "GO-GO-GO!" the officers yelled. Leeming signaled to everybody else to stay back. I held my breath.

Then, quickly, one of the SWAT team members appeared at the doorway. He gave a thumbs-up. Simultaneously, in Leeming's hand the radio crackled. "We've got an injured white male adolescent in the basement. Surface blood. Other kids are okay." An ambulance came careening down the block. Leeming, Peterson and several of the other officers dashed towards the house.

The emergency medical technicians rushed in too, and for several long moments nobody emerged. I ran a dozen bloody scenarios through my mind, trying not to feel responsible. Finally, the squad carried out a stretcher. The face of the boy who lay on it was swathed in bandages. "Jason, Jason, you okay? You okay?" Dan Bloomfield screamed plaintively.

But nobody answered. The boy was swiftly carried into the ambulance, which sped off, police escorts fore and aft.

Leeming stuck his head out and waved me in, shouting for Bloomfield to be brought in too. Shelly's perfect living room was a shambles: chairs and tables overturned, windows broken, ceramic dogs shattered. A policewoman was trying to comfort Erin and Sarah, who were cowering in their pajamas behind the sofa. Both little girls were whimpering. On the television, a situation comedy was cackling amid the chaos.

A very tall, dark-haired young man who could only have been Harry Godwin slumped in a chair. He was handcuffed, a husky police officer on either side of him. He looked dead-eyed, staring at the wall.

"Your boy's going to be okay," Leeming told Bloomfield, who had embraced his whimpering daughters and was wide-eyed at the scene around him. Leeming raised his hand and showed us a plastic bag. Inside was a small pistol. "Jason's got cuts on the forehead, that's all. Prince Charming here claims they were in the basement fighting over the pistol Harry probably stole. The gun didn't hit anybody when it went off, but Jason banged his head on a corner of a workbench. Your son says he was going to go to the police to tell what he knew and get his mother freed. Harry was trying to stop him. Jason says when they heard the bullhorn they panicked and hid. We found them in the basement behind the oil burner. That's the story. We'll sort it out later."

At the sight of Godwin, who had now added two more traumatized children to his lengthy list of victims, a wave of anger swept over me. "I know about your record in Newton, Harry," I told him. "We know about the Cyberskulls files. We know what you did to Wendy Mosley and Lila Tomlinson." He seemed taken aback at that, briefly shifting his gaze from the wall to my face, then back. "Lila's giving a statement now. So is Tobias. So, shortly, will Jason. You're looking at a long list of problems, Harry."

He turned his head. I wasn't impressing him. He had utter

contempt for people in authority. How else could he have done what he did? He was a plain-looking kid, not remarkable except for his height and the vacant eyes you sometimes see on kids arrested for drive-by shootings, for whom violence is just background noise. He was in uniform: baggy shorts hanging low, Nike Airs high up the ankle. His thin knees shot up over the edge of the chair.

"How could you hurt Jason, Harry?" Dan Bloomfield blurted out. "He was your best friend."

The room had grown quiet now, with the crime scene technicians using the back door. The half dozen or so people in the room were listening to me. I had called the party. Thank God I hadn't come alone.

I signaled to Leeming, who ordered Bloomfield taken out back. The little girls were sent upstairs to play video games with one of the younger officers.

Danielle Peterson pulled out her tape recorder and read Godwin his rights. "I want to talk to a lawyer. I want to talk to my parents" was all he'd say. The expression on his face was bored, as in I've-been-here-before. I don't know if I've ever been so enraged in my life.

"I think I know what you're thinking, Harry: that nobody actually got raped and you won't do serious time. But I say you'll be in institutions for a long time. Because we haven't gotten to the big stuff, Harry. The big charge is murder. You killed your principal. You came here and stole the gun. You took it into the school. You pulled the trigger."

At the word "murder," every cop in the room froze.

"You knew Shelly Bloomfield was coming to talk to Ms. Rainier-Gault about Jason," I continued. "You waited until she unlocked the school door—she left it open for Mrs. Bloomfield—then you slipped inside, went into the library and waited. You knew your family would be the next one she would call. You had talked your way out of trouble before, but this would be tougher. You knew they were closing in on you and that the charges were serious. You'd always believed that people winked at this stuff, that it was a game you could get away with, that girls didn't like to come forward, that school administrators and parents didn't take it all that seriously. You could cop a feel, squeeze a butt here and there and so what? Who'd really care? But you ran into a woman who was onto you and was determined to stop you."

"Look, I've given him his rights. He's said he wants a lawyer," Peterson murmured. "Anything he says can't be used until one gets here. Don't let this go on too long. And don't bully him."

"Turn off the tape," Leeming told her. "Officially, this interview ends now. But let Deleeuw finish. I need to hear this and I want the boy to hear it too." Peterson clicked the tape off.

I looked around. The debris was not just of a living room but of a family. Godwin definitely looked more frightened now. He was losing his dull stare. The murder accusation seemed to have jolted him. I guess he thought he was clear of that, that Jason's poor old mom would take the fall for it. I had struck home.

"You couldn't stop yourself from going after these girls. I'll give you the benefit of that, maybe. You were—are—disturbed and you never got the help you need. The people around you share the blame for that. But you *could* stop this woman, this principal, from nailing you. If you hurried. You were worried about what would happen after the conference. After Shelly worked on Jason some more, Ms. Rainier-Gault might know a lot more. You couldn't afford that. So you waited until Shelly left, got into her car and drove away. Then when Rainier-Gault stood up, you shot her from right across the hallway, as easy as popping tin cans. She never even saw you. Then you skateboarded back here, pronto. You intended to put the gun back where you found it, but then you heard one of the Bloomfields' cars pulling into the drive. So you picked up the top few logs and threw the gun into the woodpile."

I looked around. Peterson looked alert and tense, Leeming impassive. Another detective was taking notes. Godwin stared at me.

"He knew where the gun was kept?" Leeming asked.

"George Bastable will testify that Harry knew about the gun. He heard Jason tell him about it, offer to show it to him. I'll bet Jason and Harry did a lot of target practice up on the Brown estate or in the woods behind the old railroad yard."

Leeming had heard enough. He waved to the officers. "Take him out of here. Call his parents. Tell them we're investigating him for sexual assault and murder and they might want to meet him at the station with a lawyer." Godwin had to duck his head to avoid hitting the door frame. He gave me a long last look, not a hateful one particularly, more of a smile. A sort of fuck-you smile. Then he spat on my shoe and let the cops lead him away. He hadn't said a word.

Dan Bloomfield, in his kitchen, was reflexively going the macho route. He demanded that I be removed from his house and that he be allowed to see his son. He bellowed he'd sue the cops for brutality. He was on the edge of out-of-control. Reality had yet to intrude. I was only too happy to oblige.

"Let me say a few words, Chief," I suggested. Leeming nodded. It was working well so far.

Harry Godwin might have been hopelessly screwed up and deserving of some compassion due to his age, but I had nothing but contempt for Dan Bloomfield, Grade A slime.

"Be quiet, Bloomfield," I snapped, after making sure he was still in handcuffs. He was big, and had his swing connected, I'd probably still be on the ground. "When you're done suing the department, maybe you can explain to them why you didn't tell anybody that George Bastable called and warned you that Harry Godwin was planning on getting hold of your shotgun. That several of Jason's buddies knew exactly where it was, that Jason was practically giving guided tours."

That took a bit of wind out of his sails.

"You might also tell them that you confronted Jason and that he told you Harry had probably taken it that day. You might explain that your son told you about the sexual assault diaries he and his friends so proudly logged in his computer. You made him tell you the night I was here, and then you called Shelly and got her to fire me because I was getting too close. You told her Jason would end up in a lot of trouble if I didn't go away. You knew Godwin was a sick loser and you also knew or suspected that Jason was involved, or at least knew about what Harry had done.

"But why tell me or the police about these things when it all tied in so nicely with your plans to dump Shelly? So you said nothing while your wife was accused of murder. You were willing to let her go to jail rather than implicate your son in a murder or wade through a messy and expensive divorce. Let the state handle it all for you."

It was a sick litany, and the sickest part was that Bloomfield hadn't committed any provably illegal acts. Just immoral ones.

"Were you trying to protect Jason?" I asked him. "Maybe you were worried that he'd killed Rainier-Gault. So you made a trade-off, his mother and your wife for his freedom. Or are you just a complete scum who saw a unique opportunity to get rid of a woman you had no feelings for anymore? Which was it, Dan?"

I think it was the image of Shelly Bloomfield sitting in the county jail that made me lose it. Or maybe the memory of my first encounter with her and Austin in the park as she enthusiastically volunteered her domestic philosophy. Maybe her sad, betrayed voice on the phone. I don't remember exactly what happened, only that I shouted some obscenity at the top of my lungs and was reaching for Bloomfield's throat when suddenly I was on the floor, gasping for breath under the weight of a thousand pounds of cop.

Leeming was furious, and rightly so. He threatened to deck me himself if I tried such a stunt again. Nonetheless, my little outburst had had its effect. Bloomfield was sweating; his bluster was gone.

The police had more than enough to chew on; they could take it from here. Leeming told his detectives to take Bloomfield to the station and make arrangements for his kids. It might be hard to get at him legally, but he sure wouldn't have a pleasant day.

I felt queasy. I was sitting quietly on a stone bench in the shade when Danielle Peterson came out into the yard.

"You okay, pal?"

"Yeah. I'm sorry for that. It was unprofessional."

"True," she said. "But we've all lost it. No harm done here. Wish you'd gotten to him."

"Yeah, me too. Sometimes when you're right, you wish you were wrong. That woman gave her whole life to her family, and her husband and most beloved child zipped their lips and shrugged their shoulders while she rotted in jail for murder."

"Does your client, if she *is* your client, know that her son and husband were selling her down the river?" Peterson wondered.

"I think she knew," I said. "First, it was just a suspicion that Jason was involved in more than strap-snapping. But she tried to fire me right after Dan called her and told her I was looking at Jason's computer. She'd seen some of those files, probably more than she'd let on. It even dawned on her, I'm sure, that Jason might somehow need protection from murder charges. She was going to confess to the murder. She'd spent her whole married life protecting Jason and making life easy for her husband. She was ready to protect them right up until the end.''

I took a sip of coffee from the mug that Peterson handed me. Coffee magically materializes wherever cops are around. I dialed Jane on Benchley's telephone. "Sweetie," I told her, "it's okay. It's over. Gunshots fired, but not at me. Nobody got hurt. It's a pretty sad victory. I'll explain the whole thing when I get home.''

I buttoned my blazer. It was getting chilly back there out of the sun. Or maybe I just felt chilled.

"You know, Danielle, Dan Bloomfield never seemed upset enough that his wife was in jail for murder. Now I know why.''

"Congratulations," she said. "You made us all look like amateurs. I was always a little twitchy about Shelly, but I'd just begun to think about daddy. Tell me, how'd you fix on Harry as the shooter?''

There were plenty of things I still didn't know, but it was time the cops took over.

"After Nate Hauser told me that Harry was capable of everything I thought Tobias was doing, I stopped obsessing on Tobias and began to look around. I found out about Harry's record in Newton, which made me think he could have been involved in the attacks on Wendy Mosley and Lila Tomlinson. That could have provided a motive to do away with Rainier-Gault, if she'd gotten wind of that stuff. After all, Wendy Mosley was coming around. One day soon she might name her attackers.

"Then, when I looked at the crime scene, I noticed that bookcase. If the killer fired from the library, which seemed likely, the case would have hidden him from sight while providing a handy place to balance a gun. But that meant a tall killer.''

"I figured the shooter was in the library, too," Peterson mused. "But I have to say, towards the end of the week I was thinking of the hubby. I knew about the girlfriend; we were trailing him. Last week, instead of visiting his wife in jail, he was in the city paying a call on Ms. Braverman, not exactly the behavior you would expect from a worried husband. Then for a while I contemplated joint murder charges, husband and wife. Both had motive. She'd sacrifice anything for that boy.''

"You're not wrong about that, Danielle," I said softly. "She would sacrifice everything. She did. But you don't know her. She's not the sort of person who could ever pull out a gun and execute somebody. That takes somebody who's dead inside. Somebody like Harry. Or like I thought Tobias was.''

"Speaking of which," she said, "you think Tobias didn't know who killed his principal?''

I shook my head. "Tobias was so traumatized, maybe he didn't want to know anything. He was swept along. The sexual drive was powerful, peer pressure even more so. And nobody saw the signs. Nobody said, 'Tobias, I don't like your friends. I don't want them in our house. I don't want you hanging around with them.' Maybe that's all it would have taken.

"I think Harry confided in Jason, because he needed to control Jason, to find out what Shelly knew, and he needed that shotgun. He knew that that little pistol he lifted from somewhere wouldn't do for killing the principal.

"I might be giving him too much credit, but I wonder if Harry was thinking of setting Shelly up all along. He saw how she was with Jason. Everybody was always saying it: 'Shelly would do anything for that boy.' Everybody would immediately think of her as a suspect, especially when after the principal suspended Jason. Harry probably told Jason that if the principal found out about the attack on Wendy, he'd wind up in a special school after all. And we know from Tobias that Jason has gotten pretty tired of his mother watching him so closely—''

"Yeah, maybe he was more than ready to fight his own battles. Even ready enough to watch his mother go to jail." Peterson shook her head. The neighborhood dogs were still barking. The kids on the block would have lots to tell their friends on Monday.

"I think Jason couldn't go through with that, not in the end," I said. "I bet that really is what he and Harry were fighting about. Jason was probably weakening, freaked out because he knew we had the files—I'd told Tobias—and realizing what life without Mom might be like. I'll bet he couldn't really do it.''

"You're a romantic, Kit.''

Leeming came out into the backyard and ordered everybody down to the police station for statement-taking. I looked back over my shoulder at that wretched house for what I hoped was the last time.

Peterson was still curious. "Deleeuw, you're only a one-man

band. How'd you get all this stuff on Harry Godwin and Dan
Bloomfield? If you don't mind my asking."

"I do mind your asking. Write it off to my intuitive skills."

We both were silent for a minute or so. Neighbors peered out of
their houses, looked at the Bloomfield house, shook their heads. I
suspected the Bloomfield family would be gone within weeks.
There was really no family left.

We walked slowly towards the street, fatigue stiffening my joints.
Peterson muttered, "This woman was completely betrayed by her
husband and son. You couldn't give more than she gave. It's just
unbelievable. If the husband wanted out, why didn't he just leave?
The adultery laws don't mean squat anymore. He could have had
his new girlfriend." I remembered she'd gotten married only six
months ago and sighed.

"I don't think he plotted it. I think he saw his opportunity and
seized it. This way she's out of the way for good, no muss, no fuss.
Nobody would blame him for divorcing a murderer. He might
even split on great financial terms. His new girlfriend likes good
food and expensive jewelry. And maybe he was angrier than Shelly
imagined at all the time she put in with Jason. The real partner-
ship was between Shelly and Jason, not Shelly and Dan. Maybe
Shelly got lost in her own notions about child care. And Dan
might also have been afraid that Jason *had* killed Rainier-Gault, or
at least helped with plotting her murder. That's one answer I
don't really have. All I know is, Shelly's conviction—remember,
she was prepared to plead guilty—sure would've simplified his life.
And he could tell himself he was doing it all to save Jason."

"But you don't buy that."

"I buy some of it. I don't believe in black-and-white judgments,
Danielle. Sometimes people have no idea why they do what they
do. Maybe Dan Bloomfield is a damn hero for sticking his neck
out for his kid. His lawyer will sure try to make us think so. I can
see a jury buying it. Here's a case filled with weak people: boys
who can't stand up to rapists; school officials who can't face up to
harassment; parents who don't want to deal with big messes right
under their noses; husbands who abandon their spouses. Who
knows what really goes on in Harry Godwin's head? Or Dan
Bloomfield's? I don't. The more I see, the less I know."

She patted me on the back. I got into the Volvo and headed

towards the police station, leaving behind the detectives and technicians, the blood and shattered dreams.

Then, on impulse, I turned around and drove down my own street, left the car idling and ran inside. I needed to see, touch and hug my family. To know that, for the moment at least, mine was still okay.

Epilogue

IF YOU CARE TO KNOW families at a glance, watch them on a beach. Are the parents talking to each other? Or does Dad stare vacantly and restlessly out to sea? Does he play with the kids or read the sports section for hours? Does Mom wind up making sand castles with them all afternoon? Can the kids amuse themselves or do their whines carry endlessly across the dunes? What kind of summer novels are the grown-ups reading? Do they bring Chee-tos for snacks or high-fiber stone-ground whole wheat crackers? Lie on towels with beer logos or tote organic rolled-up straw mats?

For Jane and me, this was a tradition of our annual Long Beach Island vacations: sitting on some windswept dune, watching the parents on the next beach blanket tell five-year-old Jonathan how disappointed they are that he tried to drown his little sister. "We're going to count to three," says Jonathan's dad, "and if you don't settle down, then no ice cream tonight. One. Two. Three." Jonathan throws his sand bucket at Dad. He screams that he has sand in his tushy. More counting to three. We had counted to three many times that afternoon.

It probably wasn't as much fun as yachting in the Bahamas, but it was cheaper and worked for us. Our own family was in that transitional stage. Emily was no longer content to build sand castles with me all day, so she'd brought a friend along. Ben was no longer content to be with us at all in public, so he surfed, trawled for girls and read science fiction day and night. In between, usually at mealtimes, we came together again comfortably and happily, giggled about other people we'd seen on the beach, yakked about books we were reading, talked about this dreadful teacher and that boy-crazed classmate.

Blair the hamster had come along on vacation too, working her wheel as frantically as she had in Rochambeau. If I'd had a real dog, I would have opened the cage and been done with her.

But then, Percentage was smarter than I thought. He had clearly figured out that limping brought an endless stream of biscuits, snacks and pats. "Oh, poor, sweet dog," I heard over and over. When he saw people coming, I swear his leg became twice as stiff. When I threw a tennis ball into the water, he plunged in about five feet, then turned around and came out, with ball or without. People on the beach praised his moxie for even trying; only we knew that five feet was as far as he'd ever gone, cripple or no.

I was always especially appreciative of Jane and my family after a case like the one I'd just finished. I deeply loved being together, acutely conscious as I was of how short-lived our time together really was. My work kept me from getting smug. I had a great marriage and we had two reasonably happy, successful kids, but so had the Tomlinsons. Shelly Bloomfield would have said the same a few months back. Families break easily, and once they fracture, it's tough to piece them back together.

As it turned out, I did see Shelly one more time. She stopped by the little cottage we rented, to say thanks and good-bye. She was moving to Boston. With Jane's help and encouragement, she'd landed a job with a nonprofit foundation based in Cambridge that helped parents whose kids struggled with learning disorders and emotional difficulties. She would help advise parents of their rights when their kids were denied proper treatment, and she'd suggest ways parents could work with their kids and the schools. And she'd be great at it.

Shelly was moving alone for now. Temporarily, she'd lost the family on which she had centered her life. She'd broken down when she was released from jail; her children were sent to live with her mother while she was recovering. She hoped to bring them to Massachusetts as soon as she was settled; her therapists thought she could and should.

"It's amazing, isn't it, Kit?" she asked as we visited quietly on the screened porch behind the cottage. "A year ago I believed my duty was to stay home and parent my kids myself. Now I'm not positive I can or should be a parent at all."

I think we both knew she didn't really believe that. But Shelly had to work it all through again, in a different way. Much of what she'd avowed in her old life wouldn't serve her very well in her new one.

The authorities were still sorting through the murder of Nancy Rainier-Gault. I had gotten it mostly right, according to Peterson and a grudging Leeming.

Harry Godwin had killed Nancy Rainier-Gault on his own, the police believed, although Jason had figured it out quickly enough and remained silent.

Dan Bloomfield hadn't known about the killing before it happened. He couldn't be charged with anything, the county prosecutors had decided. They couldn't prove he deliberately withheld evidence, and cheating on your wife was no longer a crime in New Jersey or anyplace else that I knew of. Nor was looking the other way while your wife faced murder charges. Under intense legal pressure, Bloomfield offered Shelly a generous divorce settlement, one that would enable her to construct her new life in Boston. He knew he couldn't live in Rochambeau any longer and moved to Manhattan. With malicious glee Peterson, who had made it her business to annoy Dan Bloomfield at every available opportunity, told me the buxom girlfriend had dumped him within days of his move into the city. Seems she'd received—anonymously—a pretty damning police report on her beau. We take justice where we find it.

Peterson, who'd also kept me advised of the police and legal maneuverings, said she suspected Bloomfield didn't want to go near a divorce court proceeding and that had spurred his magnanimity. But the truth was we might never really know his motivations. I believed he wanted Shelly in jail and also that he was terrified his son was a murderer. All I really knew for certain was that Shelly Bloomfield had been betrayed in the most fundamental of ways, by a husband I suspected had been unfaithful for years, and by a son she had sacrificed so much of her life to help.

Jason told the police that he suspected Harry had killed the principal. But Harry had convinced him that he would be institutionalized if sexual assault charges were ever brought against him. Harry assured him a smart lawyer would get his mother off. Smart lawyers get everybody off, he said. Jason, it turned out, wasn't so hot at thinking for himself. And Godwin was skilled not only at preying on young women but in bullying his more gullible peers into joining him, then intimidating them into silence.

Jason told the police he didn't think he could go through with their plan if his mother was convicted. Harry had asked if that meant he would rat on his best friend. Would he go to the police? It was then, in their wrangling that Saturday morning, that Harry brandished the pistol he had stolen from his uncle and the gun went off.

Jane thought it would take a good therapist years to get things working between Jason and his mother again. Though it was vital that they try, she was skeptical that they could do it, at least for many years. Jane's theory, which she'd been honing during our strolls on the beach, was that Shelly had sacrificed too much of herself, that Jason felt suffocated, and that he was rebelling in part against the confining nature of their relationship.

Shelly wasn't wrong in arguing that parents were primarily responsible for the care of their children, but her ideas about the acceptable ways to do it were too narrow for the times. If some parents were too distant, Jane mused, Shelly was in too close. That sounded right to me.

I couldn't imagine how she would fully recover from the knowledge that she had given so much for a family willing to see her accused of murder, hauled off in handcuffs to face a trial, when there were things they could have done to stop it.

The woman sitting in the deck chair on our porch had lost her feistiness, probably for good. I missed that part of Shelly. She had also shed some of her self-righteousness and combativeness. She seemed no longer to view one mode of mothering as superior to the others. Life is complex for both men and women, but the pressure on women seems worse to me, especially when it comes to child-rearing. All their choices feel difficult and risky.

"I always thought I was doing the right thing," Shelly told me in the softer, flatter voice she used now. "I thought I was doing the most important work there is. Now I don't feel so secure about what the right thing is. I want my children back. I'll work towards that as quickly as I can, but I'm still not over the shock. What Dan did . . . I can't handle it yet. I just know that when we—me and the kids—are back together, I want it to be in a healthier way. I want us all to have our own lives, as well as our life together as a family, for better or worse. I know it will be hard.

"But I'll be grateful to you, Kit. You stood with me, even when I tried to brush you off. I was ready to confess. I know now that wasn't really saving my family; that was sacrificing all of us. I'll always be in your debt."

The nicest words I'd heard in my new career. This detecting stuff could be okay.

I walked her down the gravel road to her car. "Kit, I never paid you. I know, you said don't worry about it, but I do. I'm going to send you checks from time to time, when I can. Not large checks, but I'll pay you, I swear it." I nodded, thinking she needed to make the gesture. She handed me the first one right there— drawn on an account that carried only one name—for $100. We agreed that I'd sign it over to the Nancy Rainier-Gault Award Committee.

When Shelly drove off in her spanking new Saturn, we were both in tears.

A whole generation of therapists, educators and mothers and fathers would be busy for years dealing with the aftermath of this case.

The Cyberskulls gang were all charged with varying degrees of sexual assault and battery. Except for Harry Godwin, all pleaded guilty. Tobias and Jason would avoid trials and probably be sentenced to indeterminate therapy and counseling, with their records expunged after several years of model behavior.

Godwin would most likely never stand trial for sexual assault, either. Neither the Tomlinsons nor the Mosleys wanted to subject their daughters to more stress and public exposure. But the murder charges, even though he would probably be tried as a juvenile, would ensure that he spent some years in juvenile institutions. Peterson told me twelve- and thirteen-year-old kids were involved in more homicides all the time, though not usually in places like Rochambeau. If their uncles didn't own guns they could steal, kids could buy guns themselves right outside their schools.

I thought that Shelly could and would rebuild her life. But I didn't feel too optimistic about Harry Godwin's future. The real fault lay with the grown-ups. Harry should have been treated years earlier. His first assaults should have been taken more seriously, by school officials, the police, his family. If they had, one person's life might have been saved, a lot of other people spared considerable pain.

I suspected Jason might have helped Harry beat up Ben and poison Percentage. But given the other crimes, I doubted that the attacks on my son and dog would ever be resolved. I was mistaken, it turned out, to assume that Ben knew more than he had let on. He just didn't want to talk much and, in the time-honored and resilient ways of adolescents, had put it behind him. According to reliable neighborly sources, even this peripheral involvement in the school's greatest-ever scandal had elevated Ben's status, especially in the eyes of a doe-eyed eighth-grader named Moira.

Charges against Jamey Schwartz were dropped. He had to go into counseling like the others, but the general feeling was that he was a small fish who should be thrown back and given another chance.

The Tomlinsons had, as predicted, hired a battery of the best psychiatrists in and around New York; they already had the best lawyers. I had the sense they would come through okay. They had undertaken their recovery with the same energy that had previously gone into their successful careers.

Ruth Tomlinson had called to thank me and to tell me she was taking six months off from her travels to see the kids got the proper attention and counseling. The family would be spending August together in Maine, she said. "Even Gifford," she added.

Tobias had many complex issues to deal with, they all now understood, and they would deal with them together. He still felt a lot of guilt and shame and rarely ventured out of the house. Ruth reported that Lila was slowly returning to herself. She was even looking forward to returning to her lacrosse team, to school and to her friends in the fall.

Wendy Mosley didn't fare as well. The family decided to move after all, when it became clear she would never be comfortable in her old school again. The girl battled depression, anxiety, deep isolation. I had never met her and now doubted I ever would. She'd refused to see me the two times I came to her home.

If there was a bright side, it was that the town and the school system moved quickly, instituting a sweeping new plan to deal with sexual harassment. Study units were added to the curriculum, girls would be encouraged to report incidents and unwanted overtures, and the authorities promised to respond quickly and forcefully. It would probably take a number of suspensions until the boys in the school figured out they meant it.

Nate Hauser said Rainier-Gault would have been pleased. The trick, he told me, was to make sure no one let up and forgot in six months. "My contribution and penance," he said, "is to not let that happen." Chief Leeming had something of the same idea. The police department and the county prosecutor's office had sustained pretty severe criticism from people in the town about the time it took to stop these boys. SHOUT bused in from the city to rally in front of police headquarters for a week or so. They wanted assurances the department would respond more quickly, and the chief had promoted Danielle Peterson, giving her particular responsibility for revamping the Rochambeau PD's response to harassment and sex crimes.

I had gotten another ripple of good publicity, but none of us wanted to encourage much media contact, given the sensitivities involving kids and sexual assault. And the outcome of this case wasn't something to celebrate. I was grateful when, after a month, the whole affair had quieted down.

As for the Rochambeau Harpies, we met for a postmortem and thank-you potluck dinner. It was a hoot. The Harpies, who already knew twice as much as me and the police combined, had informally continued to gather information about the case and about a lot of other things I didn't want to know. They decided to meet every so often to talk about women's and family issues, an agenda that could keep them busy well into the new century. But it might provide a way for those in the workplace and those at home—and those with one foot in each place—to understand one another better and resent one another less. The tribes had stopped shouting for a bit, at least in Rochambeau, and started listening to one another. And the Harpies had volunteered to be available for detecting backup whenever I needed them.

I'm jealous of women, in some ways. They are still undergoing a great revolution. Most of the time, men can only sit by slack-jawed and watch. It's no trendy social spasm, it's a great upheaval with a lot at stake: the kind of families we have, the nature of our relationships, the kind of parents we are, the lives women lead and the way children live. I hope I survive it.

As for me, I plan to meet with Willie when we both get back from our vacations. The adjacent telemarketing operation in the American Way has gone bankrupt, making a small two-office suite available right next door to Deleeuw Investigations. Tenants aren't lining up to sign leases. All I have to do is knock down one paper-thin wall.

I owed Luis, as usual. If there was real justice in the world, he would have headed a high-prestige Manhattan law firm, defending the biggest and most celebrated cases and making gobs of money. Since there wasn't justice, I'd arranged for an extremely trendy New York trattoria to surprise Luis at the Lightning Burger with a catered meal. It was spectacular. Tasteful floral arrangements. The first tablecloths ever to appear on Lightning Burger tables. Candles. Crusty fresh bread. A Tuscan theme: polenta con funghi. Capellini in brodo. Scampi. Scallopini. All washed down with an excellent Orvieto. Murray Grobstein the Sneaker King, the Latvian fried-dough makers and other Mall denizens were all invited. I silently toasted the Cicchelli family of mannequins, who smiled benevolently on our royal repast from across the way.

After Shelly said good-bye, Jane and I walked down to the beach and set up our rickety beach chairs. We watched the tide come in. We also saw the mom we'd come to recognize, reasoning once again with recalcitrant Jonathan.

"Jonathan," she told him firmly, "your father and I aren't happy. You shouldn't have used your whiffle bat on your sister's head. Remember, we discussed this? You said you wouldn't do it again. Now, we'll have to take your Barney away for the rest of the afternoon." Jane bet me five bucks the mom wouldn't make good on the threat. We were watching to see who prevailed.

The drama is eternal, this family stuff. It is the great sweepstakes, and usually it takes decades to discern who's won or lost, how it all turns out. Meanwhile, all of us are pilgrims struggling up the path.

Just a few years ago, when I was working in Wall Street, I saw the world as Us and Them. "Their" kids got arrested, shot, were emotionally disturbed. Mine got straight A's and sailed off to Brown. I know better now. There is the thinnest of boundaries between me and Them, between my family and theirs, and you could find yourself on the other side of it in a snap.

One way or another, said my dear old friend Benchley, we would all walk through the fire. When I or the people I loved took that walk, I hoped someone would be there to help.